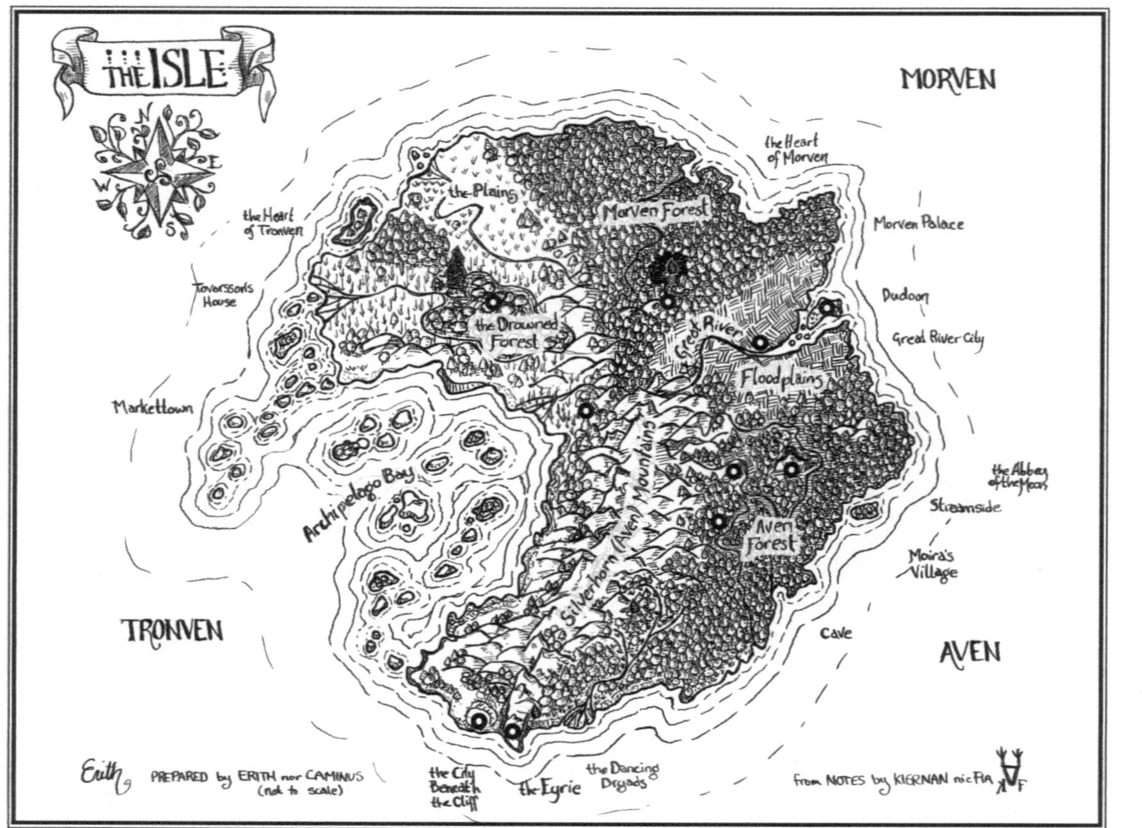

THE ISLE
N
E
S
W
MORVEN
the Heart of Morven
the Plains
Morven Forest
Morven Palace
the Heart of Tronven
Dudoon
Great River City
Taversson's House
the Drowned Forest
Great River
Floodplains
Markettown
Archipelago Bay
the Abbey of the Moon
Streamside
Silverhorn (Aven) Mountains
Aven Forest
Moira's Village
TRONVEN
Cave
AVEN
Erith PREPARED by ERITH nor CAMINUS
(not to scale)
the City Beneath the Cliff
the Eyrie
the Dancing Dryads
from NOTES by KIERNAN nic FIA

A CARESS OF WATER

Three Realms, Nine Monarchs

A CARESS OF WATER

written by

NICO SILVER

illustrated by

NIK SYLVAN

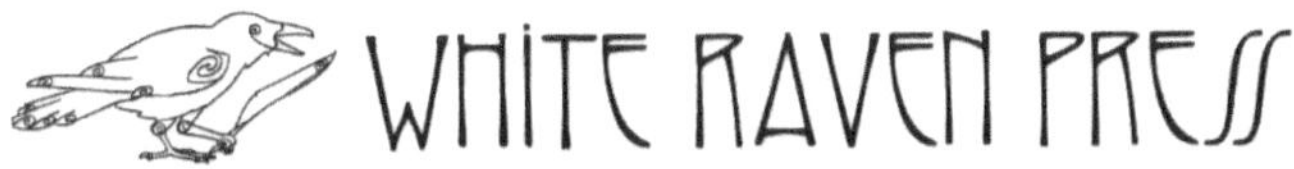

ISBN 978-1-998212-38-5

White Raven Press
North Cowichan, British Columbia, Canada

Cover illustration: "Kier and Fionn: The Kiss" © 2024 by Nik Sylvan.

Cover design and border by Nik Sylvan.
Title typefaces: Rivanna NF Pro by Nick Curtis and Eva Antiqua by Spiece Graphics, used under license via MyFonts, www.myfonts.com.

for Granny Norton and Auntie Roberson
(who might have been okay with the smut):

This is your fault, too.

Author's Note

Just like last time, there is a lot of enthusiastic, consensual sex in this book between two men in love. It gets pretty graphic, so if that's not your thing, maybe this book isn't for you.

There are also scenes of sexual harassment and sexual assault (this does not happen between our main characters, who are sweet and gentle with each other). These scenes are not meant to be titillating; they're terrible and that's how they should be viewed.

There are brief mentions of pedophilia and incest, though no actual scenes including the former.

There are scenes of violence, which include stabbing, blood, and death-by-beheading. There are also general references to not wanting to be alive.

There is a lot of swearing, including (especially) the f-word. Kiernan swears a lot, sorry.

And, finally, there is still not quite a happily ever after – yet. This is book three, and it ends with our heroes in a good place, but there is more to come. I promise there will be a happily ever after for Kier and Fionn before the series finishes.

If I've missed anything you think should have had a warning attached, please do let me know. You can always reach me by email at nico@nicosilverbooks.com.

I: THE EYRIE

1
Fionn

I HARDLY HAD TIME to change out of my travel clothes before Healer Kah came to fetch me personally.

She clasped both of my hands in hers and smiled, the expression turning her stern – and exhausted – face kinder.

<My Seer,> she said, and I wondered when hearing the language of my own people would feel normal, instead of reminding me that I was an outsider. <The salt-leaf you sent from Morven Forest was a gift from the spirits. Thank you.>

<Have there been…?> I hesitated. I only knew what the messengers had told us before we left Morven Forest: that the fever had hit the Eyrie hard, and many were ill. For all I knew, half my people might have died while I was on my way back.

The King might have died.

<No deaths,> she said, and I breathed easier. <But…> She looked away and my stomach plummeted.

Healer Kah let go of my hands and went to the huge window that made up most of one wall of my sitting room.

<Is it bad?> I asked.

<No one has died,> she repeated. <We've been able to keep the fever from spreading, and a few of the milder cases have recovered fully.>

<And the worst cases?> I reached up to stroke Flame's head and then Smoke's. As if they could sense my worry – and more and more I suspected they could sense a lot of things – my two feathered tree serpents had tucked themselves around my neck, one little dragonish head nestled beneath each ear.

<We're keeping them stable,> Healer Kah said. <They might recover, given enough time, but we'll run out of salt-leaf eventually.>

<And this is why no salt-leaf grows in Aven now,> I said, moving to stand by the window next to her. <Because they had no seer to complete the healing.>

<And they prepared it inefficiently,> she replied. <Thanks to you, what we have will last much longer.> She watched me, waiting, I think, for me to elaborate on my comment about seers and healing.

<In Morven Forest, I spoke to a dryad.> I leaned my forehead against the glass. I had been able to save Kiernan's life despite his terrible injuries, because Daphnis had told me a seer's healing magic was so much stronger when they left their physical body behind to work in their spirit body.

Whatever else Daphnis had done – I would always feel badly for letting him take on my guilt, but at least one of his actions was unforgivable – he had enabled me to save Kiernan. Except I had almost lost myself in the process, when the spirits of the forest had called me to join them – and Daphnis had echoed their calls – and I had accidentally woven my magic so deeply with theirs that I nearly gave in. It would have been so easy, and so pleasant, to join them as something greater than I could ever be alone, but also as something no longer embodied.

Healer Kah continued to watch my face. <What did they say? This dryad?>

I closed away my surface thoughts – Kah wasn't a seer, but as an experienced healer she could read a lot more than most people, and there were things I felt, things I thought, that were private. Things that were dangerous, here in the Eyrie.

<He taught me how to use salt-leaf bark to leave my physical body, to heal in my spirit body, where I can use much more magic without burning myself hollow.>

<Did you try it?> Her voice was intense, as if she was fascinated, but also worried about how I might answer.

<Prince Kiernan saved my life,> I said, and Kah blinked at what must seem to her to be a sudden change of topic. <He took a sword thrust meant for me, and it almost killed him.>

She pressed a hand to her mouth. <Does our King know you were attacked?>

I shook my head. <I haven't seen the King yet.> I could not bring myself to say "our" King. Not anymore. <Councilor Rocsh will no doubt inform him.> I pushed away from the window and went to the fireplace to lift the kettle off the flame. The first thing Neeka had done after helping me carry my things here was to put water on for tea.

I sighed and inhaled the fragrant steam as I filled the tea pot. <The dryad was right. I used salt-leaf bark and healed the prince in my spirit body. I was… so very much stronger.>

<This is wonderful!> said the Healer, true excitement in a voice I was used to hearing as level and measured and nearly unemotional. <I suppose I owe you an apology for doubting that salt-leaf would be any use at all.>

I shook my head. <I believe my spirit body would allow me to use enough magic to heal those who cannot recover from the fever on their own.> I let a little of my fear creep into my tone. It sounded like such an easy solution.

Her eyes lit up, fierce with hope.

<But…> I had to look away from the expression she bore. <I almost lost myself in the process.>

<What do you mean, "lost yourself"?>

I poured tea and handed her a cup, using the pause to gather my thoughts. <I was so strong,> I said. <I called on the Three Realms, and all of them came to my call. Land, Sea, and Sky rushed through me and poured into the strongest healing magic I've ever felt.> I took a sip and let the heat seep into my belly for a moment before I continued.

<I called on the Sidhe Lady of the Forest and all the spirits I could feel crowding around me.> I met the Healer's eyes. <They love him. The spirits of Morven Forest see Prince Kiernan as a son, almost as one of their own, and they love him. They all came to my aid – to *his* aid – and helped me heal him. His injuries were so terrible.> I paused to sip my tea again and my hand trembled when I lifted the cup to my lips. <And I nearly went with them when they departed back into the otherworld or scattered away into the forest's magic.>

I held Healer Kah's gaze as she stared at me.

<Did they force you?> she asked. <Did they try to make you go with them?> She sounded more fascinated than worried.

<They… *offered*… and it filled me with longing. They were so welcoming. I would have become part of something so much larger. I would have had unimaginable power. But I would have lost myself.> I stared into my tea. <I don't know if I can resist that pull again.>

<How did you resist then?> She finished her tea and set the cup on a table.

I had to give her an answer, but I couldn't tell her that Kiernan had called me back, that he had held my physical and spirit bodies both, and told me he loved me, that he needed me, and I had chosen *him* instead of the magic and acceptance that the spirits offered.

I couldn't tell her that if Kiernan was here with me now, I would not be afraid to heal my people in my spirit body, because he held my heart and he would always call me home again.

I considered Healer Kah a friend and mentor, but ultimately her loyalty was to the King and so she mustn't find out I still loved Kiernan, would *always* love Kiernan. Because, as kindly as she was to me, she would tell the King of my disloyalty, and the King would… Well, I didn't know what the King would do, but it would not be good.

So I shrugged. <It turns out that feathered tree serpents can spirit travel,> I said. I had only *seen* it in a vision, but I had no doubt that Smoke and Flame could leave their own bodies and join me in spirit form if they chose.

<And your two loyal companions guided you back to your body.>

I finished my tea so I wouldn't have to answer. I wouldn't lie if I could avoid it; even letting her believe that Smoke and Flame had called me back felt wrong. But I could not risk telling her the truth. I could not risk the King learning it.

I turned to look at the small pile of bundles on my sitting room floor. Almost none of it was my personal belongings. Those had been left behind in Morven Forest and would be sent to us on the next ship traveling this way. Most of the pile was salt-leaf and other medicines. We had left in a hurry and I'd had to prioritize, bringing only that which could be carried by bird folk flying.

<I'll have most of this sent to the infirmary,> I said. <I'll prepare more poultices and syrups this evening and then…> I paused.

<You intend to try your spirit healing?> Kah's hand was

warm on my shoulder.

<I do.>

<Rest first, before you do anything else,> she said. <You've had a long journey, and you're exhausted. Push yourself too hard, and you'll be useless to us.>

I nodded. <I will. I'll unpack and have someone bring you these.> I waved at the pile of bundles. <Then I'll bathe and rest. Neeka will help me prepare the remedies once she's rested, too. After the evening meal.>

When Healer Kah was gone, I sat on the nearest couch and the serpents slipped from my shoulders to curl up in my lap.

Bright sad, said Smoke.

Miss Dark, said Flame.

"How do I do this?" I asked.

He loves, said Flame.

We love, said Smoke.

"Love." I looked at my hands. My fingers were long and slender and pale, and I loved how they looked against Kier's darker skin. They had grown more calloused from all the practice I'd had working a mortar and pestle to prepare herbs. I had toiled nearly nonstop aboard the *Sea Spray*, learning to work with the rise and fall of the deck instead of struggling against it. But if the fever was as widespread as Healer Kah had indicated, then there was still so much more to do.

I pressed a hand below my belly button, where I could feel the warmth of my connection to Kiernan. I was too far away from him now to be able to sense his emotions, but whatever had brought him such pain as I was leaving seemed to have also restored our bond, so I could at least feel that he was alive.

The ache of being so far away doubled me over and I curled into myself, pulling my feet up onto the couch to tuck myself into a ball of misery. Smoke and Flame curled close to me, purring softly.

And I let exhaustion take me down into sleep.

I woke when Neeka tapped briskly at the door and walked in, servants bearing the evening meal following behind her. I sat up and rubbed my eyes. They were dry and gritty, and I didn't feel as if I'd really slept at all.

<Time to eat, sleepyface,> Neeka said, but her voice was gentle instead of teasing. She had left a potential new love behind in Morven Forest, and I had told her much more of my past with Kiernan than I had told anyone else, so she had some idea of how I was feeling. She also shared my worry for our people's health.

I was about to tell her I wasn't hungry, so I could get to work on the poultices immediately, but my belly rumbled, loud, and Neeka laughed.

<You don't have to stay,> I said, as the servants left. <Unless you haven't eaten yet.>

<I haven't,> she replied. <And Sifka moved out while we were gone, so my room feels empty.>

<I'm sorry,> I said, lifting the lid off a serving dish to see what it contained. Roasted wildfowl stuffed with wild river grains. It smelled delicious and my mouth watered.

<I'm not.> Neeka uncovered a plate of root vegetables drizzled with honey. <I told you we hadn't been getting along and agreed to spend our time apart thinking about what we wanted?>

I nodded, mouth full of roast meat. I lifted the last cover to find bright green spears of steamed spiral-stem. I picked one up and bit off the tip. It was crisp and perfect.

<Well, you already know what I decided.> She blushed and looked at me with her chin up.

I swallowed my food and grinned at her. <You decided to find out what it was like to kiss a Sidhe Palace Guard,> I said, and ducked away from her half-hearted smack.

She grinned back. <Sifka made her choice, too, and moved out. She took most of our furniture with her.> She picked up a slice of roast fowl and examined it. <I'm not sad, but it does make my room terribly quiet. And empty.>

After we ate, we sorted the bundles of herbs, sending most of them to the infirmary with one of my guards. Then we divided up the preparation chores between us; I took on the poultices, while Neeka opted to monitor the boiling down of syrups. Then, finally, late in the evening, we had done as much as we could do for the time being.

I stood at the counter in my bathing room, so tired I was dizzy. I put out a hand to steady myself, and when I heard Neeka come in the door behind me, I tried to straighten up.

<Are you okay, Tokka?> she asked. <Maybe you should lie down. It's late.>

I shook my head to clear it. I'd had a vision of nearly this exact scene, deep under Morven Forest in the sacred cave.

<I'm fine.> I turned to look at her. <I just don't want anyone to die. Not if there's anything I can do.>

She gestured at the clutter on my counter, the results of our evening of toil. <We've made enough poultices to last Healer Kah for a few days, at least, even if more people fall ill.> She put her hand on my forehead, and I scowled.

She laughed. <You feel warm. You should rest.>

<Yes, Mother,> I said, and she laughed again. <Will you put the kettle on while I pack all this up?>

She nodded. <Promise you'll rest,> she said.

<If I do fall ill…> She narrowed her eyes at me like she suspected I might be up to something. <And I have seizures, tell Healer Kah not to use her muscle-relaxing tea on me.>

She frowned. <But it keeps you from thrashing around.>

<And yet, I don't feel any better when I wake.> I scooped a handful of crumbled leaf remnants into my hand from the counter and brushed them into a clay jar. <And I think it interferes with my visions.>

She nodded and filled the kettle, then left me to package up the medicines we had made. When I was done I put a scoop of salt-leaf bark into a linen pouch and tucked it in my pocket.

Smoke and Flame flitted in from the cracked-open balcony door to join me as I went into my sitting room to give Neeka the last of the packages for Healer Kah.

You go, said Smoke, a hint of rebuke in her voice.

We follow, said Flame.

I shook my head, glad for once that Neeka's magic didn't include understanding the speech of serpents.

I sat on my favorite couch and pulled a blanket over my lap. It was getting colder, especially with the door always left ajar for Smoke and Flame to come and go. I would have to consult a builder for a better solution before it got any chillier.

I smoothed my hands over my lap and frowned. Something was different. I'd had a vision of this, of Neeka helping me make medicines and me waiting for her to leave so I could add salt-leaf bark to my tea. But it wasn't the same. It had been even colder outside in my vision, nearly winter, as if the events playing out had happened later in the year by several ninedays at least in my vision than they were actually happening now.

It didn't matter, though, did it? The future was changeable. Perhaps we had returned sooner than my vision had told me we would, or the fever had struck sooner. It was comforting, in a way, that my vision had not been exact. It meant it *really was* true that the future could be altered. It meant our choices, our actions, *mattered*.

<I'll take the remedies to Healer Kah,> Neeka said, taking the kettle off the flame and pouring it into the teapot. I smelled winterleaf and sweet bean pod. <If you agree to go to bed.>

<You, too,> I said. <As soon as you leave those at the infirmary, go get some sleep. We may be hard at work again tomorrow.>

She nodded and put her hand on my forehead again.

<I'm not feverish,> I said, pushing her hand away, but smiling. <Only tired.>

She frowned at me but gathered up the results of our evening's work and left. I got up to lock the door behind her. It wouldn't keep the King out, but it might make him reconsider coming in, and I hoped he was too busy and too tired from doing his job and organizing the efforts to keep the fever from spreading, that he was in bed himself in his own rooms, and too weary to visit me.

I took the bag of salt-leaf from my pocket and dropped it into the pot with the other herbs. I had no idea how strong it needed to be, or if the winterleaf and sweet bean might change how it worked, but I had to try.

As soon as the water soaked into the linen bag, a scent like wood smoke rose from the teapot and the tree serpents stirred where they had curled up in my discarded blanket on the couch. They raised their heads to watch as I poured tea into a cup.

We follow, Smoke said.

We keep safe, said Flame.

"You can't follow me this time, little friends." I settled back on my couch and pulled the blanket over my legs. I sipped the tea. It was not unpleasant, though sharper than I preferred. It was too hot, but I drank it as quickly as I could, and as soon as I set the cup on the table, Smoke and Flame went to it and lapped up the final drops. Then they came back to the couch and curled up on either side of me.

"I should get into bed," I said, but it was too late. My whole body felt flushed and suddenly I was standing, looking down at myself and the two little balls of feathers and scales curled beside me.

My back twitched — not in my spirit body but in my physical self — and then one of my wings. I looked undignified, sprawled and spasming irregularly, and I had to look away. I hoped Kiernan never saw me like that.

But he had. He *had* seen me. He had held me and watched over me while I had a vision, and he still loved me. He still wanted me.

He had been sad when I said I looked repulsive. I was beautiful, he told me. Lovely and strong, and he was honored to be allowed to watch over me while I was vulnerable.

I swallowed a lump in my throat and looked back at myself. I couldn't see the beauty Kiernan saw, but perhaps I wasn't repulsive, only laid bare. I turned away and took a step towards the door. Deep in the Eyrie, my seer-sight could detect the flickering glows of my people, hundreds of them, each a slightly different color according to the nature of their magic and the state of their health. The ill and the feverish looked sickly and flickered the most.

I headed for the door.

You wait, said Smoke.

We follow, said Flame.

I turned to watch, surprised though I shouldn't have been, because I *saw* this in a vision, as the tree serpents left their physical bodies to flit around me in their spirit shapes.

"I should have expected that, I suppose," I said, and felt surprised all over again not to hear a reply, a raspy voice in my head saying, *You can never tell, with tree serpents*. But that was something that had happened in a vision, when I had walked out onto my balcony to meet the white raven and found myself in the cave beneath Morven Forest.

Now, I was *not* having a vision, but spirit traveling, and here my beloved wasn't holding my hand and waiting for me to wake. I was alone but for my serpents, with an infirmary full of deathly ill people who needed me to heal them.

I stepped through the door and followed the guttering glows down deeper into the Eyrie, Smoke and Flame flying close beside me. I felt sick in my belly, knowing that even in my spirit body I could do too much and burn myself hollow. Or I could give in to the lure of the spirit world and drift away into magic. But there was also a tightness in my back that made me stand up straighter. I was a seer, and a healer, and I was finally about to do one of the things I had been born to do.

2
Kiernan

I HAD KNOWN, as soon as I started to run, that I would never make it to the coast before Fionn's ship left. So when my stag bounded out of the trees, I pulled myself onto his back and turned him back towards the Heart of Morven.

I had the presence of mind, at least, to stop and pick up Daphnis's severed head, and to stop again at Dec's cabin for a blanket to wrap it in. It would have been cruel to walk onto the palace grounds carrying it uncovered, for all the dryad servants to see.

The expression of confusion on his face would probably haunt me for the rest of my life. I would have given a lot to have had some other course of action I could have taken than cutting off the head of the person who had been my first lover and my first real friend.

A lot, but not anything. I would give *anything* to see Fionn safe and happy, and for that I needed magic.

The Captain of the Queen's Guard met me as I slipped off my stag's back and headed for the walkway that spiraled up into the canopy of the giant oak that was the Heart of Morven.

«Our Queen wishes to see you,» he said. I half-expected him to speak Islish, but of course he wouldn't, now that our foreign guests were gone.

«I was just going to her.» I held out the blanket-wrapped bundle. «Will you take care of this?»

He glanced at it, then took it from me. «The traitor's head?» He watched my face closely for a response.

«His name was Daphnis.» I thought I saw him relax, just the tiniest fraction, and a muscle tugged at the corner of his mouth.

He nodded. «Your mother awaits you in her chambers, lad,» he said.

I nodded back, and waited, and finally saw his eyes widen, heard him suck in a breath, when he noticed. I had always thought him more observant, but I suppose his attention was more on my expression than on my forehead.

«Your antlers…» He stopped himself from saying more, schooled his face into stillness, and pretended disinterest. He was my Queen's trusted ally, and couldn't appear to have sympathy for me instead, whether he felt it or not.

«At least I can feel the forest again,» I said and turned away to enter the Palace.

Padraig, too, was waiting for me, and he fell into step beside me as I went in the door. I caught him staring out of the corner of my eye and ignored it for as long as I could. Finally, tired of the glances he kept darting at me, and the number of times he drew in a breath but then didn't speak, I stopped, turned, and said, "What?" deliberately using Islish to see how he would react.

He took my arm and pulled me into a nearby alcove, out of the way of servants rushing past. He ignored the pleasant view of one of the gardens out the alcove window to stare at me instead.

"What the fuck happened?" he said, low and urgent. "Cousin, you've got no fucking antlers." He touched one of his own and then reached to brush my hair aside, and I flinched away. My forehead, the two ovals where my antlers had once sprouted, was raw. Even the brush of moving air hurt. But I could feel the forest. I could touch my magic, even if I couldn't use it. Daphnis's dryad magic pooled in the core of my being, unfamiliar and – so far – unusable.

And I could feel Fionn, far away and getting farther, but *there*, warm and present in my belly.

"I had Daphnis… remove them."

"You what? Why? Is he… Did you kill him?"

I cocked my head a little sideways. "I know you have a brain, cousin. Use it."

"Fuck. Kier."

I tilted my head to look down at him, putting on my best haughty prince impression.

"My Prince," he said. He didn't spit the word, like Sean used to do; instead, he said it as if he really meant it. It made something twinge in my guts. "That's how she took your magic. The moonsilver on your antlers was enspelled. Fuck."

"Daphnis is dead," I said, and though I tried to keep my voice neutral, I could tell from the way his eyes softened that he knew it hurt to say. I hadn't thought he'd known anything about my past with the dryad, but perhaps he had. Perhaps he knew more about a lot of things than I had given him credit for.

His hand curled around the back of my neck, and he moved closer.

"Don't, Pad," I said. I didn't think I could bear kindness right then. I needed cold, emotionless stillness to get through the meeting with my Queen.

"Don't what? Comfort you? You don't always have to be so fucking strong." He pulled me into his arms, and I knew I needed to move away. But I was so tired.

"Yes, I do," I said. "I can't show any weakness, Padraig. You know she uses weakness." I moved to pull back and he held me tighter.

"Let the servants see us," he said softly. "Let them talk, like we decided. Your Seer might be gone back to the Eyrie, but we can still protect Erith by letting everyone think you and I are… involved."

"Like *you* decided," I said, but I kept still and let him hold me. I even rested my hands on his hips, but that was all. It would be so easy to let him comfort me, but I suspected his idea of comfort involved a lot fewer clothes than mine, and as pleasant as that would be, *his* naked body was not the one I yearned for.

We stood that way for a long moment, until I said, "I have to go see her."

"I know." He moved away far enough to rest his forehead on mine, careful not to get too close to my raw antler wounds. "I wish you would let me distract you. Erith wouldn't mind."

"You should treat Erith better. Treasure him."

"I do. He gives my life meaning. But I think he'd enjoy having you join us."

Then I did pull away, because his offer was starting to sound tempting. The man I was would have given in with hardly a thought. But I was not the man I used to be, and I wouldn't hide my heartache in fucking.

Padraig stayed outside the Queen's door to wait with her guards, while I went in. And stopped dead, trying not to stare.

My Queen sat on a couch, elegant and regal as always, but she looked… ill. Exhausted. Weak, almost.

Her bronze skin looked as if all her blood had leached

away, leaving her strangely pale, and her cheekbones were rendered sharper by the tension in her face. I had never seen my mother look *vulnerable* before.

She stood as I walked in and took my elbow when I would have sunk to one knee. I met her eyes in surprise and found myself unable to read her expression. That was becoming disturbingly more common – until recently, she had never even tried to hide her thoughts or emotions. She never had to, because she was more powerful than anyone around her.

«Sit,» she said, indicating the large, too-soft chair she always gave me.

«I don't think I can sit there, my Queen. Not with this.» I gestured over my shoulder at the sword strapped to my back.

Her eyes moved to look at it. «Of course. Where is the other?»

«In my rooms. I haven't had the chance to get the harness altered to carry both.»

She nodded and indicated a hard wooden dining chair for me, so I moved it closer to her couch and we sat.

«Tea?» She gestured at one of her servants, a faun who looked enough like Erith that she was probably a relative, who moved away from the wall to lift a kettle off the fire and carry it to the sideboard.

«Not wine?» It was a small dig, and I knew she would recognize it as such, but I was feeling reckless. She was already going to give me some terrible punishment for circumventing her spellwork; what was a little comment about her fondness for wine on top of that?

But she only said, «I don't think wine would improve my headache.»

«Are you unwell, my Queen?» I shifted my sword to get more comfortable on the chair, giving me an excuse to look away without obviously avoiding her gaze. I had never known her to be ill, or tired, or even out of sorts. It was not a comforting thought.

When I looked back up, she was studying me and, if she was surprised to see me without antlers, she didn't show it.

«There was a backlash,» she said, gesturing to her own antlers, and I saw faint dark marks around the moonsilver that decorated her tines that looked like scorch marks. «Your magic against mine.» The very idea that the removal of my antlers had injured her, even in such a small way, was both unsettling and oddly comforting. She was a strong magic user and I had never known her to miscalculate before.

«My Queen?»

Her smile was stiff, but then relaxed into something almost genuine. This meeting was *definitely* not going how I imagined it would.

«I'm proud of you, my son,» she said, and I almost fell off my chair. My long practice in not showing her any vulnerability was probably the only thing that kept me still, that prevented me from even twitching in surprise.

«My Queen?» I repeated, feeling slow and stupid. She always was several steps ahead of me.

She waited until the faun had poured us each a cup of tea before she spoke again. «Can you never call me Mother?» she said.

The tea sloshed in my cup, and I realized my hand was shaking. I put the cup down and pressed my palms against the tops of my thighs.

She sighed and sipped her tea. «You found a way around my punishment, as I knew you would. »

I stared at her, unable to keep my surprise entirely contained. I couldn't think of anything to say, so I said nothing.

She set her cup down. «It was not in any way I had

anticipated, hence the backlash.» She smiled and stood, and when she put both hands on my face, I was very glad I had put my tea cup on the table.

She stroked a lock of my hair back from my forehead and I held very still so I wouldn't flinch. «You are so like your father,» she said, and I could have sworn I heard something wistful in her voice.

«I have his hair,» I managed to say, knowing my continued silence would tell her more than my words, and not wanting to show her any weakness.

«You have much more than his hair, even if it isn't visible to most.» She touched my face again, stroking her thumb beneath my eye and I held very still. I had seen her take a man's eyes with her claws once, when he had made an inappropriate comment about one of my sisters. «You are so like *me*.»

I tried to find something to say, to hide the way her words hit me like a punch in the gut, but what *could* I say? I hated her. I loved her. I respected her. And she disgusted me.

She smiled again and it had that same wistful look.

«Go to Dudoon,» she said. «Then Great River City. Set up an embassy for me there.»

«Yes, my Queen.» I said it automatically.

«My sweet boy,» she said softly. «You always were too kindhearted for your own good. I hope I have been able to make you strong enough for what is to come.»

I could barely force air in and out of my lungs. She had never before in my life said anything that loving to me. She had never before touched me with kindness or indicated she cared what happened to me. Even as a small child, she had always been cold and distant, someone to be on one's best behavior with. I had wanted so badly to please her, and I had been terrified of her. I had *never* been her "sweet boy."

«What is to come, my Queen?» I finally managed, seizing on the one part of her words that made any sense at all.

«Ask your Vogel Seer friend,» she replied, and the way she said it made me wonder if she knew, despite my attempts to hide my feelings, that I loved him with my whole being.

MORE THAN A NINENIGHT passed after the Queen had called me to her rooms to tell me to go to my father. During that time, I had packed most of my clothes, draped cloths over my furniture, and had chosen five more of the Palace Guard to serve as my Prince's Guard. I had selected a small number of books to bring with me, made sure the things the Vogel delegation had left behind were packed securely, and I had convinced Erith to ask around among the palace staff to see if anyone was interested in a new job at a Sidhe embassy in a mostly human city.

A surprisingly large number of fauns, werewolves, and assorted other peoples showed up at my door to interview, and by the time I left Morven Palace I had enough new employees to fill every role I could think of, and then some.

"They like you, my Prince," Erith said shyly when the long evening of interviewing was over, and the list he was keeping filled several pages. His Islish was soft and pleasant; he had been using it at every opportunity since I had asked if he wanted to come to Great River City with me.

I had sent a letter ahead to my father asking for help finding a building in the city to rent or purchase. I wanted somewhere we could have both offices and housing, and I didn't want to have to wait until we arrived to search for somewhere my people could feel safe. I didn't know what kind of reception we would find with Morven's human Monarchy.

The day we left, I was already exhausted, but at least I hadn't had much time to pine over Fionn. The closer we got to the river, though, the better I slept and the more relaxed I felt. I had a job to do, and it was far away from my Queen. It was closer, if only a little, to Fionn.

I sat my horse at the top of a hill looking down towards Great River, watching the long train of my new staff moving slowly closer to the city. The rooftops were just visible from this vantage.

My horse – a gift from my Queen along with three dryad servants and a string of pack mules, because a riding stag would not do well in the city – was a small, light-boned creature that didn't like to stand still any more than I did. We were both going to have to practice.

Beside me, Padraig and his horse were much calmer. His mount was a loan from his father, the most renowned breeder of horses in Morven. «I've never left Morven Forest before,» he said, his voice low.

"Speak Islish, Pad," I said. "You might as well get used to it now." I shifted in the saddle and my horse pranced in place, then settled for tossing his head. On my shoulder, Coal stirred and then slipped off to circle us in the air. His flight was still wobbly, but he'd taken to it eagerly as soon as his feathers grew in.

"I've never left Morven Forest," my cousin repeated.

"I don't think any of them have, either." I nodded towards our people, many of whom were glancing behind themselves as they left the shelter of the trees.

"They all volunteered," said Padraig. "Except the dryads."

I shook my head. "I had Erith ask the dryads if they preferred to come with me, or to return to my Queen's employ and stay in Morven Forest."

"Of course you did." The corner of his mouth quirked up.

"Spirits forbid you ever act like a prince and command anyone to do anything."

"Are you taking over from Sean then? Will you remind me at every turn of how unprincely I am?"

He looked at me. "Of course not. And I'm insulted that you asked." But his mouth curved into a grin. "I expect your dryads would much rather face the unknown with you than stay at home and work for our Queen." He looked back at our people.

I nodded. "I did promise them fresh soil to root in, delivered every few months. I've asked my father to look for a building with an outdoor courtyard."

"You mean to give your dryads their own garden."

I couldn't read his voice. It might have been friendly, or it might have been disgusted. I knew he didn't have the same bigotry towards non-fey peoples as many noble Sidhe did, but I hadn't been able to figure out if that also extended to enslaved people.

I had thought my cousin was easy to read, but the longer I knew him the more I discovered he was very good at hiding his feelings behind surface thoughts.

"I'd rather give them their freedom," I said, watching his face. "But since I can't, a garden seems the least I can do."

"What kind of reception will we get, do you think?" He switched his reins to one hand to stretch his fingers, then swapped to stretch the other hand. I realized that, for all his easy stillness, he was nervous.

I shrugged. "My father – General Druison – will be glad to have an embassy to complain to, when he feels his over-Monarch is being unfair."

"His over-Monarch, who is also his wife? Don't your parents talk to each other?"

"My parents can't stand each other. They've been

separated since before I was born, remember?" But I was thinking of the uncharacteristic softness of my Queen's face when she said, "You are so like your father."

I shook my head. "He'll also be glad we chose Great River City and not Dudoon to locate ourselves."

"You grew up there, right? When you weren't in the Forest?"

I shook my head again. "I've only been to the city a few times, on formal occasions to meet my uncle."

"The King of Great River Monarchy." It wasn't a question, just a re-statement of facts we had gone over many times since I was told we would be leaving.

"He doesn't like me very much," I said, earning me a glance and a half-grin.

"What did you do to deserve that?"

"I was born." I nudged my horse forward, back onto the narrow road behind my people. I heard Padraig cluck to his mount and follow.

We made camp on a ridge above the city, with the dark edge of Morven Forest just barely in view through the gloom behind us. The whole way here, we had travelled during the day and slept at night, because even though the Sidhe were largely nocturnal, Great River City and the human Monarchy operated by daylight hours. I knew it was uncomfortable for many of my people, but we had to be able to function by human rules.

There were farmhouses within view, and smoke from the chimneys of cabins and other dwellings tucked into the edge of the forest. Tomorrow we would face a whole new word, but for tonight we could rest and prepare.

Once everyone was occupied in setting up camp, I carried on alone, turning away from the city and heading upriver to where a ferry would take me to the island in the mouth of the river.

Approaching Dudoon as the night grew its blackest, I had to make myself breathe slowly to calm my racing heart. This fortress had been the one place I could truly be free of my mother. It had also been where I had learned not everyone liked the fey – most especially my own brother.

I rode up to the gate and stopped when the two guards on duty stepped in front of me.

"Humans only, elf," one of them said.

The other muttered something about the small size of my horse and the probable tiny size of my cock, and they both snickered.

"Last I heard," I said lazily, "General Druison only required half-human ancestry."

The first guard shrugged and the second snickered again.

"I don't suppose I could convince you to send word to the General that he has a visitor?"

"General Druison doesn't visit with fey," said the guard who had speculated on the size of my tackle.

"Tell him Kiernan Druison is here," I said, keeping my voice dry and unemotional. "He's expecting me. Wake him if you have to."

I watched as both guards' faces drained of blood when they realized who they were talking to.

"Unless, of course, you'd like me to demonstrate the knife skills I'm famous for?" I hated the rumors about me, both here and in the Forest, but they did have their uses.

My horse danced under me, and I calmed him with a hand on his neck.

"Prince Kiernan," said one of the guards, stammering in his effort to get the words out quickly. "Of course you can just ride through. You'll find the General in the hall."

I smiled, pulling my lips up so he could see my long

canines, trying not to revel in the fear I smelled on him, and rode past. I ignored every stare and glance, every muttered comment from the people in the main courtyard. I was used to it. I'd grown up with it. At least most of the soldiers inside the fort remembered me and none of them got in my way.

The stable hand who scurried out to meet me and take my horse's reins offered a hesitant smile. I recognized him and hoped the flush that came to my face as I remembered him folding me over a hay bale in the stable loft didn't show too badly.

"My Prince," he said. The title was mine through my father as well as my mother, but not everyone here used it for me, since my father didn't use that title either, preferring "General." "I'll make sure your horse is well looked after. He's a pretty little thing." I flushed again; he'd said the same thing about me once, and from the look in the man's eye, he remembered it, too. And fuck, when I had I turned from the confident little shit who couldn't be embarrassed no matter how obvious the innuendo, to a blushing fool mortified to be recognized by a past fuck?

I knew the answer, of course. It had happened when I fell so completely in love no one else interested me anymore.

"Thank you," I said, sliding from the saddle and lifting my pack to my shoulder. I handed over the reins and the young man – Colin, I remembered – brushed his fingers over mine taking them.

"You're welcome to share a drink with me, if you need somewhere to escape to." He nodded towards the stable. "I'm stablemaster now, and the loft apartment is mine."

I nodded and walked away, not trusting myself to speak. It used to be so easy to navigate flirtation like this, even when I wasn't interested. But Colin had been enthusiastic and attentive, the perfect antidote to the self-pity I'd felt as a youth after my Queen sent all the dryads to the pleasure garden.

"Fuck," I muttered, trying to push aside the memories of escape to the hayloft, and Colin, over and over. I startled as a light weight dropped onto my shoulder.

Nyah, said Coal, slipping inside the collar of my shirt and nuzzling my neck.

I squared my shoulders. There wasn't much point in trying to look bigger since I was nearly a head shorter than the shortest soldier in Dudoon, but at least I could avoid slouching. I summoned every ounce of confidence I had and several I didn't and pushed open the Hall door.

The huge room went quiet as I walked in. My father sat at the head of the main table, eating a late meal with his commanders. I wasn't at all surprised to find him still awake in the middle of the night; as a child I had thought he never slept at all.

"If it isn't the cockiest little shit smear in Morven," said a voice far cockier than mine had ever been.

Coal reared up on my shoulder, spread his tiny wings, and hissed.

My older brother laughed. "And he's got a pet to match: tiny but convinced he's scary."

"Good to see you, too, Duncan," I said, meeting my brother's eyes. "Girls still weep when you try to chat them up?"

The tension went out of the room as some of the soldiers laughed. Most of them didn't like me, but I was good with a sword, even with the apparent disadvantage of my size, and all of them respected me.

It also helped that my brother was a dick to everyone, not just to me, and was only given respect because he was the General's son.

"Kiernan." My father stood from his chair and beckoned to

a servant, who scurried forward with another seat. "Join us."

"Hello, Father," I said. "My Queen sends her regards."

3

Fionn

MY PREVIOUS SPIRIT TRAVELS had not prepared me for this. I walked through the door to my rooms without opening it – eyes squeezed shut and terrified I would get stuck halfway – and past my guards. The two men didn't react in any way as I passed and the color and brightness of the light that glowed within them told me they were both weak in magic.

The floor felt solid enough beneath my feet, but the walls had a not-quite-real texture when I brushed my hand against them. And though I couldn't exactly see through the walls with my eyes, some part of my seer senses could *see* the magical glow of the spirits of my people.

At first, I tried to look at them all, to understand them, but there were too many and it made my head hurt. So instead, I tried *not* to look at them, and it helped.

I headed for the infirmary, wondering if there was a faster way to travel, if perhaps I could imagine where I wanted to be and have my spirit body manifest there. I didn't dare to try, though; I was too afraid of getting something wrong, of making a fatal mistake that would trap me and doom my people to a slow death of incurable fever.

It was a temptation, too, to leave the Eyrie entirely, to spread my physically inadequate wings that somehow let me fly in spirit form and head north to find Kiernan. If our connection was restored, then maybe he had enough magic now to see me in my spirit body – and he must, because Daphnis' magic had let him see me once before – and to touch me.

A memory of his hands on my skin while I was in spirit shape tugged at my thoughts, but I put it firmly aside. As much as I longed for Kiernan, I had work to do. First, I would see my people healed. Then perhaps, I could indulge my own desires.

Approaching the infirmary, I could sense more and more clearly the extent of the sickness affecting my people. Every cot there was full, their occupants' inner glow faint and sickly, and extra cots had been crowded in wherever they would fit.

I stood in the doorway and stared. There were so many, and Healer Kah had told me these were only the worst cases; anyone who could still manage to look after themself was quarantined in their own quarters and tended to there.

How could I even begin to heal all these people? I took a deep breath to steady myself and reached for calm. I had healed Kiernan's terrible wounds, had even undone where previous healing had gone wrong and re-healed him. Alone, each of these fever patients would need far less healing than he had needed.

Perhaps I couldn't heal everyone in one night, but I *could* heal them, one at a time.

I moved to the middle of the room, and one patient stirred on their cot as I passed by. When I glanced at him, he stared, eyes wide.

<Healer?> he said, voice raspy. <Healer, I think I'm hallucinating.>

One of Kah's assistants emerged from the back room and hurried to the patient's bedside. She laid a hand on his forehead and closed her eyes. With the mask over her face, I couldn't see her expression, but I could *see* her healing magic reaching out to him. It couldn't drive out the fever, but it could tell her if he had worsened or improved.

<You're not any worse,> she said. <What do you see?>

<Our Seer,> he replied, looking at me. <He's right there.> The man tried to lift a hand to point but failed. The healer turned anyway, a puzzled frown on her face. Then suddenly, clarity, and I knew she saw me.

<Are you really here, my Seer?> she said. Her eyes flicked up and down, examining me, then quickly returned to my face and I remembered, with a rush of embarrassment, that in spirit form I was always naked, that even the extra feathers glued to my wings to make me presentable were gone.

At least, being Vogel, my genitals were tucked away in my sheath, and nudity among my people was not anything remarkable. It was hard, though, to shake off the conditioning I had received at the Abbey of the Moon, that told me an unclothed body, however sexless, was obscene and shameful.

The healer was still staring at me, and I realized I needed to reply.

<I'm here,> I said. <I'm spirit traveling, so I won't be visible to everyone.>

<But how?>

I shook my head. How didn't matter. <I'm here to heal. In spirit form I can use more healing magic without burning myself hollow. But I don't know how many I can cure of the fever before I need to rest, so please show me to the worst off first.>

She stared a moment longer, then nodded. <This way. We put the worst cases closest to the preparation room. And the children.>

I followed her to a cot where a thin child – perhaps seven years old – lay pale under the white infirmary sheets. Their tanned face looked leached of color, except for bright spots on their cheeks. They looked like a caricature of a sick patient.

<I'll get you a stool.> The healer hurried into the back room, and I looked down at the child. As if they could feel my eyes, they opened theirs. They were bloodshot and unfocussed, but a remarkable shade of golden yellow. The child's feathers and short-cropped hair were a darker shade of the same color, almost amber in the soft light of the infirmary.

<Hello,> I said, and the beautiful eyes focused on me.

<Seer?> they said. <Have you come to bless me? I'm going to die, aren't I? I don't want to die.>

I smiled, trying to keep the desperate sorrow, my fear and doubt, from showing on my face. I even banished the thoughts deeper into my mind in case this child had magic and could read me the way Healer Kah or Seer Siona could.

<I'm here to make sure you don't die, little one,> I said. <What's your name? I'm Seer Tokka.>

<I'm Lisna,> they said.

<Strong spirit,> I commented, though they probably knew the meaning of their own name. It felt good to say it aloud; it felt like a good omen. I sat on the stool the healer brought me. She hovered nearby for a moment.

<I'll be close if you need anything,> she finally said and retreated across the aisle to check on the other patients.

<I have a friend named Nikna,> I told the child. <It means "strong mind.">

The child smiled, but the effort of speaking seemed to have exhausted them, and their eyes drooped closed. They appeared to sink into the mattress.

I bit my lip, then reached out to take Lisna's hands in mine, and closed my eyes. The Eyrie was built on a cliff where all Three Realms – Land, Sea, and Sky – met, both in tangible form of cliff, ocean, and air, and in the magical sense. That magic flooded to my call and Smoke and Flame swirled around me in a tight spiral. I didn't even have to see them to know they were there, and their movement started to make me dizzy.

Too much, said Smoke.

Go slow, said Flame.

I breathed deep and pulled away from the magic, narrowing my connection to the Realms, slowly, carefully letting it flow through me but not overwhelm me like it had done when I healed Kiernan.

My serpents stopped their dizzying flight and settled onto the child's pillow, one of each side of their head. They purred softly and the Eyrie's magic swirled around them, making a glow of pale blue around serpents and child. The child sighed and their breathing eased.

I concentrated on my hands where they held the child's and let healing magic move through me, into them. Something large and powerful and ancient brushed against my senses and I almost snatched my hands away. But it was not the child's magic I felt – though theirs was strong for one so young. It was something else. Something *other*.

She comes, said Flame quietly.

The Lady. Smoke's voice was reverent. I hadn't known tree serpents could even feel reverence.

I nearly opened my eyes to stare at them and was glad when I kept my concentration and continued to feed magic into the child's body, because a bright light was forming on the other side of the cot, and it made my eyes ache even through closed lids.

I breathed slowly, feeling out the fever, and pushing it, moving it to the surface of the child's body and away. I sought for the sickness that caused the fever and snuffed it out, smothered it in healing.

Little silver one, said a voice in my mind. The bright light on the other side of the cot dimmed, but I still kept my eyes squeezed shut.

The Lady, Smoke had said. Did my serpent refer to the Lady of the Skies? She who was the Eyrie's representative of the Goddess Above the way Morven's Lady of the Forest represented the Goddess Below? The very idea filled me with awe and fear, and I tried not to think about it too much, even as the ancient presence touched my mind again.

Let me aid you, Vogel Seer. I didn't want to, but I opened my eyes. I had *seen* the Lady of the Forest in a vision, but this was different. This Goddess was *here*, was present right in front of me.

She stood on the other side of the child's cot, a tall woman with skin the color of a clear summer sky and hair the white of clouds. Her locks seemed not to feel the pull of the earth, but floated around her in long, fine strands like mist. Her wings were every shade of the midnight sky and her eyes… Her eyes were the same sun-gold as those of the child on the cot between us.

I stared and tried to say something, anything, but no words came out. She smiled, brushed her fingers over the child's forehead, and then was gone. But her magic remained, strengthening me and letting me more easily regulate the magic that wanted to rush through me.

Smoke and Flame slid from the cot to my lap and from there to my shoulders.

She loves, said Smoke.

She heals, said Flame.

The child opened their eyes, and for an instant I could see deep into their spirit. For a long time we stared at each other and I felt like I was laid just as open.

<Lisna,> I said. <The Lady of the Skies has blessed you, but not to go to the afterlife.> I smiled. <I think she wishes you to live a long and full life, to use the magic you have been given.> Because this child's magic was pure and strong. They would be a healer, but also something more than that. Not a seer, but perhaps not so different.

They blinked at me, sleepy, but no longer feverish. <Thank you, my Seer.>

<Tokka,> I said. <But my dearest friends call me Fionn.>

<Thank you, Seer Tokka-Fionn.> Their eyes closed again, and they slept.

I brushed hair from their face and noticed that on one side it was a darker shade, almost orange, and on the other golden. It was a subtle difference, but now that I noticed, it seemed obvious. Their feathers were similarly divided, darker on one wing than the other, and even their freckles were brighter on one side, split in a clean line down their face and neck.

I looked around for the healer and she walked quickly over. <Did you know?> I asked. <That this child is…?>

<Male and female both?> she finished for me. <Her parents don't know what to do with her. Officially, she's a girl, but physically, she's both.>

I bit my lip, thinking. <She's very strong in magic. Or she will be, probably soon.>

<Healing magic?>

<That and more. She feels somewhat like a seer, but… not. And… I think I feel fire magic in her.> I brushed hair back from the child's face again. <Take care of her. Perhaps…> I hesitated, because I still believed Kiernan would come for me

and take me away from here, so my future at the Eyrie was uncertain. <I'd like to help train her, when her magic comes.> As if I was capable of training anyone, as untrained as I still was myself. But I if could learn enough, I could pass it on, and at the very least I could help ease the transition into magic-using. And I knew exactly the person to help someone so young learn to control magic. Kier had come into his magic even younger.

<If you *saw* her magic, that could be very soon, indeed,> said the healer. <I'll ask Healer Kah to speak to her parents.> She paused, a sadness on her face. <Her father, I think, would be glad to be rid of her, to be able to devote his time to her brother. Her mother will do as her husband wishes.> Her tone of voice told me what she thought of women who follow whatever their man wants and I had to hide a smile.

<I don't mean to adopt her,> I said, but my words lacked certainty. The thought of raising a child wasn't one I'd ever had. I was a man who was only attracted to men; the idea of having a family had never occurred to me. And yet I would not abandon this child. I didn't think I could abandon any child who needed me, and *this* child would grow up to be something new and special.

I wondered what Kiernan would think about being a father to an adopted child. And then I realized I was thinking about him as if we were married and I pushed the thought aside.

The healer smiled. <We can always find a place for her here, especially if she'll have healing magic.>

I stood up to go to the next patient and swayed on my feet, suddenly dizzy. Smoke and Flame pressed their heads under my ears and purred, and my vision cleared. Surely I could heal a few more before I needed to rest. There were so many here who needed help.

IN THE END, I healed seven more – all of them children – before I was completely overcome by lightheadedness. The whole time, I felt the Lady of the Skies touching my magic, but eventually – even with her help – I had to stop. I was mortal and frail and could only do so much.

I woke in my own bed and had the absurd thought about how startled the healer must have been when I suddenly disappeared. Unless I *had* walked back to my body and was simply so weary I didn't remember the journey.

I wondered how I had moved from my couch to my bed but then I smelled it: thick floral perfume.

The King's arms tightened around me, and I wanted to weep.

<Good morning, little seer,> he said.

<My King.> With effort, I kept my voice even. A headache lurked behind my eyes and I needed a cup of pain relief tea or it would soon erupt into something incapacitating.

<Was it a useful vision?> he said, his voice a deep rumble in my ear.

<It wasn't a vision, my King,> I said, burying my face against the pillow to keep the morning light from stabbing my eyes.

<And yet you were twitching and seizing. It was difficult to hold you still.>

<I was spirit traveling,> I said. <And it's best not to hold me still when I'm having a seizure.> I pressed a hand to my head. <My King, I have a headache. I was healing all night in my spirit body, and I need to rest.>

<Is that so?> He kissed the back of my neck and stroked a hand down the length of my body.

I shivered and tried not to think too clearly about how I had been dressed when I left my body on my couch, and how I was now naked, the King's chest pressed to my back, his hips nestled close against the top of my tail.

He kissed me again and then slipped out of my bed, reaching for a sleeping tunic and robe discarded on the floor. <I'll tell your attendant you require her,> he said, and I think I managed to pronounce a <Thank you> before he left.

I curled tight under the blanket, wings and tail clamped against my back and legs. There was a dampness under my tail that I didn't want to think about. I hoped I had soiled myself while I was out of my body, because otherwise it meant the King had…

<Goddess, please no,> I whispered.

I heard the outer door open and close quietly, then Neeka's footsteps as she passed through my bedroom to open the balcony door and to fetch water from the bathing room. She passed through again and I heard her stirring up the fire in my sitting room.

My head throbbed. I clenched my teeth and slid a hand between my legs, reached back for the wetness under my tail, between my buttocks. I didn't want to know, but I *needed* to know. I withdrew my hand and cracked open my eyes. The early morning light hurt but I had to look. The damp substance on my fingers glistened, translucent white.

I bit back a sob. At least there was no blood.

And then, suddenly, I flung myself from the bed, ignoring the two serpents who streaked in through the open balcony door chittering in distress, and scrambled for my bathing room. I leaned over the sink and vomited.

<My Seer?> Neeka said, her voice soft from the other room. <Tokka? Are you ill?>

I wiped my face and swung the door shut before sitting on

the commode. I squeezed my muscles to try to force out whatever of himself the King had left in me while I was twitching on my bed, my spirit self elsewhere.

I threw up again, spattering the floor between my feet, and I tried to hold back a sob.

The door opened and Neeka looked in. I didn't tell her to go. She was the one person – saving maybe Kiernan – who I could bear to see me squatting on the commode and vomiting.

She knelt carefully in front of me, avoiding my mess, and took my face in her hands. <Is it something you ate? Shall I send for Healer Kah?>

I shook my head. <I'm not ill.>

She brushed her hand over my forehead.

<I need my tea,> I said, and she nodded.

<Get in the bath,> she said. <Have a hot soak. I'll clean this up later.> I let her help me up and into the hot pool, and let the water soothe me.

When Neeka returned, I sat on the edge of the pool with only my feet submerged and drank the tea, feeling my headache retreat enough that I could think clearly.

<Call for a cleaner,> I said, and she shook her head.

<I don't think you want anyone around you, do you?> she said, kneeling to clean up the mess I had made. When she had finished, she said, <Did our King…?> But she couldn't say whatever else she had been about to ask.

<Last night I spirit travelled,> I said. <I was able to heal some of the children who were taken worst by the fever.>

<And it's left you ill yourself.>

I shook my head. <Exhausted and with the worst headache I've ever had, but not ill.>

She crossed the room and sat next to me on the edge of the pool. I leaned my head on her shoulder, and she put an arm around me.

<Then what?> she said.

<I… I think I tried to do too much and passed out. I suppose my spirit body vanished from the infirmary. Or at least I don't remember returning to my body.>

I paused and pressed my face into her shoulder, breathing in the comforting scent of soap and winterleaf that always clung to her. Then I took a deep breath, and another.

<When I woke up,> I said, turning the teacup in my hands but not really seeing the design of clouds swirling around it. <The King was in my bed – *I* was in my bed, when I had left my body on the couch.>

<Oh, no,> Neeka said softly, her arm tightening around me.

<I think he… No, I *know* he… he…>

<You don't have to say it, Tokka.>

<I haven't seen him since we returned yesterday morning. I haven't had a chance to tell him what I read in the Founding Laws.>

She turned her face to breathe into the top of my hair. <It doesn't matter, Tokka. Even if he could legally take you as his pleasure boy, it's still wrong to… to do that while you *slept*, while you weren't even present in your body. That's – >

<Please don't say it,> I said and the tears I had been holding back began to leak from the corners of my eyes.

<It was wrong,> she said, but didn't put a name to what our King had done, what he had been doing all along, because even when he had seemed to give me a choice, I had never believed I was allowed to refuse. Not until I read the Founding Laws.

<Tell him next time you see him,> Neeka said. <In fact, once you're rested, go to him. I'll come with you, and Trikta and Konta. Tell him what you learned. Surely he won't continue once he knows it's against the Founding Laws.>

<He already knows,> I said. <Councilor Rocsh and I believe he's hidden the Eyrie's copy of the Laws so no one else can learn.>

<But *you* know now, and the Councilor. Our King may be selfish and jealous, but I don't believe he would keep doing this once he knows others are aware of the law.>

I straightened up and examined my hands clenched around the teacup. <You once told me the King was a generous and skillful lover.>

She slouched, leaning her elbows on her thighs. <It's what I had heard,> she said. Her voice was full of misery. <I thought it was true. I didn't know… he preferred… boys.>

<That he wanted me because he could pretend I hadn't reached my majority yet? Because I'm smaller than other Vogel?>

<I thought he wanted you because you're beautiful, and unique. Tokka, my Seer. I'm so sorry.> She put her face in her hands.

I leaned into her again. <I don't blame you, Neeka. You didn't know, so you could hardly have warned me.>

She lifted her head to look at me. I could tell from her eyes that she did blame herself, at least partly.

<And even if you had known, what could you have done? Even if *I* had known, I still could not have refused him.>

<I think I hate him, Tokka,> she whispered. <It's treason, but I really think I hate our King.>

<Me too,> I said softly. <I didn't even hate the Abbess of the Moon or the Alfar King, and they wanted to sacrifice me. I didn't hate Sean nicFia, who wanted to kill me but hurt Kiernan instead. But I really do believe I hate the King.>

4
Kiernan

"You had a birthday," my father said as I perched on the stool that had been fetched for me, grateful that I hadn't been brought a regular chair that would leave me feeling like a child at the grownups' table.

"Yes, sir," I said.

"How old are you now?" asked Duncan. "Twelve?" He laughed, but only a few of the nearby men chuckled with him, and even they didn't really sound amused. It was a tired joke we had all heard far too often, that I looked young, that I aged slowly because of my half-fey ancestry.

"Thirty-seven," said my father before I could answer. I was glad, because my answer would have been to break my brother's nose.

"If you were full Sidhe," he continued, "That would be equivalent to what, twenty-five for a human?"

"It's not really exact," I said. "And I *am* half-human." And so non-human-appearing I had to constantly remind people of it. Or choose to let them forget.

"Wouldn't know it to look at you," muttered Duncan. I knew part of the issue was envy. He looked every day of his forty human years. He was middle-aged and I was still barely past my majority and we were only three years apart. My father and I both ignored him.

I knew what my father was really asking, though. Humans – or at least those in the upper classes of Great River Monarchy – had traditional gifts that were given at specific ages. When I'd turned thirteen and had showed up on his doorstep having run away from my Queen's Court, he gave me a skinning knife he'd been given by his father when he turned nine. And when I reached nineteen, he sent me a bow suitable for a fifteen-year-old human boy. Presumably there was another such gifting occasion at twenty-five.

"You don't seem to be lacking in blades, but if you want one from my armory, you're of the age to choose one."

"I'd like that." Where I would strap on another sword, I had no idea, but I wouldn't turn it down, even if steel was duller and heavier than moonsilver. My father's armorer made excellent weapons.

"I count four on you," Duncan said, eyeing my twin knives and two swords. "What are you compensating for, little brother?"

I smiled, showing him my teeth. "I didn't know you could count." Someone snickered and my brother scowled. I knew I'd pay for that later, but only if he managed to surprise me in a dark alley somewhere.

"Obviously I need something to fend off suitors with," I continued. "But I don't suppose you have that problem." Several of the men at the table laughed outright. They knew, as I did, that Duncan had never figured out that what women actually want is to be treated as people, and not as prizes to be won, or problems to be solved.

I didn't bother to tell him that the blades he had counted were only the ones he could see. I had three small but deadly faun-made throwing knives in each boot, a curved werewolf-smithed gutting blade under my coat in the small of my back, and our father's skinning knife tucked under my right arm.

"Would you like to choose now?" My father continued to ignore Duncan, as he usually did, which might explain why my brother was such a dick: it was the only way he could get anyone to pay attention to him.

"As long as you don't send Duncan to supervise."

He snorted. "I don't know why you two can't get along like grown adults."

"He'd have to be grown first," Duncan muttered.

My father pushed his plate away, drained his goblet, and stood. "Come on then." He looked at Duncan. "You stay here."

My brother scowled but didn't argue.

I wanted very badly to point out that my father didn't only avoid Great River City because he was needed in Dudoon. He also stayed away because he didn't get along with *his* brother any better than I got along with mine.

Instead, I just got up and followed him out into the gateyard, keeping my back straight and trying not to be so conscious of the fact that I was short compared to every person there, even my father, who wasn't especially tall for a human.

We crossed the gateyard without speaking and headed through the main keep and out the other side to another courtyard at the rear and then to the base of the tallest tower. The first three floors were the armory: shields on the ground floor, armor on the next, and weapons on the third.

We climbed the stairs, and it wasn't until we stepped inside the weapons room and the door was shut behind us that my father spoke again.

"You didn't have to lose the antlers, son," he said. "You never had to do that."

I paced the room, pretending to examine a rack of spears far too long for my height, and then a row of double-bladed axes.

"I didn't do it to fit in," I said. "I stopped trying to fit in when I was thirteen and finally realized it was never going to work."

"I know," he said, his voice quiet. He wasn't a loud man by nature, but there was something almost gentle in his tone.

I turned to look at him. "Do you ever speak to her? Write letters?"

"Of course." He looked away and it was his turn to pretend to examine a row of weapons.

"She took my magic," I said.

"Like when you were a child, and she sent you here for the first time."

"No." He glanced up and quickly looked away again. "When I was a child, she took my antlers so I couldn't use magic, but I could still *feel* it. This time… I had someone else do it." I picked up a sword and swung it experimentally. It was too large for me, but it was well-balanced and felt comfortable in my hand.

"She put spelled moonsilver on my antlers," I said. "It didn't just block my magic; it *took* my magic. It took my connection to the forest, took… It took everything." I swung the sword again. "I know you don't have a lot of magic, but you do have some. You must have an idea how that would feel."

He turned away from the arrow he was inspecting and I put the sword back on its rack. He gripped my shoulder, and I had to work to hold still, to not break his grip and drop him to the floor as I had been trained to do. As *he* had trained me to do.

"I'm sorry," he said, and he sounded like he meant it. "We talk about you, in our letters, and not much else, but she didn't tell me that."

"It was excruciating. And empty." I pulled away and ran my hand along a row of daggers, each sheathed in plain leather. "I wanted to die, General." I almost called him "father," but couldn't quite manage it. I had grown up calling him "General," or "Sir," like everyone else in Dudoon.

"I'm sorry," he said again. "But you held on. You lived. And you escaped her spells."

"At the expense of being able to actually *use* my magic, yes." I held out a hand and summoned wisplight. A thin and vague pool of bluish glow flickered in my palm for less than a heartbeat and then dribbled away to nothing.

It was pathetic, but it was more than I had been able to do when I left my Queen's palace. I dropped my hand and resumed examining weapons. I wasn't sure why I had told him any of that, about wanting to die. I didn't want pity, especially not from him.

On the far wall was a cupboard, closed and locked. I had always wondered what was inside but had never dared ask. Now, as I approached it, my father said, "Here," and tossed me a key.

"What's in there?"

"You don't remember?"

"I've never seen inside," I said. I fitted the key into the lock, and it snapped open easily. I wondered why I had never thought to pick the lock as a child. It wasn't a complicated one. "I haven't even been in the armory for years."

"Not since your mother gifted you with your fancy ancient fey weapons. You didn't need my steel anymore."

"Steel is heavier than moonsilver," I said. "I'm not exactly a large man, General." I didn't add, "compared to a human," because he already knew I was taller than most Sidhe, and heavier built than any Alfar or Huldr.

He snorted. "You might be a shortass, but you're stronger than half my men, and quicker than all of them."

"Are you complementing me?" I swung open the door of the cabinet to reveal stands holding bright-bladed swords, knives, a few axes, and one very large spear point. Every one of them was beautiful, and most of them were probably worth more on their own than the whole rest of the armory.

"I did a lot of things wrong as a father," he said, and sighed. I resisted the urge to turn around and stare at him. My father was not one to admit mistakes. He wasn't one to *make* mistakes.

"I grew up," I said. "So did Duncan. You kept us from killing each other."

Another sigh. "Duncan is a smarmy shit who thinks he should have everything handed to him because his father is a General and his uncle is a King."

I laughed, but it was dry. "He is kind of a dick, but I don't think that's your fault." I bent to look closer at a leaf-shaped dagger on the bottom shelf. It had a blackened steel blade with some kind of design etched on it. The shape reminded me of fey designs, though it was clearly human workmanship.

"Maybe not." I heard him shift to lean against a shelf. "But you…"

This time, I did glance up.

"You needed affection, and I gave you a sword. You hungered for knowledge, and I gave you exercise. It's a mystery to me how you turned out to be a decent man."

I turned away again, confused, the prick of tears in the corners of my eyes. If he had ever once spoken to me like this growing up, I might not have resented coming here so much.

I could hear the smile in his voice when he spoke again. "Even if you did fuck your way through half my staff and a not a few of my soldiers."

That startled another laugh out of me, and it felt more genuine this time. Something loosened in my chest, and I felt… okay.

"Some of them will be happy to have you back." I looked at him again to see his smile turn into a grin.

"Well, I'm not going to be fucking anyone this time."

"Not even my stablemaster? I'm fairly sure he was looking at your ass when we crossed the gateyard."

I turned back to the cupboard. I could feel a flush creeping up my neck and was glad the tone of my skin would hide it if it reached my face. "Not even Colin," I said.

"So is it true, then? You were gelded in Aven?" I could tell from his voice that he was poking fun at me, so I gave him a very serious look.

"I'm sorry, Father. You won't get any grandsons out of me."

His eyes widened and he made a choking sound, and I couldn't hold in my laughter.

"You little shit," he said. "I almost believed you. But what did happen?"

I lifted the knife from the bottom shelf of the cupboard so I wouldn't have to look at him. In my hand, it looked long and elegant. The design on the blade, now that I could see it clearly, was a complicated knot of twisted lines and curves, with the head of a strange beast – a dragon, maybe – reaching down the blade.

"I fell in love," I said, and swung the knife. It whistled through the air, quick and nimble. "Where did this come from? It's light." I held it up for him to see.

I could feel his curiosity, but he answered my question

instead of following up on my statement. "That was your uncle's. Our grandfather gave it to him, and before that it was *his* grandfather's. We don't know when it was made, but family legend says it was brought to the Isle from the Continent, before the Founding. It supposed to be an alloy of steel and moonsilver, made by a process no one knows anymore."

I swung it again. It felt good in my hand, like it belonged there.

"Some say there were three of them, once, but no one knows where the others are."

"If it's a blade of kings, what's it doing here?"

He reached past me to pull the blade's sheath from the shelf. He ran his fingers over the leather – it was tooled to match the blade, though it was much newer.

"Waiting for you." He held out the sheath.

I stared at him. "Shouldn't it go to Eamon?" The King's oldest son was a few years younger than me, and the Crown Prince.

My father's look was unreadable, and he turned it on me for what felt like a long time. Finally, he said, "No. If you want it, Kiernan, it's yours."

I took the scabbard and slid the knife home. It fit snugly and settled in with satisfying click that I felt as much as heard. I realized that I *did* want this knife, more than I had wanted the fey weapons my Queen had given me.

"You know, she didn't even say 'Happy Birthday'?"

"She doesn't remember those things. You know that."

"Of course." I swallowed. It was true, but it still stung, just as it had every year. "Does it have a name?" I said, nodding at the knife. Naming weapons didn't have the same significance for humans as it did for fey – fey named blades adapted to the hand of their owner and burned the hand of anyone else.

"Legend says it did once, but it's been long forgotten."

I nodded and walked the rest of the way around the room, lifting down a few other swords to try, but I had made my choice as soon as I had touched the antler hilt of the etched knife.

"She does love you." My father's voice was soft, that almost-gentle tone filling it again. I turned to see if he was trying an ill-considered joke, though I already knew he wasn't.

"You don't believe it," he said, his brows drawing together. For a fleeting moment it was like looking in the mirror at my older self.

I thought of her telling me she was proud of me, that I was like my father, like *her*. I shook my head. "She's never acted like it."

"She wanted you to be strong. *Needed* you to be strong."

"She almost *broke* me."

"But she didn't and look at you now."

"Antlerless, magicless, and banished from Morven Palace? Again?"

He shook his head and put a hand on my shoulder. "Kiernan. Son, you defeated her at her own game." His voice held no gentleness now, only something that could have been fierce pride. "She punished you, and you escaped." He sighed and dropped his hand away. "She wants you strong, but she also fears you becoming too strong to control."

It was my turn to shake my head. "I need to get back to my people before morning. Did you find us a building?"

He ignored my change of subject and said, "We did the best we could with you, son. You were not exactly an ordinary boy."

"Did you never think that maybe I wanted to be? That I wanted to be treated like every other child on this fucking Isle?" I wanted my words to come out angry, but they only sounded tired.

He shook his head and stepped past me to lock the cabinet. "I wish you could have been an ordinary boy, Kiernan."

When he turned back, his face was all business, any trace of emotion gone. "I've been corresponding with an agent in Great River City. You can meet with him tomorrow. I believe we've found you the perfect location, but they want payment up front, in coin."

"That won't be a problem."

His eyebrows shot up, but he didn't comment. We walked back down the stairs, and through the keep to the gateyard. The stablemaster appeared when our footsteps scuffed across the stone, wiping his mouth with the back of his hand like we had disturbed him at dinner, though it was now deep night.

"General," he said. He didn't salute – he wasn't a soldier – but he stood straighter and looked at the ground in front of him. "My Prince." He snuck a glance at me, and I winked. He blushed and it made up for my earlier embarrassment at remembering our past. I had nothing to be embarrassed about, after all, and at least I could still *pretend* to be confident.

"My horse, please," I said, and he nodded and moved quickly away.

"Come back when you can stay longer," my father said.

"I will." I wasn't sure I would, but he didn't need to hear that now.

"Make sure you present yourself to your uncle once you've seen the agent and settled your people."

"Of course."

He looked like he wanted to say more, but in the end he just nodded and stepped back as I mounted my horse and rode out the gate.

I held on as I rode away, as I crossed the wide river on the ferry, as I followed the riverbank west towards where my people were camped. Then halfway back I pulled my horse to stop and leaned over his neck. The tears were hot and stinging and my heart ached in my chest.

Coal curled tight around my neck and pushed his little head beneath my ear.

"Fuck," I said, and it came out half sob.

Coal purred and it vibrated into my skull, easing something just enough that I could sit up and nudge my horse into a walk again.

Love, said Coal.

I DIDN'T EXPECT A WELCOME party when we rode into Great River City, which was good, because we didn't get one. But the agent was where he said he'd be, and he showed us to the building he'd found.

It was old, and there were repairs needed before the cold weather really hit, but it occupied an entire block of its own, and it was well-built. It wouldn't take too much to convert the bottom floor into offices and reception rooms, and there was plenty of space on the other floors for small a private room for each of my staff, and a suite for Padraig. There was a kitchen and a dining hall, and even a small stable. We could keep our riding horses there, but the pack animals would have to be kept elsewhere or sold. Maybe I should send the mules back to Morven Forest.

The topmost floor was smaller than the rest but had a large balcony and a private bathing room, and even though it felt selfish, I decided to claim it for my own. There was even a perfect room for a library.

Best of all, the building wasn't a solid rectangle on its block; instead, it formed a square with an open courtyard in the middle. It was barren, but by spring we should be able to have it flourishing as a garden. A small forest oasis hidden in the city.

I handed over the coin – the price was high, but my Queen had provided well for us and promised more money if we needed it – then I signed the paperwork and took the keys. The Sidhe Embassy had a home, and I could breathe a little easier, knowing my people would be safe.

Padraig and Erith helped me get everyone organized; Erith especially had turned out to have a talent for it, and I didn't think I'd have been able to manage half as well without him. Once everyone had been given a task and the cleaning and unloading had begun, I called the three dryads to me and led them out into our courtyard.

They stood in a row in front of me, eyes on the ground, hands folded, waiting.

"This is to be your task," I said and one of them, a short, green-haired person who was slight even for a dryad, glanced up at me and then quickly away.

I held back a frustrated sigh. I didn't know if these dryads had been treated worse than Daphnis had, or if they were just meek by nature, but my efforts to engage them in conversation on the way here had not been spectacularly successful. It wasn't their fault, of course; it had never been safe for dryads to be anything but subservient in my mother's court.

I paced across the courtyard and paused to poke at a cracked flagstone with my foot. "I want a garden here," I said. "Somewhere we can all come to relax, to feel we're not so far from Morven Forest." I turned back to them and caught another, much taller, dryad looking at me. They took longer to look away.

"And I would very much like it if you made yourselves a home here, a space of privacy just for the three of you."

At that, all three looked up, met my eyes, and then looked

away. Only this time, none of them looked at the ground. Instead, they looked around themselves at the courtyard. It wasn't much to look at now, but it had potential.

"By Founding Law, your people are enslaved. By magic they have been kept that way." They all seemed to draw closer to each other without moving, and they didn't look at me, but I could feel their attention on me anyway. "I would change that if I could. And maybe someday, things will be different."

Now they all looked at me openly.

"Until that day, I want you to feel as if *here*, at least, you are the equal of anyone else who works for me." I had to look away from their stares and paced across the courtyard again. "I'm not permitted to pay you in coin, but anything you need, for this garden or for yourselves, only ask and I'll see you get it."

"My Prince?" said the tall dryad. I turned and they met my eyes. I could see their breathing was quick, like they were afraid, but determined not to show it.

"Yes, Pitys?"

They blinked, the only sign that they were surprised I knew their name.

"Does the Queen know?"

"She does not, nor will she."

"What sort of garden do you want us to grow?" asked the mid-height, very pale dryad.

"Beith, is it?"

They nodded.

"Create a garden you three would like to live in. A garden we creatures of Morven Forest will feel at home in. If it means one large space, or several small ones is up to you three to decide."

"Can it be wild?" asked the third dryad, one of the shortest I had seen aside from dryad children, and slender as a reed.

Their skin was the pale yellow-green of the inner bark of a salt-leaf tree and their hair the green of new leaves. "Can we bring trees from Morven Forest here?"

"Yes and yes." I smiled. "And you are called Syrinx?"

They said, "Yes," in a soft musical voice that made me wonder if they could sing.

"Do you all call yourselves 'they' or do you use something else?" Daphnis was the only dryad I knew who had used something other than 'they,' but that might only be because he was my friend and felt comfortable asking.

"I use 'they'," said Syrinx.

"Pitys uses 'they' and I use 'she'," said Beith. "My Prince."

I nodded. "Thank you. I'll leave you to explore. Please let Erith know if you have any immediate requirements. I'll have your pots of soil brought in and you can expect more to arrive in a few moons."

"My Prince?" Syrinx stepped forward hesitantly.

"Never be afraid to speak to me," I said gently. "I am not my mother."

"Why are you doing this? We're only dryads. Slaves."

"You're people," I said. "One of my dearest friends was a dryad, until my Queen took him away from me."

"You mean Daphnis."

I nodded. "I will never be King, but you're still *my* people and I want to do as much for my people – *all* my people – as I can." It wasn't a great answer, and it sounded too much like I was claiming them as possessions, but it was the only answer I had. Someday soon, I supposed I ought to find a better one.

For now, like everything else I did, I had to hope it would be good enough.

5

Fionn

Councilor Rocsh came to see me after the noon meal. I was still groggy, though I had slept again, but at least my headache had retreated, and I could think straight. I planned to sleep even more before the day was done, because I wanted to spirit travel again that night, to heal as many as I could. If it meant sleeping all day so I could manage it, I would.

I would do it even if it meant I woke every morning with the King in my bed.

<Councilor.> I inclined my head, and he bowed his in return and seated himself gracefully on the couch I indicated. I sat, too, and my serpents curled protectively around my neck. They liked Rocsh but could sense my overall unease and were acting suspicious towards everyone from the servants who brought the meal to Neeka, who always gave them treats.

<You look tired, my Seer,> the Councilor said.

<I am. It was a long night.>

<Neeka told me you were outside your body, healing our sick.>

I nodded and took the cup of tea Neeka handed me. I held it cupped in my hands but didn't sip it. I was so full of all the teas she had made me that day I was surprised my insides didn't slosh when I moved.

<I intend to do so again tonight, and tomorrow, and every night for as long as it takes.>

He sipped from his cup. <I've spoken with our King about the Founding Laws. He insists he has no knowledge of the whereabouts of the Eyrie's copy and that he has never read the full section detailing the obligations of Monarchs and Seers, only the summary.>

<I see.>

He smiled gently and leaned across the table to squeeze my hand briefly, before settling back on the couch. I had once thought him an emotionless person, but the longer I knew him, the more I could read his subtle expressions.

<I gave him the transcription I had made of the relevant sections. He was… not pleased.>

<Thank you, Councilor.>

He watched me without speaking for a moment, and I wondered how much of my thoughts he could read. I had never looked at him with my Seer senses and it seemed rude to do so now, so I didn't know how much magic he had or what its nature was. Kiernan had told me Rocsh had said he could read the intentions of others, but that was all I knew.

<If he still insists, Seer Tokka,> he said, his voice carefully even, like he didn't want to spook a wild animal. <I hope you will let me know. You should not have to struggle alone, and if necessary, I will present the matter to Council. I do hope it won't come to that, but I will act if you need me to.>

<It would be uncomfortable for the King to have his transgressions made known, I suppose.>

A hint of a smile touched his wide mouth, and he said,

gently, <It was your feelings I was hoping to spare, my Seer.> He sighed. <I am sworn to work for our King, but if I must choose, Tokka, it is you I will protect.>

I couldn't help but stare at him. Once, I had believed him to be the King's truest ally, but over the moons I had lived in the Eyrie I came to realize more and more that Councilor Rocsh put our people above all else, and the health of our Monarchy over the wishes of its King.

In Morven Forest, I had begun to believe he was an ally not of the King, but of me as our Seer, because I was the representative of our people to both the spirit world and to King and Council. Now he almost sounded as if it was *me*, not just as the Eyrie's Seer, but as myself, that he wished to protect.

<Thank you, Councilor,> I finally managed. The words seemed entirely inadequate, but it eased something in my chest to know I had an ally among the Council, among the nobility.

I knew the King would seek me out, sooner or later, and not just to show up in my bed. There would be a conversation, or more likely a lecture, and I had no notion how it would go save that he would be displeased.

He would likely never let me forget he was disappointed in me.

But that was for later. For now, I had people to heal. When Councilor Rocsh left, I had Neeka make me a sleeping tea – yet more tea! – and crawled into bed. Smoke and Flame draped themselves over my pillow.

We watch, said Smoke.

We keep safe, said Flame.

"Thank you, little friends," I replied and then I let the sedative in the tea do its work and pull me into sleep.

I woke feeling almost refreshed and let Neeka fuss over me while we ate our evening meal together. Then I sent her home, told my night guards that I must not be disturbed while spirit traveling lest something go wrong with the healing, and I drank a cup of salt-leaf bark tisane.

As before, Smoke and Flame lapped up the final drops and joined me in spirit form, and we headed for the infirmary.

This time, Healer Kah was tending the patients herself, and she immediately sensed my presence and hurried over to me. She took my hands and smiled, and it was comforting to find I was mostly solid to her.

<My Seer,> she said. <I heard you were here last night, that you enabled several of my patients to go home to their families.>

<Is Lisna still here?>

<For now, she has gone back to her parents, but Healer Renta told me you believe she will become a healer.>

<Yes. She… there was a lot of magic dormant in her. Healing magic and other things I couldn't read. She will be very strong, whatever talents she has. And…>

Something must have showed on my face, because Kah looked at me with concern. <What is it?>

<I saw… You probably won't believe me.> I laughed, but it felt – and probably sounded – forced. I wasn't even sure *I* would believe me.

<I believe, my Seer, that *as* a seer you see things most of us cannot.>

I drew in a steadying breath. <The Lady of the Skies was here. She aided me, helped me regulate my use of magic so I didn't use too much at once. And…> I looked down the row of cots. There were just as many as there had been the previous night, so I had to assume more patients had been brought it – those who had been tended at home by their families, perhaps.

<Go on.> Kah's voice was warm, and I knew from watching her work how she could draw her patients out, to get

them to trust her, in order to learn things they might not otherwise reveal, that could help her heal them. I realized now that it was also a magical ability, something that enhanced her healing magic but could be used separately from it.

Healer Kah, could, I thought, be very dangerous if one had secrets. I carefully buried my thoughts behind a shield of nonsense ideas as Seer Siona had taught me.

<The Lady of the Skies has taken an interest in Lisna. Though she stayed with me as I healed, she only became visible when I was healing Lisna. She touched the child's forehead, stroked her hair. I believe the Goddess Above has chosen Lisna as a favorite.>

<Did the child see her? And for what was she chosen?>

<I don't know.>

There was no more I could say about my experience, so I had the Healer take me to my first patient of the night, perched on my stool, and let myself slip into the proper state of mind for healing. It was not quite a trance, and not quite seer-sight, but something of both, and it was much easier to do in my spirit body. And though she did not make another appearance, I could feel the Lady of the Skies nearby, her terrifying and comforting presence brushing against my magic.

This time, I healed ten patients before I had to stop, and this time I didn't black out. I realized, as I pulled myself free of the magic, that Healer Kah had stayed close, lending me her own magic, and it was she who decided when it was time for me to rest.

I walked back to my rooms, weary even though my spirit body wasn't affected the same way as my physical body would have been. I felt as if I had been scraped out with a serrated spoon like the kind we used at the Eyrie to eat certain thick-skinned fruits.

I was barely aware of being back in my body before I

slipped into sleep. In the morning, I had the same terrible headache, but I was alone in my bed. Neeka later told me that the King had come, and my guards had passed on my instructions, and he had left without protest.

So it went for the rest of the nineday. I slept each day while Neeka helped the healers prepare more poultices and syrups for the herbal part of the fever cure. At night I spirit travelled and performed the magical part.

We soon learned that all parts of the cure were more effective of done in the correct order, with the right amount of time between. So while I slept, Healer Kah administered the syrup to drive the fever to the surface of the body in the morning. In the afternoon, she applied the cooling poultices, and at night, I would use healing magic to drive out the fever and sickness for good.

It was exhausting, but my endurance improved with each night and soon all of the worst cases were cured and we could slow our treatments, allowing me more time to rest.

The whole time, the King respected my request to be undisturbed at night. But of course, it couldn't last.

HE CAME TO MY ROOMS on the day Healer Kah insisted I take off to rest. The only patients left in the infirmary were those who were strong enough to recover on their own, given time, and since we still had plenty of salt-leaf on hand, we could give them that time.

I sent Neeka away to enjoy herself in the City Beneath the Cliff, and even got Trikta and Konta to agree to take the day for themselves. The guards who stood outside my door were less familiar but seemed competent enough. And it wasn't likely that anyone would attack me in the Eyrie – my guards were more ceremonial than functional, anyway.

I was seated at my loom, working on weaving the thread I had spun from my own hair into a ribbon with a complicated pattern that was only visible when the light hit it just so. It was my first attempt to make an offering like the ones I had seen depicted on the walls of the caves below the Eyrie. The pattern I had adapted from one in the book Kiernan had given me at Autumn Balance, and I was pleased with how it was coming out.

I was so absorbed in my task that I didn't hear him come in and I shrieked when his hands came down on my shoulders. I couldn't help but think Kiernan would be disappointed in me, that I'd let someone sneak up on me, though he'd likely only smile and tease me gently.

<Making yourself a pretty ribbon for your hair, little Seer?> the King said, sliding his hands down my chest.

For a long moment, I froze, not knowing what to do. Then I stood up and stepped away. <My King,> I said, inclining my head slightly. <I'm weaving an offering, such as our ancestors used to leave for the spirits.>

<How fitting for a Seer.> He smiled, showing too many teeth. <But do you not kneel for your King anymore?>

<My King.> I bit my lip, hard, and then made myself relax. I mustn't be afraid, and I mustn't seem anxious. I pulled calm around myself like a cloak and lifted my chin. <According to the Founding Laws, I am nearly your equal in rank.>

His eyes turned hard, and I breathed carefully, slowly. I knew that look, and it was dangerous. He didn't like to be defied.

<I'm hearing a terrible lot about the Founding Laws lately, little Seer. But that doesn't change the fact that you belong to me. Your precious Founding Laws say that, too.> He raised a dark blue eyebrow.

<My King,> I said, struggling to maintain the proper respect in my voice when all I wanted to do was scream at him. <The word used to convey belonging is an archaic one. It refers not to ownership, as a slave is owned, but instead evokes a sense of duty, of unbreakable obligations.>

<Is that so?> His voice held a note I knew meant he was on the edge of fury, but I couldn't stop now.

Kiernan had said I no longer needed to be afraid to return here, but I *was* afraid. I was terrified. I buried it deep, worried that even so far away he might feel it, and fret.

<It is, my King.>

<That still sounds like you are mine to command.>

<The obligations go both ways, my King.> I took a deep breath, glad that my serpents had gone off to see if they could catch some fish with the wild serpents that gathered near the beach. <I should be paid, to begin with.>

<Is that the issue, little Seer? Money? You are housed, fed, and clothed. What have I not provided for you?>

<According to the laws, my King, I am owed a wage in addition. Money of my own to use as I wish.>

<Owed?> His anger was seeping closer to the surface of his words.

<According to the Founding Laws, my King.>

<And you know this how?>

<I read them in Morven. The Sidhe Queen was gracious enough to allow me to consult their library.>

<And what else are you *owed*, little Seer?> There was a challenge in his voice. He dared me to say it, to deny him what he most wanted of me.

<I am to have voice in your Council and to be the one who oversees our people's spiritual life.>

<You have those.>

<And...> I hesitated, fear knotting in my belly.

<And?> The edge of anger became razor sharp.

<And we are not permitted to…>

<To what, little Seer?> He stepped closer, and I backed away until I reached the window. I cursed myself for letting him corner me.

<To have… relations, my King.>

<Is that what the Founding Laws say, little Seer? That a Monarch may not have relations with his Seer?>

<Yes, my King.>

<And how does the word "relations" translate? Is it an archaic term as well? Is it as slippery as the word for "belong"?>

<It is very clear, my King.>

<Enlighten me.> He stood so close I could feel the heat from his body as clearly as I could feel cold from the window seeping into my wings.

<A Monarch may not dictate with whom a Seer shares their bed,> I quoted. I had read it over so many times in the Morven Palace library that I knew the words by heart. <And it is inappropriate for a Monarch to take any of their own Seers as lovers, as it could create a conflict of interest.> I had to force air to keep moving in and out of my lungs. <That is what the Laws say, my King.>

<Show me these Laws that so conveniently make my possession of you illegal.> He pressed even closer, his body pinning me against the glass.

<I cannot, my King.>

<Really? And why is that?>

I made myself meet his eyes. His deep blue stare bored into me, but I refused to look away, to back down. <Because someone has removed the Eyrie's copy of the Founding Laws from the library. It has gone missing.>

<And I am to simply believe you?> He put his hand on my

face and ran his claws over my cheekbone. <Pretty little boy, I own you, and you know it.>

<Councilor Rocsh has read the Laws, too, my King. You may ask him. I believe he also had a transcription made of some sections.>

<And did you tell Councilor Rocsh that I'm fucking you, little Seer?>

<He had already guessed, my King. The whole Council suspects.>

He leaned closer and I closed my eyes, bracing myself for I knew not what. But he only kissed my forehead, surprisingly gently.

<Nobody knows anything, little Seer, and we will keep it that way. Once, you enjoyed my touch, and I believe you will again.> He pressed the full length of his body against mine and the thick scent of his perfume filled my nose. <Today, I will let you think on your options. When I return, I think I will begin your education all over again. Another cleansing bath in the sacred pool might do you good.>

He stepped back and I wanted to sob in relief. I made myself stay calm and serene. I didn't say anything. I didn't know *what* to say.

<When I return in a day or so, I expect you to be obedient, as you were when you first came here. Do as I wish, and I will give you everything. Money, jewels, pretty clothes. Pleasure such as you have not felt before.>

I still didn't move. I doubted the King could hope to match the pleasure I had already experienced with Kiernan, but I said nothing. I didn't even blink.

<Defy me, little Seer, and I will make sure you learn your place the hard way.>

He turned to go.

<If you wish to see for yourself, my King, the relevant

parts begin halfway through the Founding Laws, in the section titled "Seers and Monarchs."> I was surprised my voice came out so calm. I sounded detached and unconcerned.

I did *not* sound like the youth my King wanted me to be.

He laughed without turning. <How will I read it if, as you claim, the book is missing?>

<That, you will have to answer yourself, my King.> I braced for his anger, but he only waved a hand in the air and left.

I kept myself still and upright until the door closed behind him. I forced air in and out, kept breathing slowly, waiting until I knew he was really gone. And then it was as if all the strength went out of my legs, and I sank to the floor. My hands were shaking. My whole body trembled. I curled over my lap, hands pressed to the stone floor to keep them still, and I breathed in desperate gasps.

He had been angry. Terrifyingly so. And yet he hadn't exploded, hadn't hit me, or even forced me to pleasure him. Perhaps the King could be reasoned with, after all. Perhaps I wouldn't have to resort to laying my shame bare for the Council to see and judge. Maybe I could dare hope.

I sat that way, slumped on my floor, until I heard a tap at my door. I stood quickly, smoothing out my tunic and making my face serene and expressionless. It was only servants bringing my evening meal, and they left the dishes on the table and quickly departed. The food didn't interest me, though I knew I needed to eat after all the healing I had done. I needed to stay strong. Since coming to the Eyrie, I had lost weight and hadn't managed to put any back on. Since I had already been thin to begin with, I couldn't afford to lose more. So I uncovered the dishes and inhaled the scents, hoping the smell would make me hungry. The first dish held prawns and shellfish on skewers, dripping in butter, while the second was crisp cold greens that must be the very last of the season, grown in a glass house somewhere. Under the last cover was a slice of some kind of tart, creamy-looking and studded with sugared dried fruit.

A cool breeze brushed the back of my neck as Smoke and Flame pushed open the balcony door on their way in.

Sea bugs, said Flame, landing on my knee and staring intently at the skewers of seafood.

Is good, said Smoke.

I held out a skewer for each of them, then made myself eat the rest. The serpents had no interest in the greens, but I ate them, my appetite finally returning when the tart oil they were dressed in met my tongue. I cleaned the plate and then eyed the dessert.

"Do you want some?" I asked.

Smoke and Flame each sampled a little of the tart, declared it too tangy, and curled up on the hearth. I tasted it tentatively. I wasn't given sweets often at the Eyrie, and had almost never had any, aside from seasonal fruit, at the Abbey. Even in Morven Forest I had only sampled a few desserts, so I didn't know what to expect.

It *was* tangy, flavored with some kind of citrus, and creamy on my tongue though I didn't detect any dairy in it. The fruit, though dried and chewy, still retained its flavor, but sharpened almost to sour. The sugar that preserved it balanced the whole in my mouth.

I ate the whole slice and sat back. I couldn't remember a time when I'd actually eaten everything that was brought to me, without Neeka's help, at least. Usually there was far too much food for one person.

Finally, I let myself relax. My people would soon be safe from the fever, and Councilor Rocsh would convince the King to obey the Founding Laws. That the King had neglected to mention Rocsh had already spoken to him and instead played ignorant bothered me, but I pushed the thought aside. I could concentrate simply on being a Seer again and would no longer need to be afraid.

And maybe soon, Kiernan would regain his magic and come for me.

6
Kiernan

I PRESENTED MYSELF to the King of Great River Monarchy first thing after the evening meal. I had let Erith dress me in my finest, most uncomfortable clothes and shaved the soft fuzz that always tried to grow along my jawline as if my hair wanted me to look a little human but refused to actually grow into a beard. I buckled on my swords and my twin knives – all Sidhe named blades – and reluctantly left the rest of my weapons behind. It was, apparently, rude to carry hidden armaments in the presence of royalty.

It was hardest to leave behind the knife my father gave me, but I hadn't had my belt adapted for it yet, or really even figured out where it would fit.

Each of my guards, and I decided that for this occasional I would bring all six, also had a named sword and at least one knife. And, to make clear the statement that Morven Forest was not only a Monarchy of Sidhe, I also brought Erith along as my secretary and attendant.

"Are you sure, my Prince?" he had said, as he helped me

into my coat. He was too short to settle it over my shoulders the way Daphnis used to, but he had a better eye than I did for which trousers went with which shirt and which pair of boots.

"Being my secretary comes with a pay raise, and you've already been doing the work."

"But… in court? I'm a faun. Won't my presence insult the King? They say he doesn't like non-humans."

"If he's insulted by non-humans, he's going to be insulted by everyone I'm taking with me. And by me, for that matter. I don't very much care if a faun in his palace insults him more than an honor guard of Sidhe or a half-human nephew." I smiled encouragingly at him. "He needs to know from the beginning that I treat all my people as equals. And besides, you're a very good secretary."

He blushed as he handed me the circlet of moonsilver my Queen had insisted I needed. With no antlers anymore to bear the customary silver tines worn by Sidhe royalty, she felt I needed something to indicate my status. And so, to make sure no one doubted my princeliness, I was forced to put on something far too much like a crown for my liking.

It was pretty, at least, made to look like leafy vines wrapping around my head, holding up small, stylized antlers above each eyebrow. I had wondered if my Queen was mocking me or making some kind of point I wasn't getting.

I settled it on my head and then made sure Erith had knives of his own, worn openly as he was permitted to do as a member of my personal staff. A row of delicate throwing knives was sheathed across his chest – made by his own father, he had told me – and a longer dagger hung from his belt. Dressed in my green and grey livery and standing proudly straight, he looked a far stretch from the awkward and fearful young man I had hired.

"You look handsome," I told him, and the tips of his ears

turned pink. "I hope Padraig appreciates you."

As we entered the long receiving hall in Great River Palace, Erith walked a half-step behind me, ready to scurry forward if I needed him. My guard followed in pairs close behind, Padraig nearest my right, where he would be best able to protect my non-dominant side.

The hall echoed with our footsteps; there were few people there to muffle the sound. I hadn't expected a welcome party here, either, but I suppose I had hoped for something more than a few bored-looking courtiers. It seemed very nearly rude, in fact, and was probably my uncle's way of letting me know he wasn't pleased with my presence, or with the establishment of a Sidhe embassy.

Even the Vogel King had given us more of a turn out and the Sidhe weren't even *his* over-lords.

I stopped at the foot of the dais and looked up at my uncle. He shifted on his throne and looked back. The Queen's seat was empty, but my cousin Eamon, at least, fulfilled his duty to visiting royalty and sat at his father's right hand, watching me expressionlessly.

"Kiernan nicFia," my uncle said.

My guards fell into place around me, two to each side, two behind. They moved smoothly and I had to work not to smile. The drills I had put them through had paid off, even if there weren't many people present to observe.

Erith stepped forward and bowed low. "King Iain Druison nor Great River," he said, his bright voice filling the vast space. I had to bite back another smile at how this shy young man had managed to find a store of self-confidence. "May I present Prince Kiernan Druison nicFia nor Dudoon nor Morven, Ambassador to Great River for the Queen of Morven Forest and the Sidhe Monarchy." He made sure to carefully enunciate every smallest part of my title before stepping back to his place.

"A faun, nephew?" My uncle's face bore a slight sneer, a look of utter disdain, and I felt Erith slump a little next to me, could almost feel his confidence deflate.

"You did well, Erith," I said, so softly only my staff could hear me, and he straightened up again.

Next to my uncle, Eamon shifted in his seat. I resisted the urge to look at him, to see if he was objecting to his father's disdain or supporting it.

"I value all my subjects equally, King Iain. I have werewolves and humans on my staff as well. I was given to understand Great River was a progressive city, with opportunities for all inhabitants of this monarchy."

I thought Eamon snorted but I could have misheard, and I still didn't dare look away from my uncle. The King sat very straight on his throne, his dark brown hair slicked back and held in place by a ridiculously large crown. It looked heavy and I found myself hoping it was uncomfortable.

"The outsiders' quarter has a… variety of occupants. But Great River is a human monarchy. It will *always* be a human monarchy."

I wasn't sure what his emphasis meant, but he seemed very concerned that I understand his position.

"I haven't come to change that, King Druison." I drew out the word "king" just enough that he would be reminded that he should be addressing me as "Prince." "Not unless my Queen instructs otherwise." And that was to remind him who he answered to. I'm fairly sure he hated the fact that, because his was a vassal monarchy, and I was the son of his over-monarch, I was very nearly his equal in rank. "I'm here, as my Queen requested, to set up an embassy for Morven Forest, as a first step towards improving trade, for the benefit of both our peoples."

"Of course." My uncle waved his hand dismissively and looked at his son. "Prince Eamon," and he emphasized "prince" for my benefit, "will be your main liaison for all that. Consider him *my* ambassador."

"Of course," I said, deliberately copying his phrasing. Now I felt I could really look at my cousin. He looked back with open curiosity. He'd been a baby when I was first presented to my uncle, and I had been a tiny child of six, homesick and unable to fit in. We had never spent any real time together, only sat next to each other at infrequent banquets over the years and even more rarely sparred with wooden swords under my father's supervision.

"Prince Kiernan," my cousin said, and his voice, though formal, held none of the hostility my uncle's had. "I've a banquet planned for fourthday next that I hope you will attend. I'll forward an invitation once I know where to direct it."

I inclined my head with more respect than I had showed my uncle, knowing I was playing a dangerous game, but also knowing I had my Queen's permission to handle whatever arose as I saw fit. And as much as I hated her, it felt good to have my Queen's trust, to be useful to her in a way that didn't include killing or spying.

"I'll have my secretary send the address to your secretary."

After that, there was a list of formal acknowledgements, greetings passed on, and the like, none of which meant very much, but all of which had to be properly addressed. I wasn't offered a place to sit, or refreshments, or anything. I knew my Queen, when I told her, would find it incredibly rude.

Finally, I turned to go, my Guard smoothly stepping aside and falling back into place behind me. We walked back through the near-empty hall and out into the huge courtyard in front of it. The palace of Great River was much larger than it needed to be, a statement of power and a gesture of defiance.

Most of the citizens lived in the city or the surrounding countryside and most of the soldiers lived in Dudoon. Every part of the palace echoed.

It echoed especially when running footsteps approached from behind us.

My guards surrounded me, so efficiently I had to smile. Erith stayed close but shifted to place himself where he wouldn't be in the way if I had to draw a blade. I was grinning at my people's good training when Prince Eamon panted to a halt in front of me.

"Cousin," he said, leaning one hand on the edge of the doorway we'd just passed through to catch his breath.

"You couldn't send a lackey to catch me up?" I said, but I let the grin stay on my face, and he answered it with one of his own. At thirty-two, he was still relatively young for a human, but old enough to have all the responsibilities of an adult.

"I'd have to find one first," he said. "Father doesn't like to have too many staff crowding him."

"I noticed his hall was awfully empty." I turned back towards the gate, and he fell into step beside me, my guards making room for him.

"I think he was trying to provoke you into saying something undiplomatic."

"He's going to have to work a lot harder if pissing me off is his goal. I can be entirely unperturbed just to make *him* annoyed."

"I told him that." He sounded amused, then apologetic. "He doesn't like you very much."

"I'm used to it."

"I could never figure out why."

I considered what I should say. Eamon seemed friendly. He was my cousin, but I'd already had one cousin try to kill me, and Eamon's father was the unhappy King of my mother's vassal monarchy.

"I'm half fey," I said. "For a lot of people – and not just humans – that's enough."

"Well, I hope you won't avoid visiting because of him."

I didn't say I had planned to do exactly that. "I'll visit when I need to, regardless of how he feels about me."

"Good. I –" I stopped at the gate and paused, waiting for him to finally say whatever it was he had run after me to say. "I hope we can be friends."

I forced myself not to stare, and instead of answering, I offered my forearm for him to grip the way humans did when meeting and parting. He took my arm and held it briefly. He was strong, his grip firm.

"Let's see how your banquet goes first," I said, but I smiled.

WHEN WE RETURNED to the embassy, I got a thorough scolding from Coal as he coiled around me in the air, chittering and saying, *Nyah*. He was not impressed that I had made him stay with the dryads while I went to the palace.

"I'm sorry little friend," I said, holding out both hands to stop him from thwacking me repeatedly in the face with the end of his tail. It didn't hurt, but it did become irritating very quickly. "I thought it best to introduce King Iain to our embassy's diversity a little at a time."

I saw, out of the corner of my eye, one of the dryads watching me, their expression unreadable except for the slight curl of amusement at the corner of their mouth.

"Did he behave himself, Syrinx?" I asked, finally managing to coax Coal onto my shoulder.

The dryad blinked but showed no other sign of surprise at being noticed. "Yes, my Prince. He disposed of some grubs for us, that would have eaten whatever trees were decided to plant, come spring."

I turned to look at them fully and they lowered their eyes. "Thank you," I said, and they nodded.

Coal forgave me later that evening, when I fed him poached shrimp from my own plate as I sat on my balcony wrapped in a thick wool blanket and looked out over the city. We had almost no furniture, and there was still so much work to do, but I felt like I had accomplished something just be being here, by finding a group of very different people who could work together to help me, to help our Monarchy.

I wondered if Fionn felt the same growing sense of pride about his work as a healer and seer. I wondered if he was making sure to rest enough, to not push himself too hard trying to help everyone at once. I knew Neeka would look out for him, but there was only so much she could do against his stubbornness.

Our connection was warm and strong in my belly, but it told me nothing about how he was feeling. He was too far away.

Coal crept into my lap, his tiny scaled belly fat with all the shrimp he'd eaten, on top of the grubs from his afternoon in the garden. I scratched between his ears, and he said, *Love*.

A smiled curved my lips. "Love," I agreed.

Coal fell asleep draped over my leg, and I leaned back in my chair. It was not the most comfortable seat; it had been salvaged from the building's basement and needed new upholstery. My staff had also found a corner stacked high with old military cots in useable condition. They were also not the most comfortable, but no one would have to sleep on the floor while we waited to get furniture.

As daylight drained completely from the sky more and more points of other kinds of light lit up the city. Most were flames – lamps and candles and fireplaces – but here and there I saw bluish and purplish and greenish wisplights. My uncle disliked magic as much as he disliked non-humans, but he couldn't prevent people from using it any more than he could prevent other peoples living in his city, especially as some of those peoples had been here longer.

The long day's work, the aftermath of stress from visiting my uncle, and all the strange and conflicting feelings I had only half-confronted after seeing my father had left me exhausted, and even the fact that my chair was jabbing me in the side couldn't keep me from drifting off.

I WOKE LONG AFTER full dark, in the deepest, coldest part of night. It wasn't unusual for me to wake at night, alert and unable to fall back to sleep. I was adaptable, but being awake all day didn't feel natural. Most Sidhe – and I was like most Sidhe in that way – preferred to sleep away the brightest parts of the day and the darkest parts of the night. We saved our waking times for dawn and dusk, like forest creatures, though a full moon was likelier to keep us awake than a dark one.

Waking at midnight was unusual even for these last few unsettled ninenights. Falling asleep in my chair might have had something to do with it. So might have the cold, or hunger.

Coal had eaten most of my supper, and while he snored on, I woke when my belly grumbled. I moved the little serpent to his basket and carried him inside to my office – or what *would* be my office, eventually – and settled him on the edge of the hearth. Then I headed for the stairs. There was bound to be bread and cheese in the kitchen, at least.

I should have stopped and gone back when I heard Padraig's voice, but I was only half-awake and didn't really register what he'd said until it was too late and I walked through the kitchen door to find him, sleeping tunic hiked up, with Erith bent over the table in front of him.

<There's a good boy.> *That's* what he'd said, and if I'd realized it, I'd have known not to enter. Unfortunately, I didn't realize until after I met his eyes, and he grinned.

<Join us, cousin?> He thrust against Erith again and the faun squeaked. I looked at the younger man and he wouldn't meet my eyes. He was flushed bright red from embarrassment.

"You know people have to eat off that table, right?" I said, and made myself keep walking, past the table and across the room. I opened the door to the pantry and found a loaf of bread covered in a cloth and already sliced. There was no cheese, but there was butter and a pot of honey, tightly covered against ants.

I kept my back to the two fucking on the table, ignoring the sounds they were making. Padraig, at least, didn't seem bothered that I was there, to judge by his breathing. I covered three slices of bread with a precise layer of butter and then drizzled them with honey.

The sweet smell of the honey made me think of Fionn and the sweet flavor of his… I shoved the thought aside as I shoved the bread back into the pantry and picked up my plate.

When I turned to leave, Padraig grinned at me again and pumped his hips more enthusiastically. Poor Erith looked like he was hoping the ground would open up and swallow him.

"I didn't take you for an exhibitionist," I said as I passed them.

"I didn't think there'd be anyone in the kitchen this late, and Erith just looked so fucking delicious." He stroked a hand down the faun's back. "You *are* welcome to join."

"Take him to your room," I said. "He deserves better treatment from you."

Padraig shrugged. "I'm almost done, anyway." His breathing grew ragged, and I walked quickly away.

When I got to my suite, I had the sudden urge to cry, so I abandoned the bread on the table next to my bed and climbed out the widow to the roof. The balcony just didn't seem high enough, or far enough away from the kitchen.

I was cold outside and would soon be colder, but I ignored it and sat leaning against one of the chimneys, staring into the sky. I didn't know if Padraig meant for me to find him fucking Erith – he'd offered several invitations to share his bed since we left Morven Palace, always assuring me that Erith wouldn't mind, though Erith himself had yet to say anything one way or the other.

I think he was offering comfort in the only way he knew how, and not so long ago, I would have gladly accepted, because sex was the only way I'd known how to accept it.

Now, seeing him and Erith, smelling the sweetness of honey, feeling the heart bond warm inside me, only made me miss Fionn more. Even watching Erith grow in confidence at his own abilities hurt as much as it delighted, because he reminded me of Fionn in so many ways. They had both been shy and uncertain when we'd met, they were both gentle and kind, and they had both grown more and more sure of themselves as they were allowed to find out what they were good at.

I leaned against the brick of the chimney and felt tears prick my eyelids, but they didn't fall. I hadn't told Erith yet, but I planned to speak to the headmaster of Great River University, to see about getting him a place as a student.

My stomach rumbled again, and I wished I had brought the plate of bread out with me, but I didn't want to go back in yet, in case Padraig decided to come looking for me. I should have locked my door, just in case. So I ignored my hunger and let my mind drift, trying not to think about Fionn.

The night sky wasn't as dark here as it was in the forest, and the stars weren't as bright, either. There were always lights on in the city, and behind me, if I cared to turn and look, I would see the palace lit up like a festival bonfire. In front of me, rows and rows of houses and inns and shops each had a light on somewhere to stave off the dark of night.

South across the river was a second palace, a second city, almost a twin to Great River, and almost as brightly lit. It was home to the royal family of Aven's human Monarchy, and its family tree was so entwined with Great River's it was a wonder they hadn't merged generations ago. Except they had different overlords, which I supposed would go a long way towards preventing them joining.

I looked away, downriver towards the dark fortress of Dudoon, which was lit only where absolutely necessary. Something bright caught my eye against the dark sky. Was it the first beginning of sunrise caught on the underside of a cloud?

But it was a clear night, and sunrise was still far away. No, it was a bird, pale and large. I thought of Fionn's white raven, that had taught him spirit flight and had brought him to me those times I had needed him most. I had never seen it, but maybe tonight I would.

It soared closer and an absurd hope filled my belly. I felt for my connection to Fionn and found it bright and true – and very strong. He was close.

I pushed myself to my feet and balanced on the slope of the roof, one hand on the chimney to steady myself. I watched him fly closer.

He circled, as if unsure of which way to go, then dropped

close to the rooftops, caught himself, and rose higher in the air. Then he seemed to decide and headed straight for me. Before he reached me, two long feathered shapes arrowed out of the sky and dove at me, chittering in excitement.

We fly, said Smoke.

In spirit, said Flame and as I looked at them closer, I realized their shapes were paler, less substantial, and I laughed.

"I didn't know you could spirit travel," I said, as they landed on my shoulders, purring. Their already light bodies felt insubstantial, barely there.

We guard, said Flame.

We guide, said Smoke

Bright comes, said Flame.

I scratched them both under the chin, ignoring the not-quite-solid feel of them under my hands, and watched Fionn soar closer. His face was alight, full of fierce joy – whether at flying or at seeing me I didn't know. And didn't care. What mattered was that he was happy.

"Coal is inside," I said. "On the hearth."

The serpents slid from my shoulders and went to find my window, and I held out my arms. Fionn dropped neatly onto the roof, folded his wings, and said, "Hi." His smile was shy and sweet and perfect.

"Beloved," I said, and pulled him close. He felt half-substantial, but he was warm, and maybe he was only in his spirit body, but he was *here*. I buried my face against his neck to inhale his sweet musky scent.

He kissed the top of my head, and then I heard his sharp inhale and braced myself for his pitying look as I leaned back to meet his eyes.

"Oh, beloved," he said softly, but it wasn't pity in his eyes. It was anger. Was he angry I'd lost my antlers, or angry that

I'd had to?

He raised a hand, and I felt him gathering magic. I caught his wrist before he could touch me and gently moved his hand to my lips.

"No, beloved," I said, my mouth brushing his fingers. "If you heal me, they won't grow back."

"Oh!" He traced my lips instead and let his magic flow back into the Realms. "That's how you restored our connection." He smiled, tentatively. "That's the pain I felt as our ship sailed away."

I nodded. "I'm sorry you had to feel that. I asked Daphnis to do it. Dryads are very strong, and it was… relatively fast."

"Is Daphnis…?"

I shook my head.

"I'm sorry," he said.

"I made it quick for him," I said, pushing aside the memory of the dryad's scream as his hands caught fire from the magical flame on my antlers, my Queen's last punishment for anyone who tried to help me.

Fionn put both hands on my face, traced my cheekbones with his thumbs, and said, "I still think you're very handsome."

I laughed. "I'm very glad you do."

"Will you kiss me, Ambassador?" he said, teasing.

I pushed up onto my toes to reach his lips, and he opened his mouth to let my tongue in, angled his head to let me in deeper, and slid his tongue alongside mine. There was fire between us, like I'd never felt with anyone else. It was the heart bond, maybe, or maybe it was just that we were perfectly matched.

"Maybe we should go inside?" he said. "Before one of us loses our balance and falls off the roof?"

I took his hand and we climbed down, not to the window,

which was awkward to get into, but onto my balcony. And then I looked at him more closely. "You're naked, pretty bird."

He blushed, pink just touching his cheeks and the tips of his ears. Looking at him made me flush, too.

His mouth quirked up on one side. "It's rather convenient, don't you think?" He pulled me towards the balcony door. "You, on the other hand, are very inconveniently still wearing clothes."

7
Fionn

*I*WILL LEAVE YOU TO THINK *on your options,* the King had said, and had told me he would return in a day or two. And while the thought made my stomach hurt, I *was* glad that I needn't worry about him bothering me anymore that night.

His visit had left me too unsettled to sit long at my loom, or to let the rhythm of my drop-spindle soothe me. Even a soak in my hot pool wore off quickly and I simply washed and climbed out again. I put the kettle over the fire in my sitting room and paced, both serpents watching me from the basket of unspun wool next to the hearth.

We fly? Flame said, her voice hopeful.

We three, said Smoke.

"I can't fly," I said, absently. Then I stopped pacing suddenly and stared at them. In my spirit body, I *could* fly, and of course they knew that. And Daphnis's magic had given Kiernan enough connection to the Realms that he could see me in spirit shape. He could even touch me. And perhaps whatever he had done after that, that had returned our connection to full strength, would also increase his ability to *see*; it might ensure that even if Daphnis's magic faded, my spirit shape would not.

I went quickly to my bathing room to fetch salt-leaf bark. I had plenty left should the fever break out again. Thanks to Kiernan and our trade with the Sidhe, we had enough of all parts of the tree to last a while. The smoky steam rose from the pot and this time I decided not to include winterleaf or sweet bean pod.

We go, said Smoke.

We fly, said Flame.

"Yes." While the tea steeped, I dressed in my favorite sleeping tunic and folded back the covers on my bed. Then I locked my door, banked my fire, and put out my lamps. In bed, I cupped the tea in my hands, impatient for it to cool enough to drink. Smoke and Flame waited, one on each side of me, staring into the cup as if that would help it cool faster.

Finally, I drank it down as quickly as I could, leaving a little in the bottom for the serpents, then set the cup aside and settled into bed. Smoke and Flame curled up on each side of my head.

I was used to leaving my body by now, having spent a nineday healing each night. The serpents were used to it, too, since they had accompanied me every time. Soon we three were looking down on our physical bodies. I watched as my back spasmed, like I was having a vision, but there was nothing I could do except return to my body, and that was not in my plans until much later.

We go, said Flame.

Hurry, hurry, said Smoke.

I laughed and followed them out onto the balcony,

stepping easily through the closed door. I was used to that now, too. All I needed to do was close my eyes and act as if the door didn't exist.

The sky was dark over the sea, and the stars brilliant. I knew the wind was cold – I felt it, but it didn't seem to affect me much in my spirit body. I stretched, relishing the feeling of being naked, now that I was alone and not trying to heal people. It was hard, sometimes, to be so comfortable unclothed in my physical life, because I had been raised in the Abbey to be ashamed of my body. And even though I had learned early, from my extensive reading, that not all cultures felt the same about nudity, it was difficult to set aside those thoughts. I only hoped that one day I could be as confident naked as Kiernan was. I hoped I could be as unbothered by being *looked at*.

The sea was even darker than the sky, with no brilliant stars to make it seem less foreboding. It frightened me to look on, it was so big and so powerful, but I didn't hesitate to step up onto the stone railing. I balanced easily and tried not to think about the sheer drop and the unforgiving water below. I had never flown on my own; the raven had always been with me to guide me to Kiernan.

Drawing a deep lungful of air, as if I was about to plunge into a pool of water and needed to hold my breath, I spread my wings, and I jumped. The wind caught me, and held me up, and I let out an involuntary shriek of joy.

Smoke and Flame circled around me, dipping and diving, and chittering encouragement. I flapped my wings and rose into the sky, out over the sea, and then circled back to follow the coast.

By ship, everything had seemed so close, and yet took forever to reach. From the air, things seemed so very far away, yet I passed by landmarks almost as quickly as I spotted them.

I wondered, if I could fly in my physical boy, would I travel as quickly, or did spirit shape give me added speed?

The landscape changed in subtle ways as I flew east, then followed the curve of the Isle to head north. Some trees became more common and others less so, and the sandy beaches of Aven gave way to the rockier shores of Morven. At first, I simply wanted to get to my destination as quickly as possible, but soon my thoughts were overtaken by the sheer preposterousness of my situation and I laughed into the wind.

In my physical body, I could not fly – I would never fly because though my wings were perfectly developed in form and shape, they were vastly underdeveloped in size. They might break my fall and keep me from injury if I dropped from a height, but they would never carry me into the sky.

And yet here I was, in spirit shape, my tiny wings holding me up as well as they would have done if they were full-sized. And they *glowed*. *I* glowed, something like wisplight trailing behind me.

I climbed into the sky, rolled over, dove down, and swooped back up. Smoke and Flame circled and cavorted alongside me, as if my joy were infectious. And very soon, I forgot all about the King and his threats.

I laughed, and my serpents chittered back.

We fly! said Smoke.

We three fly, said Flame.

I climbed and dipped and dove and swooped again. And then I saw the gleaming ribbon of the Great River flowing down from the mountains to the coast. The twin human cities faced each other across its width and on an island in the river's mouth crouched the dark bulk of the fortress of Dudoon. It reminded me of the Abbey of the Moon, only even more frightening. I had made sure to stay far away from the Abbey on the way here – it was one reason I decided to follow the coast and hadn't even looked inland. I had no desire to ever see that place again.

I flew more cautiously as we approached Dudoon, suddenly unsure of myself. How was I to find Kiernan? I had thought I could remember where his room had been, but would he even have the same room now as he had as a child? Would he be in the main keep, or would he be awake and working, setting up his embassy in a more prominent part of the fortress? I circled a few times, wary of the men I saw on the dark walls and tower tops. The highest tower appeared not to have any guards, so I landed there to try to think what to do.

"How do I find him?" I said softly. I supposed I had hoped I would somehow just *know* where he was, the way I could feel his emotions when he was near.

Smoke and Flame landed on my shoulders and nuzzled their little heads again my cheek.

You see, said Smoke.

With heart, said Flame.

I smiled and scratched under their chins. "Of course." I stilled my thoughts and let myself feel the heat in my belly where my connection to Kiernan lay. Then I opened myself to my seer-sight – so much easier to do in this shape, and so much stronger. The magical glows of the people nearby flared up too bright for a moment, until I tempered my *sight*. And the silver thread that was my heart bond with Kiernan stretched out from my belly button into the dark night.

West. He was west of me.

"He's not here," I said, but that was okay; I knew which way to go now. This time I felt no trepidation when I climbed up onto the battlements and flung myself into the air.

Smoke and Flame streaked ahead of me, circled back, and flitted ahead again, as if they wanted me to hurry.

In flight, the silver thread vanished, and I couldn't seem to fly and use my seer-sight at the same time, so I simply headed west until the shape of Great River City resolved from a geometric dark patch dotted with light into the shapes of individual buildings. There, the palace was blazing with lights, and around it clustered smaller buildings, each with their own lights, glows, and flickering flames.

This city was so much bigger than the City Beneath the Cliff. I didn't know how I could possibly find anything here, on foot or from the air.

I paused, circled, and tried to open my seer-sight again, to find the silver thread. I fell. I beat my wings desperately and caught myself before crashing onto a rooftop, but the thread was gone. I could feel the connection, I just couldn't see it.

I hesitated, wondering if I should chance landing so I could look again, circling and unsure what to do. Smoke twisted in the air around my head, and Flame did the same at my feet.

We lead now, said Smoke.

You follow now, said Flame. They streaked away, no hesitation in their choice of direction. I followed, flying as fast as I could to keep them in sight. And then I saw him, standing on a rooftop, watching me, as if he had known to wait for me. I saw Smoke and Flame reach him, and greet him, and then vanish beneath the roof.

My heart felt full, but there was fear in my chest, too. What if was too satisfied in his work to want me? He had everything he had wanted, now; why give it all up to steal me away from my King and become outlaws?

As I got closer, I could see the look on his face. His hand stretched out, and my fears vanished. He was smiling, and a tear had escaped his eye to run down his cheek and I don't think he even noticed. The hand he held out to me was strong and sure… and then I saw it tremble slightly.

I folded my wings and landed on his roof a few steps away. My tongue seemed to forget how to make words and all I could get out was, "Hi." I felt suddenly shy.

"Beloved," he said, and I thought my chest would burst with joy. He pulled me close and buried his face in my neck.

I shivered, but I wasn't cold; I was flushed. I bent to smell his hair, to breathe in his fir-forest scent, and kissed the top of his head. And froze. Where were his antlers?

"Oh, beloved," I said, my heart aching for him. The breeze blew back his curls and I could see the bony ovals where his antlers had been, raw and unhealed. Without even thinking, I gathered healing magic and raised my hand. He was in pain – I could feel it through our bond – not strong, but persistent.

He caught my wrist as I reached out and brought it to his mouth instead, to kiss my fingers.

"No, beloved," he said, his voice gentle, deep, and smoky. "If you heal me, they won't grow back."

Of course! That was how he had restored his connection to the forest, to the Realms. To me.

He told me, and I could hear the sorrow in his voice, how he had Daphnis remove his antlers to escape his Queen's spellwork, and it had worked, but there was magical, unquenchable fire, and he had killed Daphnis to spare his suffering.

I cupped his face in my hands, tracing his cheekbones with my thumbs. They were sharper – he, too, had lost weight since we'd met, and he looked tired.

"I still think you're very handsome," I said. He *was* handsome, and beautiful, and he made my body ache to be close to him.

He laughed. "I'm glad."

Then I bit my lip and dared to tease him. "Will you kiss me,

Ambassador?" And he did, burying his hands in my hair and pulling my face to his, reaching his mouth up to mine, and I thought I would surely catch the roof on fire, I burned for him so.

"Maybe we should go inside," I said, remembering we were on a rooftop, and I might have wings, but he didn't.

He helped me climb onto a balcony that was empty save for a small table and a rickety chair, and when we were both down he stepped back, keeping hold of my hand. He looked me up and down.

I knew I must be blushing; I felt the heat under my skin.

"You're naked, pretty bird."

I think he knew I was always naked in spirit shape, but his voice was teasing, daring me to come up with a cheeky reply.

"It's rather convenient don't you think?" I said, pulling him closer and turning us both so I could push him towards the door leading inside. "You, on the other hand," I continued, "Are very *inconveniently* still wearing clothes."

"Am I?" he said, his beautiful full lips curling into a grin. "I hadn't noticed." He reached back for the door handle, opened it, and led me inside.

It was dim, the only light the glow of coals in the fireplace, but it looked very empty. He pulled me farther inside to a door across the room, which he locked. Then, suddenly, he scooped me up into his arms and I let out a startled laugh.

He carried me across the room to another door and through, paused to lock that one, too, then kept going.

"You have a lot of empty rooms here," I said, nuzzling his earlobe.

"We just moved in," he replied. "I haven't had a chance to send anyone out to buy furniture. That will be my sitting room and back there was my office."

"And this room?" I said as he paused in the middle of the

space.

"My bedroom."

"Trying to get me in your bed again?" I teased. I touched his face, tracing his dark eyebrows and the curve of his ear.

He set me on a soft surface, checked that my wings and tail were comfortably tucked under me, and stepped back. "I've succeeded, it seems." His grin grew wider, and I looked down to see I was lying on a cot piled with blankets, a cloak folded up at one end for a pillow.

"I don't think this bed is big enough for both of us," I said, lying back and looking up at him.

His lips curled again, and he tugged at the laces of the loose shirt he was wearing. "Oh, I plan to buy a very large bed to replace it. Once that can accommodate a pretty bird man's long, beautiful legs and plenty of wrestling."

I smiled at his reply and let my lips part as he pulled his shirt slowly over his head, revealing the sculpted muscles of his belly and chest, a little at a time. When he tossed the shirt aside, he met my eyes and his were dark and hot.

I stretched on the bed and watched as his eyes left mine and drifted down the length of my body. I knew I was blushing again, but I would *not* be ashamed. I wanted him to look at me, to like my body, to desire me. I licked my lips and put both hands on my chest, stroked them over my ribs and belly, and slipped my fingers into the soft feathers that covered my sheath.

He made a low noise in his throat. "Fionn," he said.

"Kier," I replied, and stroked my hands lower, sliding them between my thighs and pushing my legs open, just a little. "You still have clothes on."

He breathed raggedly and, still watching me, undid the buckle of his belt. He only had a single knife on it, a curvy one I had never seen before. He set the knife aside carefully, then undid his trouser tie and let the fabric slide down his legs.

I let my gaze linger on the thick muscles of his thighs, drift down to his shins, and back up, pausing to rest on the bulge in his undergarment. He was already so hard, and it was because of me, from *looking* at me.

I licked my lips again and moved my hands back up my body to rest behind my head, as he dropped his undergarment to the floor and stepped closer.

Before he reached me, I swung my legs over the side of the cot and sat up, reaching for his hips to pull him to me. His hands found my hair again and I buried my face in the crease of his hip, inhaling his musky scent. I could feel the hardness of his erection next to my face and traced it with my fingertips, up to the end to press against the slit, then lower to feel the shape of his tip.

"Goddess Below, Fionn," he breathed.

"Mmm," I replied, running my palm down his length and then curling my fingers around him. I lifted my head just far enough to slide my lips over him, teasing his tip with my tongue and making him moan. I sucked for a moment, then looked up at him. His eyes were closed, his dark brows drawn close over his nose, and he was breathing quickly.

"Did you know," I said, running my fingertips over his erection again, "That Vogel have almost no gag reflex?"

"What?" he said, blinking down at me.

I let one corner of my mouth curl up, then bent my head to slide my lips over him again. And I kept going until I felt him hard against my throat, *in* my throat, and my lips brushed the soft curly hair at his base.

He groaned deep and tightened his hands in my hair. He pushed his hips against my mouth as I sucked. His breathing went even more ragged.

But then he went still. "No, Fionn, wait."

I stopped moving, too, and looked up at him.

"You feel so fucking good," he said. "But I don't want to come yet. Fuck. Not yet."

I moved my mouth away and he shuddered, then dropped to his knees next to the cot.

"Pretty bird," he said, his voice full of wonder. He stroked my face and leaned in to kiss me, to press me back onto the cot as if he wanted to devour me.

"My Kier," I said, when he lifted his mouth to climb onto the bed and straddle me. I nudged his leg until he shifted it between mine — first one, then the other.

He leaned his weight on one arm and traced my chest with the other hand, so softly my skin tingled in response. He trailed his fingers over my belly and brushed gently over my sheath. With one finger, he traced my seam, and I couldn't even wait for him to tease me; my erection slid out, hard and slippery.

I wrapped a leg over his back and opened my mouth to his when he kissed me again. I pulled him closer, making him press the full length of his body down on mine. His erection pressed against mine, slid against mine, and I couldn't keep my voice silent any longer. I thought I was going pulse right then, but he levered himself up onto one arm again and wrapped his fingers around both of us, pressing our hardnesses together.

I reached down and slipped my hand between our bellies to curl my fingers around us, too, my thumb curling across his fingers and his thumb pressing against mine.

I pushed my hips against his and cried out again as we slid together. And my first pulse came, slow and shuddering from my base to my tip.

Kiernan gasped as my semen splattered my belly and we slid together again. "Fionn," he growled, and tightened his fingers, and thrust himself against our hands.

I pulsed again, just as slow. I could feel it grow and throb until I splattered more fluid on my belly.

With my free hand, I grabbed his hair and pulled his mouth hard against mine so I cried out into his mouth when my third pulse came and my fourth started to build.

"Please, Kiernan," I whispered against his lips. "Don't stop."

"I love you, Fionn," he whispered back, and thrust against me, against our hands, against my erection, harder and faster until I wanted to scream, I was so aroused. And then I did, nearly, as my fourth pulse overwhelmed me, and I spilled again, hot and hard, almost hitting my throat.

"Fuck," Kiernan said.

"I love you," I whispered and pulled his mouth against me again, so I didn't know if his yell had words or not, but his semen joined mine on our bellies and he relaxed.

He lifted his head and smiled. "My pretty bird," he said. He let go of us, trailed a finger through the beautiful mess on my skin, and licked our mingled fluids off.

I took his hand in mine, dipped his finger again, and sucked the salty-sweet taste off of it.

8
Kiernan

MY COT WASN'T BIG ENOUGH to curl up on and relax together, so we sat side by side and I wrapped a blanket around us. For a while we just rested, leaning together, sleepy and content. I could feel through our bond that Fionn was happy and sated, and from the other room, I could hear Smoke and Flame and Coal softly chittering to each other, although if they were talking, I couldn't make out the words.

For a sweet and precious moment, everything was right with the world.

Fionn sighed, deep and long, and turned his face against my hair, careful not to brush against my forehead.

"You're tired, aren't you?" I said.

"I'm okay." His breath was warm where it slipped between my curls to tickle my scalp. It felt almost pleasant on the raw stumps of my antlers.

"Did you stop the fever?"

"Oh! Yes!" He sat up straighter and the blanket slipped off his shoulders. He tried to pull it back up but he couldn't seem to hold onto it, as if every physical thing except me was not really solid to his spirit shape. I tugged it up for him and held it snug around him.

"We sent the salt-leaf you gave us ahead with the messengers," he said. "So Healer Kah was able to begin treating people before I even got there."

"That's good."

He nodded and when he looked at me his eyes were shining. I couldn't help but smile at how happy he looked. "When I arrived, I spirit travelled, like when I healed you. Nobody died, Kier. Not one person."

"You saved them all."

"I had help." He traced a finger along a fold of the blanket. "I told you your Lady of the Forest spoke to me in a vision?"

"You did." I freed a hand from the covers to lace our fingers together. "You said she helped you heal me."

"Yes, but… I only *spoke* to her in visions. But when I was healing at the Eyrie…" He paused and his silver brows dipped together, like he was puzzling something through. I could watch him think all day and not believe my time was wasted.

"There was a child," he said. "My first patient. I healed all the children first, but this one was… remarkable. So full of magic, not awakened yet, but there. And Kier…" He paused again and his eyes were full of wonder. "When I was healing them, the Lady of the Skies appeared and… not just as a vision. She claimed the child, or… perhaps chose them. And every time I healed after that, I could feel her helping me, as I felt your Lady of the Forest, just brushing my magic, strengthening me." His voice was as full of wonder as his eyes.

I leaned over to kiss his cheek. "Every day you come into your magic more and more. They say seers once acted as messengers between the spirits and the people, even between the gods and the people." Then I teased, "Someday, bards will sing ballads about the great Seer Tokka of the Eyrie, who spoke to Goddesses."

"Stop it," he said, but he was smiling, and he did not sound displeased.

"You said 'they' when you spoke of this remarkable child." I might not have noticed, because the usage was common among the fey of all monarchies. But I knew it was not permitted among the Vogel, who were less forward-thinking. "I thought your laws only allowed 'he' or 'she' as assigned by the attending healer."

"Yes." He frowned. "Officially Lisna is 'she', but… Kier, they're such a remarkable young person."

"So you said." I smiled. "Perhaps you could tell me about them."

"The healer who was on duty the night I healed Lisna told me they were officially 'she' but… well, Lisna has the reproductive parts of male on one side and female on the other. I *saw* when I healed them."

"Divided down the middle?"

"I know it sounds strange."

I shook my head. "It's very rare, but it happens to birds. I saw a redbird like that once, years ago. It was bright red on one side of its body, and pale orange-brown on the other. Male on one side, female on the other."

"Yes! I read a book in the Abbey that said it could happen in birds and some insects. But the book didn't mention the Vogel people." He scratched his nose. "I didn't get a chance to ask Lisna what they wished to be called, though I suppose in the Eyrie there's no choice, anyway."

"Another law for you to change, beloved?"

"Yes." He looked away as if lost in thought and I felt anxiety creeping into him.

"Fionn?"

He looked back at me and I could see worry in his eyes, too.

"Did I say something wrong? Your smile is gone."

He shook his head. "No. Only… when you mentioned changing laws I thought…" He looked down at our hands, twined together on my knee. "You have important work here. You're making a better future for your people."

"As you are for yours." I said it softly, beginning to understand what distressed him.

He looked at me again, and bit his lip, then relaxed his mouth as if he realized he was expressing a nervous habit. "Do you still want…" He looked away. His eyebrows dipped even closer together, and his nostrils flared.

"Do I still want to be with you?" I said and he swallowed hard.

"Yes." It was almost a whisper.

"Fionn." I made myself stay quiet and calm when what I wanted to do was turn his face to mine and say very loudly how much I loved him.

He pulled his legs up onto the bed and wrapped his free arm around them. His hand in mine tightened. He finally looked up.

"I want, with everything I am, to be those two old men you saw in your vision, happy and in love in their own house. You and me, together," I said.

He bit his lip again and I didn't think he realized he was doing it.

"Do you still want that?" I asked, voice still soft, and I let the blanket slide away so I could stroke the smooth feathers of his wings.

He nodded. "Yes." His voice was still barely above a whisper.

"Do you still want me to steal you away from the Eyrie?"

His eyes slid away from mine. "Yes," he said. "But Kiernan, you're needed here."

I stroked his wings again and felt him relax.

"I –" I sighed. "I do want to make the lives of my people – fey, human, dryad, all of them – better."

He swallowed.

"But I would give it all up, everything, if you ask."

"I could never ask for that." He pulled his hand from mine to wrap both arms around his legs, to curl up tight, and it felt like he was retreating from me.

"If you need me, Fionn, I will leave everything. Even if you *don't* ask." I paused and touched his knee, then bent to kiss his shoulder. "If you don't want me, then… then I won't."

He stared at me; eyes wide. "Of *course* I want you. Kiernan, I *hate* being apart from you."

"So we keep to our plan, then?"

"Our plan?" He looked so confused I almost laughed, but instead I leaned closer and kissed his ear. "You help your people at the Eyrie, I help my people here, and as soon as my antlers grow enough to let me use my magic again, we run away together."

His lips curved up. "And we travel the Isle helping those who need us."

"Yes."

His smile grew into the one I loved so much, the one where he seemed to light up, to glow. "You still want that?"

"I do. Very much."

"Me, too."

I TRIED TO SLEEP after Fionn left, leaping off my roof with Smoke and Flame leading the way and disappearing upriver; he wanted to follow the mountains this time and stay far away from the Abbey of the Moon.

Lying on my cot, I spent a long while trying to steer my thoughts away from possible ways to make my antlers grow faster so I could use magic sooner. Then I tried calling up wisplights and flame, watching with dismay as light glowed in my hand only to dribble away before it became much of anything. Finally, thinking I was trying to light the candle on the nearby table, Coal belched out a thin stream of fire that melted the whole thing to a stub.

We both stared at it in shock until I said, "I didn't know feathered serpents could make fire."

Coal said, *Secret*, in a smug voice and curled up to sleep on my pillow, and I realized I had forgotten to tell Fionn that Coal's first – and until that moment, only – word was "love."

While I was thrilled that Fionn was able to visit me now, that I'd forgotten to tell him the one thing I had most wanted to share made me realize that it wasn't enough. It would never be enough to have to steal moments here and there, to meet secretly in the dark, or in caves, to never truly be allowed to be together.

Finally, after tossing around for what felt like an eternity, I slept. Until a feeling of dread in my belly woke me when dawn was still only a pale reflection on the underside of the clouds gathering out over the distant sea. I was muddle-headed and felt a headache coming, so I got up and dressed in last night's clothes, buckling on my belt and one knife.

I didn't yet have the means to make tea in my rooms, so if I wanted something to hold off the headache, to maybe help me sleep a few more hours, I would have to venture into the kitchen again. I only hoped Padraig and Erith didn't decide to use the table while I was there.

I took the plate of bread and honey that I hadn't got

around to eating the night before and ate it as I descended the stairs and followed the long hall. It had hardened a little but still tasted good, and I felt a little better after. Coal insisted on licking the dribbles of honey left on the plate when I was finished.

In the kitchen, I did not find my cousin and my secretary sporting on the table. Instead, I found one of the dryads, Syrinx, studying a book that was propped open in front of them.

When they heard me, they startled, closed the book, and made as if to hide it. Then they realized they'd been caught, and sat very still, looking down at the tabletop.

I put my plate next to the sink and rounded the long table to pick up the book.

"I'm sorry, my Prince. I'll put it back," the dryad said, their voice carefully toneless.

I studied the cover, then flipped it open to look at the title page. *On the Building and Maintenance of Bridges*. "This looks like riveting reading," I said, trying to make my voice light. "But where did you find it?"

"Erith left in on a bench in the garden, my Prince. I… I should have given it to him immediately."

"Well, I'm glad you didn't leave it outside in the weather."

"What is my punishment to be, my Prince?"

"I… what?" I blinked. But of course, a dryad would think they deserved punishment for reading. They were supposed to be inanimate objects unless given a task.

I put the book back on the table. "Are you literate?" I asked, though I supposed the answer should have been obvious. But few dryads could read and even fewer could write. They weren't allowed anything that might seem like bettering themselves.

"I –"

"I'm not going to punish you for reading, or for knowing how to read, or for wanting to learn, Syrinx."

They looked up in surprise when I said their name and then quickly looked away again. I knew why they hesitated to answer. My Queen would have sent them back to the pleasure garden, or worse, for knowing something that was supposed to be above their station. And she would also have punished them for lying if they pretended not to know. To Syrinx, answering my question either way was dangerous.

"When I was in the pleasure gardens, my Prince, I was the favorite of a noble lady who liked me to read her love poems while I… while we…"

"While she used you?"

They met my eyes again and this time didn't look away. Their irises were the color of the first new leaves of spring. "Yes," they said.

"Can you also write?"

Their nostrils flared, the only sign that they were again uncertain of how to answer. Finally, they said, "Yes, my Prince. I'm slow, but I can write."

"You read Islish," I said, tapping the cover of the book.

"And Sidhe, my Prince." They looked at their long fingers. "Dryad language has no written form."

"Or none that anyone has bothered to remember."

That got me another quick glance, another surprised look, that I would care enough to understand the difference.

"Yes, my Prince."

"Do you wish to learn? To be educated?" I had asked that once of Erith, and his answer had been so eager it still made me smile to remember.

Syrinx again answered with caution. "I am a dryad, my Prince. Enslaved peoples are not permitted to study."

"Maybe," I said, and realized I was looming over him. I

turned away to fill the kettle and light the burner so I could make the tea I had come for. "But no one can stop you from learning."

"My Prince?"

"What things would you like to learn, if you were allowed?" I rummaged in a cupboard for the headache tea, then added the leaves to the pot.

"I would like to know how things work, my Prince." Their answer was so similar to the one Erith had given me, I had to turn back to the teapot to hide my smile.

"Like bridges?"

"Bridges and buildings, plumbing, weaving, making cheese. Everything."

This time I let them see my smile and Syrinx, hesitantly, smiled back.

"I've written to the Headmaster of Great River University, to see about enrolling Erith," I said.

"Will they allow a faun to attend?"

"I believe I have presented sufficient arguments to convince them. It is only *mostly* a human school. There are students from other peoples." I lifted the teapot from the counter and put in on the table. "But I don't want him to go alone. I want him to have someone with him, in case he needs support, or help. Or protection." I held Syrinx's eyes for a long moment, then turned back to the cupboard for cups.

"Or protection?" they said softly. "Who will you send with him?" Their voice was carefully neutral again, but I could see what might be hope shining in their bright eyes. I noticed their hands were clenched together on the tabletop, as if trying to keep that hope at bay, because it was too bold for a dryad to want something.

"Do you enjoy working in the garden?" I said, suddenly realizing they were here, reading about bridges, instead of rooted in the courtyard with the other dryads.

"I enjoy being in gardens, my Prince, and forests. But…" They laughed softly and it made me glad to know they felt comfortable enough, finally, to show emotion to me. "I must seem a terrible excuse for a dryad, but I find I don't especially enjoy growing things. Making them grow, I mean."

"Tea?" I asked, pouring two cups without waiting for an answer. "I'm afraid it's the pain relief kind, but it's still nice."

"Are you not well, my Prince?" they said, staring at me before adding, "I would very much like some tea."

"Just a headache," I said. "I slept poorly." And very little, though I didn't tell them that. I slid a cup across the table and Syrinx picked it up with something like wonder on their face and sipped carefully.

"You don't enjoy growing things," I said, pulling out a chair and sitting. "But you want to know how things work?"

"Yes, my Prince. I… yes." They stared into the teacup, sipped again, then said, "I want to make things, my Prince, to craft things with my own hands instead of growing them." They laughed again, a note of self-deprecation in their voice. "As I said, I'm a terrible excuse for a dryad."

I inhaled the steam from my tea and drank. I could already feel the headache retreating, and the feeling of dread along with it. "I don't know," I said. "Who decided that dryads have to like gardening?"

They looked at me in surprise again. "I suppose it is because our magic lies there, my Prince."

"What little was left to you, after the Founding."

More surprise that they tried to hide by sipping their tea. I wondered if I was altering Syrinx's whole view of fey-dryad relations. I hoped so. I hoped to alter *everyone's* views. And I still hoped, someday, to free the dryads.

"Yes, my Prince."

I toyed with my teacup, lifted it to drain the last of the liquid, then set it aside. Syrinx still held theirs as if it were a precious jewel.

"I need someone to accompany Erith to the University, to help him study if he needs it, and to protect him from whatever dangers might present themselves to a faun attending a mostly human institution."

"Who will you send, my Prince? One of your guards?"

"I don't think an ambassador's secretary quite rates a guard of their own," I said. "I had thought of sending one of our human staff."

"Of course, my Prince. I'm sorry."

"You have nothing to apologize for." I tapped the side of my empty cup. "An ambassador's personal secretary – a *Prince's* personal secretary – *might* be considered high enough status to have an attendant, though." I met Syrinx's eyes.

They stared back, understanding growing on their face.

"You may have solved a small problem for me, Syrinx." They blinked, but didn't dare to answer yet. "It would mean he would also need help with his secretarial duties. And I suppose I would need a new attendant of my own. I can't expect him to be secretary, valet, *and* student."

"I could help, my Prince," Syrinx said, and I could hear the eagerness they tried to hide. "I was attendant to a Lord's youngest son, when I came out of the Gardens, before the Queen gifted me to you. He was most displeased when she did so."

I let my mouth curl up. "Did you enjoy being a personal attendant?"

"I might, for someone like you, my Prince."

"And will you accompany Erith to class? Study with him?"

Their eyes glowed when I asked the very thing they had been hoping for, but probably still believed I wouldn't give.

"Yes, my Prince. Oh, yes!" They clutched their teacup so hard I was worried the clay might crumble – dryads were exceptionally strong. But their smile was worth a thousand pottery teacups. An infinite number of teacups.

"Excellent." I pushed myself to my feet. "That's one less detail I need to worry about."

"I'm happy to serve, my Prince."

The dread had left me when I drank my tea, but now it came roaring back worse than before, only now it didn't feel like anxiety, it felt like fear.

"What is it, my Prince?"

I clutched at the chair back to steady myself. Fionn's terror was so strong he might have been standing next to me. Then it was gone, and I felt pain, a disorienting blow that left me reeling.

"Fionn." I fought to breathe, to hold off the fear. It wasn't *my* fear. Oh, Goddess, why was Fionn so afraid?

"My Prince?" I realized that Syrinx was holding me up, his strong arms around my shoulders, helping me to a chair. And then, as quickly as it began, the fear and pain and disorientation were gone. I slumped over the table, breathing hard.

"My Prince, what has happened? Shall I fetch a healer?" Syrinx was perched on the next chair over and had his arm around my shoulders. I knew they must be very worried if they had broken their training and dared touch me without permission.

"I'm… I'm fine. I felt Fionn, he was afraid. Someone hurt him." I felt helpless. Someone hurt him and I hadn't been there to protect him. I had failed him.

"You have a heart bond." Syrinx's voice was full of wonder. "I've never met anyone heart-bonded, but they say the bird folk have such bonds much more frequently than other peoples."

I pressed my face into my hands. I hadn't even known heart bonds existed until I met a married pair of Vogel fishers who told me what my connection to Fionn was. "He's so far away," I said, my voice coming out muffled.

"Your beloved… his name is Fionn?" Their arm was warm across my shoulders, but it was his presence that comforted me most. "That's… the Vogel Seer? Seer Tokka? I saw him when the Vogel delegation was in Morven Forest. He smiled at me."

"He… yes. Not many people know," I said. "It's safer that way." I turned my head to lay my cheek on the cool wood of the table. "His attendant and his closest guards know. One of the Vogel Councilors. Padraig nicFia. Erith. Daphnis knew. And now you."

"I won't tell anyone if you don't wish it known, my Prince."

"I want everyone to know," I said, and snorted something resembling a laugh. "But now, it's safer if no one else knows. And I know you won't say anything." And I did. I don't know how, but my magic – crippled as it was – whispered that here was someone I could trust.

And then I was on my feet again, fear so intense in my belly I thought I would be sick. I crossed the kitchen before I even knew I was moving.

"My Prince?"

I was vaguely aware of Syrinx following, but I couldn't ignore the urge to flee, to get away. *No, don't take me back!* Then pain again, pain I recognized. Long talons gripping my shoulders, digging in and breaking the skin. I had felt that pain when I tried to escape the Vogel King's guards and one of them had caught me, long toes gripping me and tossing me to the hard sand of the beach.

When I managed to shove the fear aside, I found myself

halfway down the hall, Syrinx's arm around me again, not trying to stop me but only trying to keep me standing.

When I looked at him, he was blurry, and I realized I was crying. I *knew* that pain. Someone had grabbed Fionn by the shoulders, heedless of their wicked talons penetrating deep into the shoulder muscle to scrape against bone.

I gasped in air and leaned on Syrinx, and pushed the fear and pain aside so I could think. It ebbed away gradually, leaving only a deep uneasiness behind.

"What can I do, my Prince?"

I reached out for the wall and leaned against it, letting Syrinx step back.

"He's afraid, and hurt." I rubbed tears out of my eyes impatiently. "He's supposed to be *safe* in the Eyrie, Syrinx. He's their *Seer*; they're supposed to keep him safe." I made myself breathe slowly, feeling for the calm I used when fighting. I could face a man twice my size, armed only with a knife, and feel completely free of worry. I used that now, though it was a very different enemy I faced. I needed a clear head.

I pushed away from the wall and turned to climb back up the stairs. "Will you start as my attendant right now, Syrinx?"

"Of course, my Prince."

"Good. You can help me dress to see my father, General Druison of Dudoon."

"May I ask the occasion, my Prince?"

"I need a ship."

9

Fionn

I LANDED ON MY BALCONY with an uneasy feeling in my belly, and no idea where it originated. And then I almost tripped over the bodies of my two serpents, limp on the stone floor.

I dropped to my knees, unable to keep in a cry of anguish and reached for them, hesitant to touch them but needing to know. Smoke and Flame in their spirit bodies streaked past me, and I watched as they returned to their physical forms, first turning pale, then misty, and then seeming to be absorbed.

Then Flame stirred and I let out my breath.

Hurts, said Smoke, lifting her head.

Cold, said Flame. I gathered them into my lap, glad that they were solid enough to me that I could lift them. I ignored the tears that dripped down beside my nose and let the warmth of my healing magic wash over them until their little bodies no longer felt so cold. They began to purr and slipped into the air to circle me.

The uneasy feeling persisted. Why were they outside at all,

when we had all three left our physical bodies in my bed? The only answer I could think of was one I didn't want to face. But I couldn't avoid it unless I planned to simply stay in my spirit body forever and live out there on my balcony. I climbed to my feet and saw that every lamp in my bedroom was lit, spilling light out through the glass. I could also see light coming from my half-open bathing room door.

For a long moment I stood frozen. I didn't want to go in there. I didn't want to return to my body, knowing what I would find, knowing who would be waiting for me in my hot pool.

He had promised me time to think. I don't know why I should be surprised that he had changed his mind. The longer I knew King Sarkot, the more I knew he was very far from an honorable man.

King waits, said Smoke softly, hovering near my ear, then flitting away.

We protect, said Flame.

"No, little friends," I said softly. "You can't protect me, even if you could get inside. You mustn't attack him; it would only make everything worse."

I pushed away the dread in my belly with effort, and held onto calm, then stepped through the door and crossed the room to my body. I looked small and lost, one wing twitching sporadically, but there was a soft smile on my face. Had my body reacted to my spirit self spending the night with Kiernan, making love and talking quietly? Had it been more aware of being safe and loved in Great River than of being… than of whatever had happened here?

I reached out to brush hair out of my own face and was drawn back into my body and… I was standing on a hill with Kiernan, overlooking a camp of tents bustling with people.

"They're here for you, pretty bird," he said, and I had an

impression of antlers, different than he had in Morven Forest, before I was pulled away and left shivering in darkness as Kiernan cursed the damp kindling, his own inability to call magic, and the cold. As I sat up to help him re-start the fire I was hit by a wave of deeper darkness and pulled away.

I was on my back on a hard wooden floor, a cluster of wisplights holding back the shadows with a flickering glow. I held my knees pulled almost to my chest and Kiernan leaned over me, his muscular arms strong columns on either side of my shoulders. His deep green eyes burned as he looked at me, as he thrust into me, and I cried out softly as I pulsed.

"I'm sorry, pretty bird," he gasped. "I want to be gentle, but I can't…"

I let go of my knees to wrap my legs around him, to dig my fingers into his backside and my claws into his skin.

"Don't hold back, beloved. I don't need you gentle, I need you fierce."

"What if I lose control?" He dipped his head, so his hair brushed my chest, and he thrust into me again, his muscles straining to hold back.

"Lose control," I said. "You are safe to lose control with me."

And darkness again. Something hurt inside me and there was a buffeting sound from the window, as if a bird was flying against it, over and over.

I pushed myself upright. Not a bird, but two serpents. I saw them and they saw me and hurled themselves at the glass again. I shook my head, and they landed on the balcony floor to watch me through the window.

Everything ached. My back muscles felt as if I had been seizing all night, though I knew I only twitched a little when I was spirit traveling. And inside. I pressed a hand to my belly and found myself sticky, white drying and starting to flake.

Under my tail felt sticky, too, and… I had spilled all over the sheets, big splatters of white, drying into a crust.

I flushed in shame. I had never had *that* happen while I was spirit traveling, though it was true I had only been intimate with Kiernan once before in spirit shape. But was it so different from pulsing in a dream? *That* was hardly shameful.

More thin light spilled across the floor. Not my lamps this time, but the rising sun reflected off the clouds far out at sea. A splash echoed from my bathing room, and I wanted to burrow into my blankets and hide. And I wanted to hurt my King.

He had come into my bed again while I was out of my body, had violated me while I had no way to even know he was there, let alone fight back. He had probably believed he was pleasuring me while my body responded to Kiernan and I making love together, halfway across the Isle.

"Goddess Above," I whispered, trying not to shake, not to cry.

Something leaked out of me onto the sheets, and I couldn't look; I didn't want to see the evidence that I was nothing more than a pleasure boy to my King, to use as he saw fit, no matter what I wanted. And suddenly, I needed to throw up. For someone with little gag reflex, I certainly seemed to vomit a lot.

I climbed from bed and headed for my bathing room. I didn't want to see the King, but I also didn't want the cleaners to have to mop sick off my floor. Bad enough they would have to deal with the mess on my sheets.

I made it to the door and lunged for the commode without even looking to see him in my hot pool. If I had looked, I might have seen him lean out of the pool as I came in, and grab for me. He had a hand locked around my ankle before I could cross the room.

<Come here, little seer,> he said.

I tugged at my leg, but his grip was hard and cruel, his claws digging in. He was taller than me, larger and stronger, and he pulled me towards him as he slid back into the hot water.

<My King, I need to –> I couldn't finish. I fell as he yanked on my ankle and spewed the contents of my stomach across the floor as my cheekbone hit the cold tile. My ears rang, my head spun, and I tasted blood.

<I said, come here little seer,> the King said. <I believe I told you very clearly that I would not stand for any further disobedience.>

<My King, you said…> I shook my head, still trying to pull my leg away as he dragged me closer. I pushed against the floor, trying to get up, and the room seemed to tilt and spin around me. <You gave me a day,> I finally managed to say. I shook my head, trying to clear it, and almost threw up again. <My King, I don't feel well.>

I slid into the pool, cracking my chin on the edge and crying out, though I wanted to show him no weakness.

<Poor little Tokka.> The King gathered me into his lap as if I was a child. He kissed the top of my head, and I tried to pull away.

My breath was coming in ragged gasps, and I couldn't stop the room spinning long enough to form a coherent thought.

<You gave me four pulses, little one,> he crooned into my ear, and, despite the heat of the water, I felt cold. <No one has managed that since my first night with my Queen, when she was still a trembling and fearful girl.>

<I was not even *in* my body,> I said, and the words came out slurred. I squeezed my eyes shut.

<And yet you *did* enjoy it,> he said. <Because you also had

four.>

<No.> But I couldn't manage to put any strength in the word.

<You know, little seer, as pale and colorless as you are, you *do* look so like your mother when you try to deny the passion you feel.>

If I thought I had felt cold before, it was nothing to what I felt then. I shivered, and I couldn't stop.

<You're shaking so, little one. Not having a vision, are you?> His arms held me tight, but he didn't hold me to comfort me the way Kiernan did. He held me to imprison me.

<You knew my mother?> I said. It was the only part of anything he had said so far that stayed in my thoughts. I opened my eyes, and the room tilted, so I shut them again. <Why did you never tell me before? Do you know who killed her? Do you know... do you know my father?>

<So many questions. Be a good boy, and someday I'll answer them.>

Why would the room not stop spinning? <My King, please.> Suddenly I didn't want to flee; I wanted answers. Magic flooded me and my ears rang louder. <How did you know my mother? Why did no one ever look for me?> The magic surrounded me and to my surprise, he answered.

<She was the Eyrie's Archivist,> he said. <She thought she could gain a better position by fucking her King – >

<No,> I said, cutting him off, certain, somehow that the last part was a lie. Magic echoed in my voice.

<No,> said the King, faint surprise in his voice. <No, she only wanted to care for her books and her documents, but she couldn't refuse me, though she wanted to. I was her King, and I fucked her bent over her own desk, every day until she admitted she loved me.>

I couldn't breathe properly, could only pull in air in

sucking gasps, but I needed to hear it. All of it.

<She got pregnant, and still she asked for nothing except what she needed for the library, the archives. She told me she loved me; she said the words, but she meant none of it.> He sounded like he had only just realized that fact, like the thought of being unattractive to someone was unfathomable.

<She never once refused me, though she wanted to, and one day, she told me she had spoken to a human seer in the city, who told her that her child – *our* child – would be a seer, too.>

Then it penetrated my thick brain what he was actually telling me. <My King, are you – > I felt sick again and tried to climb off of his lap.

<I will take care of you if you behave, little seer. I will not give you back to the Alfar.>

<My King, tell me.> I still couldn't frame the question and the magic that had sustained me was leaking away again.

The King stroked a hand down my wings, but it felt nothing like when Kiernan did it. There was no caring, no gentleness, only ownership.

<My oldest child,> he said. <It's a pity you're so stunted, or you would be my most perfect child.>

A truly horrible thought occurred to me. If the King could take *me* to bed, knowing who I was, what of his other children? Surely he wouldn't? They really *were* yet to reach their majority, while I only looked like it because I was small. And no one else knew but him, that I was… I was…

He laughed suddenly, and it was a horrible, cruel sound. <You will not like what happens to you if anyone finds out,> he said. <Pretty little seer. You think your life is terrible now.> He laughed again. <Let it torment you, that you should be my heir, but instead you're my pleasure boy.>

I screamed suddenly, not in fear but in anger, surprising

even myself. I heard Smoke and Flame fling themselves at the door again and I tore away from the King, pushed away and stepped up onto the bench to climb out. I found my foot in his lap and dug in my talons and shoved myself out of the pool and crawled across the floor.

I didn't look back; I couldn't bear to see if he was following, I just dragged myself to the door, heedless of the mess I slid through, and hauled myself to my feet. I staggered out the door and onto the balcony, where my serpents swirled around me in the air. I was soaking wet and naked, and the air was frigid and I could not go back.

I could not stay here, not knowing what I knew. So I didn't even think as I threw myself over the railing and plunged towards the dark sea. I spread my inadequate wings and felt the air tear at them, but they caught, and I slowed. I wasn't flying; I wasn't really even gliding, but I was moving away from my rooms, down towards the sea, and – far too slowly – around the bulk of the cliff.

The water was black below me, and restless, heaving against the cliff. Was there a storm out at sea, that darkened what had earlier seemed to be only a partly clouded sky? I sobbed into the wind and beat my wings hard. The black waves were too close and getting closer. I was falling too fast. I wouldn't die when I hit the water; it probably wouldn't even hurt very much. But what if I didn't make it along the cliff to the beach? I had never learned to swim. There was no place at the Abbey of the Moon deeper than the baths.

No. I could not go back. I would sooner drown, sooner be battered by the waves against the base of the cliff. *Please don't make me go back.*

But I heard the sound of wings behind me, and a rush of air, and I screamed in defiance and fear as talons caught my shoulders and yanked me upwards. My scream turned to a sob of pain as his long claws broke my skin and dug deep into muscle. I heard as much as felt him reach bone and scrape against it. I screamed again and the sound was snatched away by the rising wind.

And then I fell, wings still awkwardly half open. I hit the stone floor of my balcony hard with my knees and the glass of the door with my face. The same cheek that had smashed on the tile now bashed against the glass and I saw red and black.

The King said nothing as he grabbed my hair and hauled me to my feet, but I caught a glimpse of his face before he opened the door and shoved me through. I saw rage, pure and unfiltered.

Smoke and Flame circled him, hissing and biting, and I thought fiercely at them, *No! Stay away. I won't have him hurt you.* I felt their reluctance, their anger, but they obeyed, slipping out the balcony door and away.

<Guards!> the King bellowed, grabbing my arm and pulling me into my sitting room. A confused attendant – the King's – poked his head through the door from the anteroom, saw me, and went white. He scrambled to open the outer door and beckon to the two King's Guard who waited outside. I saw no sign of my own Seer's Guard, and I was thankful that it was too early for Trikta or Konta to be up yet.

<My King,> said the Guards, as if they were one person in two bodies.

He shoved me towards them, and I tried to stand straight, to pull serenity and calm around me. I knew I must look pathetic, soaking wet, naked, bloody, and bruised, but I could pretend to be above it all. They hesitated, but each took one of my arms when the King said, <Hold him.>

I lifted my chin and ignored the tears burning in my eyes. <You break the Founding Laws, my King,> I said, and was surprised to hear my voice come out strong and even. I touched the Three Realms and let magic soothe me. I couldn't heal myself, but I could let it lend me strength. I didn't dare look out the window for Smoke and Flame, but had to trust they were safe outside, and that he wouldn't hurt them.

The King's attendant hovered near the door. <Shall I call Healer Kah?> he asked timidly.

<Call the featherworker.>

<The… featherworker, my King?>

<Did I not speak clearly? Call the featherworker. When he has gone, then you may call a healer.>

The attendant nodded and scurried away.

I watched the King, keeping my head high. I felt deep, ugly shame at what he had done to me, but I refused to show it. Not to him.

<What do you intend to do?> I said, deliberately leaving off his title.

He glanced at me but ignored my question and paced back and forth across the room until a very sleepy-looking man carrying a basket full of feathers and glue hurried into my room and bowed.

<You require my services, my King?> he said. He looked at me and the color drained from his face, the habitual scorn there turning to shock and horror. I knew he didn't like me much, but apparently, he also didn't think I deserved my injuries.

<Clip his wings,> said the King, his words precise and without emotion.

<My King?> the featherworker hesitated, looking from me to the King and back.

<Clip. His. Fucking. Wings.> The King let a fraction of his rage spill into his words.

The featherworker looked terrified, but he said, <My King, my profession exists to enhance wings, to design facial

feathers that communicate more than our natural feathers can, to create *beauty*.> He looked like he might be about to soil himself in fright, but his nostrils flared wide in indignation. <I will not, I *can* not, do as you ask.>

He turned and began to leave the room.

<You will find no more work in the Eyrie,> the King snarled.

The featherworker winced, but did not turn back. He paused long enough to draw a large and elaborate pair of shears from his basket. Even from where I stood, I could see the royal crest – a pair of stylized wings flanking a crown – on them. <So be it,> he said, resolve in his voice. <I will not clip his wings. If you require me to do so, then I renounce my Royal Commission.> He set the shears on the table and walked out, closing the door softly behind him.

The King stalked to the table and snatched up the shears, snarling. <Hold him,> he growled at the guards. I felt them shift behind me, as if they were exchanging glances, but they each strengthened their grip on my arms.

I tried to keep my breathing calm, when I wanted to scream. I tried to remain still, when I wanted to thrash, to wrench myself away and run for the door to escape, to get away.

<Do not make this harder on yourself, little seer,> the King said as he moved closer, eyeing me like a wolf eyes a stag – or at least how the stories made such a hunt seem.

I closed my eyes and made my face still and blank, made my whole body still. I wanted to fight, to scream, to strike out with my claws and my talons and rend flesh, to scrape against bone as he had done to me. But he was stronger, the guards were stronger, and I knew I was helpless. The only thing I could do was try to retain my dignity.

So I breathed, remembering the Abbess's lessons. If I

could stay calm and serene while she hit my bare back with a leather strap, for the crime of reading when I was supposed to have been dusting the library, then I could stay calm and serene while the King… Goddess, I couldn't even think the words. Of all the things he had done to me, this somehow seemed the worst, even though my wings weren't even functional anyway.

I heard the snick of the shears and managed not to flinch. I held myself still and focused on breathing as he yanked my right wing open and clipped so close to the skin, I was afraid he would cut me. I even managed to be still when he wrenched open my left wing and *did* cut me as he recklessly hacked off feather after feather.

I felt a tear trickle down my face but ignored it as he cropped away the feathers of my tail and I felt their ragged ends scrape the backs of my thighs. I was glad for the strong hands holding my arms, because I didn't think I could have kept calm and remained standing, both.

And finally, it was over. I heard a clatter as the King tossed the shears aside and they hit the stone floor.

I opened my eyes and saw I stood in a drift of white and silver, my added-on feathers and my natural feathers scattered over my feet and sticking to the blood pooling on the floor.

Blood?

Oh, of course. He had stabbed my shoulders with his talons, and I had bled all down my body and onto the stone.

<You are mine, little seer. Don't forget that.> He jerked his head at the guards, who let go of me and preceded him to the door.

<King Sarkot,> I said. I swayed but remained standing.

<Now you can call the Healer,> the King growled, and his attendant hurried away.

And finally, they were gone.

And finally, I let go of the last traces of magic I had clung to. I let go of my serenity, of the Abbess's harsh lessons, and I slid to the floor, collapsed in a pile of feathers and blood and bruises.

Finally, I let myself cry, let myself feel relief when Smoke and Flame chittered at me from the balcony so I knew they were okay.

I waited for the healer, because what else could I do?

10
Kiernan

THE CITY WAS BARELY WAKING up as I rode through, but my horse shied at every shadow anyway. When we reached the outskirts and the hard-packed dirt road upriver, I gave him his head and let him run a little and when I slowed him again, he was calmer.

I didn't think he liked being cooped up in the city any more than I did.

This time, the guards at Dudoon's gate moved aside immediately, even though they were not the same men as last time. One of them called out, "The General's in his office, Prince Kiernan," as I rode by. I nodded and kept going. Leaving my horse with an apprentice stablehand, I entered the main keep and hesitated in front of my father's door.

He'd chosen an easily accessible room for his office rather than one with a view, which summed up his personality entirely. He was efficient and disciplined and would always choose whatever path would make his fortress operate most effectively, even if it meant his own discomfort.

Not for the first time, I wondered if I had inherited my desperate need to be useful from him.

The fear and pain I felt through my connection to Fionn had faded, leaving me with a lurking unease. The urgency to get to him was no longer overwhelming, but it was still strong. Maybe I couldn't have prevented whatever had happened, but the sooner I got there, the sooner I could stop anything *else* from happening.

I knocked with a lot more confidence than I felt, and when I heard my father say, "Come!" I opened the door.

He was leaning over his desk, frowning at a map of Dudoon. When he looked up, his eyes widened, but he didn't smile. I don't think he had ever smiled at me even when I was a child. My last meeting with him had been an exception in many ways.

"Kiernan." He nodded at the knife on my belt. "It suits you."

I still wasn't used to not having my twin knives strapped to my thighs, but something had made me want to carry this knife, especially here.

"I need a ship," I said, not bothering with any formality or preamble. My father was a straightforward man, one reason, I think, that he had not enjoyed living in my mother's court, where everything was an elaborate ritual.

He straightened and turned his frown on me. "You need a ship."

"Yes, sir."

"And you think I'm going to give you one."

I had not, of course, thought I could simply show up in the General's office and leave a short time later with a seaworthy vessel under my command. I had only hoped he would listen to me.

I faced him and kept my own voice as uninflected as his

had been. "I need to get to the Eyrie, and I hope you might lend me a ship, or else give me passage on a vessel already heading that way."

He came around his desk, studying my face, his frown deepening. "And why do you need to get to the Eyrie?"

"I…" I hesitated. I couldn't just say "personal business" and hope he wouldn't pry. And I knew my father had loved my mother, once, but I didn't know what their love had looked like; he was gone from Morven Forest before I was even born. I couldn't have guessed if *he* would have sailed away from an important position if he believed my mother was in danger, or if he would have put duty before love.

I suspected the latter but hoped for the former.

He reached around me and closed the door, then retreated behind his desk to sit and contemplate me. I had spent enough time in his presence to have learned how not to fidget when he did that, just as I had learned never to show emotion to my Queen.

He waved his hand at the chair opposite him, too big for me to sit comfortably but the only other seat in the room. I adjusted my knife on my hip and my swords across my back and sat. My feet dangled just above the floor.

"Kiernan?"

I realized I hadn't answered him yet. "It's Fionn," I said.

"And Fionn would be?"

Of course, I had only told him I had fallen in love in Aven, not who with or what had happened after.

"He's the Vogel Seer."

"Unusual name for bird folk." He leaned back in his chair and tented his fingers. I knew he was calculating the same way he worked out a conflict. He'd evaluate and re-evaluate with each new piece of information, but once he made a decision, there would be no changing it.

"He wasn't born in the Eyrie. His Vogel name is Tokka. And…" I fumbled for the best way to explain what Fionn was to me, to convince my father to help me.

The General snorted. "You fell in love with a Vogel Seer. Of course you did. Apparently, it runs in our family to fall in love with the exact wrong people."

I stared at him but couldn't think of anything to say to that.

"My first wife, Duncan's mother, was a farmer's daughter," he said. I hadn't known that; I had only known they divorced while Duncan was still a baby, so he could marry my mother. "I thought my father would disown me when I married her. If I had been his heir, he probably would have. Lucky for him, she tired of me quickly and left me for a blacksmith as soon as Duncan was weaned."

"But I thought –" I cut myself off.

The corner of his mouth twitched up, but it wasn't exactly a smile. "You thought I divorced her to marry the Queen of Morven Forest." He did seem amused, and it stung, that something that had caused me so much pain was funny to him.

"That's what Duncan told me."

"That's what Duncan wanted to believe himself, because he wanted someone other than his mother to blame. And he wanted a better reason to hate you than you being half fey."

I stared at him with my mouth open for a few moments before remembering to shut it.

"I don't suppose your mother told you our marriage was as much a love match as a political alliance?"

I shook my head. "She never said much of anything on the subject."

He sighed. "According to the peace treaty, she was supposed to marry your uncle. The alliance was meant to unite the two Monarchies. But your uncle was already betrothed to a daughter of the Floodplains Monarchy across the river, and your mother and I…"

He reached out to shift the map on the surface of his desk. "We had met the summer before, at a Midsummer celebration intended to begin the process of negotiating peace. It was hosted in Great River Palace, and we danced half the night and parted agreeing to write each other. We fell in love through letters, and through the few times we were able to meet in person. The treaty was re-negotiated when all parties agreed I was an acceptable substitute for my brother."

"You still love her." I resisted the temptation to swing my feet back and forth in agitation. It was bad enough I felt like a child in this chair; I didn't have to *act* like one, too.

"Yes, but you've always known that. I just couldn't stand to live in Morven Palace, and she couldn't stand to have me there."

I laughed without mirth. I had grown up believing my father was obsessed with the beautiful Sidhe wife who had sent him away; it never really occurred to me it might actually be love. "It's not an easy place to live."

"And yet, you kept running away from Dudoon to return there."

"And running away from Morven Palace to return here." I shifted my knife to a more comfortable position, trying not to fidget with it. "I'd have given anything to just live in the forest. Palaces and fortresses are not for me."

"Yet you went and fell in love with a Vogel Seer. You can't haul *him* out into the woods to live in a cabin without running water."

I could; he had told me so, but I didn't say that.

"He's been hurt. He's afraid and in pain." I breathed out my nose, long and slow, trying to think of some way to convince the General to help me. "I need to borrow a ship, or to beg passage. I need to get to him."

He cocked his head to one side. "You feel his pain?"

I looked away, studying the maps and lists attached to the walls. This office not only didn't have a view, it didn't even have windows. "We're heart-bonded," I said, reluctantly. I had learned never to offer too much, not even to my father who was a fair man, because anything offered could be turned back to wound.

"Heart bonds are a fairy tale," he said. "Like dragons and the Prince Who Will Unite An."

"Not for the Vogel. They're rare, but I've met other heart-bonded bird folk."

"And you're not Vogel."

"But Fionn is." I stood up from the chair, or rather, I hopped down from it. "I wouldn't ask if it wasn't important."

He didn't react to my sudden movement, not even as I gave in to worry and started to pace.

"Is he being hurt now, as we speak?"

"No." I was relieved he wasn't, but reluctant to say so, because it weakened my argument.

"Kiernan." His voice was grave. I stopped pacing and turned to face him. "I understand, I truly do. If I ever thought your mother actually needed me… I do understand." He pushed himself to his feet and leaned on the desk again. "But I can't give you a ship, and I can't give you passage."

"But –"

"I'm glad you came to me, instead of trying to do everything without help." His voice was dry, and I might have smiled at how well he knew me, if I hadn't been so anxious. "But you came here to do a job, an important job, and if you fail to do it, your Queen will be extremely displeased."

Not "your mother" anymore, but "your Queen." I knew he was warning me, and I knew he was right.

"I need to go to him."

"You *need* to go back to Great River City and get your embassy established. You need to make sure it's running, that your staff can carry on day-to-day operations, that your uncle is used to the idea enough that he'll ignore you."

He straightened up from his desk. "Because if your Queen finds out you left all of that undone, abandoned your people to their own devices in a strange city, she will find a lot worse punishment for you than taking your magic."

I stared at him, angry and frustrated, and completely unable to argue against him. "There *is* no worse punishment than her taking my magic."

"She could have your sweetheart killed, son," he said, gently, and I remembered her once casually mentioning giving Sean permission to kill Dec. "If your lover is not in pain now, chances are he's safe enough for the time being. Something terrible may have happened but it's over, and unless you figure out how to step back in time, there's nothing you can do for him."

I opened my mouth to protest, and he cut me off with a gesture. "Go back to Great River and do your job. Once you've got your staff trained to the point that they can carry on without you for a little while, *then* think about rescuing him."

He was right, and I hated that he was right. If I left too soon, my Queen would notice, and her punishment would not fall only on me, but on my staff.

And without my magic, how much use was I to Fionn anyway?

Maybe… maybe he would spirit travel to me again and I could ask him what he wanted me to do.

"Come back in a moon or two, and if the storms aren't too severe, I'll see about getting you to the Eyrie."

"A moon." I had to work to stay fully upright, to not slouch my shoulders in defeat.

"Kiernan." His voice was almost gentle. "Your Queen means to see you do great things."

That had me jerking my chin up. "My Queen waited thirty-three years to even acknowledge me as legitimate, and even then, she merely made me her lackey, her assassin. Her *spy*."

He raised his hand, and I stopped. "And in those thirty-three years, and the four years since, you have trained and worked hard and become the most gifted swordsperson I have ever seen."

I could only stare at him. More complements? He'd said more nice things about me in the past few days than in my entire life up to that point.

"If you are equally as strong in magic, as strong as your mother believes you to be…" He shook his head.

"She never taught me spellwork." I managed to keep the resentment out of my voice. I was an adult, not an unwanted younger child. Not anymore.

He laughed, and this time he sounded genuinely amused. "The exalted Queen of Morven Forest once confided to me that Sidhe spellwork is a crutch for the less powerful."

I stared at him. Again. "But she's not less powerful than anybody. She's –"

"One of the most powerful magic users on the Isle. In the *history* of the Isle. That is true, and yet… She once said she regretted studying spellwork because it made her pure magic less effective." He shrugged. "I have so little magic I might as well have none, so I can't say I understood her, but I do know she believed that you would be more powerful without learning spellwork." He paused, glanced at the map on his desk, and back at me. "And she had reason, though she never shared it with me, to leave your magical training to her Seer."

He leaned to grasp the door handle but paused before he opened it. "She believed you would be stronger than she is." Then he opened the door and gestured for me to leave. I went, too confused to come up with any more questions or arguments, though no doubt I would have many before I got back to the city.

H E SAID 'NO', MY PRINCE?" Syrinx was waiting for me at the door when I returned to the embassy. I let our stablehand take my horse and looked into the dryad's kind eyes.

"He said 'no'."

He held the door open for me and followed me up to my rooms. The sun was well past noon and showed every speck of dust that floated on the air, every patch of grime on the woodwork, and every dirty smudge on the windows. I hated how much my father was right that I had too much work here to run off to the other side of the Isle.

"What will you do now?" Syrinx waited until I'd removed my swords and then helped me out of the stiff, formal jacket I'd worn to Dudoon.

"I don't know," I said, buckling my swords back on. I pulled off my boots and socks and stretched my toes, then picked up my knives. "I'll be in the basement."

Since I needed a place for my guards to train – and any others of my staff who were interested – and I had designated the courtyard as a garden sanctuary, I had decided to use the building's cavernous basement. Once we'd moved the pile of cots and random furniture upstairs to be used until we could buy suitable replacements, the space was empty save for the furnace and boiler in one corner and a large cloth-covered object in another. It covered the entire block the building occupied, except the center, which was a solid core of earth and stone underlying the courtyard. It gave us a big square of four rectangular spaces, easily divided into areas for sparring with different weapons. I planned to have cushioning mats made for one or two of the rectangles, and weapons racks, and anything else we might need.

For now, it was a convenient unoccupied place for me to practice forms. I shifted my long knife back on my belt to make room and strapped on my twin blades, then settled my swords more comfortably on my shoulder. Then I stood still and breathed, feeling the packed dirt floor under my bare feet, and connected to the Three Realms as I used to as a child when I first came into my magic.

Breathing in, I drew magic up from the land and breathing out, I let it flow back to the sea. Breathe in and the tide of water magic rushed into me, out and it rose to the sky like sea spray. In to draw down the magic of the sky, and out to let it fall back to earth. Magic swirled in and out of me in an ancient cycle, and I was the spark, the green flame at the center of it. I still couldn't *use* the magic, but it was enough, for now, to feel it. It made my skin tingle.

And then, without thinking, I reached over my left shoulder with both hands, and drew my two swords, Winterborn and Brightheart, each named for someone I loved. They had not been made to work together, unlike my knives; they weren't even especially well-matched. Winterborn was heavier, and pulled down at its tip, making it a good blade for chopping and slashing, but more difficult to control. Brightheart was slender and light, a good thrusting weapon that could still deliver a good slash, if I kept in mind the lack of heft behind it.

I began to move, Winterborn in my dominant hand. In

some ways, practicing blade forms was like dancing. I could dance alone, or with a partner, or even many partners. I could wield one sword or two, or use knives instead, or only my bare hands.

When I began to feel the strain of movement, of swinging two substantial weapons – because even moonsilver becomes heavy – I tossed both swords in the air and caught them in opposite hands, taking Brightheart in my left hand and Winterborn in my right. Immediately, the balance was different, and I had to adapt the way I moved.

I had thought to come down here to clear my head, to think, but sword forms are best done in the absence of thought. So I practiced, and I moved, and grew tired. I sheathed both swords together, slipping them back over my shoulder to rest in their scabbards, and just as I was about to draw my knives to continue, I heard a shuffle, as if someone had been watching and wanted to let me know they were there.

I refrained from cursing aloud. I needed to be more cautious about getting lost in my practice. I should have known they were there. I should have known they were coming even before they started down the stairs. But I had wanted to lose myself in nothingness, and so I had.

I turned to find three sets of eyes staring at me. Three people stood on the stairs as if they had paused mid-step near the bottom.

«Holy fuck, cousin,» said Padraig. «I knew you were good, but that's ridiculous.»

Beside him, Erith clutched some papers in his hands and stared openmouthed. Syrinx simply watched, composed and serene, their eyes bright and curious.

"Did you come to practice, or did you want something?" I met Padraig's Sidhe words with Islish.

"Erith has papers for you to look over and was nervous about disturbing you."

"You never need to worry about bothering me," I said, and Erith smiled. "Unless Seer Fionn visits and we retreat to my rooms." His smile grew to a grin.

Padraig looked around the empty space. "Shall I organize training for your Guard?"

"Sooner is best," I said. "They're good, but they could always be better."

He nodded and headed back up the stairs.

"I need a bath," I said. "I don't suppose the hot water is repaired yet?"

"It's… well… It's warm, at least, my Prince." Erith fell into step beside me as I ascended to the main floor. Syrinx followed.

"What papers do you have?" I held out my hand and he passed me a sheet filled with his careful writing.

"This is the final list for the furniture order, my Prince. Except for whatever you need for your rooms." Then he handed me a second sheet with a list of shop names and prices.

"This is everything we need?"

"Probably not, my Prince, but it should be most of it."

"I suppose we'll wait until this is all delivered and installed to see what we missed?"

"Yes, I thought that best. If you agree, my Prince." He sounded hesitant.

"You would know better than I do what everyone needs. I trust your judgement."

He ducked his head. "Yes, my Prince."

"I wonder if you should call me 'Ambassador' instead?" I made my voice sound as if I did indeed wonder, and he stared at me.

"But you're a Prince, my Prince, and a Prince is a much

higher rank than Ambassador and…" He trailed off, seeing the curl I couldn't keep from showing on my mouth.

"If I had my way, Erith, you would all call me Kiernan."

"Yes, my Prince Ambassador." It was his turn to hide a smile.

We reached my rooms, to be met by Coal, who was circling over a table loaded with covered dishes. No doubt there was far more food that I could eat alone, and I made a mental note to have Erith help me look over the menus. There was no need to be so lavish when we weren't at court, and I had no desire to see food wasted.

"Your evening meal, my Prince?" said Syrinx.

"A bath first," I said, and added as he bustled away, "I *can* do it myself." He ignored me and continued to the bathing room.

"My Prince, I had an idea," Erith said, hesitant again. He followed me into my bedroom, taking my swords as I stripped them off and leaning them near the hearth. In the bathing room, Syrinx was frowning at the taps, watching the water flow into the big copper tub. It looked slightly bluish, but I'd bathed in worse.

"An idea?" I hung my belt, all three knives still attached, on a rickety chair, and stripped off my shirt.

"About… about getting to the Eyrie. If General Druison won't help you, I mean." When I turned to look at him, he almost cringed and I hated the thought that even now he might expect me to be as quick to anger as my Queen was.

"I told him, my Prince," said Syrinx, shutting off the water. "I know I shouldn't have, and I'll take any punishment you give me." They met my eyes calmly. "But Erith is my friend, and he cares for your happiness."

"Conspiring against me, are you?" I smiled when I said it, and both the others smiled carefully back. "What was your idea?"

Erith held his papers to his chest as if they were a shield and said, "Perhaps Prince Eamon would give you a ship."

I blinked. It hadn't occurred to me to ask my cousin. I knew the King would never help, simply on principle, but Eamon had seemed almost eager to be friends. Was he too eager? Or just as lonely as I had been?

"You think Prince Eamon would help?"

Erith shrugged. "He seemed nicer than King Iain. And he has a whole fleet of ships, I'm told."

"Prince Eamon does? Yes, yes of course he does." When my cousin had come of age at nineteen, my uncle had put him in charge of Great River's fleet.

"And his banquet is coming up. You could ask him then."

"It's worth a try." I dipped my hand in the water to test the temperature. It was *almost* hot. "Was that all the papers you had for me?"

He held out the envelope he'd been clutching to his chest. "This came, too," he said. The paper was thick and soft, cream with elegant writing in bright blue ink. Scholar's blue.

I took it, glanced at it, and handed it back. "Are you pretending you can't read suddenly?" I said, teasing gently.

"Why would I get a letter, my Prince?" He held the envelope as if he was afraid of what was in it. I wondered if he recognized the seal of Great River University on the flap.

"Read it and find out," I said. "And in future, you don't need to show me any mail you get. No one does. Your correspondence is private unless you wish to share it." I turned my back, stripped off my trousers, and climbed into the tub.

I heard Syrinx from the other room, scolding Coal. "No, little one, you can't eat until our Prince is ready."

"Erith?" I said. He was still standing there, starting at the envelope. "I don't require assistance bathing."

"Oh! No, of course, my Prince." He still didn't move.

"Open it," I said, reaching for the soap.

He slid his finger under the flap and unfolded the paper. It was a single page, and he read it quickly, his eyes getting bigger and bigger. "Is this real, my Prince?" he whispered.

"What does it say?" I looked up to meet Syrinx's eyes at the door. It was a good thing I wasn't shy about bare skin, because it seemed my bath was going to be public today.

"It says…" He looked up at me and started to cry. "My Prince, it says I have a place at the University. To start after Midwinter."

11
Fionn

THE TIGHTNESS STARTED behind my eyes almost immediately, but I was too weary to even raise my hands to press against my forehead.

"Goddess Above, not *now*," I said, but I had never been able to hold back visions before. Why should it work this time?

I was standing on a cliff overlooking the sea. The view was not so different from the one off my balcony, only from a little higher up, perhaps. The sun was just rising to my left, and I heard laughter as two people, two Vogel, strolled past me arm-in-arm to stand on the cliff's edge.

They didn't see me; I was only watching a vision of what had already happened, or maybe something yet to come. I could not take my eyes off the people in front of me. The man was tall, with large elegant wings and his long hair blew back from his face to tangle with his feathers. He was shining white and silvery grey, almost blinding bright in the sun. He wore a kilt of pale blue, and his bare chest was freckled blue-grey.

I wanted to weep, because he looked as I would look in a

decade or two, if I hadn't been born too small, with wings that could never carry me.

The Seer laughed again and put an arm around the other person. I thought it was a woman, as tall and elegant as he was, until they turned and the sun caught the shift in their feathers; they were sunny gold on one side and a paler color on the other, divided down the middle of the person's body.

Was this a future vision, then, of a grown-up Lisna and… but no, this Vogel's colors were softer than Lisna's, and the Seer's clothing matched what I had seen painted on the walls of the caves below the Eyrie. The past, then.

I realized, then, who I was looking at. The man was the last Vogel Seer, the one who had died soon after the Founding, after his existence guaranteed that his people – *our* people – would have a Monarchy of our own. Because only people with seers were given monarchies at the Founding. And I had seen this vision before, or one like it, when Kiernan and I had accidentally made use of the shrine below the hills of Aven and I *saw* so many things, and then forgot most of them.

The gold-feathered person kissed the Seer's cheek and gestured at him with graceful hands. He smiled and placed a hand on their belly. They were pregnant, and, I realized, unable to speak aloud, using gestures to make words instead. Had our ancient language had a silent component? I was intrigued at the idea.

The wind gusted, bringing tears to my eyes and blinding me, and then it was night, and I had to turn around to see the Vogel Seer, kneeling alone at a shrine on the cliff's top. His eyes were closed and he breathed evenly, quietly singing words in Trillka, the language we only used now for names. I tried to hear the words, aching to sing them, too. It was a prayer, a song of gladness and sorrow, for speaking to spirits and facing death calmly.

This time, it was not the wind that brought tears.

Three men emerged from a small tower on the east side of the cliff. They wore golden masks like the ones King Sarkot's Guard wore, and two of the men carried spears. The third had rope.

The Seer didn't fight them, but he did weep, his tears catching the light of the nearly full moon.

A different darkness crept over my vision and I wanted to cry out, to flee, because I found myself on the roof of the Abbess's tower at the Abbey of the Moon. Only the perspective was lower. The tower was lower, and this was not the Abbey, but a fortress that had been there before the Abbey was built.

Three fey stood around the edge of the roof, one tall and pale-haired, one smaller and red-haired, and one middle-height with hair that seemed to blend into the night.

"This will not bring the peace you think it will," the Seer said. His words were in Old Islish, which I had never heard spoken aloud, yet I understood it as clearly as if he had been speaking the modern language. "Subduing the dryads is not the answer, and you know well how many of your own people disagree with you."

"We do not need your agreement," said the Sidhe. His hair, the color of dried blood, was pulled back in a moonsilver clasp, and silver decorated the tines of his large antlers, as well. I realized I was looking at one of Kiernan's ancestors; his eyes were the same deep green.

"We only need your blood." The Alfar woman held up a sickle-shaped blade that caught the light of the full moon as brightly as the silver tips of her long, curving horns.

The Huldr person remained cloaked in shadows, as if they drew the darkness around themself to hide them from the moonlight. All I could tell of them was that they had straight dark hair and some kind of horns or antlers reaching up from their brow that looked like the twisted branches of a dead tree.

And then I was on the floor in a pool of congealing blood and damaged feathers, with Healer Kah tugging on one arm, and Neeka on the other.

<Goddess Above, please Tokka,> said Neeka. She sounded like she had been crying, like she was still crying and choking out words between sobs.

<He's still breathing, Neeka,> said Healer Kah, her voice calm and soothing, but with an edge to it I had never heard before.

<I'm okay,> I said, but even I could barely hear my voice. I tried to speak louder. <I'm okay.> But I was *not* okay, was I?

<He's awake!>

<Just get him into the bathing room. There's so much blood I can't even see where he's injured, let alone how badly.>

Between them, they got me into my bathing room and perched on a stool. I managed to help a little, though my feet wanted to drag. I clutched the sides of the stool with both hands to keep from falling off, and tried to ignore how it hurt to sit. Neeka held me steady, her hands strong on my waist, while Healer Kah wet a towel and began to wipe my skin. I pried my eyes open and realized I must have been thrashing around in my own blood on the floor while I had my vision. I was so covered my skin didn't even look the same colour.

As she worked, the Healer gathered her magic, and I felt her hands – her whole being – go still when she uncovered the punctures in my shoulders.

<Neeka,> she said, her voice frighteningly calm. <Will you go make a pain relief tea? Make it very strong. And let those serpents in so they can see he's alive.>

I blinked and tried to focus. <Smoke. Flame.> My voice sounded raw. Had I been screaming?

I saw a sudden blur of movement and color.

Bright hurt, said Smoke.

Locked out, said Flame.

I lacked the energy to reach out to pet them, even if I could have followed their quick flight, but I managed a smile. "I'll be okay," I said. "Go with Neeka and let the Healer tend me."

They grumbled but left the bathing room. Healer Kah shut the door quietly behind them.

<Tell me what happened.> She resumed her cleaning, concentrating on my shoulders so she could see the damage. <This will hurt,> she said, and pried open one of the punctures to rinse it. My nose pricked with the sting of alcohol before the sharp pain hit, and I managed, barely, not to flinch.

<I tried to flee,> I said, bracing myself as she rinsed out another puncture. <He brought me back.>

<Our King?> I could feel her anger, in her hands, in her voice, and even in the way it slipped into her magic as she tended my wounds. She was the strongest of our Healers at the Eyrie, but our healers were weak compared to those of the Sidhe and the other fey, and for now she couldn't do more than stop the bleeding. It would take her time and many days to close the wounds.

<You're angry.> I did flinch when she rinsed another wound, and another, and when she spread salve on them all and began to wind a bandage around me.

<Not at you, Tokka.> Her voice went gentle. <If our King did this – > She cut herself off as anger seeped back into her words.

Bandage in place, she took the towel to the sink, rinsed it, and turned back to cleaning my skin, looking for more damage.

<I can do that,> I said, trying to take the towel, trying not to be useless. But my arms didn't seem to want to cooperate.

<No, you can't. And you must move as little as possible while you heal.>

I bit my lip and let her wash me. She went still again when she finally looked at my wings, but then she just kept working, cleaning and bandaging the cut from the King's carelessness with the shears, tending to the scrapes on my knees and hands, and finally examining my cheekbone.

She held my eyes open and stared into each of them in turn, shaking her head at what she saw. Her hands and her magic were cool on my face, easing the bruising and soothing my headache.

<Stand up, so I can look at the backs of your legs.>

I did as I was told, holding onto the stool so I wouldn't fall, and something in the way I moved must have told her things I couldn't put into words. She rose from examining my calves and gently touched my back. <Bend over the stool a little farther, my Seer.> Her voice was so gentle it almost set me weeping again.

<Why?> But I already knew. I ached inside, and her magic wasn't strong enough to even let her see why, let alone heal me.

<Did he force you?> Her hand smoothed my feathers, warm and comforting, as she moved my tail to one side.

<I don't know,> I said, trying not to shake. If I started, I wouldn't stop, and Healer Kah couldn't heal me properly if I was trembling violently. I held back tears. Once, I had gone years without crying because the Abbess would have beaten me for it. Now, I hardly seemed able to stop. <I was not in my body,> I said. <I was spirit traveling.>

I bit my lip hard as the Healer's careful fingers pushed into me and her magic found the ache and sting. She withdrew and went to the sink to wash her hands. Very carefully, I sat on the stool again.

<I thought I told you to rest, my Seer,> she said, but there was no rebuke in her tone.

<I can fly,> I said in a whisper. <In my spirit body.>

The look she gave me was full of understanding. She had wings that could carry her on the wind, but every Vogel must surely have contemplated the horror of losing their ability to fly.

<So you were flying in spirit shape, and our King crept into your bed?>

<Yes.> This time, I couldn't stop the trembling, I twisted my fingers together, hard, and reached for the calm of my magic.

<And when you returned to your body, you fled from him?>

<No, I –> I didn't dare trust her, no matter how I wanted to. She was the King's healer.

She took my face in her hands and looked into my eyes, and I realized she was opening herself to my Seer *sight*. <Tokka, my Seer, I will not lie to you. I am a healer, *your* healer, and you can tell me anything and know it will not get back to our King. Not from me.>

And I *did* know. I could *see* her truthfulness, and her anger at the King. Her fury.

<When I realized what he had done, I… I wanted to throw up, but he was in my bathing room. In the hot pool. He grabbed me.> I touched my cheekbone carefully. It still ached, but Healer Kah's magic and salves had helped.

<I fell and he pulled me in with him.> I looked away from her eyes and she let me go, turning to put away her things and clean up the bloody towels.

<Take this.> She handed me a jar of salve. <Every morning when you get up and every evening before bed and every time you eliminate, until the jar is empty.>

I looked at the jar in my hands, unable to look at her.

<Inside you, Seer Tokka. It will keep infection away. Unless you'd rather I poke my fingers into you every day?> She turned back to tidying. <And no sex for a nineday at least. Two is better.>

<Yes, Healer.> I forced the words out.

<What happened after he pulled you into the pool?> Her eyes were hard now, but not because of me. Because of *him*.

<He told me…> For a moment I couldn't breathe. I almost dropped the jar of salve when I swayed on the stool, but Healer Kah's strong hands steadied me, gently grasping my arms above my elbows. <He told me he knew my mother.>

She sighed. <Enough, for now. I think Councilor Rocsh needs to hear this, and I don't think you should have to tell it twice. And I think it's long past time we went to the Council about our King's behavior.>

<He'll punish you,> I said, grabbing for her arm and wincing when pain shot through all six punctures at once.

She shook her head. <I am Head Healer of the Eyrie, and it is my duty to ensure the health of my people. *All* of my people. I will not let him continue this –> She waved her hand. Then she slipped her arm around my shoulders. <Now into bed with you. You need rest more than anything now.>

I let her help me up but balked when we approached the bed. <I can't,> I said.

<He won't bother you again, my Seer, you have my promise.>

<The sheets,> I whispered, shame flooding through me.

<Neeka? Can you change the bedding while I find our Seer a sleeping tunic?>

My attendant bustled in from the other room, a cup of tea in hand, and for a little while I stood still and let them tend to me like I was a child. And finally, I was in bed, as comfortable as I could be, with a serpent on the pillow in each side of my head.

<You gave me sleeping tea,> I said, trying to hold back a yawn.

<Yes, I did, my Seer,> said Neeka, smoothing the covers over my chest. <You need sleep.>

<I'm not a child.> But I sounded like one.

<No,> said Healer Kah. <You are not a child. But you *are* injured, and you *will* rest. Neeka will be here if you need anything, and Trikta and Konta are just outside your door. This afternoon, you and I will speak to Councilor Rocsh.

THE CONVERSATION with Councilor Rocsh turned out to be less terrible than I feared. I hardly even needed to say anything, because Healer Kah had already told him what I had told her, and the rest he was able to figure out from my tentative explanations.

When I said, <He told me he knew my mother,> and followed with the King's description of the archivist, the Councilor went pale.

<Her name was Liska,> he said, when I stopped speaking. <When she got pregnant she decided to go home to her parents to bear her child. We *thought* she had gone home, but then she never sent letters, never sent for us to visit her as we expected. By the time Nikna and I went looking for her...> His voice was strained, as though he was having difficulty getting the words out, and I wanted to hug him for feeling so badly for me.

I blinked away tears. I was getting so *tired* of tears. <Her name was Liska?>

Councilor Rocsh smiled, but it was sad, and there was a

strange undercurrent of anger. <She was loved by everyone here. She was smart and kind and, though she was quiet, she could talk to anyone.>

I stared at my hands but looked up when Healer Kah touched my shoulder softly, careful to stay away from the bandages. <The rest, I think, is between you and the Councilor. I'm needed elsewhere.>

When she was gone, I sat staring into the cup of water on the table next to me.

<Was it our King?> Councilor Rocsh said, voice low. <Did he get her pregnant?>

I couldn't look at him; I was afraid his kindness would have me bawling again. <He said she couldn't refuse him, because he was King.>

His hand was warm on my knee, but I could feel the tension in his body.

<He said she had a friend in the City Beneath, a human seer, who told her that her child would be the first Vogel Seer in generations. I didn't know it was possible to know that but… if the friend was a skilled enough Seer, perhaps she *could* have known.>

<I'm so sorry, my Seer.>

I forced my eyes to meet his, holding in my emotions and drawing in a calm and serenity I didn't feel. For a moment I saw raw grief in his eyes, and then it was gone and I believed I must have imagined it. <I had a vision, Councilor. I was just coming out of it when Neeka and Healer Kah found me.> I glanced away, then back. <It was of the past. I saw… The last Vogel Seer was sacrificed by the three fey Monarchs after the Founding to… to gather enough magic so they could enslave the dryads. They believed it was the only way to stop them from continuing to resist.>

His sharp indrawn breath told me this was not something

he had known. And how could he? I had never read it in any of the histories I had scoured, not even the ones that described the process of the Founding. It was not noted in the Founding Laws, or any law books that came after that I had ever heard of. The only thing that *was* recorded was that the dryads were enslaved because they refused to make peace, and that magic of some unspecified kind ensured they remained so.

<What if… What if the King… I was to be a sacrifice, too. What if the Alfar knew of the ancient magic that enslaved the dryads and wanted to repeat it to subdue more people and give them rulership over the whole Isle?>

<Speak no word of this, my Seer.>

<What if the King…?>

He put his fingers on my lips, gently but firmly, the way Kiernan used to do before I told him I hated when he silenced me.

<I will look into this, Tokka, you have my promise. In the meantime, say nothing, not even to Neeka. This is a very serious accusation, and we must be cautious. We must have undeniable evidence.>

I bit my lip and nodded.

<And I *will* make certain our King does not trouble you again… with the other issue. You will still have to work alongside him, as his Seer, but the rest… I promise that will stop. I thought I had said enough before, but I misjudged him. That will not happen again.>

I nodded again. <I can work with him. So long as he doesn't touch me.>

<And if we are correct, and you are indeed… Well, you'll make a fine Prince, my Seer.>

When he had gone, I slept again and then tried to dress myself for a council meeting, only to have Neeka and Healer Kah team up to send me back to bed. I didn't want to be an invalid, but I was still exhausted from the spirit travel and healing I had done, and even with Kah and the other Healers' magic, my injuries healed only slowly.

Every morning and evening, I applied Healer Kah's salve and let her clean and re-bandage my shoulders and draw her healing magic into me. The only thing Neeka would let me do was read, so I read, researching the spiritual life of the Eyrie and our Monarchy, and sending my guards back to the library again and again. When I was too tired for research, I read fairy tales.

When I was finally allowed up again, I went to the first council meeting I could, to find that the chairs had been moved, and instead of the uncomfortable chair next to the King's throne-like seat, I had been given a seat that matched those of the rest of the Council.

And when all the Councilors had arrived, the only empty place was at the end opposite the King, between Councilor Rocsh and the green-feathered man who had supported my request to accompany the delegation to Morven Forest.

He smiled when I sat down, and I knew I could find the strength to do this. Nothing was said, but the Council had adapted for me, to protect me, and I was beyond grateful.

The King came in at last and we all stood and bowed and sat back down. He didn't even glance at me as the meeting began, and I breathed easier. Until we adjourned and he slipped his arm into mine as I was heading for the door.

<Dine with me,> he said. I had to fight not to snatch my arm away, but only pulled it firmly from his grasp.

<My King, I don't think that's appropriate.>

<In your rooms, my Seer, with your attendant and your Guards standing over you. I only wish to talk. There are things still unsaid between us.>

I swallowed and looked around for Councilor Rocsh. He

was waiting as the rest of the Council left and watching the King closely.

<My King?> he said, and his expression made his pleasant face appear severe. I would not have wanted that look turned on me.

<Don't fret, Councilor,> the King said. <I have taken your words to heart.> His smile had too many teeth. <I have no desire to be judged by the whole Council, so I will behave myself.>

<You can begin by refraining from touching me again,> I said quietly, so no one but he could hear.

He scowled and took a step away, but didn't protest. When we reached my rooms, Trikta and Konta hesitated. Their place was outside my door, and even though they didn't know the details, they knew I didn't want to be alone with the King.

<I will be on my very best behavior, my Seer,> the King said, his voice filled with contrition. I turned my Seer *sight* on him, and he did seem to be telling the truth, so I nodded.

<The King wishes to speak to me alone,> I said, and my guards nodded and took their places, Trikta giving me a look that I think was meant to tell me they would break the door down if I called for their help. Neeka waited until the noon meal had been delivered before she retreated into the anteroom with the King's attendant. She hesitated, then finally shut the door.

I gestured to a couch and the King sat, hands folded in his lap like a student about to recite a lesson. I uncovered the dishes, knowing I should eat, though I didn't feel able. I was still store, still healing, though all that visibly remained of my injuries were small pale scars that would eventually fade to nothing.

<I am to apologize to you,> said the King.

I frowned at his phrasing. He had been told to apologize,

but didn't sound like he felt he should. I didn't look at him, focusing instead on the food, making myself choose a slice of spiced meat and lay it onto a piece of thin crispy bread. I made myself take a bite, and chew, and swallow.

<Are you?> I finally said.

<My Healer tells me I should get on my knees and beg your forgiveness. Councilor Rocsh says I should stay away from you and instead spend the time studying the Founding Laws.> He picked up a small round fruit and popped in into his mouth, then scowled and took it out again. <I detest preserved fruit,> he said.

Feeling contrary because I was frightened, I chose another of the same fruit and ate it. It was oddly soft, but sweet with the sugar syrup it had been preserved in, and a little bit tart. It was, I realized, a very small plum with no pit and the skin still on.

<And will you apologize?> I said, pretending to be calm, aloof, when I was finding it hard to keep the plum from gushing back up along with the porridge I'd had for morning meal.

<Will it make any difference?> He tilted his head to watch me, and he almost looked like the charming and handsome man I had at first thought him to be, the man I had almost wanted to seduce me.

<I will not let you into my bed again, nor visit yours.> I picked up another plum, drawn to the sweetness despite my unhappy belly, but I couldn't manage to eat it. I put it down again.

<Because it violates your precious Founding Laws.>

<They are *our* Founding Laws, and that is only one reason of several.>

Out of the corner of my eye, I caught a flicker of movement and realized the warmth in my belly wasn't only the heat of sickness at the King's open desire.

<Because you are my son,> he said, and my guts cramped to hear him say it so plainly. <Yet no one but we two knows this, so what does it matter?>

I didn't tell him Councilor Rocsh knew, and Healer Kah had probably guessed. I stood abruptly and walked away from him, around the table to a clear spot on the floor in front of the hearth, recently cleaned of my blood and feathers.

<I rather think Healer Kah is right. You *should* get on your knees and apologize to me.>

He stood and rounded the table, his eyes burning, not with anger, but desire. He thought I was going to forgive him, that the begging for forgiveness was to be some kind of sex play. I made myself meet his gaze with every bit of icy serenity I could summon. He looked at me a moment longer, then knelt and bowed his head.

<Tokka,> he said. <Little Seer. My beautiful, beautiful boy. I am so sorry. Punish me. Tell me how I can make things better with you. Tell me what I need to do for you to love me again.>

I bit back the reply that I had never loved him in the first place. I felt only disgust when I looked at him, and anger, and betrayal.

<Beg,> I said.

12
Kiernan

THERE WAS A TIME, once, when I enjoyed courtly events. Once I reached my majority, though – and probably a good few years before that – I mostly used such events as a place to meet pretty men and women, after which I'd quickly escape to someplace quieter to fuck whomever I'd met.

Now, I could think of few things I would like to do less. I'd have sooner washed laundry or pulled my own teeth out than go to my cousin Eamon's banquet.

But I had no choice. Even if he hadn't organized it in my honor, I was in Great River City representing my Queen now, and it was my duty, my *job*, to attend.

It was my duty, in fact, to attend, to look spectacular, and to charm everyone there. As my Queen's representative, of course. At least I had a lot of experience, even if it didn't amuse me the way it once had.

So, that fourthday, I had one of my staff who was good with scissors trim my hair, I shaved my chin fuzz all the way up to my ears, and I bathed in fir-scented water. I *gleamed,* when I stepped out of the bath. It had, thankfully, been plenty hot this time.

I stood in my undergarment in the middle of my bedroom while Erith and Syrinx argued over what to dress me in. That Syrinx was actually arguing seemed a good sign – he was comfortable enough with me to make his opinion known instead of simply doing as he was told.

I envied my Guard, who only had to put on their cleanest uniforms.

"I think this one," said Erith, holding up a tunic with an elaborate border on the hem.

"Perhaps the deep green would be better, to match his eyes," countered Syrinx.

"But it's too plain."

"It will be under a jacket."

"It might get warm, and he'll want to take off his jacket."

"I won't be taking off my jacket," I said. "It would be too informal." I didn't think they heard me, or if they did, they ignored me. It was, I supposed, a consequence of treating one's staff fairly. They weren't afraid of me, so they were free to do as they liked.

I sighed.

Erith set the tunic aside and went back to my wardrobe – newly delivered that day. It still wasn't very full – I had been too busy scrambling to get the Embassy functional to shop for clothes or have a tailor stop in.

"May I make a suggestion?" I said, raising my voice. The fire was low, and I was getting a chill, standing there nearly naked.

They turned to look at me, eyebrows raised. I felt like a piece of furniture that had suddenly come to life and begun speaking.

"The dark grey trousers make my ass look spectacular."

Erith's ears turned pink.

"Pair them with the short green jacket with the pattern of branches on it, so as not to *cover* my spectacular ass."

Erith's cheeks turned pink.

"Then add whichever shirt and boots look best."

They both stared at me for a couple of heartbeats. Then Syrinx's mouth curled up. "Henceforth, they shall call you Prince Kiernan of the Fine Backside."

Erith looked scandalized, but I laughed. Syrinx was not only arguing in front of me, they were making jokes at my expense, and I was delighted.

"I *have* dressed myself for a banquet before," I pointed out. "And we want them to remember me. So, make use of my best feature."

"You have many good features, my Prince," said Erith, and then his whole face flushed as he realized how his words could be taken, especially with me standing there with only a small bit of cloth covering my tackle.

In the end, they agreed on the green shirt and deep grey boots embossed with a leaf pattern over-painted with subtle tones of green and brown. I added my belt with the knife my father had given me, and strapped Winterborn across my back. Of my two swords, it was the one I'd had longest, so I was more effective with it than with Brightheart.

I'd have liked to have strapped on every weapon I owned, but Eamon would probably be insulted.

We rode to the palace, me leading the way, with Erith perched nervously on a pony next to me and two of my six Guards behind us. The other four had stayed back, two to guard to Embassy, and two to sleep.

"You'll be allowed to eat with the palace staff, once the main courses are over," I told Erith. "Padraig and Màiri will take turns eating, so one of them will go with you."

"I can eat later, my Prince."

I smiled. "You're allowed to have a little fun tonight. The food will be the same as we nobles will be eating, unless Eamon is a lot stingier than I thought. Indulge."

"I'm nervous," he said softly.

"You won't be alone, and not all humans are as terrible as my uncle. Some of the palace staff are even non-human."

He held his reins too tight, but his pony was used to nervous riders – one reason I had selected that particular mount – and simply ignored Erith's hands and kept walking steadily alongside my horse.

"Yes, my Prince."

"Will there be dancing, do you think?" said Padraig. "It would be a shame for you to waste that particular pair of trousers on an event where you're sitting down the whole time."

"I don't know what Eamon has planned. Drinks and mingling after the meal, probably. I only hope whatever it is, it isn't too elaborate."

"Or too much like our Queen's banquets."

"Ah, yes, you were forced to perform at the last one." Màiri's voice was teasing. She was easy to get along with and I was very glad I'd offered her the position in my Guard. Her father – Captain of the Queen's Guard – had been less pleased to have her taken from Morven Forest, even if Prince's Guard was a large step up from the Palace Guard she had been.

This time, there *was* a welcoming party for us. Grooms stepped forward in the courtyard to take our horses and valets wielded clothes brushes to remove horsehair and road dust. Erith looked terrified as a tall, thin man in grey and maroon vigorously brushed him off. Finally, a butler led us into the palace and through the halls to the main dining room.

When we stepped through the door, everyone already

there turned to look, and those seated rose to their feet. Erith seemed to shrink next to me as they all bowed and watched us with thinly-veiled judgement.

"Steady," I said. "They're not looking at you." Except some of them probably were. Fauns tended not to travel much outside Morven Forest – they seldom had the money or the permission to do so.

Prince Eamon stepped around the head table and came forward to meet us, clasping my arm warmly when he reached us.

"Prince Kiernan," he said. He smiled at Erith and Màiri and then held out his hand to Padraig. "And you must be Padraig nicFia, cousin of my cousin. I didn't get a chance to greet you last time."

"For the next three years, I'm only the Captain of my Prince's Guard," Padraig said, but he clasped Eamon's arm.

The Prince of Great River shrugged. "I hope our cousin won't be offended, but tonight you shall be Lord nicFia, because I've had a place set at the head table for you, next to Kiernan. Unless you are also a Prince."

Padraig glanced at me, as if for permission, and it was my turn to shrug. "I'm not a Prince unless my Queen decides I am," he said. "And I'm a little far out on the family tree for that to be likely."

"Well, you can't very well turn down an *invitation* from a Prince," I said. "And you can guard me just as effectively sitting next to me as standing behind me."

Eamon nodded happily and led us down the center of the big room, letting everyone get a good look as we made our way to the head table. "I had a very interesting letter recently," he said.

"Did you?" I replied politely.

"Indeed. The Headmaster of the University wanted my

opinion on admitting a student." His lips curled and I could see he was trying not to look at Erith.

"Does the Headmaster of Great River University usually ask your advice on which students to admit?" I slid into the chair he indicated, noting that he'd given Padraig and me chairs with slightly longer legs, so we wouldn't appear too much shorter next to our tablemates. Erith and Màiri took their places behind me, next to Eamon's guards and attendants.

"He does not, no, though he will occasionally ask my opinion on other matters, since I make sizeable contributions towards the running of his institution." He raised his hand, and suddenly everyone else was sitting and servers began bustling about with platters and pitchers. "Naturally, I read his letter with especial care."

"And what did he require?" I selected a slice of roast fowl from a plate offered to me and watched as the server skillfully added a drizzle of sauce.

"The prospective student was non-human, and he wanted to know if it would be permitted to admit them."

"Is the University human-only, then?" I nodded to a server offering roasted vegetables and from another I accepted a cup of something cool enough to cause condensation on the outer surface.

"It isn't, strictly speaking, though it is unusual for non-humans to even apply. Thus, the number of non-human students at any one time is very small."

"So why ask your advice for this particular student?"

"The prospective student was from another Monarchy as well as being non-human," he said, taking a sip from his cup. "And the Headmaster wanted to be certain not to… violate any royal policy on the matter. Normally, the University requires students to be citizens of Great River Monarchy, but this student came with a royal recommendation."

I could practically feel Erith listening intently behind me and had to hide a smile. Padraig leaned around me to say, "And what was your advice?"

"I believe education should be available to all those who have an aptitude for it. If it were up to me, I wouldn't even charge the students tuition. And anyway, having the Prince of Morven Forest owe me a favor didn't seem like a terrible idea."

"So you told the Headmaster to admit the student?" I asked, snagging something bread-like from a passing tray and breaking off a piece to taste. It was flaky and buttery, and I had to resist the urge to call the server back for another.

"I did." Eamon let his smile grow into a grin.

"I am grateful," I said. "And I'm also confident the student will make the University proud."

"I expect he will." Eamon glanced over his shoulder, met Erith's startled gaze, and smiled.

"Speaking of favors," I said, turning my cup in my hands. "I have another to ask." I set the cup aside to apply my knife to the perfectly crisped cut of lamb that had just been added to my plate.

"Indeed?" said Eamon, raising an eyebrow and trying to look haughty. "I'm going to have to think of something really good to ask in return." The smile tugging at the corners of his eyes gave him away and I was glad my uncle and aunt had decided not to attend this function, even though I knew I should be insulted. He seemed much more relaxed without his father scowling next to him.

"How can I serve you, my Prince?" he said, and the corners of his eyes crinkled even more.

I resisted the urge to stick my tongue out at him as I would have done when we were children.

"I'm pretty sure you're *my* Prince," I said. "Here in Great River, anyway."

He looked puzzled and opened his mouth to answer but was distracted by a server with a tray of candied fruit.

"I need to get to the Eyrie," I said. "Soon." I pushed a slice of vegetable around my plate with the point of my knife. "The General said he might get me passage in a moon or more, but I need to leave as quickly as I can."

He turned back to me, sugared strawberry halfway to his mouth.

"Is this a diplomatic trip?"

I put a piece of lamb into my mouth and chewed slowly. It was perfectly cooked and delicious.

"It's… It's not," I said. "It's personal." I ate another bite of lamb, then a bit of roasted turnip. Then I met his eyes, hoping my instincts were right and I could trust him. "I've spent every moment I've been here working to make sure my staff can function without me for a while."

"This is about you falling in love, isn't it?"

I didn't answer.

"It is. Of course it is. I didn't believe for an instant you'd been gelded." He sipped his drink and regarded me seriously.

"Does everyone think I've been gelded?"

He shrugged. "Well, you're not trying to fuck everyone in sight, so yes."

"I need your help, Eamon. The General said he *might* find me passage, but not until I've been here long enough for him to believe my Embassy won't fall apart if I leave for a while."

"Give me three days."

I blinked. "You'll help me?"

He grinned. "I'm a romantic. I have a small vessel I use for delivering messages. I'd wager she's even faster than one of your pretty Sidhe ships. The crew is on leave, but I can get them mustered and ready in three days."

I didn't know what to say. I had expected I'd either have to argue my case or offer up some useful piece of information my Queen wouldn't have wanted shared in order to get his help. Finally, I just said, "Thank you."

"You'll owe me one, and I hear that's no small thing among the Sidhe."

"This favor is no small thing," I agreed.

I STOOD AT THE TOP of the great white cliff that thrust out from the coast of Aven into the sea, watching the little boat that had dropped me on the docks in the City Beneath the Cliff as it grew smaller in the distance.

Prince Eamon had kept his word and had a fleet little vessel, encouragingly named *Silver Lining*, equipped and ready for me three days after the banquet.

I had gathered my staff in the kitchen of the Embassy and explained where I was going and why and told them they had my permission to travel back to Morven Forest if they preferred. I explained that it was possible our Queen might decide I had done wrong, and punish *them* for my actions, and I wanted them to have a chance to leave if they chose.

To my surprise, though not to Padraig's, if I was any judge of facial expressions, not one of them left. In fact, one of the humans, whose main job was organizing the household workers, had asked permission to speak and then told me he would rather stay and risk our Queen's ire than return to working in her palace. The rest of them nodded in agreement.

Then Padraig made a ridiculous speech about how they would all work together to make the Embassy run so smoothly our Queen would never even know I was gone. He had been practicing copying my handwriting, he said, so he could even sign my official reports, which Erith would of course write, as my secretary. Then he and Erith had caught me between them in a hug.

"And we're all going to want to meet this mysterious person who has so captured your heart," he finished, as if he hadn't already met Fionn.

In the City Beneath, I had followed instructions once given to me by the old Vogel couple who had first recognized I was heart-bonded with their Seer. They had told me how to get from the other side of the Eyrie cliff, over the top, and down into the City. All I needed to do was reverse the directions, following the almost invisible path away from the crumbling wall to the cliffside, and up.

My plan was to climb down the other side to the cave entrance I had found there – which I had entered even after being told it was too easy to get lost – and follow it to the ancient shrine and then up into the Eyrie. Last time I had gone there, I had not reached Fionn, though I had seen him. All I'd managed to do was get caught by two angry King's Guards who kicked the shit out of me.

I knew where Fionn's rooms were located, from my one brief glimpse of him as I had sailed away and left him there, but I had no idea how to get to them from inside. Once I made it into the occupied parts of the Eyrie, I was going to have a difficult task, and this time I had little magic with which to call concealing shadows.

As the boat vanished around the curve of the shore, I turned away from the view and looked around. The clifftop was nearly flat, dotted here and there with collapsed towers and other rubble. Once, it had been as magnificent as the still-used parts of the Eyrie. A gleam of light on water caught my eye and I picked my way carefully across the expanse of stone.

The tiny pool was nearly an exact circle and reflected the clear blue sky perfectly. Spaced around it were three short stone pillars, two of them fallen, but one still intact. It had a hollow in its top and I knew it was a lamp, like the one in the caves deep beneath the Eyrie. This was a shrine, I was certain; perhaps a place to honor the sky and the spirits of the dead, as the shrine beneath the Eyrie had once been used to honor the spirits of earth and the bodies of the departed.

Nyah, said Coal, and he launched off my shoulder, circled the pool, and chased after a dragonfly. It was so peaceful here, with only the sky and the stone, that I was tempted to stay and rest. But I could feel Fionn deep in my belly, warm and close. He was anxious, perhaps a little afraid, but it didn't feel urgent. It didn't worry me, but it did make me want to keep moving.

"Come on, Coal," I called, realizing he had flown out of my sight. "Let's go find Fionn."

He didn't reappear and I cursed under my breath. I closed my eyes and let magic wash over me, so strong here where land, sea, and sky all met that it almost overwhelmed me, so strong I could actually *use* it, if only a little. I could feel the inhabitants of the Eyrie below me, vague presences that made little swirls and eddies in the magic. And there was my connection to Fionn, like a delicate silver thread, leading almost straight down into the rock. It vibrated with his tension.

And there, the bright red spark that was Coal, and two others, one shading into orange, and another nearly purple. I opened my eyes and three serpents streaked over the edge of the cliff to circle me.

Is Dark, said Smoke.

Is here, said Flame.

Love, said Coal.

"Hello little friends," I said, watching them zip through the air, wanting to grab them and pet their little feathery heads, to feel them twine around my neck. "I missed you. Will you tell Fionn I've come for him?"

Smoke landed on my shoulder and nuzzled my cheek.

Bright hurts, she said.

"He's hurt now?" I felt suddenly cold, despite the brilliant sun that had kept the sea wind from feeling too cutting.

Flame landed on my other shoulder.

Is healed, she said.

Is King, said Smoke.

King, said Flame, and growled.

"The King hurt him?"

They flowed off my shoulders into the air and twisted around me.

Dark come, said Flame.

Come now, said Smoke.

They streaked away around a crumbled tower and might as well have vanished.

"I can't just climb down the cliff," I said. I took a few steps after them. "Can I?"

Secret, said Coal, and flew around my head three times, then followed the other serpents. But instead of disappearing around the tower, he circled back.

Secret, he said again, and I wished he had learned more than two words.

I adjusted my pack and followed him, careful over the tumbled stone. He kept coming back, then flying ahead, and I realized he wasn't leading me to the cliff edge, but to a ruined tower. Its roof had fallen, some of the stone collapsing into the hole, but most of it onto the cliff top, where it formed a pile of rubble. It had been a small structure, probably only a single level, and barely big enough to qualify as a room's worth of space. I peered down. There was a stairway, intact until about halfway down, where it simply ended.

"If I go down there, little one," I said, "I'm not coming back out the same way."

Secret, said Coal, and flew down into the space, vanishing behind the stairway where it was broken. I sighed and contemplated my options. I had rope, but I had no idea if I was going to need it later on, so I was reluctant to use it now. But if I jumped down, and the passage led nowhere, it was going to be very difficult to get back up. If I used the rope, I could make sure I had a way out, and then come back to retrieve it later, but the serpents' words had made me uneasy, and I didn't want to waste any more time than necessary.

"Fuck," I said. "I hope you know what you're doing." But Coal was somewhere below me and didn't answer.

I climbed carefully down the intact stairs, avoiding the fallen chunks of stone. I expected to find evidence of people here before me, but then again, the space was too tight for a Vogel to spread their wings, and I didn't think they'd be any more eager to be stuck down there than I was.

On the last intact stair, I stopped and tried to see what might be awaiting me down below, but it was dim and even with my night-dweller's eyes I couldn't see much. Coal reappeared, said *Nyah*, and flew back into the dark.

"Oh well," I said, and slipped over the edge of the stair to hang by my hands. I took a breath and let go. I landed on a chunk of fallen stair and almost twisted my ankle but managed to catch myself. A dark opening led away from where the bottom of the stairway would have been, so I followed it.

The passage spiraled like the staircase had, then suddenly came out through a wood-framed doorway, so ancient it felt almost as hard as the stone under my hand, and into what looked like it might once have been a sitting room. Everything sparkled faintly with a thin coating of salt. Ancient furniture, still miraculously intact, squatted around the room. There was a big stone fireplace in the center of the room and what would once have been a wall of windows but was now mostly empty frames. Shards of glass were scattered on the stone beneath. One section high up on the wall was still brilliant with color and showed and green and blue feathered serpents in flight against a pale blue sky.

I walked across the room, passing a hearth where I dropped my pack, and entering a door to what must once have been a bedroom. Beyond that, I found a bathing room, water still running in its hot pool. Satisfied that there was nothing dangerous here, I went back to the first room. The balcony had been cleverly built so that it would be nearly invisible from outside unless you were looking at it from the exact right angle. I avoided broken glass and leaned carefully over the edge. All I could see was cliff and sky and sea. But I knew, having seen it from the ocean, that to my left as the cliff bent back towards the beach the Eyrie was in ruins. Below me and to my right it was intact, with rows of balconies and windows.

If I was correct about where on the cliff this room was – above the currently occupied levels and near the centre of the cliff's outthrust rock – Fionn's rooms should be almost directly below me.

I went back into the room, closed my eyes, and touched my magic. When I opened my eyes, my connection with Fionn was visible again, stretching down into the rock below my feet. He felt close, and by the angle of the thin silver thread, he was somewhere near the fireplace, perhaps in his own sitting room. It was just after noon – perhaps he was sitting down to eat.

I laughed, for the first time in a long time feeling real hope.

And I was very glad I hadn't used my rope to get down here.

THE
II: CITY BENEATH

13
Kiernan

I FELT FIONN'S ANXIETY simmering in my belly, pushing me to move faster, to rush. But I knew that hurrying could be the worst thing to do. A badly-tied knot might come undone and leave me to plummet to my death. Or worse, it might hold long enough to get me down to Fionn's balcony, only to slip and drop him instead.

So I made myself go slowly and deliberately. I tied a knot every arm-length along the whole of the rope to make it easier for Fionn to ascend it. I tried to picture the outside of the Eyrie in my mind, to figure out where best to attach the rope, but the balcony had been invisible from the sea. I breathed deep and called on my weak magic again to let me *see* approximately where Fionn was. He was still almost directly below, so I hoped that meant his rooms were laid out the same way as these ones.

Then I tested several places for tying the rope. There wasn't a lot of fallen rubble here in the room, and the balcony had a solid edge instead of a stone rail, so the only real option was the window frame. It was carved stone with ancient wooden inserts that had held the glass. I was nervous of the higher areas, because windows were constructed more for vertical than horizontal pressure – or so I assumed, never having had the opportunity to study window construction. So I finally chose a spot lower down where several elegant arches of narrow stonework came together.

To be certain, I used more of the rope's length than I really liked to loop it around two more similar joins, tying it in each place. If one part of the stone crumbled, I hoped the others would hold.

When I leaned over the edge of the balcony to look down, Smoke and Flame flew up to meet me, and Coal slipped off my shoulder to join them.

Dark come, said Smoke, her tone bossy.

Bright needs, said Flame, a little more gently.

They circled me, but though they urged me to hurry, they didn't seem too agitated. In my belly, Fionn felt nervous, but not terrified.

"Watch out for guards for me, will you?" I said. "Or anyone else flying by."

We watch, said Flame.

We guard, said Smoke.

Nyah, said Coal.

I tool one final look over the edge and then gathered up the rope and lowered it until it dangled freely, swaying back and forth in the breeze. Then I checked my weapons, pulled off my boots and socks, glanced around to see that no one was near, and climbed over the side.

Raised in the forest and climbing trees since I could walk, I had never been troubled by heights. *This* height, though, was something beyond my experience. It was higher, even, than the cliff I had dangled over in Aven Forest, so I decided the best thing was to simply not look down. I didn't need to see the rope to climb down it, anyway; my toes found each knot and, though they were hardly the grasping digits Fionn's were, they steadied me as I lowered myself with my arms.

For a while, all I saw in front of me was pale stone. Then I felt space open up in front of my feet. A few more moments of careful climbing and I was hanging in front of another balcony.

The clear glass window closing this balcony off from the room inside was intact and spotlessly clean. Within, I could see a delicately carved desk up against the glass holding a row of ink bottles. Farther inside, couches clustered around a low table, a stone hearth filled a large part of one wall, and on one of the couches was Fionn.

He sat on the edge of his seat, in profile to me, and was so still and calm he might have been a statue. But there were shadows under his eyes and tiny lines of tension around his mouth. His wings were tucked close to his back, but the feathers looked ragged. On another couch, his back to me, was the King of the Eyrie.

I crept the rest of the way down the rope and crouched against the window. I could hear their voices, muffled only slightly by the glass between us.

Fionn said something in Voglish. I had tried to find references so I could study the language, but had only begun to learn it, so I only understood that he said something about an apology. It sounded like a question. But I could feel his emotions and I could tell that he didn't want an apology. If I had to guess, I'd say he only wanted to keep the conversation going until the King was satisfied with what he said and left.

The King asked a question of his own in return, and as he spoke the movements of his head made the light pull purple highlights from his midnight blue hair. His wings were so big they draped behind him like a robe.

<I will not let you in my bed again,> Fionn said. It probably showed something about me that the only phrase I fully comprehended had to do with sex. I decided not to think about that too closely. But the tension in my belly eased at Fionn's words. I knew, of course, that Fionn had not wanted to be his King's lover, but some part of me couldn't help but wonder if he might crave the safety that position would bring.

He plucked a tiny plum from a platter on the table, looked at it, and set it down again. The King said something about Founding Laws that made Fionn's eyebrows pull together as he replied.

I shifted carefully along the glass towards the door, reached for the handle, and turned. It was locked. When I looked into the room again, I thought I saw Fionn's eyes flick towards me, then away. My connection to him grew warmer. Did he know I was there? Should I wait until the King was gone or should I interrupt them?

The King's next words hit like a fist in the gut, and I froze with my hand still stretched out towards the door handle.

<Because you are my son.> It was almost a question, and poor as my Vogel was, I understood every word. I felt sick, and saw my reaction mirrored on Fionn's face. How long had he known? Would he have told me, or would he have felt too ashamed? Because I could feel his shame in my belly as if it was my own.

I swallowed down the sick feeling and made myself look away to examine the door handle. From the corner of my eye, I saw Fionn suddenly stand and cross the room to an open spot near the hearth. Whatever he said next came out as hard as the stone I crouched on. Whatever it was, it made the King stand, too, and step around the table. He looked at Fionn, expressionless, and then suddenly knelt at his Seer's feet.

I had felt the urge to do that more than once myself, not to pleasure him – though I had done that, too – but to *worship* him. Fionn should be given every honor. His King should *grovel* before Fionn for what he had done.

I made myself look back at the door. It was locked from the inside, with no keyhole I could wriggle a wire into. It was not a lock that could be picked in the normal way. But it was a simple mechanism, and there was a thin space between the door and its frame. I reached down my leg. Most of my throwing knives were above me, sheathed in my discarded boots, but I had one strapped to each calf, too.

The knife I pulled free was delicate, faun-made, and meant for sticking point-first into flesh. But it had a flat, slender blade.

I heard the King say Fionn's Vogel name, Tokka, in the middle of a longer string of words, something about beauty. I caught most of the next phrase, <Tell me what I need to do for you to love me again.> I looked away from the door. He was sideways to me but focused wholly on Fionn. I only hoped he would stay focused and not catch my movement from the corner of his eye.

Fionn looked at him, cold and regal. <Beg,> he said, and I flinched even though his words were not directed at me.

The King closed his eyes and raised his hands. I tuned out his words again, because Fionn had moved farther into the room, away from me, making the King turn his back to the window – on me – again. He didn't look at me, but I was certain he knew I was there. He pressed two fingers to his lips and turned them outwards, as if sending me a kiss. He did not seem to be asking me to wait.

I eased closer to the door and slipped my knife into the gap, feeling for the catch. It resisted and I apologized to the knife in my hand and the person who'd made it; it was a poor way to treat a good weapon.

The King dropped his arms to his sides, and looked up at Fionn, as if awaiting judgement.

The lock snapped open, and the King began to turn, but Fionn put both hands on his face and he stopped.

<My beautiful Tokka,> said the King. That I could understand. <Have I begged enough?>

I eased the door open and slipped silently through.

"It will never be enough," said Fionn. The King jerked slightly at the switch to Islish. "You cannot possibly apologize enough."

The King laughed as if Fionn had made an amusing statement. <I will beg at your feet every day, little seer. I will be what you want me to be.>

Fionn dropped his hands from the King's face and moved away, around the side of the room past the hearth. Towards me. He met my eyes, and I reached over my shoulder for the hilt of my sword.

He nodded, just a slight tilt of his chin and the King began to turn, to see what he was looking at.

Fionn glanced back at the King. "I will never forgive you," he said, and I felt hurt and anger, hatred even, surge through our bond. Then calm.

"Are you sure, pretty bird?" I said, in a voice pitched so that only Fionn would hear me.

"I'm sure."

I said nothing to the King of the Eyrie as I hopped over the couch and the table full of food, said nothing as I drew my sword, and still nothing as I removed the King's head for him – for Fionn – in one smooth motion, my Sidhe moonsilver blade barely hesitating through muscle and bone.

FIONN AND I BOTH STOOD frozen, waiting for the King's body to topple over. It seemed to take forever, poised over his bent knees like his corpse was still begging forgiveness.

His head hit the floor first, landing with a softer sound than it seemed like it should have. Then his body leaned, tilted slowly to the side, and crumpled. Blood seeped out onto the floor, and I stepped away from its spreading pool.

Finally, I let my arm relax, then flicked my sword to the side, scattering drops of blood over a couch covered in a tasteful pattered fabric in shades of green. I took a napkin of thick cream linen from the table of food, wiped my blade, and slid it back over my shoulder into its scabbard.

I found myself afraid to look at Fionn. What if I had misinterpreted, and he would be upset that I had just beheaded his Monarch? I would not feel regret for doing it – he had hurt Fionn, and death was the best he deserved. But if Fionn had wanted him to live… I *could* regret doing something my beloved would disapprove of.

"You came for me," he said softly, and I gathered my courage and faced him. He wasn't smiling – there was a tear sliding down his cheek – but he held out a hand towards me.

"I will always come for you," I said, moving carefully away from the dead King to round the couches and take Fionn's hand. His fingers were cold, so I tucked them between my palms.

"But you don't have your magic back," he said, raising his free hand to brush the hair from my forehead.

"You needed me," I said. "I felt your pain and fear. I wanted to come sooner. I *tried* to come sooner."

I stopped when his hand dropped to cup my cheek in his palm. "You're *here*," he said.

I smiled. "I'm here."

He looked at the King, then away. "Thank you."

"Beloved." I tried to put every tiniest morsel of what I felt for him in my voice. "We need to go now."

He nodded. "Yes. Yes, we do. But Neeka…"

"Just us two," I said. "Write her a letter and leave it where only she will think to look. But hurry."

I glanced towards the balcony where the rope dangled, swaying in the sea wind, plain to see for anyone who looked.

"I'll just… I'll just write a quick note." He let go and turned for his desk. I watched him pull out paper and pen and write a few lines in his impossibly beautiful handwriting, then tuck it into his basket of wool waiting to be spun. He picked up his spindle and turned it in his hands.

As he straightened up, I grasped his shoulders. "Dress in your warmest clothes, pretty bird. Pack a bag, but only essentials. Undergarments, a sleeping tunic, a change of clothes."

"Medicines?"

I moved my hands to his face. "Of course, but only what you know you'll have a use for." I smiled again. "Pack lots of your foot cream."

That got me a smile.

"Go on. I'll keep watch."

He hurried away and I listened to him moving around in his bedroom. I glanced at the window in time to see Smoke pass by in one direction, then Flame in the other. Coal swooped through the open door and landed on my shoulder, burrowing under the collar of my shirt.

Secret, he said.

"Yes." I noticed a satchel hanging near the door and crossed to lift it off its hook. Soft voices came from the other side. Neeka and a deeper voice – the King's attendant? They seemed to be having a friendly argument over something. A card game, maybe?

I crossed the room again, this time to the table of food. Each platter was lined in waxed cloth, making it simple to wrap up the food in small packets. There were two kinds of meat and three of cheese, plus preserved fruit, bread, and crispy savory biscuits. They fit in the satchel – after I dumped out flakes of bark and leaves – with room to spare.

Over in one corner near the window was a loom, more elaborate that I would have expected. I realized that Vogel weaving technology was even more advanced than Sidhe looms and I wished I had time to make a diagram for Syrinx and Erith to puzzle over. The loom was warped with fine gleaming white thread and had a length of very narrow cloth started on it. I stroked my fingers across it and smiled at the softness. It was cloud silk. A basket of thread spools and another of unspun silk – Fionn's own hair, I realized, that had been cut when he first arrived here – were tucked beneath the loom.

I bent and pulled the baskets closer, tucking a spool of thread and as many handsful of silk as would fit into the top of the satchel before slinging it over my shoulder. I threaded a strap through the buckle to hold the bag closed.

I heard Fionn move from his bedroom to his bathing room. Bottles and jars clinked as he hurriedly packed.

I touched the weaving on the loom again, just a brush of my fingertips. As I turned my head, I could see it had a subtle pattern woven into it, invisible until the light shifted.

When I heard Fionn come back into the room, I said, "You've weaving offerings."

"Yes," he replied, coming to stand next to me to look down at his work.

"Do you want to bring it?"

He looked at me, then back at the weaving. "Am I never coming back?"

I slipped an arm around his waist. "You don't have to leave if you don't want to, beloved, but *I* can't stay. I just killed the Vogel Monarch."

"Leave it," he said softly, leaning his head on mine. "If I return someday, I'll finish it. If not… I'll start something new."

Smoke streaked in through the open door. *Guards come*, she said.

"How close?" I pulled Fionn towards the balcony. He had two bags over his shoulders, full, but not bulging.

Beach, said Flame, zipping in to join us.

"The beach by the city, or by the ruins?" I reached for the rope and held it steady.

City side, said Smoke.

"Can you distract them? Delay them?"

We go, said Flame.

We hinder, said Smoke, and they both streaked away again.

"Time to climb, pretty bird," I said.

Fionn looked up the rope. "All the way to the top of the cliff?"

"Not all the way. Only halfway. You'll see."

He took hold of the rope, and I felt his fear.

"Okay, pretty bird?" I put a hand on his back, and he turned and leaned his forehead on mine.

"I can't fly," he said.

"Then don't let go." I kissed his cheek.

He faced the rope again and nodded.

"I'll hold the bottom steady. You just climb."

"What if they see us?"

"They won't. Smoke and Flame will keep the guards away."

"I… I can't climb very fast," he said, but he reached up for a knot above his head and pulled himself up. I could see the hesitation in his arms and remembered his shoulders had been injured, were maybe still hurt. But there was no choice now. I leaned back on the rope to hold it tight. He felt with his foot, and I watched his long toes curl around another knot.

"Just climb. Don't worry about speed, just don't stop."

I heard faint chittering from far around the bulge of stone; the serpents were doing their best to delay the guards, and I wished I had thought to ask how many guards there were.

Above me, Fionn climbed, clinging with hands and feet both. I didn't think he could hear the serpents and I was glad. He'd get there faster if he didn't try too hard.

Then there was a shout from the direction of the city, and his foot slipped off the knot he was holding and skidded down the rope. I heard his quick intake of breath and felt the stab of pain before he calmed his thoughts.

"You're okay, pretty bird," I said. "Just keep going."

"Was that a guard?"

"They haven't seen us."

He made a gasp that sounded like he was holding back tears, but he kept going. He winced every time he grasped the rope with the foot that had slipped, but he kept climbing.

I leaned back to try to see if any guards had come into sight of us, but from where I stood, I couldn't see much of anything.

Above me, Fionn climbed, then I heard him say, "Oh!" and a moment later I felt his weight leave the rope. He leaned over the balcony high above and opened his mouth to call out, but I shook my head. His eyes widened and I knew he understood. If the guards were close, we needed to be quiet.

I scaled the rope quickly, ignoring everything else, including the drop below and the wind tugging at me. I couldn't ignore it when Smoke streaked by behind me just as I was reaching the edge of the balcony and turned to see she had something shiny in her mouth. I threw myself over and onto the floor.

"Inside," I whispered, and Fionn faded into the shadows of the room.

I looked at the rope, still hanging free and visible, but I didn't dare try to bring it in. A guard flew past, the sun bright on his bird mask and his red and yellow wings, but he was looking ahead, cursing the boldness of feathered tree serpents in Voglish, Islish, and probably Trillka.

Then Flame zipped by, followed by another guard, yelling something about a thief.

"They've seen us," said Fionn, fear making his voice raspy.

"I don't think so." I leaned out just enough to look after the guards, then started pulling up the rope. "Smoke stole something from one of them. That's what they meant by 'thief'."

"I thought you didn't know Vogel."

"I know a few words. I've been studying."

He crouched next to me, helping me pull the rope in and carry it inside. "I hope she doesn't get caught." Then he turned to look around. "It's just like my rooms," he said. "But… Oh." His voice went very soft as he glanced into the corner, the same one where below us, his loom waited for him to someday return.

"Oh, Kiernan," he said.

14
Fionn

I DON'T KNOW WHY I was so afraid to climb that rope; perhaps it was because this time, if I fell, my ruined wings wouldn't even slow me down.

Before, I would probably have made it down without injury, definitely without death. Now, there was no chance of me surviving such a fall.

But Kiernan's deep smoky voice, his quiet words, his very presence, gave me courage and I took hold of the rope and climbed. And maybe I slipped once, burning the sole of my foot on the coarse line, but I did it. I made it to the top and over and Kiernan climbed up behind me and somehow the Eyrie's guards didn't see us as they flew by in pursuit of Smoke and whatever trinket she'd stolen from them.

Once inside the room, I breathed easier, until I looked around, and then I couldn't breathe at all. The room was nearly identical to my own, save for the doorway on the side wall where I had bookcases. It led into a dim passage and its wooden door had fallen from its frame but lay mostly intact on the floor.

Even the wooden furniture and metal fittings were preserved, though probably too fragile to ever use again. What sunlight leaked into the room sparkled off salt crystals that the sea wind had deposited on every surface. I could even see where Kiernan had crossed the floor, disturbing the glittery layer.

But none of that, as wondrous as it was, had stolen my breath. I had started to turn around to face Kiernan, to wrap my arms around him and kiss him, when an ordinary object in the corner caught my eye. A drop spindle, moonsilver adornments gleaming, had rolled under a piece of furniture as if it had been dropped and forgotten only yesterday.

I stared for a moment then realized *what* piece of furniture it had rolled under. It was a weaving loom, nearly twice the size of the one I had downstairs. Its wood had shrunk away from the joints and its metal parts had corroded, so it had come loose and fallen apart in places, but it almost looked like it could be repaired and used again. Nearby there was a spinning wheel, and a bench, and another, smaller loom leaned against the wall.

Remnants of silver textile still clung to the heddles.

"Oh, Kiernan," I said, when I got my breath back.

"What is it?" He turned away from coiling the rope.

"These were a Seer's rooms."

"There hasn't been a Seer in the Eyrie besides you since…" He trailed off and came over to put a hand on my back.

"Since just after the Founding," I said.

"That was more than a thousand years ago. Could this room have been abandoned so long?"

"One thousand, four hundred, and twenty-seven years," I said. "Assuming the way we count the years since the Founding is accurate."

He reached out a hand tentatively towards the loom, as if it would crumble under his fingers. "Amazing," he said, his voice full of awe.

"They must have closed off his rooms after…" I stopped and turned to face him, and my cloak slipped off my shoulder with one of my bags. He grabbed it and as he moved to settle cloak and bag back into place, his hand brushed the ragged feathers of my wing.

His face went still. His whole *body* went still. "Pretty bird," he said, his voice soft. He stepped around me and I had to make myself stay in place, to not turn with him to hide his view of my shame. He lifted the bags off my shoulders and set them on the floor, then pulled my cloak away, too.

"Goddess Below, Fionn." His voice was full of anger, but his hands were gentle on my wings. "Did *he* do this to you?"

I didn't need to ask who he meant by "he."

"I tried to escape," I said.

He smoothed my wings down with both hands and embraced me, pressing himself against my back. "What did he do that you needed to escape?"

I swallowed and tried to relax into his arms. I felt hot with shame. "He came into my bed while I was spirit traveling. He wanted me to… to keep being his pleasure boy. Even after he told me he knew my mother. That he…"

"It's okay, beloved," he said. "You have good reason to be upset." He turned his face into my back, breathing warm between my shoulder blades. "I'm glad I killed him." His voice was muffled, but hard. I was afraid he would pity me, but it was empathy I heard instead, and anger on my behalf.

"It doesn't matter," I said, trying to sound unconcerned. "I can't fly anyway."

His arms tightened around me. "It *does* matter. He mutilated you. He used you and he frightened you and he hurt you. It matters very much."

"They'll grow back when I molt." I put my hands over his. But he was right. It *did* matter. The feathers would grow back, eventually, but in the meantime, anyone who looked at me would wonder what I had done to deserve such punishment. "Until then, my shame is visible for everyone to see."

He stiffened, and let go of me, then turned me to face him, still impossibly gentle. He put his hands on my face and stroked my cheekbones with his thumbs. "You have nothing to be ashamed of." He said it firmly. "And I should have been here to protect you."

I looked away from his eyes. "My own father used me as his pleasure boy. How is that not shameful?" I didn't even try to keep the self-disgust from my voice.

"You didn't know he was your father," he said. "You only knew he was your King, and *everyone* thought that made you his property. I never should have brought you here in the first place."

"*He* knew." I tried to pull away and he slipped his hands behind my neck.

"Then that is *his* shame, not yours."

"How can you still want me?" I said, hating the whine that crept into my voice, hating how I could feel so sure of myself one moment, and so in doubt the next. I could stand other people judging me, I could look down on their scorn, but not Kiernan. His judgement I could not face.

"Oh, pretty bird," he said, his voice soft, but insistent. "You're sweet and kind and generous." He pulled my face down to kiss my forehead. "You're smart and curious and you look at the world with such wonder I can't help but share it." He kissed my lips, but softly. "You're beautiful, handsome, *and* pretty. You're brave and you're strong, and for some reason you believe I can be all those things, too. You make *me* believe it." He kissed me again. "And you needn't take on someone else's shame. *You* have not done any wrong, only had wrong done to you." He kissed me harder. "And if I have to beat the fuck out of anyone who tries to say otherwise, I will."

My skin flushed at the thought of him fighting for me.

"Would you kill for me?" I said, my voice small. I felt sick for wanting it, but I *did*.

"I *have* killed for you, beloved," he said, sliding his hands to my chest. "Twice."

"Twice?"

He smiled. "Come with me. There's something else I want you to see."

He took my hand and led me through what would have been the bedroom into the door on the far side. In my rooms, it led to the bathing room, and it seemed to do so here, too. Scuffs in the coating of salt showed where he had walked through and back.

Many of the tiles were cracked, and much of the colored window glass had broken and fallen to the floor. The sink was cracked in two, but the commode was intact, and I could even hear water flowing through it. And the hot pool, cracked around the edges, still steamed. The water looked clear and clean.

Kiernan let go of my hand and began to unbuckle his sword.

"What are you doing?" I asked.

"This is best seen from *in* the water, unless I miss my guess."

"Are we safe here?"

"It's blocked off from the rest of the Eyrie, and nearly invisible from outside. We should be safe to stay for a while."

I frowned but didn't resist when he unclasped my belt and drew my tunic over my head. I pushed his hands away when he reached for my shirt. "I can do that."

"I like undressing you." But he let go to strip off his own clothes and didn't wait for me before slipping into the water. I followed more slowly.

"Here," he said. "Lean back." He moved behind me, his hands smoothing my ragged wings. I expected him to flinch away from them, but he didn't touch me any differently than he ever had. It made me feel better. Like he cherished me, even if I was damaged.

I leaned back against him and he settled my head on his shoulder and slid his hand under my back until my body was held up by the water, floating.

"Now look up."

I looked. The ceiling above us was crumbling slowly with age and salt and moisture, but enough was intact to see it had been painted like the night sky. A fireball streaked across one edge of the painting and feathered tree serpents flitted through the dark.

And in the middle…

"I saw him in a vision," I said. The Seer had huge wings, outspread to hold him aloft, and long hair that twisted around him in the sky. I had hair that long once.

The style was more naturalistic than the paintings I had seen in the caves beneath the Eyrie, or the one on the ceiling in the shrine below the Aven Hills. Except for the paint that had flaked away, he looked almost alive.

"What was he doing?" Kier said in my ear. "In your vision."

"First, I saw him looking out over the sea, laughing with another person. His… his spouse, I suppose. They were pregnant. They were… like Lisna."

"The child you healed? The one who was both male and female?"

"Yes."

"In Morven, we call that 'between.' Man and woman both, or neither, or some combination of the two. Most dryads are between, with both male and female parts, able to both sire children and bear them."

"Between," I said. "I suppose that's better than making them choose only man or woman. Or being told which they must be." I looked up at the painted sky. "The Seer's spouse… they spoke with their hands, with gestures." I held my own hands out of the water and tried to imitate the way the ancient Vogel had moved.

"You're sad," he said, and I realized he was feeling my emotions through our bond again. I gently pushed them aside. It was hard enough to feel one's own, let alone share another person's.

"Then I saw him at a shrine, on the top of the cliff, I think. He was praying. Or perhaps communing is a better way to describe it, speaking to the local spirits, singing to them. Guards came for him and took him away."

I felt his lips on my neck, not seductive, but comforting. His arms slid around my chest to hold me tight.

"And then I *saw*… They sacrificed him." It was hard to breathe. "The Founding Monarchs. They sacrificed him for a blood spell to enslave the dryads."

Kiernan went still, his hands pausing where they had been stroking my skin. "So that's how they did it." He sighed. "Was it all of them? All nine?"

"I only saw three. Alfar, Sidhe, and Huldr."

"All fey. The three Triarchs."

"They were at the Abbey of the Moon, or where the Abbey *would* be. Where the Abbess's tower is now."

"Goddess Below," he breathed. "I wouldn't be surprised if the Abbey was built to protect that magic." He sounded thoughtful. "Maybe I can go there again, and find it, and break it."

"Maybe," I said. "But the Alfar at least must know about it. Somehow, they knew to sacrifice *me* there, to conquer the rest of the Isle. Only –"

"Only what, pretty bird?"

"He wasn't a virgin; he was to be a father. So why did I have to be?"

"Maybe it takes more magic to enslave an entire Isle full of people that it takes for only one."

"What if they try again?"

"I won't let them." His voice was fierce, and I shivered despite the hot water. But it was not a shiver of fear. "But I wonder…" he said softly. "I wonder if Sean tried to kill you to prevent it happening again. If his motives were actually about protecting our people, the Sidhe, and not about causing war or disrupting trade. Or hurting me."

"I think the King… He said my mother knew I would be a seer, that her friend who was a human seer told her when she first learned she was pregnant. I think he… I think the King might have killed her himself and sold me to the Alfar."

His hands rubbed my arms, and I felt comforted. How could he be so good at making me feel stronger just by touching me kindly?

"What would he gain from selling his people's only Seer? His own son? Fionn, you should have been his heir."

"He liked money and power. Maybe having the Alfar leave him to rule as he saw fit was enough. They are our over-monarchs, but they don't try to govern us, only collect their tithes."

"I'm not sorry I killed him," he said.

"Neither am I." I floated a moment in silence, staring up at the figure on the ceiling. "Am I a horrible person because…"

"Because you wanted your King dead? No. I don't think you could be a horrible person if you tried." His lips brushed my ear as he spoke, and I shivered again.

"I *like* it when you… when you defend me," I whispered. I felt pressure behind my belly muscles. "When you fought Dag because he wouldn't leave me alone…" I flushed even hotter than the bath could make me. "I got… I became aroused, to see two handsome men fighting over me."

"That doesn't make you horrible, pretty bird." He sounded like he was trying to hide the amusement in his voice.

"And you *have* killed for me," I said. My erection pushed against the inside of my sheath. How could I be stirred at the thought of someone's death? Except it wasn't the death that made me amorous, it was the thought that Kiernan would do something so final for me.

"I have and I would again." His hands slid from my arms onto my chest. "Does it arouse you, beloved? That I would do anything for you? Even take life?"

"Yes," I whispered. The ache in my groin was almost unbearable.

"It arouses you, that I would do violence for you? Because I would. I will. If Dag bothers you again, I'll flatten him."

"He's so much bigger than you."

His hands traced the shape of my pectoral muscles and followed the crease between my belly muscles downward.

"He's nothing." His voice rumbled. "I would take on three big hairy werewolves for you. Ten. A dozen." He found my hips and one hand lingered there, steadying me in the water. The other slid over my thigh. "I would raze the Eyrie to the ground if I had to, to protect you."

My breath was coming out in hectic little pants. I turned my head to find his neck with my lips then captured his earlobe between my teeth.

His fingers brushed softly over the feathers that covered my sheath and I let go of his ear to gasp.

"Why?" I asked. I lifted my head just enough to watch his middle finger trace the line of my seam and then I couldn't hold my desire in anymore. My erection pushed slowly out of my sheath and Kiernan groaned in my ear.

"Why would you do those things?"

"Because I love you, Fionn." He ran the tips of his fingers over my erection. His breathing was ragged, but his hands were steady. He dipped his fingers into the base of my sheath and pulled them out slick with lubricant. That hand he moved behind me, slipping between my buttocks to press against my anus.

"Because you're mine and I'm yours." He curled his other hand around my hardness, stroking slowly as the fingers of his other hand traced circles behind.

"I *am* yours," I whispered as he pressed his fingers carefully into me. He couldn't reach far enough to bury them deep inside me, so he massaged me just inside until I had to push against his hand, to slide my erection in his fist. I pulsed and a thin dribble of white floated away into the water, pulled down by the flow that had kept the pool clean for a millennium and more.

"Pretty bird," he said. He nuzzled my neck and kept his hands moving, a little faster now, still teasing but promising release. My second pulse was stronger and my third stronger still.

Then was the long pause that always came before my fourth, that always made me wonder if there would *be* a fourth. With the King there never was; with Kiernan I never had less. Once I had even had five.

"Don't stop," I said, even though his hands never faltered. He shifted position to reach me better, pressed farther inside me and found the place that felt so good when he rubbed. I gasped and thrust against his hand.

"Faster," I said, and he slid his hand over me, into me, faster. "Harder," and he rubbed harder, pressed harder.

My pleasure built in slow agonizing waves, and I floated helpless as he touched me, rubbed me, fucked me with his fingers.

"I would kill for you, too," I said, and I felt a shift in his emotions through our connection. His hands remained steady, pushing my pleasure until I wanted to scream. "Oh Goddess," I said, more moan than words. "I would kill for you, Kier." And my vision went grey around the edges even though my eyes were squeezed shut as my fourth pulse crashed over me, leaving me tingling from scalp to toes. This time, the ribbon of white the water tugged away was thick and seemed endless as it spiraled into the depths of the pool.

Kiernan moved his hands away slowly and wrapped his arms around me again. I let myself sink until I was sprawled in his lap.

"Feel good, pretty bird?" he said, kissing my cheek.

"Mmmm." I was too spent for words. Four pulses left me drained in the best way, sated and not wanting to move.

For a while we just sat together in the water, letting it make our muscles limp. Then I twisted around to look at him.

"I *am* yours," I said, not whispering this time.

His kissed the end of my nose. "And I'm yours, beloved." His green eyes were steady on mine. "If you could," he said, "would you marry me?"

I think my heart stopped for a moment; I know my breathing did. "But I can't," I said, too surprised to answer.

His mouth quirked up at the corner. "But if you could?"

"Of course I would," I replied. "But even if I could, *you* couldn't."

"Why not?"

"You're the Prince of Morven Forest. You need an heir, and I can't give you one."

His smile grew. "I'm a Prince, but I'm not my Queen's heir. It doesn't matter if I have children."

"But you're *an* heir."

"I'm the backup. I have two older sisters. And besides, even if I *was* to inherit, there are other ways of getting an heir."

"What do you mean?"

"My great grandfather married a between with male tackle. So they made a contract with the daughter of a highborn Sidhe to be his… the proper term is 'Mother of the Heir' or 'Father of the Heir' depending on the role."

"Oh." I tried to puzzle that through.

"It's the same if a Monarch or their spouse is infertile or can't produce an heir for some other reason. It's a contract that's almost as prestigious, and as binding, as a marriage contract. They say more than one lord has pretended to need a Mother or Father of the Heir just to get another alliance in addition to marriage."

"Oh, that's very practical."

"It is."

"Do you want children?" I said, suddenly hesitant. What if he wanted many, and would always be finding someone else to have them with?

But he shook his head. "I'm not *against* the idea, but I don't know that I want them."

"What if we adopted?"

He touched my cheek. "Are you thinking of a certain remarkable Vogel child?"

I hid my smile against his chest. "Perhaps. But I think Healer Kah will take her in."

"Do *you* want children?"

"I'm not interested in women."

That got me his infuriating smile again. "That doesn't mean you're incapable of getting one pregnant." He ducked the swat I aimed at him. "Or you could find a between or a man with female tackle. You *do* have options."

"Sit on the edge of the pool, and I'll show you the only thing I want," I said.

He blinked at my sudden intensity but braced his arms on the edge of cracked tile and pushed himself out of the water. I rested my chin on his knee and looked up at him.

"If I have children, I'd rather adopt them. *You're* the only one I want to… to spill into."

He pushed wet hair off my face.

"You're all *I* want," he said.

"I know." I felt the abrupt return of confidence and wondered how I had ever doubted him. Why did I keep slipping into uncertainty even when I could feel how he felt in my own belly?

I nudged his thighs apart. "Look at you," I teased. "You've gone all soft."

He looked down at his groin, where his penis was limp against his leg.

"I guess I really *don't* want children," he said and laughed when I jabbed his calf with my finger.

"Just lean back," I said, and without waiting for him to do so, I took him in my mouth and sucked, and slid my lips slowly up his length, and by the time only his tip remained against my tongue, he was hard and breathing fast.

"Remember I told you Vogel have no gag reflex?" I said, when I moved my mouth away.

"I'm pretty sure you said, 'very little' gag reflex." He seemed to be having trouble forming words.

"Close enough." I plunged down on him again, so far I felt

his tip press against the roof of my mouth, then the back of my throat, then *into* my throat and my lips brushed the soft curls at his base.

"Fuck." He groaned. "Oh fuck." As I sucked and slid and swirled my tongue his "oh fuck"s grew louder and less coherent until he arched his spine, threw his head back and spurted hot into my mouth.

15

Kiernan

LATER, DRIED OFF AND DRESSED, we made a bed of blankets and spare clothes in front of the bedroom hearth, and I broke up an ancient dresser for wood. It seemed safe enough to build a fire, since the chimney connected to the others below it and our smoke would blend with that of the other rooms.

It was a shame to ruin a piece of furniture so old, but I chose one that was already damaged enough that it could never be used again.

I unpacked some of the food I'd taken from Fionn's table, and we made sandwiches of it, and of course I made tea — Fionn's favorite winterleaf and sweet bean pod, of which he'd packed a large packet.

"Where will we go?" he asked. He sat on the hearthstones, as if being closer to the fire gave him comfort. He held his tea cupped in his hands and seemed to content to inhale its steam instead of drinking it. He stretched out a leg and I scooped his foot into my lap and examined the rope burn on his sole.

"We can't stay in Aven." I leaned over to reach for his bag, and he took it before I could, rummaged, and handed me a clay jar, as if he knew exactly what I was looking for. "Is this good for burns, too?" I opened it when he nodded and the scent of swordleaf hit my nose and made me sneeze.

"I hoped we could go back to Moira's village. I'm sure she and Col would take us in."

"I'm sure they would." I thought about Seer Moira who had taught Fionn so much in the short time we hand stayed with them, and her gruff but kind werewolf husband Col. "Are you eager to see Dag again, pretty bird?" I teased.

He shoved me with his foot, and I laughed and almost dropped the jar of foot salve. Moira and Col, and even pushy Dag who had not taken Fionn's hints to leave him alone, had done more for us than most people I'd known my whole life.

It was Moira who'd told me to stop being an idiot and tell Fionn I loved him. She didn't use those words; she had been much nicer. I hadn't listened and had ended up nearly dying to reach him in the Eyrie to make up for it.

"I wish we could," I said. Moira had treated both of us like family and had not hesitated to put even a prince to work in her kitchen. I liked her very much. "But I don't want to endanger them. Not again." I spread salve on Fionn's foot, moving carefully over the burn. The redness seemed to fade quickly, and I felt him relax under my hands. I massaged one of his big, claw-tipped toes and he sighed, leaned back, and sipped his tea.

"Of course." When I let go of his foot, he tucked it close and let me take the other one. "Could we go to Great River? To your Embassy?"

I concentrated on the arch of his foot while I considered, but I already knew the answer. "I can't grant you asylum. I don't think I can even claim diplomatic immunity for myself. I killed a King, pretty bird. If anyone manages to follow us, I can't lead them there, to let them connect us with Morven." I bent double to kiss the top of his foot before rubbing firmly along the bottom of each toe. "It will get around very quickly if you show up there after disappearing from the Eyrie. My Queen would very soon figure out what happened, even if no one else realized I was responsible." I paused, tracing my thumb over the flexible scales on the upper surface of Fionn's foot. "I should probably try to avoid an inter-Monarchy incident, if I can. At least until I can figure out how to make it seem justified."

"It *was* justified," said Fionn. "You were defending me. Maybe…" He frowned and looked at his hands, still wrapped around his empty teacup.

"Maybe what?" I rubbed the sides of his foot with my thumbs.

"If we turn ourselves in, to the Council, maybe they'll see that what you did was necessary. That you killed him to protect me. Maybe they won't arrest you."

I wrapped my fingers around his slender ankle. "Councilor Rocsh might believe that. Or he might see me as a threat to his Monarchy. To you, even." I studied the top of his foot. "But the King's Guard would kill me before we ever got to see the Councilor. No, I think we need to disappear for a while. Let the ants' nest we've stirred settle down. Then we'll figure out what to do next." I didn't say that I hadn't planned to leave my staff alone for so long, that I needed to get back before my Queen suspected I was up to something or else they would suffer punishment in my stead.

Perhaps it made me a terrible person, but the only one whose happiness and wellbeing concerned me just then was Fionn.

"So we'll be outlaws? Like we tried to avoid by going to the Eyrie in the first place?"

"Do you want to go back? You only have to say, and I'll find a way to get you back to your people. You could go to any Guard in the City Beneath the Cliff and they would return you the Eyrie safely." It hurt to say it, to even suggest that I would be willing to let him go now that I had him again.

"You couldn't come with me," he said, his voice small.

I set his foot gently on the floor and put the lid on the salve jar. It hurt to think about him walking away from me again, but if it's what he wanted, I would do it.

My stomach tied in knots while he stared into his teacup, sipped and found it already empty, and set it aside.

"I can't go back there," he finally said, and I could breathe again. "Maybe one day, but not now." He met my eyes and his silver irises caught the firelight and turned to gold. "You came for me like you said you would, so let us be outlaws while we find a way to be together."

I nodded. "We'll go to Tronven."

"Have you ever been there?"

"No." I'd been all over Morven, even to the plains where the reclusive Hirsch lived. I'd seen a lot of Aven – all save the Alfar's mountain cities. But I'd never been to Tronven; I'd never had reason to. "We'd best stay clear of Huldr lands, at least to begin with. Humans and other folk will be curious, but unlikely to bother us, and the Siegel probably won't care about us an all, if we even meet any."

"The humans of Tronven trade with the people of Aven. Word might get back. I'm not exactly inconspicuous." He smiled and tugged at a lock of his silver-white hair.

"It probably will, but how often do your people listen to humans or anyone not Vogel?"

"The bird folk in the Eyrie, approximately never." His smile twisted a little. "And any Vogel who are likely to talk to humans also don't talk to those in the Eyrie."

I squeezed his knee. "Siona told me once the seers of the Isle protect each other, even over the interests of their Monarchies. They have a network of their own outside Monarchy boundaries, and you should be part of it."

"Moira said something like that, too, but I'm not a part of it, even if I should be."

"But they'll help protect you, pretty bird, like Moira did when we escaped from the Abbey."

He leaned forward to wrap his arms around his knees. "I'm frightened, Kier." His eyes glistened, but I wasn't sure it was from tears. "But… For the first time since I came to the Eyrie, I have real hope. Maybe I can just refuse to return until the Council changes the laws so we can be together."

I smiled at that. I had killed his King and somehow given him hope. "We'll be together," I said, putting all my conviction into my words.

"Yes." He was quiet for a moment, then he said, "I don't like being helpless, Kiernan. I want you to teach me to fight."

I touched his hand where it clenched around his arm. His claws dug into the fabric of his sleeve. "Beloved –"

"I know. Seers mustn't take life. But can't I at least learn to defend myself?"

"Do you know why Seers mustn't kill?" I said softly.

He shook his head. "Everyone keeps telling me I mustn't, but no one will tell me why."

"When I was a boy, there was a faction in my Queen's court that thought our people would be better off without a half-human Prince. Perhaps they thought I was somehow a threat, or maybe they wanted to re-start the war with the humans of Great River."

I shifted into a more comfortable position. "One day, they sent an assassin after me."

Fionn's eyes fixed on my face.

"He was a lord in my mother's court, someone she had let get close to her. Someone she had trusted. It isn't easy for a Sidhe to deceive another Sidhe. We can't lie, and some of us have magic that helps determine if people are sincere. So he very nearly succeeded." I didn't remind him that being half-human, I *could* lie, and he didn't mention it.

"Oh, Kier." His voice was breathy.

"He came after me with a knife, when I was in the forest helping Siona harvest medicinal herbs. I was excited to be allowed to find and cut the plants all by myself, so I was incautious. I was still trusting, then." I failed to keep the self-deprecation out of my voice and Fionn put a hand on my shoulder. "He nearly reached me, but Siona's herb knife reached his eye, and then his brain, before he could carry through his strike. I ended up with only an easily healed scratch on my arm." I stared at the place on my forearm where, even though I didn't even have a scar, I could still see the stripe of my own blood. It was the first time someone had intentionally tried to harm me.

"Siona killed someone to save you?" Fionn's voice was quiet, almost tentative, but his hand on my shoulder was strong. I tilted my head to rest my cheek against his fingers.

"She did. Craig nicStane – my Queen's Captain – found us, much later, huddled next to the man's dead body. I was crying, but not because I was afraid. I was crying because Siona was blind."

"But she was always –" He stopped suddenly as he realized. "Siona *wasn't* always sightless." His voice rasped. "She lost her vision because she saved your life by killing someone."

I kissed his hand. "That is why you mustn't kill. A Seer who kills loses something precious for every life they take."

I looked at his face finally, and I saw understanding there, and something fierce. Determination, maybe.

"So teach me how to defend myself without taking life." His hand tightened on my shoulder. He met my eyes, looked away, then looked back. "But if I had to, Kier, I would risk whatever loss I might face and kill to save you."

I wanted to tell him no, to not even think that way, that my life wasn't worth his vision, or his hearing, or whatever the spirits might take from him. But I didn't. We were heart-bonded and so I knew he felt as strongly about me as I did about him. And there was no question that I would kill for him, as many times as I had to, no matter what I lost each time.

So I nodded. "Okay, pretty bird. I'll teach you."

"You will?" He let a smile grow on his face. "I was sure you would say no."

"I can't deny you anything," I said, laughing. "I thought you'd figured that out by now."

"Can we start now?"

"In the morning. But if you're going to learn to fight, you first need to learn to take care of your weapons."

"I don't have any weapons."

"Then it's a good thing I have more than one normal person needs." I reached for my sword belt, set aside, but close enough I could reach it quickly if I needed to. Fionn watched me, eyes bright.

I pretended to consider all of my weapons, even laying them out in front of us, from my skinning knife to my swords. I already knew which I was going to give him, but it was fun to make him wonder.

"You do have a lot of knives," he said. "What's that one?" He pointed at the leaf-bladed knife my father had given me.

"An ancient blade made from both steel and moonsilver. The technique is long forgotten and only a few such weapons remain." I drew it and handed it to him, hilt-first. He held it carefully. "My father gave it to me for my birthday. He said it was my grandfather's, and his grandfather's before that. Supposedly, there were once three, but the other blades were lost."

He examined the design and then handed it back to me. "Well, you can't give me this one."

"These are faun-made throwing knives that Padraig and Erith gave me. Erith's father made them." I showed him the slender blades, then pointed out the skinning knife and the werewolf-crafted gutting knife.

"And that's Winterborn," he said, pointing to one of my swords. "And Brightheart." He pointed to the other. "I don't think I could use a sword."

"Give me your belt," I said.

He reached for his pile of clothes and handed me the wide leather belt with its ornate clasp and beautiful tooling. I slipped my twin knives off my belt and onto his.

"But Kier," he said, "You can't give me those, They're too much a part of you."

"Stand up," I said, getting up myself and taking his hand to pull him after me. He stared at the belt in my hands. I slipped it around his slender waist and settled it on his hips and then bent to buckle the sheaths to his thighs. I drew both knives and handed them to him. He took them carefully.

"These are Sidhe named blades, given new names when I was gifted them by my Queen." I touched a finger to the crossguard of each. "You shouldn't even be able to hold them."

He looked at me, startled. "That's why your Queen thought I was innocent of attacking her. Because if I had used your knives as she saw her attacker doing, I'd have been burned."

"But we both know you *can* hold them." I touched his hands. "They accepted you when you borrowed them, even though everything I've ever learned about named blades said they shouldn't have."

"Why?"

"I don't know." I trailed my fingers up Fionn's arms to his face. "But they accepted you. Their names are Sinister and Dexter, which mean 'left' and 'right' in the Dryad language." I snorted. "I suppose I wasn't very imaginative when I named them. I was only eighteen, and thought I was clever to know Dryadic."

"You know the Dryad's language?"

"Back then I knew about six words. Now, maybe sixty."

His lips curled and parted slightly. It was hard not to lean closer and kiss him, to forget about teaching him and pull him against my body instead.

"It's tradition for the new owner to rename them, to claim them for their own."

"Do I have to?" He turned his hands to examine the knives from another angle.

I shrugged. "I don't know. They've accepted you already, so perhaps not."

"I think I want to keep their names. Because to me they're a part of you, and I want to keep them that way."

I couldn't stop myself from kissing him then. Just a little. When I pulled away, I said. "Now that you're armed, I'll teach you how to care for your weapons. Tomorrow, I'll begin to teach you how to use them."

FIONN WAS AWAKE before I was; I felt him stir next to me and slide out from under the blanket, but some part of me knew it was him, and that we were safe, so I fell back to sleep.

I still didn't love being awake all day and sleeping all night, but I had managed when I lived in Dudoon with my father, I managed at the embassy, and I would manage now.

I opened my eyes and stretched when I smelled tea and warm bread.

Fionn smiled at me and said, "Hi," in his soft, husky voice and my whole body responded by flushing warm. My cock twitched and I had to push away amorous thoughts.

I returned his smile and said, "Good morning, pretty bird."

"Will we leave today?" He handed me a cup of tea when I sat up and turned back to the hearth. He had put a fallen chunk of stone in the middle of the coals and was using it to toast slices of bread and melt cheese on top.

"Not today. Perhaps tomorrow. Today I'll start teaching you to use those knives." I gestured at his belt, laid out carefully on the hearthstones, twin blades arranged side-by-side.

"Before we start –" He used a sliver of wood to slide the bread onto the one wooden plate I had thought to bring and set it between us.

"Mmm?" I sipped my tea, letting the heat seep into me.

He turned to face me fully and tugged at one of the feathers next to his face. "Will you cut these off for me?"

I watched him over the rim of my cup. The steam felt good on my skin, and I inhaled it, letting the sharp, sweet scent wake me.

"Are you sure?" I asked.

"They aren't even accurate," he said. "They were never accurate."

"What do they say?" I snagged one of the bread-and-cheese slices and took a bite. It was good; the cheese was sharp and salty and the bread crispy.

He touched the large feather in the center that looked like it had come from a white argus pheasant.

"This one says I belong to my King." His voice caught on the last word, and he swallowed a gulp of tea. "The rest say…" He looked at the cup in his hands. "They say I'm not seeking a partner. That I'm not interested in sex at all."

His knee was warm when I put my hand on it and squeezed. "I'll cut them off for you."

"Thank you."

"What should they say?" I finished my bread and watched while he took a bite of his and chewed. I could watch him do small, mundane things all day and never feel bored.

"If I was a normal Vogel in the Eyrie, they should say…" He hesitated and took another bite of his breakfast. The tips of his ears turned pink. "They would say I'm unmarried and interested in men, but that I have a committed partner. And that I have no children." He met my eyes.

"A committed partner?" I said it softly and smiled. I felt warmth all through me and it wasn't from the tea.

"Aren't you?" His tone was just a little challenging, and his eyes sparkled.

"You know I am." I pushed up to my knees, took his teacup, and set it aside. He didn't resist when I pulled him onto my lap, but he did keep eating.

When he had swallowed the last bite, I kissed him. For a moment, he let me, then he pulled back to rest his forehead on mine. "Can you cut these adornments off first?" he asked. "I'm tired of telling anyone who sees that I'm someone else's property."

He pressed his face against my palm when I cupped my hand around his cheek.

"You belong to no one but yourself," I said, stroking his cheekbone.

His lips curved in a soft smile. "I belong to you."

"Only because I also belong to you," I said.

He sat very still as I carefully cut away the feathers that had been glued around his face. They were so skillfully attached that it was difficult to separate them from his hair and his natural feathers.

"It's okay if you cut my own feathers," he said. "I don't even care if you cut my hair. I just want them gone."

In the end, I only detached two very small natural feathers and a few strands of hair. He relaxed and sighed, and I stroked his hair back from his face.

"You almost look like the shy young man I met so long ago at the Abbey of the Moon."

"That wasn't even half a year ago." But he smiled.

"Are you ready to play with knives?" I said, and he nodded.

First, we sat side by side and I showed him how to hold the blades so his fingers, his whole hand, and not his wrist, acted as a pivot for movement. Then I showed him how adding wrist and elbow and arm movements made the knife into a flexible – and sharp – extension of his body. After he practiced that for a while, I gave him the two scraps of wood I'd carved into basic knife shapes the day before while he had practiced blade care.

I took the two real knives myself and showed him move-by-move the first of the blade forms I had learned as a boy, so young I'd only just begun to walk. He was hesitant at first, and awkward, like he didn't know how to hold himself.

"Just relax, pretty bird. You don't have to be perfect. Just move, one step at a time. When you've got all the steps, then we'll work on the rest."

He nodded and tried again, and then I stood beside him, and we did the moves together, over and over until I saw from his smile that he was starting to *feel* the steps.

"That's it," I said. Then I changed position, moving in front of him so we were practicing face to face, so he could see how everything worked in relation to an opponent. I kept enough distance that each step and strike came nowhere near me, not because I was worried he'd hurt me, but because I didn't want *him* to worry.

He smiled wider, so I moved closer and closer until our weapons touched sometimes, as if we were really fighting, but not.

"Oh!" he said suddenly, his voice full of delight. "Kier, it's like dancing!"

I let my grin take over my face as we kept moving. I felt full and warm that I was able to share something of how *I* felt about blade work.

"Yes, it is. It's very much like dancing."

"I like dancing," he said, and I could have sworn his motions became just a little more elegant with each step. I didn't say it; I didn't want to make him over-confident because I knew from my own journey learning to use blades that too much confidence could be worse than none at all. But I could tell that teaching him was going to be a joy. It already was, and we had only just begun.

When his breathing started to falter, I stopped him to rest and drink. Before he was completely rested, I had him stand again and began to take him through a second form.

"It's important not to exhaust yourself," I said. "Especially when you're first learning." He nodded and followed my lead, made a mistake, and corrected himself.

"But," I said, pausing to adjust the way he held out one arm. "It's also important to keep going until you start to feel you're getting sloppy and push beyond that. Because that's when you can teach your muscles to be efficient. When you're so tired you don't even think you can move your arm again, your arm will find a better way to move, and your muscles will remember."

He nodded and began the form again. I noticed the slight tremble in his arms and how he tensed to try to compensate.

"Don't clench your muscles," I said. "Relax them."

"That doesn't make sense." But I could tell he was trying anyway.

"To your mind, no, it doesn't make sense. But your body understands."

When he completed the form, I stopped him. "That's good for today."

"Was I terrible?" He set aside the wooden props and took his knives from me to clean them.

"You were not terrible," I said. "You did very well."

The smile he turned on me lit up his face. And then his eyebrows drew together, and his eyes went unfocussed. I took the knives out of his hands and set them aside and caught him when he crumpled.

16
Fionn

IT WAS HARD NOT TO HOLD too tight to the knives when Kiernan put them in my hands. My instinct was to grip them as hard as I could so I wouldn't drop them. But he was patient, gently uncurling my fingers and showing me how to hold on most firmly – but not too tightly – with my first finger, so I could easily change the angle of the knife with my other fingers.

When he showed me how that grip gave the knife much more flexibility and range by stripping off his shirt so I could see how his muscles moved as he changed arm and hand position, I had to work hard not to stare. His muscles moved smoothly under his skin and his veins stood out as he flexed and shifted, and I wanted to drop my weapons and touch him.

I was nervous and awkward, wanting to do everything perfectly the first time, as I had when he showed me how to dance in Morven Forest, but he just smiled and showed me again and again until I figured it out. When he began to move *with* me, first at my side, and then facing me, I felt myself slip into the rhythm of it.

"It's like dancing!" I exclaimed and immediately felt stupid – until I saw the delighted look on his face.

By the time he let me stop I felt like I had accomplished something, even though I knew I was only at the very start of learning. I wanted a long soak in the hot pool, and I wanted him to take me to bed to spend what was left of the day pleasuring each other. Instead, I felt tightness gather behind my eyes. I tried to fight it as he took the knives out of my hands and set them aside. But when I did give in to the vision, I knew that Kiernan would catch me.

My eyes cleared and I pressed the back of my hand to my forehead, then took up my spindle again. I had a spinning wheel in the house, but some days I just wanted to sit on the porch and let the action of the drop spindle carry my thoughts away. The breeze was picking up and it kept catching at the deep grey wool I was turning into thick yarn to make a sweater for Kiernan's birthday. I was learning to knit, and eager to take on a project bigger than endless potholders.

A little brown bird landed on the porch railing and chirped at me until Smoke appeared from out of the forest and chased it away.

"You mustn't eat the neighbors," I said when she returned and draped herself around my neck. She was getting heavier, and I thought she might lay another clutch soon.

Too many bones, she said and purred against my jaw.

Flame appeared a moment later, chittering and cheerful, too excited to make words. She dove for my lap, settled herself, and then slid away into the air again a moment later.

Then I heard it, the rustle and crack of something approaching through the forest, though I didn't need either the serpents or the noise to alert me. I could feel him there, nearly as bright a spark in my awareness as his father was.

As soon as he cleared the trees onto our lawn, he slipped

off his deer's back and strode towards me. I set my spinning aside and met him at the bottom of the porch steps.

"Hi, Pop!" he said and leaned closer to kiss my cheek. I pulled him into a hug before he could move out of reach, and he submitted with a long-suffering sigh. As a little boy, he had loved hugs, but he was quickly approaching his majority now and apparently hugs were no longer necessary.

But it had been nearly three moons he'd been away. And he'd grown again, so he was nearly as tall as I was now. He looked almost exactly like his father, save for the height and the stormy grey eyes.

I stepped away and held his face between my hands. I couldn't stop smiling. "Did you stop by the Palace or come straight here? Are you hungry? I can draw a bath if you like."

He laughed and put his fingertips on my lips to stop the torrent of questions. I mock-scowled at him and he laughed again. "Once I get to Morven Palace, the Aunts won't let me out of their sight, so I came here first."

"Will you stay a few days? Lisna will be home soon, and I know she'd hate to miss you."

"She can come to the palace. And so can you and Dad."

"We might, but Lisna won't."

He sighed. "Where is Dad?"

"Where he usually is when he's not at home." I hooked my arm through his and we followed the path behind the house that wound through the trees and came out at an open meadow. And there was Kiernan, stripped to the waist, feet bare, with a sword in each hand. He was moving so fast the blades made blurry silver tracks through the air.

He knew we were there; he'd have known the moment Dubhghall crossed the stream. He would finish his practice before stopping.

I didn't often watch him practice anymore, not unless we

were practicing together. He was so beautiful in motion that it was hard not to drag him into bed immediately. When we practiced together, we almost always ended up making wild love wherever we happened to be.

Even now, with our son standing next to me, my heart sped up watching him. He was my weakness; Kiernan had always been my weakness *and* my strength.

With one final flourish, he completed his last form and stopped, crouched on one leg with the other stretched to the side, both arms held out with swords like silver flashes extending his reach. Then he stood and walked over to his pile of things, sheathed the blades, and turned a grin on us while pulling on a shirt.

He kissed me first, a promise of more later, and then turned to his son.

"You grew," he said, and Dubh laughed.

"You make that sound like an accusation. How do you know you're not shrinking?"

"Because Fionn would have to be shrinking, too." They grinned at each other, and Dubh submitted to another hug.

"Goddess, Dad, you stink," he said.

"That's the smell of hard work," said Kier, turning to scoop up the rest of this things.

"That's a terrible joke."

I couldn't help add, "Your father has always told terrible jokes."

"I think I'm being ganged up on." Kiernan swept an arm around my waist and we began to walk.

"How's your mother?" I said, to change the subject.

My vision went hazy again and I pressed my hand to my forehead and closed my eyes to steady myself.

When I opened them, I was in a flooded forest. Kiernan and I sat on a hill bare of trees, surrounded by water like a moat, and all around were huge trees that didn't seem to mind having their feet in the water. I heard a trickle of running water from behind us and turned to see a standing stone, no taller than I was. It had been decorated in some ancient time with spiraling designs and next to it grew a small, twisted tree that felt as ancient as the stone. Its branches rattled in the breeze and both stone and tree leaned a little over a natural basin of water from which ran a tinkling stream, iced at its edges but too active to freeze over.

All around me, spirits pushed close, curious. They swirled about Kiernan, too, and he looked around, puzzled.

"I feel something," he said.

"The spirits of this place are interested in you," I said. "In us."

As I spoke the spirits stilled and gathered over the spring. They weren't as many as I had thought at first, only three. One, I realized, was the spirit of the stone, one the tree, and one the spring. A spirit of land, a spirit of sky – the wind in the boughs of the tree – and a spirit of the sea. Then they shifted and merged into one, the genius loci of this place, as the Dryads would say.

"I feel my antlers tingling," Kiernan said. "It almost feels strange to have them again." He met my eyes, but I couldn't read his expression.

Antlers. There was something I was supposed to remember about antlers.

Then my back spasmed so badly I cried out. I could feel my limbs twitching and then pain stabbing my head.

"You're okay, pretty bird," Kiernan said, voice soft. "I'm here. I've almost got your tea ready."

I opened my eyes and blinked to try to clear them. I was on our makeshift bed in front on the hearth, my head and upper body on Kier's lap, his hand stroking between my wings.

I rolled over to look up at him. "Ouch," I said.

"That last seizure looked like a bad one," he said, reaching over me to the fire. "Can you sit up and drink this?"

I nodded and he helped me sit, putting me between his knees with my back against his chest so he could help me hold the teacup and sip from it.

I tried not to gulp it; it was too hot for that. So I sipped carefully until the pain relief took hold and I could think again. When the cup was empty, Kier took it from me and set it aside, then pushed gently between my shoulder blades so I would lean over. He checked to see that my wings were folded comfortably against my back.

"I had a vision," I said, though of course he knew.

"What did you *see*?" His hands were warm on my neck, stroking and pressing the tense muscles. I tugged at the buttons on my shirt, and he helped me take it off so he could rub my back more effectively.

"Us," I said, smiling at the memory.

"Were we old men, still stupid in love?" He worked at the muscles between my wings, and I groaned. It hurt, but it felt good.

"Not so old this time, but I think it was the same house in the woods." I curled forward over my lap so he could reach lower down my back. "You had a son. He looked just like you, only his eyes were grey, and he was taller."

"*I* had a son?" I caught the gentle emphasis on the first word.

"He looked so much like you," I repeated. I stretched out my arms and sighed. "He called me 'Pop'."

I could hear the smile in his voice. "Ah. So *we* had a son."

I had to smile, too. "Yes." I twisted around to lean my head on his shoulder, and he put his arms around me. "And then I *saw* just us two, in a forest, only the trees were growing up through water, like a lake. A forest in a lake."

"Were the trees drowned?"

"Oh, no. It was winter, but I could *feel* them, alive. It was very strange. You said it made your antlers tingle. I think I remembered something important, but the vision ended, and I've forgotten again."

"My antlers had grown back, then? Was it very far in the future?"

"No." I nuzzled his neck, breathing in his scent. He smelled like clean sweat, and I remembered we had been practicing knife forms when I'd fallen. "You said it felt strange to have antlers again, but I don't think it was very far in the future. No so far that you could have regrown them, but that makes no sense."

"Does that make it more likely to come to pass, that it was close?"

"Maybe." I put my hand on his chest to feel his heartbeat. "In the first part of the vision, you were practicing with your swords. You were so fast, even faster than you are now. And I…" I flushed hot and trailed off.

"You what?" He stroked my face and twisted his neck to kiss the top of my head.

"You had no shirt on, Kier, and you were so beautiful. You *are* so beautiful."

I felt him smile against the top of my head. "Did you want me, pretty bird?"

"Yes," I whispered. "And I want you now."

"How's your head? Your back?" He kissed my hair again and threaded his fingers through it. "Do you want a hot bath?"

"I'm fine, and yes. But first…" I leaned away and dared to meet his eyes. "First I want you to make me filthy."

His lips twitched but he managed not to smile. "Tell me what you want," he said, his voice smoky.

"Kiss me," I said. "Touch me. I want… I want to be inside you, but I want…" I felt a flush traveling up my neck but he leaned close and kissed my ear, gently nibbled my lobe.

"Tell me how you want me," he said softly, as his hands stroked my back.

"I want you on top of me," I whispered. "I want you… I want you to spill on me." I put a hand on my chest. "Here."

He let his smile grow, slow and sensuous. His hands slipped around to my chest and his fingers traced the outlines of my muscles. He let me tug his shirt over his head and pull him down onto the blanket. He put his mouth where his hands had been, tracing spirals on my skin with his tongue until I made the soft sounds he loved.

When he pulled his trousers off, and then mine, I was so ready for him my erection pushed out of my sheath as soon as the fabric was gone. I reached for him, slid my palm over his hardness, curled my fingers around him, and tugged.

He leaned away to look at me, to follow the line of my body with his eyes. Once, I would have wanted to hide, worried that he wouldn't like what he saw. But now, I felt his desire burn in my belly alongside my own, and I stretched, showing him my muscles, my skin, enjoying the heat in his eyes as he looked at me.

"Oh, pretty bird," he said, his voice low and rough. "You *are* magnificent." Then he reached out to stroke a hand down my body and trace my erection with his fingertips until I arched under him.

"Please, Kier," I said. "Before I pulse."

"Are you close, pretty bird?"

"Goddess Above, yes."

He braced his arms on either side of me and straddled me, letting our erections slide together a moment before shifting farther up my body. He moved so my hardness was behind him, pressed to the crease between his buttocks.

"Please, Kier," I said again.

He lifted himself, reached for me, and pressed my tip against himself. He made a noise deep in his throat that sounded like wanting as he used me to rub himself, around and around until I wanted to scream.

Instead, I whispered, "Please," and he eased himself down on me. I slid into him easily and pulsed even before I reached full depth. He gasped.

"I felt that. Fuck, you feel good," he said.

I reached out blindly, found his erection and stroked as he lifted and lowered himself on me, faster and faster. I pulsed a second time, and a third, and began the build to a fourth before I realized I had my eyes squeezed shut.

When I opened them, Kiernan reared above me, his head back to expose his throat. His breathing was quick, every other breath sounding like a moan, and just watching him find his pleasure from me inside him made my own orgasm build.

When he suddenly looked down at me and said my name my whole body seemed to convulse in pleasure and my fourth pulse hit so hard and so suddenly, I thought I might pass out.

"Fionn," he said. "My heart, my beloved." Then he groaned and spasmed against my hand and I got what I had wanted when he spurted semen all up my belly and onto my chest.

I think I fell asleep while he lay next to me, because when I opened my eyes again, I was cold and there was a white crust dried onto my skin and my erection had subsided and retreated back into my sheath.

"Do you want a bath now?" Kiernan murmured when I stirred, and when I said, "Yes," he stood and scooped me up into his arms and carried me to the bathing room.

THE NEXT MORNING, we woke early and packed our things. I had thought we would travel at night, but he said the path down the cliff was too treacherous to follow in the dark, and it would be less suspicious to walk through the City Beneath in daylight.

He helped me strap on the knives – I couldn't help but continue to think of them as his – and we settled our bags and packs over our shoulders.

The serpents zipped out first to check for guards. There were some, they said, patrolling the air near my balcony, but none on the cliff top.

"I wonder if they even know it's possible to get up there," Kiernan said as he peered cautiously out over the balcony. "Without wings, I mean."

"How did you find out?" I tugged him away from the edge and back into the safety of the ancient Seer's sitting room.

"A nice old couple told me how to get from the beach to the City by climbing over the top. It's not an easy path, at all, so I'm not surprised few people use it. Especially since most of your people can just fly around the cliff over the sea."

"Surely someone has flown up there? They must check to make sure the chimneys are clear once in a while."

He took my hand, and we entered the dim hallway, following its curve to the base of the ruined stairs.

"Maybe it never occurred to anyone to look for hidden entrances."

I bit my lip, then realized what I was doing and stopped. It was a childish habit I was trying to be rid of. "If I ever return, I suppose I'll have to post guards up here."

"And cut off my secret way of visiting you?"

"If I ever return, you won't have to visit secretly."

He didn't say anything to that, only pointed up the stairs. "I'll boost you up, and you'll have to find somewhere to tie the rope."

"Or I could boost you up."

"You're lighter."

"You tie better knots."

Stop silliness, said Smoke.

We go, said Flame.

Secret, said Coal.

Kiernan laughed and I joined him.

"Boost me up then, but if the rope comes untied, it's your own fault for making me tie it."

"I believe in you," he said, and though he was teasing, I also knew he meant it. He bent to offer me his clasped hands. I put my foot in them, and we counted to three together and I found myself propelled upwards. I grabbed the first intact stair and scrambled until I was up.

The serpents swirled past me and out the top of the tower.

Is clear, said Flame.

No guards, said Smoke.

Free, said Coal.

"Did Coal say 'free'?" asked Kier as I looked for a good place to tie the rope. I climbed up a few steps and decided a large chunk of stone at the top looked secure.

"Yes." I uncoiled the rope and wound it around the rock. "What other words does he know?"

"His first was 'love'," he said, and I couldn't help smiling.

"And his second?" I tugged hard on the rope to see if it was secure. It held.

"Secret."

I tossed the rope down and he caught it.

"And his third?"

"You just heard it. 'Free'." He climbed quickly up and began to coil the rope as I worked at the knot to untie it.

I refused to bite my lip again, so I bit the inside of my

cheek. I stood up from the rope and turned my back on the Eyrie below.

I had wanted so much to belong here, and maybe one day I could. For now, I would say goodbye to my people's ancient home. For now, and I hoped for the rest of my life, my place was wherever Kiernan was.

17

Kiernan

For the third time since we'd met, Fionn and I found ourselves running away. First, we had escaped the Abbey of the Moon when Fionn had nearly been made a blood sacrifice.

Then, not long after, we had run from the werewolf village where we had found shelter – and Fionn had found a mentor – when the Alfar King decided to try to stop us from journeying to the Eyrie. Perhaps he had simply wanted to avoid the political incident that could arise from him wanting to sacrifice the only known Vogel seer – which didn't happen anyway – or maybe he had wanted another try at blood magic.

Now, we were fleeing the place I had brought Fionn to be safe from the Alfar King. I tried not to think that it was a pattern that would keep repeating for the rest of our lives, but it was hard to avoid the thought. At least Fionn had *seen* better possible futures for us; now all we had to do was figure out how to achieve one of them.

I led the way across the clifftop, choosing a path as free of rubble as I could. A twisted ankle would make this a very short escape attempt.

Smoke and Flame scouted ahead, and behind, and to the sides, while Coal decided to take a nap in his basket, apparently unbothered by the motion of my walking.

As we passed the ancient shrine with its lamp-pillars and circular pool, I heard Fionn's sharp indrawn breath and turned to wait for him. I wished we had time for him to linger here.

"This is where he prayed." Fionn knelt on the stone next to the pool, facing back the way we'd come, towards the edge of the cliff and the open sky. "Where he communed with the spirits." He sat very still, as if listening. "Before the guards took him away, he sang." He took a deep, slow breath, and when he let it out, it came with a series of pure, high notes that make me want to weep, even though I had no idea what they meant. I recognized one of the syllables of Fionn's Vogel name, "ka," which meant "shining," but otherwise none of it made sense to my ears. I felt something stirring, waiting, *observing* us, and I resisted the urge to look around.

Nothing mortal was watching. I felt judged and found wanting, but in the way a parent finds a child hasn't yet measured up to their potential, but maybe one day could. It was a familiar, and not entirely pleasant, feeling.

The sound died out and I felt sadness that it had stopped, which was somehow entirely separate from the sadness the song had caused from its unintelligible words.

"It's in Trillka," Fionn said. "But I don't know all the words. Sky. Spirit, Love."

"Shining," I said, and he looked up at me.

"Yes. But it's a sad song, too. A farewell and an apology." He stood slowly and the feeling of being watched eased. "I tried to use magic to learn Trillka, the way I used it to learn

Vogelspek, but it didn't work. Not entirely. I understand its structure better, but the tenses elude me, and I know so few words."

"Perhaps too much has been lost, and even the spirits can't return it to you."

"I'm going to make a list of all the words I know, and if I return here, I want to travel around to every village and speak to every elder. I want to learn enough words that I can read the Trillka sections of the old book I found, the one Councilor Rocsh's ancestor wrote. And I want to read the writing on the walls beneath the Eyrie."

"It's in an unknown script, too, pretty bird, but if anyone can learn to read it, it's you."

He smiled, but it was sad, and I wondered if he was reconsidering leaving. He had so much to do here, so much he *could* accomplish if he stayed. And now that his King was dead, he didn't need to fear being made to... well, that.

As if he knew the direction my thoughts had taken, he said, "Let's go."

His long fingers and grasping toes were useful in the slow, steep climb down the cliff, but I felt bad for his sore foot and noticed he favored it whenever he could, but used it when he had to, and didn't complain. This journey would not be kind; Vogel feet weren't built for long distance travel and Vogel didn't wear shoes to compensate. Most Vogel didn't need to walk much distance anyway, because they could fly.

When we got to the bottom of the cliff, we paused to rest in the dappled shade of a large pine that grew so close to the rock that its roots were crumbling the edge of the stone.

Fionn sat on a fallen log, and I crouched at his feet. "Did you bring your foot wraps?" I should have asked before we left the Eyrie, but I had been thinking of what route we'd take and concerned we didn't leave anything behind.

"Oh! Yes." He pulled one of his bags around into his lap and dug through it. "Neeka was going to throw them out, when I first arrived at the Eyrie, but I begged her not to, so she had them cleaned instead. They were in the drawer with my undergarments." I pushed aside thoughts of Fionn's undergarments and him in – or out – of them and took each roll as he found it. There were two rolls of soft linen, and two of tough but flexible leather.

I lifted one of his feet and began to wrap it.

"Why does it feel like you're telling me you love me when you do things like this?" he said, as I finished one foot and started the other.

"Because I am," I said, bending to kiss his foot before winding the linen around it. His fingers combed through my hair, and I wanted to lay my head in his lap, to just stay there in the dappled sun and shadow and the crisp air of early winter and forget everything but the feel of his hand stroking my head.

Instead, I finished wrapping his foot and stood up to lead the way to the crumbling wall that separated the City Beneath the Cliff from the wilderness.

"I asked the Council to allocate money for repairs," Fionn said as we passed through one of the many huge gaps in the wall. "Over several years, it wouldn't even have cost too dearly, and it would have given many of our people much-needed work." He put a hand on a crumbling stone as he passed. "But the King refused to allow it."

I stopped him to pull his hood up to cover his pale hair. It wouldn't stop everyone from noticing him, but it would make him less obvious. We just had to hope that the common Vogel loved their Seer more than their Monarch and that the non-Vogel in the City wouldn't care either way.

When we continued, he tucked his hands under the thick

fabric, so with his feet wrapped, only the ends of his toes would give him away.

I had only been in the City Beneath once, when I'd been captured by King's Guards while trying to sneak into the Eyrie. I'd been thrown in gaol and escaped. But then I had only needed to follow whichever streets seemed to lead most directly towards the cliff and the public square at its base. It hadn't been hard to find my way.

Now, we had no such large and obvious landmark, except, I supposed, to keep the cliff at our backs and walk away from it. Or find the beach and follow the shore — but there were boats and docks and warehouses that made that more difficult than it should be.

"I know the way," Fionn said, and set off, not directly away from the cliff as I would have done, but deeper into the city.

"Have you been reading maps?" I said, because that would not have surprised me. He was curious and smart and had a good memory.

He slowed so I could catch up because his legs were longer than mine.

"No," he said, then looked at me in surprise. "We've hardly had a chance to just talk, have we?"

"We seem to keep ending up naked."

He reached for my hand. "Before I journeyed to Morven Forest with the trade delegation, I made trips into the city to speak to the people about what *they* wanted from trade with Morven."

"Fionn —" Worry grabbed at my gut even though he was talking about something that had already happened.

"I was never alone," he said. "Neeka always came with me, and I had Trikta and Konta to guard me. The King would never have allowed me to go alone." His voice faltered a little on the word "King," but he recovered. "It turns out my people *like* me. Or they did once they realized I was intending to work for them and not to glorify the royal family." He looked at me sidelong. "And once I bought things from them."

"Everyone likes you, pretty bird. Even my Queen couldn't help but be impressed with you."

"That's not the same as liking me," he said. "But anyway, I paid attention when Neeka took me to different shops." He pointed down a side road as we crossed over. "Down there is the tea shop where you found me after you escaped from gaol."

"Where you revealed who I was and made my mother come and get me." I hadn't wanted that, and for a while I had been angry with him, even while I was still hopelessly lost for him. "At the time, I'd sooner have died."

"You *would* have died," he said, "And I couldn't let you."

"I know," I said softly. "Thank you for being wiser than my selfish impulse."

He squeezed my hand and pointed down another street. "There's a bookstore that way that I've been wanting to go back to when I had time to browse. But I never seemed to have time."

"I mean to see to it that you can do all the book shopping you like."

"And here," he pulled me around the corner as we came upon a broad street with a row of trees down the middle. In spring, it would be a lovely sight. Now, the chill kept the people in, and the trees bare. "This is the main road that leads out of the city, directly towards Tronven and the fishing villages around Archipelago Bay."

"As easy as that?"

He turned to smile, and his face went still. "Kier?"

I started to turn to see what he was looking at, but he stopped me.

"No, don't look. There are guards. King's Guard."

"How far away?"

"Six blocks. Not close."

"Do they see us?"

"I don't know, but they're walking this way."

"How many?"

"Four."

"Fuck. Okay. We just keep walking. Don't hurry, just walk." I freed my hand from his reluctantly. Vogel weren't permitted to be intimate with non-Vogel and holding hands certainly made it look like we regularly broke the law. We did, but there was no need to make it obvious.

Also, I might need both hands for weapons.

We kept walking, pretending to stroll, as if we were just out for a turn around the city on a sunny day.

"Where are the serpents?"

"I don't know. I thought they were keeping watch."

I poked Coal and he stirred sleepily in his basket. "I need you to watch those guards for us, little friend," I said. "Get up on my shoulder and let me know if any of those Kings Guards see us and start walking faster."

Nyah, he said, and crawled up my sword belt to perch on my shoulder.

We walked, briskly but not so fast as to look guilty of something, just moving as if we had someplace to be. Fionn's breathing was quick and hectic.

"Calmly, pretty bird," I said, and he drew in a deep breath, getting his breathing and the speed of his heart under control impressively quickly.

The City Beneath the Cliff was probably small, on a world scale, but here on the Isle, it was one of only a handful of large centers of population. The core of it wasn't huge – we were nearly through it already – but the buildings sprawled outwards from there into craft workshops and housing blocks.

It was not a quick trip from one side to the other.

We would also probably look suspicious walking right through from one end to the other on the main road without stopping.

"What's down that way?" I nodded at a wide side street just ahead.

"A bakery, I think. And a popular tearoom."

"Shops?"

"Yes."

I turned when we reached that street, crossed, and took the next road parallel to the main thoroughfare.

"Should we go into a shop?" Fionn said. "So they won't see us?"

"Unless you know of one with a back door, we could get cornered." I dared to glance back. Someone came out of a clothing shop, loaded with purchases, and headed down the street away from us. So far, there was no sign of the King's Guard.

I breathed a little easier, even knowing I shouldn't have.

We zigzagged through the city, never getting too far from the main road, but never continuing straight for very long. Soon, we were passing more industrial-looking buildings, and then housing blocks.

Just ahead, two small boys were playing with a ball. One was Vogel, with deep bronze feathers, and the other was a dark-haired human who looked like he might have a touch of fey in his almost-pointed ears. The ball went wide and rolled our way, and Fionn bent to pick it up and toss it back. As the ball left his hands, he froze.

At the next cross street stood two red-and-yellow feathered King's Guard, gold bird-masks glinting in the sun. One held a spear leveled at us and the other had two long, sinuous shapes in his hands.

"Oh, Kier," Fionn said, worry in his voice. Smoke and Flame hung from the Guard's hands limply.

"Hey!" said one of the boys – the human child. "You're not allowed to have feathered tree serpents!" He threw a stone, and it skittered past the Guard's feet. The man ignored him, as if the boy were simply a barking dog.

"Yeah," said the other boy. "Only royalty can have serpents." I didn't bother to point out that Guards *could* keep serpents, if given permission by their King, and Seers could also have serpents, with permission or not. I didn't care what the Guards knew or didn't, and I was curious about the boys' reaction to their presence.

Nyah, said Coal softly.

The Guard continued to ignore the boys. I supposed the Vogel Monarchy was just like every other monarchy: the noble class and their servants only paid attention to other nobles, and peasants meant nothing.

"You're to come with us, my Seer," said the spear-wielding Guard, his Islish accented in a way that indicated he probably didn't use it often. "Your serpents are unharmed."

"Horseshit," I said, before I could think better of it. "They're unconscious. They don't just fall asleep when you pick them up."

The other Guard looked at the serpents in his hands and seemed surprised to find them unmoving. "They're fine," he said. "My Seer?"

Fionn hesitated. Smoke and Flame had been his companions long before he met me. He'd seen them hatch.

The Vogel boy had sidled closer while the Guards spoke. "Do you not want to return to the Eyrie, my Seer?" he said, quietly enough that the Guards wouldn't have been able to hear.

"I don't, but those serpents are my friends." Fionn twisted

his fingers together, seemed to realize what he was doing, and stopped.

"They won't dare hurt them," the boy said. "Not really." But he sounded uncertain.

"Coal?" I said.

Nyah.

"Are there Guards behind us?"

Some, he said.

"How many?"

Some. He sounded frustrated. He'd found another word, but still couldn't express numbers.

I glanced around, looking for a way out that would keep both Fionn and the serpents safe. The human boy was standing by the door to one of the housing blocks. He opened it and gestured.

"My Seer," said the Vogel boy. "We know another way out of the city."

Fionn looked at me. I needed to figure something out, and fast. "Go," I said. "I'll get the serpents and find you outside the City."

"But Kier…"

"It's okay, I have a plan." I didn't really, beyond, "surprise the guards, grab the serpents, and run like fuck," but I couldn't let him know that.

"Come with me, my Seer," said the boy. "We'll go over the rooftops."

"I can't fly," said Fionn, softly.

"Neither can Joss," said the boy, nodding towards his human friend.

"Go, pretty bird. I'll find you."

"At the end of that block, Lord Hraf," said the boy, "There's a grate leading to the sewers. There's grates all over the city. Get in there without them seeing and they won't find you."

"Hraf?" I said.

"You are, aren't you? Hraf na Tokka?"

"I suppose I am," I said. "But what if I never find my way out again?"

"It's easy," said the boy. "Keep following bigger and bigger tunnels, and you end up at the sea. Tide's coming in, though, so you might have to swim out."

"Me and all the other turds in the City Beneath," I muttered, and the boy laughed. "How do I know you're not in league with the Guard?" I pretended to be doubtful.

The boy turned his head and spat an impressive glob towards the guards, who were edging closer. "King's Guard aren't friends to ordinary people," he said.

"Will you protect your Seer for me?"

"'Course I will." He sounded mildly offended.

"He's not only my faithful Shadow," Fionn said, touching my hand. "He's also the Prince of Morven Forest and my heart-bonded companion."

"Well, then, Seer, Prince," said the boy, pulling himself up to his full height. "I swear on the spirits of Land, Sea, and Sky I'll make sure our Seer makes it safe out of the City. And if you get lost, I'll come back and look for you."

"That's good enough for me," I said. "And if you ever want to join the Seer's Guard, I'm sure a place could be found for you."

The boy beamed.

"Kiernan," Fionn said, still uncertain.

"Go, pretty bird. Seer Tokka. I'll see you soon."

He looked at the open door, then back at me, "I swear, beloved, if you get yourself killed, I'll come look for you in the afterlife."

I met his eyes and smiled. "I don't intend to get myself

killed." Then I winked at him and leapt down the street towards the King's Guard, trusting the boys to get Fionn out of harm's way.

I heard a shout as the Guards behind us realized what was happening, but they were too far away still to do much. I heard a door slam and then I was barreling into the Guard in front of me, who obviously hadn't expected me to turn *towards* him and was just staring, watching me get closer. I bent and hit his belly with my shoulder and the full force of my weight, and it was enough to knock him off his feet.

He threw out his arms to try to keep his balance and dropped Smoke and Flame to the cobbles. They hit with a pair of unpleasant slaps, but I couldn't worry about that just yet.

Coal squawked and slipped away, perhaps to check on his mothers.

"No, Coal," I said. "In your basket. Leave Smoke and Flame to me." To my surprise, he obeyed, though he complained loudly.

I hopped over the second Guard's spear and kicked the first in the face when he tried to sit up. He fell back, his head thumping into the cobbles, and he didn't move.

I cursed the awkwardness of the pack I was carrying, heavier now because one of Fionn's bags was tied to it, but I wasn't about to leave anything behind. I slipped to the side and snatched up one of the fallen serpents, tucking her through my sword belt. It wouldn't be comfortable for either of us, but I wouldn't have to worry about dropping her.

The Guard with the spear had moved between me and the second serpent, but I saw her stir sluggishly on the stone surface.

I opened my connection to the Realms – even if I couldn't *use* my magic, I could still feel it – because if these Guards had any magic at all, I'd be able to sense them that way, even if I couldn't see them. Four yellowish sparks appeared behind me, too close. I dodged the nearer Guard's spear again, grabbed it, and yanked him towards me, right into my fist.

Vogel might have kept their tackle put away until they needed it, but a well-placed punch could still hurt. A lot. The air rushed out of him, and I jerked his spear again. Before he could think to let go, I'd upset his balance, and he tripped over his fallen comrade and sprawled on the street.

I was vaguely aware of people nearby, sparks and glows in a rainbow of colors to my magic, watching from doorways and windows. No one seemed inclined to interfere, so I ignored them.

I grabbed Flame and ran for the nearest side street, a narrow one that was more an alley than a road. Which way had the boy said the sewers were? I took another turn and looked for a grate in the street. I had no doubt I'd already left behind the one he'd indicated, but he'd said there were others.

A yell behind me let me know I'd been spotted again. Damn the Vogel and their stupid long legs.

Except Fionn's legs. *His* legs were very nice.

I whipped around another corner and Flame wriggled in my hand. I draped her around my neck.

Nyah, she said, faintly.

Another corner and another street. This one was broader, and there, at the far side of the next crossroads, up against an empty-looking building, was an iron grate. I ran to it and looked in. From below, I smelled damp and rot. And lots of shit.

"Fuck." I wrenched at the grate. It was heavy, but not bolted down. It shifted, but didn't move far. I considered running again, to put more distance between me and the Guard before looking for another grate. If they saw me go in, they'd know where to look, so this escape would only work if they *didn't* see me. "Fuck, fuck, fuck." With each "fuck" I yanked, and the grate slid sideways a little more, until I had just enough room to squeeze through. I shrugged off my pack, lowered it down, and followed.

"Sorry, little friends," I said as I squeezed between stone and iron, three serpents clinging to me, into the dark and stench. It wasn't deep here, and I managed to drag the grate back into place just as I heard running footsteps.

One voice said something in Vogel, then repeated it in Islish. "Where'd the little fucker go?"

Good, they hadn't seen me. I just hoped they weren't smart enough to think to look down the sewer drains. I pressed myself further into the low tunnel, dragging my pack with me into the welcoming shadow. I wished I still had my magic and could ask those shadows to conceal me as I used to do.

There was another voice, speaking Vogelspek again, and I heard footsteps from at least four Guards move away in different directions. If four had followed and one was out cold, that only left one to pursue Fionn and the boys. Assuming they didn't just wait for him to return, thinking he'd been taken against his will.

Nasty guards, said Flame.

Not nice, said Smoke and I felt a rush of relief that they were both okay. Smoke wiggled out of my belt and made her way to my shoulder.

We go? said Flame.

"We go," I said. I shrugged my pack back on and turned to follow the low tunnel deeper into the sewers of the City Beneath.

18
Fionn

I DIDN'T LIKE SPLITTING UP; I'd only just got Kier back and I didn't want him out of my sight. But I couldn't leave Smoke and Flame to whatever the Kings Guard might do to them, and Kier was better equipped to save them and get away than I was.

So I followed the boys into their housing block and tried not to listen too closely to what happened as they closed the door.

"This way, my Seer," the Vogel boy said, leading me up one staircase, then another, and another. The human boy paused to wedge a board under the door handle and, from its perfect fit and the fact it had been propped conveniently to one side, I had to assume it had been made for that purpose. It saddened me that some of my people found such measures necessary.

As we climbed, we passed several doors on each floor, and many of them were open. People stood watching us pass – human, Vogel, and others I had no time to place. And while it was dismaying that the residents of this building had to block their outer door, it gave me hope to see so many different peoples living as neighbors.

"My Seer," many of them murmured as we passed, and I realized it was not just the bird folk who spoke, but others, too. I wondered how many of them had seen us in the street below, and how many knew I was trying to evade my own King's Guards.

I nodded at them all as we went by and wished there was time to stop and speak to them, to ask them about their lives and see if there was anything I could do to help them. But, though it seemed the Guards had gone in pursuit of Kiernan – perhaps thinking I would be easier to catch, or that I might simply return to the Eyrie on my own once I was unprotected – I had no doubt they would eventually come looking for me, and they would start with this building.

"Please," I said to the boy as he paused to slide back the bolt on the door at the top of the stairs. "Tell your people not to try to stop the Guards when they come. I don't want anyone hurt because of me."

"Oh, don't worry, my Seer. The Guards think we're all thick. We play dumb and they won't even bother to ask questions. By the time they reach the roof, we'll be long gone." He grinned. "We know how to handle King's Guard."

I tried to return his smile, but my stomach hurt with fear for Kiernan. Our connection told me nothing, which either meant he was fine, or that he had blocked his feelings off from me.

"My name is Tokka," I said.

"I know," said the boy. "I saw you at the square when you first got here."

I didn't know what to say to that, so I just followed him through the door and onto the roof. He lead me quickly across the flat expanse, and I tried to look around as we went. The people had put pots and boxes of soil here, and though everything was dead or dying as winter approached, in spring this would be a garden.

"Should we wait for your friend?" I asked, brushing a hand over the dried stems of a frost-killed winterleaf plant.

"Nah, Joss'll do the bolt up behind us and fill everyone in, so they know."

"Oh, that's good."

As we approached the edge of the roof, I didn't see any way we could possibly reach across the wide gap to the next building. I was about to comment when the boy grinned at me and kicked a rusty fitting on the roof's edge. A sudden racket had me cringing away.

"Oops," he said. "That one's a bit noisy. Rest of 'em should be nice an' quiet, so the Guards don't notice."

A slender beam of metal extended out from the edge of the roof, squealing at first and then quieting to a rushing sort of hum as is moved. It connected with the roof edge opposite with a solid "thump."

"They built these ages ago," the boy said. "Once, they were supposed to connect the whole city, so humans and all could travel rooftop-to-rooftop same as us bird folk. Talk was, they planned to make the front door of all the buildings on the roof 'stead of at street level."

"It's very narrow," I said, watching him walk out onto the beam, wings half-spread for balance.

"They were supposed to be proper foot bridges. Maybe even were, once. Now this is all that's left. My Pop and Joss's decided to start fixing 'em. Just in case."

"Just in case of what?" I peered over the edge. No one seemed to be out on the street below, so I put one foot on the beam.

"Works better if you cross quick-like. Least, that's what

Joss says." He waited for me on the other side. "Lots of the gaps aren't so wide and you can just jump over."

I shifted my cloak to the middle of my back to free my wings – not that they would do much in the state they were in, but it just felt better. Then I crossed as quickly as I could, without thinking too much about what I was doing. I looked at the beam I put my feet on and didn't let my eyes focus on the ground below.

When I reached the other side, I saw the boy staring. He quickly looked away as I resettled my cloak.

"Who done that to you?" he said, voice gruff, as he turned to lead the way across the roof.

I wanted to play dumb, to pretend I didn't know what he was talking about, but that was no way to treat someone who had helped me.

"That's supposed to be illegal," he said. "To clip a person's wings."

"The King did it himself," I said.

He hissed. "That's why you won't go back," he said, no question in his voice. "Never did like King Sarkot much, myself."

I wanted to smile at such a young child having an opinion on politics. And I wanted to weep that a child could live the sort of life where'd they'd *need* to have an opinion on politics. The children of the poor no doubt had to grow up more quickly than the children of the rich

"He hasn't done much to earn anyone's regard," I said, trying to keep my voice neutral.

The boy glanced around, then jumped the gap between buildings. I followed.

"Something big going on up in the Eyrie," he said. "There's been guards out in the city all yesterday and today, glaring at everyone and pushing folk around." He grinned, and the expression looked so natural on his face I had to smile in return. "I expect I have some idea what's up."

He approached another roof edge and this time he swung a pair of beams around from the edge to project over the gap. It was a wider distance, but the bridge was broader and easier to walk across.

"I'd a' run, too, if someone cut my wings," he said, tucking his close as if that very thing might happen at any moment.

"It's more complicated than that," I replied.

"'Course. Always is. I'm Jinta, by the way." He held out a hand and I shook it gravely.

"Tokka," I said. "Though my birth name is Branfionn."

He grinned again. It seemed to be his default expression. "The fey who was with you, was that really the Prince of Morven Forest? I heard Hraf na Tokka was tall and handsome, but I guess one out of two's close."

I laughed and walked faster to keep up. Jinta might be a child, and short, but he was quick, in more ways than one. "Yes," I said. "His name among his own people is Kiernan nicFia."

"That's Sidhe."

"Yes. Morven Forest is the Sidhe Monarchy."

"Your birth name is Sidhe, too."

"Yes." I didn't try to explain. That the Abbess had found it amusing to give me a name from the people her King planned to conquer first by using my sacrifice for blood magic wasn't a topic I wanted to get into.

We hopped another alley, and I realized I had lost track of how far we'd come. The edge of the city still seemed a long way off.

"You married?" the boy said, waiting for me to jump yet another alley.

"That would be against Vogel law."

"Never understood that, myself." He trotted across the roof, and I followed. "Mam says it was three Kings ago made that law and no one has liked it in all the time since." He paused to swing another bridge over a wide avenue. "She says just 'cause something is a law doesn't mean it's right."

"I think I would like your mother," I said, placing my feet carefully on the rusted crossmembers of the ancient bridge.

"Sure you would, till she tried to make you eat greenfish for supper. Again."

I laughed, but softly, and I think he caught my mood.

"Beats nothing at all to eat, I guess," he said.

I glanced back the way we'd come and saw no one on the rooftops except a few people in the far distance who appeared to be cleaning dead plants out of their garden boxes. It was only a matter of time before I was pursued, though. Surely I wouldn't get away so easily.

Jinta saw my look and said, "Most like they won't bother. They'll figure they can find you from the air when they get around to it. Probably letting you tire yourself out, so you'll be easier to catch."

I had to force myself still to keep my shoulders from slumping. I had been thinking like a ground-dweller, but my people were winged. Most of them could fly as easily as they could walk.

I had been stupid.

"Hey, Seer Tokka," said the boy. "Don't worry. They're also thinking the buildings will all be locked, 'cause they are. A roof door's as easy for bird folk to get to as a street door, and no one in this part of town leaves their doors unlocked. They think you have nowhere to hide."

I watched glumly as he hopped across another alley, then beckoned to me. I followed and reached him just as he banged on a metal plate set into a panel next to the building's rooftop door. He then tapped out a sequence, paused, and pressed his ear to the door.

"Here he comes," he said.

"And here they come," I answered, catching a glimpse of red and yellow wings and the flash of sun on golden metal from off in the direction of the Eyrie.

"Quick, then." He darted inside as soon as the door opened and pulled me after. "Don't think they saw us."

The door shut behind us and then there was just darkness. My breath caught and I forced myself to calm. I had never liked being unable to see, so I took a deep breath and summoned a wisplight.

And I looked directly in the face of a very old human man with bright silver eyes.

I WAS TORN BETWEEN wanting to hurry on, to get out of the city and find Kiernan, and pausing to speak to another Seer. I had met so few seers, and except for the brief times I spent with Moira and Siona, I'd stumbled through figuring out my magic on my own.

The old man blinked in the soft illumination of my wisplight, then smiled an open, welcoming smile.

"We were led to believe the new Seer of the Eyrie had no magic other than visions," he said. His voice was low and gravelly, with just a hint of old man frailty.

"There's rumors it was you saved all the nobles from fever, but official word says it was the King." Jinta snorted his opinion of that idea.

I stared at the boy, for a moment unable to process what he'd said. The old man's hand on my arm brought me back to the present.

"King Sarkot took credit for healing our people?" I said, and didn't object when the other Seer led me down a dim hallway and into his home.

He seemed entirely unsurprised by my appearance at his rooftop door, but perhaps Jinta brought him strays frequently. Or, being a Seer, maybe he'd had a vision of me. The room he ushered me into was crowded with plants, so many I almost didn't register the shabbiness of the furniture or the threadbare state of the rugs. Three small, furry carnivores padded over on silent feet to investigate me.

"No one believed it," said Jinta. "Our King never showed any magic before."

"He calls himself Lord of the Three Realms, as if he has mastered all magic," said the Seer. I chose not to correct his use of the present tense. If no one yet knew the King was dead, so much the better for me and Kier to escape quietly. Or at least less obviously.

"The only magic I knew him to do was telling lies from truth," I said, then frowned. "And I'm not even sure that was real, or just that people were too afraid to lie." I felt disloyal, somehow, for speaking of the King that way, yet I also felt more kinship with these two than I had felt for anyone in the Eyrie save Neeka and my guards, and maybe Councilor Rocsh and Nikna.

The old man laughed. "They also say you were under the King's power, ready to do anything for him. I'm glad to find out that may not be true."

"Is he really so hated?" I sat automatically when shown to a chair and one of the animals jumped into my lap and settled down as if it belonged there.

"Not so much hated as... thought to be ineffectual. Indifferent, even," said the old man. "More interested in his own wealth than in the wellbeing of his people." He gestured at Jinta. "Go fetch the tea, will you?"

Jinta pretended to be offended, but I could see his smile. He disappeared into another room, and I heard him moving dishes about.

"I shouldn't stay," I said, absently stroking the animal's soft fur. It began to purr, a sound so like Smoke and Flame made that I stared at it for a moment. "There were Guards, and I need to meet my companion outside the city. He'll worry."

"He's taking the sewers. Had to fetch two tree serpents out of the Guards' clutches first," said Jinta, returning with a steaming teapot and three mismatched cups on a tray.

"He'll be a while, then, assuming Jinta doesn't have to go looking for him." The old Seer poured and I caught the smell of frostleaf, a wild relative of winterleaf that many folk gathered in the forest when they couldn't afford to buy tea. "You have time to rest a little and let me look at your foot."

I blinked at him in surprise as he handed me a cup. "My foot?"

"You're favoring your right foot." He pointed and I resisted the urge to tuck my toes beneath my cloak and out of sight. "Your shoulders, too, but those just need rest, I think."

"It's only rope burn," I said.

"Then I have enough magic to heal it for you." He smiled and sipped his tea. "I'm Magnus, by the way. And that –" he pointed to the animal on my lap "– is Honey. The other two are Syrup and Sugar."

"What kind of animal are they?" I, who had grown up in one of the biggest libraries on the Isle, felt suddenly embarrassed at my ignorance. I thought I knew all the animals native to the Isle, as well as those brought by the humans and fey at the time of the Founding, but I didn't know this one.

Magnus laughed, but not to mock me. He sounded delighted. He petted the animal that climbed into his lap and butted its head against his hand. The third carnivore decided Jinta's lap, once he was settled cross-legged on the floor, was a suitable place to rest.

"They're cats," said Jinta.

"Oh, but… The only cats I know are lynx, and they're much bigger, with short tails." I eyed the waving appendage of the creature on my lap.

"They're like lynx, somewhat," said Seer Magnus. "Only they're tame. They originally came from the Continent, though they say the Eyrie used to be full of cats before the Founding, so it must have been even before my people came here."

I tried to remember if I'd seen any animals depicted in the wall paintings below the Eyrie, but the King had hurried me through the passages so quickly I'd barely had time to notice the pictures of seers.

"I didn't know anyone – or any creature – came to the Isle before the Founding," I said, and sipped my tea, finding it pleasant, if not quite as sweet as I preferred.

"They say that long ago, the Vogel made regular voyages back and forth to the Continent. It's why your people are such good sailors, when they could just as soon fly everywhere on the Isle and get there faster."

"There's so much I don't know about my own people," I said, thinking about the time, not even so long ago, that Kiernan told me what cloud silk really was.

"If you ever return," said Magnus, as if he knew as well as I did what my plans for the future were, and being a Seer, maybe he did, "I've books I'd be happy to lend you, and other Seers who would love to meet you."

"I'd like that," I said, so quietly he had to lean forward to hear me.

"Now," he said. "Tell me why you're fleeing the King's Guard in your own City."

I met his eyes, silver to silver, and I couldn't make words come out. I shook my head.

"I can send Jinta from the room," Magnus said softly. "Seers protect other Seers above all else. I'm sorry you had to grow up not knowing that."

Without even being asked, Jinta lifted the cat out of his lap, set his teacup on the table, and got up. "I'll be on the stairs when you're ready to go." He flashed me a grin that felt encouraging and closed the door quietly behind himself.

Instead of asking again why I was fleeing, Magnus said, "Let's have a look at your foot." I unwound the leather and linen wraps, and he took my foot between his crooked-fingered hands, leaning across the little table to reach. His touch was cool as he traced a finger over the rope burn on my sole. I tensed, expecting it to sting, but instead it tickled and then didn't hurt at all.

"There," he said. "I don't have a lot of magic, hence why I am allowed to act as Seer to a gaggle of poor folk in a crowded city, but that shouldn't trouble you anymore."

"Thank you," I said and began to wind the wraps back on. "If I do return, I would very much like to visit again."

"Then you shall," he said.

"I… can't tell you why I'm running," I said.

"You're safe with me," he replied. "This is true for all Seers. It's how we survive and thrive in a world that wants only to use us." He touched my knee then leaned back in his chair. "I won't press you, but if you tell me, I can find a story to pass on, to spread among your people in the City, so that when you do return, we will welcome and support you, even if the nobles do not."

"You would lie for me?" I said, astonished.

"Not so much lie as… pass on a selective truth."

I looked down at the cat in my lap. "I… our King is dead,"

I said softly, my stomach clenching. I expected shock, or at least surprise, but when I looked up, Seer Magnus only looked thoughtful.

"Your companion killed him?" he asked. His voice was gentle, with no accusation in it at all. I didn't need to wonder why he didn't think it was me.

"Yes." I swallowed a lump in my throat and then took a long sip of tea. I wanted to spill the entire truth to this kind old man, everything from being made my King's pleasure boy to finding out he was my own father, but the words stuck in my throat. I felt tears prick my eyes and tried to keep them in.

"I wish there was time for all the care you need, Seer Tokka," he said. "I truly wish we had that time. You need to let out what's hurting you, but if our King is dead, then our first priority must be to get you and Hraf na Tokka out of the city as quickly and quietly as possible."

"The King's Guard are already chasing him. Us."

"Well, we here in the City know how to deal with the King's Guard. We'll have them believing you're hiding in the caves before long. It'll be moons before they realize you're not here."

"I won't have anyone else endangered," I said, and he smiled at the fierceness that came out in my voice.

"We won't be endangered," he replied. He regarded me a moment, then set aside his teacup. "If you can't speak about what happened, will you let me read you?"

I bit my lip, forgetting it was a habit I wanted to be rid of. "It's… a lot, and…"

"You still don't trust me." He smiled.

"I *want* to." I took a deep, steadying breath. What had I to lose? The only thing I would expose was my own shame. So I nodded. "Do it," I said.

He removed the cat from his lap and stood, moving around

the table to perch on it in front of me. He took my face in gentle hands, and I felt a tear win free of one eye and trickle down my cheek.

"Somebody hurt you," he said softly.

I swallowed and nodded. "What do you need me to do?"

"Only sit still and lower your defenses." He closed his eyes. "Relax and let your thoughts loose instead of holding them in. Don't try to filter them. I'll see what I need to see, and I won't look at the rest."

"Will you see everything?"

"Unless you have been taught the skill of hiding only selective thoughts, yes, I *could* see everything, but I will not pry."

"I've hardly been trained at all."

"Somebody taught you good shielding practices, at least," he said. "When you return to visit, I would be honored to help teach you more. Now quiet and let me read you."

I could feel his presence, but it wasn't intrusive. He didn't press, didn't dig, he just read my thoughts and memories as they surfaced.

When he took his hands from my face, I felt ashamed because of the things he must have seen, but I also felt strangely better for sharing.

His eyes, when I met them, were full of sorrow, but he smiled. "You have been hurt," he said. "Very badly, by someone who should have protected you."

Another tear spilled over, and I wiped it impatiently away.

"But you're stronger than all that, Seer Tokka." He looked stern for a moment, and then a warm smile took over his face. "And you have the kind of love and devotion most of us only get to dream of."

Another tear, and I still couldn't make myself speak.

He laid a gentle hand on my face again. "He *is* worth

fighting for. The two of you together is worth fighting for."

"I want to make our world safe for all peoples," I said. "No government should tell anyone what they may or may not be, or who they're allowed to love."

"I believe in you, my Seer," he said, and then something that might have been mischief showed on his features. "Or should I say, 'My Prince'?"

He laughed at my expression. "Don't worry, Tokka. I won't include that in my spreading of selective truth. Maybe someday, but not yet."

"I read that before the Founding, our people had no Kings. That they were ruled by a council made up of many professions and many experiences."

"I have heard that," he said. "But what, then, was the place of Seers?"

"To advise. To speak to the people on behalf of the spirits, and to the spirits on behalf of the people. They led celebrations and made offerings."

"Is that what you want?"

"Yes. I… I think so."

"You don't wish to rule?"

"No."

He put his hands on his knees with a smack and then stood. "Your people might not give you a choice in that. I think the Vogel – the poorer folk, at least – would love a Seer Prince. And the Monarchies would require a Monarch of some kind." He lifted the cat from my lap, and it made a terrifying growl that the old man ignored. It twisted in his hands and climbed onto his shoulder. "But that's a conundrum for the future."

He led me to the door. "For the now, Jinta will take you out of the city." He smiled and kissed my forehead. "Blessings on you Seer Tokka, and make sure you return someday to visit me." He opened the door and Jinta stood up from where he'd been waiting on the stairs. "Now go. Your beloved and your future await you."

19
Kiernan

I HAD EXPECTED THE LOW, narrow entry to lead into one big passage for sewage, but instead it led into a taller, but not much wider, tunnel with a deep channel in the middle that carried runoff water and waste. On each side was a ledge, obviously built for people to walk on – for maintenance, I assumed. The whole passage sloped gradually downwards, and far ahead – almost undetectable beneath the smells of damp stone and shit – I could smell the sea.

Once away from the grate it got rapidly darker, and I wished – again – that I could use my magic to conjure up a wisplight. I stopped and tried, but the simple child's trick took so much effort to produce a thin, wavering puddle of pale blue in my hand that I gave up. How mortifying would it be to burn myself hollow trying to maintain a wisplight?

It didn't make sense, really. I had Daphnis's magic, so even with my connection to my own damaged, I should be able to use at least *some*. But I could still only feel it, not use it, as if it needed something more, something I didn't possess, to bloom..

Fortunately, there was enough light from the grate behind me and other tunnels that intersected the one I was in that my night-dweller's vision let me see the outlines of the tunnel, even if I couldn't make out much in the way of detail.

Nyah, said Coal, lifting his head from his basket to nudge my side. I rubbed his head with my fingers and he settled back down. On my shoulders, Smoke and Flame pressed closer to my neck.

"Don't like the dark, little friends?" I said, and reached up to stroke their heads, too.

Is cold, said Smoke.

"It'll be even colder once Midwinter comes," I said. "Do you want to climb inside my coat?" I opened the top buttons. It would be snug with three serpents and several layers of shirts underneath, but I'd sooner be a little uncomfortable than have my friends suffer.

Flame went first, burrowing headfirst down the front of my coat and wriggling across my belly to turn around and poke her head back out the top.

Warm, she said.

Smoke followed and tickled my ribs in the process so that I almost slipped off the narrow walkway into the smelly liquid. There was enough clear water running into the sewer that it actually didn't smell *too* bad, but I still didn't want to bathe in it.

When Smoke was settled, I lifted Coal up and he squirmed in between the two larger serpents and started to purr, sending a vibration up my sternum and making me laugh.

Is nice, said Flame.

Nice, said Coal.

The Vogel boy had said to follow the biggest tunnels, so when the one we were following dropped suddenly downward to intersect with a large passage, I climbed down the slick steps and turned to follow the direction the water was flowing – out to sea, presumably. The width of the channel I left was small enough that I could step across the water to carry on my way.

Here, it was even darker, though I could just see the shapes of side tunnels joining every so often. My forest eyes had to work hard to find enough light to even make out that much.

"I don't suppose tree serpents can make wisplights?" I said softly. Something made me want to keep my voice low, like I was intruding on a world not my own instead of making my way down a mundane tunnel beneath a populous and active city.

I paused to let the magic of the place flow through me. It was strong so close to the Eyrie, that ancient place where the Three Realms met, that it didn't take much to feel it, not even with my magic crippled and inaccessible to my use.

All around me, soft gold-green glows appeared to my magical senses, farther off in the tunnels. There were people down here other than me. Closer, the reddish colors of the serpents and my own green glow were a comforting presence. And –

I whirled around to stare at the space beside me, to see what person was standing so close to me, reaching for my knife as I turned. My foot hit a patch of slime and I slipped, lost my balance, and gathered myself to jump back, away from whomever was hidden in the shadow, even if it meant landing in the stream of sewage.

Before I could jump, a strong hand grasped my arm and steadied me, and I almost took it off at the wrist before a soft voice said, "I mean you no harm, Lord, and I apologize for startling you."

I regained my balance, and the hand retreated. A dim

shape in the shadows, tall and thin, sank to the floor to kneel with head bowed.

I sheathed my knife but didn't let go of the hilt.

"Who are you?" I asked.

"Only a dryad, noble Lord," they said.

"A dryad." That explained why I hadn't seen them. They had probably heard me coming and had gone as still as only a dryad could. I'd only noticed them when I sensed them with magic, which was an unwelcome reminder of how my magic was changed; once, I would have known they were there without having to consciously try. "I didn't think there were any dryads in Aven outside Alfar territory."

I took a few cautious steps back. "Except the dryads the Queen of Morven Forest gifted to the King of the Eyrie," I amended.

"There are dryads in the Eyrie?" The kneeling person moved slightly, perhaps in startlement, lifting their head to look at me. I assumed they didn't spend a lot of time serving nobles, because dryad servants – those in Morven, at least – knew not to react at all, to anything.

"In the lower gardens," I said. "Not in the Eyrie itself. Had you not heard?"

"Forgive my ignorance, Lord," they said, bowing closer to the stone.

"I'm not your Lord," I said. "I'm just an ordinary Sidhe trying to find my way out of this sewer so I can meet my sweetheart outside the city."

"I'm a dryad, my Lord; even the lowliest servant is my master."

"No." The certainty in my voice made them look up at me again. "I don't believe that, and I don't care what the Founding Laws say." I took a chance and let go of my knife hilt to step forward and grip the dryad's shoulder. They were thin –

perhaps it was their natural physique, but it felt like the thinness of not enough nourishment to me.

They went very still and stiff under my hand.

"Please don't kneel," I said. "And if you can, could you conjure some light?"

For a moment longer, they stayed stiff, but then they seemed to decide something – to trust me, perhaps – and they relaxed and got to their feet.

"You're Sidhe," they said. "I always heard Sidhe were strong in magic. Can you not make light?"

"I… can currently only feel magic, not use it," I said. "But I knew a dryad once who could make wisplight."

I could feel them looking at me and for just an instant, I thought I could sense them examining my magic.

"Your connection to the Realms is very strong," they said. "How could you lose the use of it?"

"Someone even stronger decided I needed to be taught a lesson," I said, keeping my voice even. I felt the brush of magic against magic again, and then a soft blue-green light appeared between the dryad's hands and moved to hover over our heads.

"You bear a dryad's magic," they said, their voice so soft I could barely hear it above the sound of water in the channel.

"Yes," I said, just as softly.

"How?" The wisplight lit their narrow face, gentling the sharp lines of jaw and cheekbone. The dryad looked as thin as their shoulder had felt, as if they hadn't eaten – or rooted – properly in a very long time. They had rough grey-brown skin, like the bark of an alder tree, and deep russet hair like a mass of thin twigs. Their eyes were the same reddish brown, wide and wondering.

"A had a dryad friend," I said, at a loss for how to sum up what Daphnis had meant to me – and what he had done to me.

"They – *he*, he called himself he – passed on his magic because he was going to be executed."

The dryad didn't even look surprised at the word "executed," which said more about the lot of dryads than any lengthy explanation could have. My heart ached for them and, not for the first time, I wished there was some way I could change the world to make it better for the dryad people.

"They must have been a friend indeed if they gave you their magic instead of passing it to another dryad." They raised a hand as if to lay it on my chest but stopped before they actually touched me. I took a step closer, pressing against their palm, and they met my eyes.

I put my hand over theirs and felt the serpents wriggle under my coat. All three poked their heads out at once and the dryad snatched their hand back.

"Daphnis *was* a good friend," I said, deciding that I didn't need to say anything more. It didn't matter what else he had done or why; he had trusted me with his magic, and he had loved me, even if it had twisted him in the end.

"You… you have feathered tree serpents," the dryad said, looking as if they were going to kneel again. Instead, they reached out hesitantly and smiled when Coal stretched his neck to butt his head on their hand.

That the dryad was relaxed enough, trusting enough to show emotion comforted me, and I smiled, too.

"That one's called Coal," I said. "And the two adults are Smoke and Flame."

The dryad scratched under Coal's chin.

"Smoke and Flame are my… my sweetheart's companions."

The dryad met my eyes again. "Your sweetheart?" Their eyes widened. "You're Hraf na Tokka. The Vogel Seer's heart-bonded." They started to bow, to kneel again, and I stopped them with a hand on their shoulder.

"How do you know about me, but not that there are dryads in the Eyrie's lower garden? Even the Vogel nobles won't admit that Fionn – Seer Tokka – and I should be together."

They smiled again, this time just a slight curl of their lips. "We know what we hear through the grates." They gestured vaguely towards a side tunnel. "All the common folk are talking about Seer Tokka's beloved, who nearly died for him." They stepped back into the shadow, away from their wisplight, and nearly disappeared. "The common folk, Vogel and otherwise, believe Seer Tokka will save them from poverty and lead them into a new golden age. They believe his beloved Shadow will help him."

"He means to try," I said. "And I will always stand with him."

"Then the common folk will help him. And you."

"Will you help me? I need to get out of these tunnels, away from the city if I can."

"You go to meet Seer Tokka?" They emerged from the shadows again, their greenish wisplight brightening as they reached out to stroke Coal's tiny head again. Coal purred.

"Yes."

"He is… leaving the Eyrie?" Their voice was carefully neutral, so I couldn't tell if they were glad or concerned.

"He is." I watched their face carefully, but they were looking at the serpents, a tiny smile twitching their lips. "He needs to get away, but he will return. He wants to help people, *all* people, including yours."

That got him to meet my eyes again. "There is no way to help my people. We are enslaved, with no hope of freedom."

"*He* has hope," I said. "And so do I. In the meantime, there are ways to make your lives easier. Seer Tokka has included soil from Morven Forest in his trade negotiations, so the dryads in the Eyrie garden will not suffer starvation, at least. He would do what he can to help you, too, once he knows you're here."

Their eyes slid away from mine, but they didn't say anything.

"Where do you root?" I touched their shoulder again and this time they seemed to lean into it a little, as if they recognized and accepted the tiny amount of comfort I was trying to offer.

"We are born down here," they said, not answering my question – not directly, anyway. Their eyes slid to the channel, where water flowed over a bed of sludge-covered stone. "We get what sunlight we can from the grates, and when our tasks bring us close to the outlets, we linger as long as we dare."

"Your tasks?"

They gestured around us. "We are the caretakers of the sewers." They let a note of grim humor enter their voice. "We repair and clean and unclog, so free peoples don't ever need to come here." They smiled tightly. "It gives us freedom, of a sort. As long as the sewers work smoothly, no one bothers us."

"But you can't leave."

"We are born here, we root here, we die here." They shrugged.

"You root…?" I looked where they had looked, at the water, the sewage.

"There are places where sediment settles deeply enough for us to find nourishment."

"That's –" I couldn't think of an appropriate word. In Morven Forest, dryads were treated like ambulatory furniture, like barely sentient servants, but at least they had sunlight and fresh air and clean soil.

"Yes," they said. "I will show you the way out." Their lips compressed. "But I must ask you to do something for me."

They lifted their chin defiantly, and I knew they were thinking the same thing I was: I could command them to do as I said, and with no other master to give contradicting orders, they would have to obey.

"Tell me what you need," I said instead, and I thought I detected a slight relaxation in their shoulders.

"One of my people is with seed," they said. "I would ask you to carry their child away from here, to somewhere they can know sunlight and good earth."

"With seed?"

"You would say 'pregnant'."

"I can't wait for a child to be born, I –"

I was so surprised to be interrupted by a dryad – because no matter how I encouraged my own to act as free people, my entire upbringing made me expect subservience – that I immediately shut up.

"You don't have to wait. They are ready to birth; they are only waiting for a sign."

I frowned. "A sign?"

"Every dryad child is birthed and planted when their parent receives an auspicious sign. For most of us, it is something simple. My birthing parent saw a rainbow cast by a drop of water on the sewer grate. Another I know watched a clump of earth dislodged from above fall into the water to add to our rooting sediment. Once a rainstorm flushed the stench from the sewers for days, and three children were planted once the waters subsided." They gazed into the darkness, eyes soft. "Thetis believes their child's birth sign will be more significant. You coming here may mean they are correct."

"Once Thetis gives birth, they will dwindle and pass on?"

"No. Thetis will remain until they implant their pollen in another."

Of course; I knew that. Dryads reproduced by infusing their pollen with all their magic and implanting it in a partner. The pollen donor would then slowly die unless they became a tree; the partner who bore the child would remain until someday they, too, chose to pass on their magic.

"Where do your people root when they pass? Your grove of ancestors? Surely it isn't down here?"

"We don't root. We let the water carry us to the sea, and then we are no more." Sadness crept into their voice.

"The child will grow up alone if I take them from here," I said.

"It is better than growing up here, a slave."

"They will still be a slave, if anyone non-dryad ever finds them. It is not only a law, it is written in magic."

"Then take them somewhere their masters will be kind." The dryad turned their look on me. "Take them home with you."

"I'm not going home. Not for… I don't know how long. I'll be traveling, and unless you know a way a dryad can root and grow without staying in one place, I will have to leave them sooner or later."

"They say the Huldr can be kind."

"They also say the Huldr can be cruel." I sighed. "And the Huldr are a long journey from here. How soon must the child be planted? Or can the other parent come with me, to root as a tree next to where their child will grow?"

They shook their head. "The dryad who implanted in Thetis was named Laurus. They have already passed on." They looked away down the tunnel. "A day or two. A child can survive a day or two without rooting. No more than that. And many of us have tried to leave, to plant our children in the clean air. We can go no farther than the tunnel entrances before magic stops us."

"What if the child can't pass the entrances either?"

"Then we are forever doomed to this." They gestured around us.

"I'll try," I said. "Of course I'll try."

They nodded.

"What's your name?" I said, suddenly realizing I hadn't even thought to ask and feeling shame for it. I needed to be better. I could say all I liked about improving the world, but what I *did* meant more.

"Alnus," they said.

"That's a strong name."

"And yet I am not strong."

"You are," I said. "You survive. Take me to your friend Thetis, and then lead me out of here. You have my word that I will do what I can for your people."

"I believe you," they said, leading the way down the tunnel. "Your Daphnis's magic shines strongly in you, even if you are unable to use it."

THE DAY WAS DRAWING down to evening, the skies going dim and grey, by the time Alnus, Thetis, and I reached an outlet to the sea on the edge of the City.

"The tide is out, but will soon turn," said Alnus, peering between the bars and leaning into the thin sunlight.

"How do I get through?" I put a hand on a bar. It was wrought iron and cold against my skin, but despite the coating of rust, the one I touched felt solid.

"The bars don't go all the way to the bottom," Alnus said. "You can swim under them."

I looked into the liquid that spilled out into another channel and then out to sea. I could just glimpse where the bars ended, halfway between the surface of the water and the bottom of the channel. When I pressed my face to the bars, I could just see the rocky shoreline to one side, and the docks of the City Beneath to the other. The channel carried mostly water, but I could see less pleasant things floating and at its bottom the sediment looked like it could be easily stirred up into a brown cloudy mess.

I was not looking forward to swimming.

Behind me, Thetis shuffled their feet against the stone. "My Lord," they said. "I will birth my child now, so that you may depart."

"Here?" I tried to keep my voice even, but I was equal parts horrified and fascinated. I had never seen a person born, though I *had* seen wolf pups and deer come into the world, and I had watched Coal hatch.

"If it is acceptable, I will go there." They pointed to a side passage.

"Of course," I said.

"I will assist," said Alnus.

"I'll… I suppose I'll swim under the bars, if a dryad child is slight enough to pass between."

Alnus smiled, as if I had said something amusing. "Dryad children are like seedlings, my Prince," they said. "We can tell they are not trees, but most people can't, especially not once they are planted. The child will fit between the bars."

"My Prince?" I said, raising an eyebrow.

Their smile grew and it felt good that they trusted me enough to let it show. "Are you not the Prince of Morven Forest?" They turned to follow Thetis, apparently not needing my answer.

"Does everyone know who I am?" I said to the empty air once the dryads had rounded the corner. It was not a comforting thought, because if people *did* know, or could guess, then it was only a matter of time before someone at the Eyrie figured out who killed their King and stole their Seer.

I stripped my pack off, and then my weapons and finally my clothes, and stuffed as much of it as I could into my pack. I checked to make sure it was tightly closed and the spells against dampness and water were still in place, though there wasn't much I could do if they weren't. I unstrapped the bag of Fionn's I had been carrying from the bottom of my pack and put it with my swords on the walkway, up against the bars where I could reach it from the other side. It would be a squeeze, but it would fit through.

The serpents flitted between the bars and into the evening.

No guards, said Smoke.

No people, said Flame.

"Can you tell how deep the water is?" I looked into the channel again, wondering if I could ease into the water without stirring up the vile sediment at the bottom.

Not deep, said Flame.

Shoulders, said Smoke.

"My shoulders might equal not deep," I said. "But it's plenty deep to me if I'm wading." I heard the dryads moving in the side tunnel, though I had heard nothing to indicate a birth was happening. I needed to stop putting off my dip in the sewer channel.

I shrugged my pack back on, slipped into the water, diving immediately and swimming under the bars. I tried not to think about the sludge. When I surfaced on the other side, I found I could stand on the bottom with my head and shoulders – and the top of my pack – out of the water, so I reached through the bars for the rest of my things and piled them on top. I refused to think about what I was standing in. Then I waited in the bone-chilling cold water for the dryads to return.

20
Fionn

*Y*OUR BELOVED *and your future await you,* repeated over and over in my head as I followed Jinta down the stairs to the building's front door. This time, there were no people watching from doorways, though I heard the sounds of daily life faintly as I passed by.

Dishes clattered behind one door, and a child's laughter pealed out from another. From a third, I distinctly heard a deep voice say, <I love you,> in Vogel, and another, not quite as deep, reply, <It's still your turn to do the dishes.>

When we reached the door, I expected to follow Jinta out onto the street. Instead, he turned down another hallway and lead me to a door at the far end.

"Some of the basements are connected, too," he said, flashing me his cheeky grin as he opened the door. I conjured a wisplight and we descended a rickety set of wooden steps.

"Not all the buildings have basements," he continued, "Because parts of the sewer run at this level, but we can get quite a way before we have to go back up to street level." He looked at my wisplight floating above us. "Once we get past Division Street, we won't have to leave the basements at all till we've reached the wall."

"There aren't any guards at the wall, are there?" I asked, ducking after him into a low passage that didn't look like it was original to the building; though it had been finished neatly with brick, it was a browner, coarser type than that which had lined the basement we just left.

"There's barely a wall," he said.

"I've seen it near the cliff. I suppose I thought it might be more robust where it faced the road to Tronven."

"Pa says it was already full of big gaps when he was a boy, and nobody's repaired it since. Started coming down in his grandpa's time, he says, and people made off with the stone to build their houses and such with."

I considered that. "Would that have been when King Sarkot's grandfather ruled the Eyrie?"

Jinta shrugged. We emerged into another basement, this one with walls of stone. A huge pile of cut wood occupied one whole wall and I wondered if the people who lived here shared the wood and the expense of buying it to burn in their stoves and fireplaces, or if they had to purchase it stick by stick from the person who stored it here.

Another brick-lined passage awaited us after we passed through several more rooms, some full of old furniture and boxes, and some with further stores of wood. A few even had rusty boilers and furnaces giving off heat and the crackling sound of flames.

"Could be," Jinta said. "He's the one decided girls couldn't be soldiers and such, weren't he?"

"He was. And ruled that Vogel must only marry other Vogel."

He glanced at me out of the sides of his eyes before

entering the passage. "That makes it awkward for you, I expect, being as you're heart-bonded to a fey."

"A little." I had to duck even more to get through the passage, and it amused me to think of the tall King's Guard trying to pursue us here.

"I suppose that means there's worse kings than what we have now." Jinta turned when we emerged and led me up a stair – solid stone this time – and along a hall.

"Roof or street?" he said as we approached a heavy door, but I'm fairly sure he was thinking out loud, not asking my opinion. "Street," he decided. "I'll go first." He eased the door open, peering out to one side, then the other. Satisfied, he stepped through. "We only need to cross." He pointed to the left and motioned to me to follow him out.

We walked quickly and I made sure my hair was hidden under my hood. On the other side of the street, he tried the door handle of a building, then knocked. I could hardly breathe as we waited, but no guards appeared, and only a few people walked down the road, intent on their errands and paying us no mind.

"Oh, it's you," said a bored voice, and the door opened. Jinta pulled me inside. The thin girl who stood facing us in the entry looked at me curiously. She looked human, but like Joss had pointed ears that suggested some fey ancestry. "What're you up to, Jinta?" she asked when she was finished inspecting me.

"Business of the resistance," he said, and the girl snorted.

"Sure," she said, and closed the door, locking it. She looked at me closely again, with clever blue eyes. "You're the Seer," she said.

"Hello." I didn't know what else to say.

"Hello, yourself. You in some kind of trouble?"

"Not your business, Nimue," said Jinta, pushing her aside

to get past.

"I'm leaving the Eyrie," I said, deciding the truth would serve me best. In my admittedly limited experience, young people reacted better when you trusted them. "My companion is waiting."

"Companion?" She smirked, like she thought I was hiding something. "You're sneaking out to visit a forbidden lover, aren't you?"

"You read too many love stories," said Jinta, but for a moment I was startled by her perception.

I smiled. "You've caught me," I admitted, and she returned my smile.

"For Goddess's sake, Nim, we're in a hurry," Jinta said, tugging at my arm.

"Can you keep my secret?" I asked. "You are correct that my beloved is forbidden to me."

"I know what that's like," Nimue said, a dreamy look crossing her face.

"You do not," said Jinta.

She ignored him. "I'll keep your secret, my Seer," she said. "I'm no snitch." She stepped out of the way. "Just make sure Jinta doesn't get himself in any trouble."

"I'll do my best."

I was still smiling when I followed Jinta down more stairs into another basement, and it lasted through several more basements and across another street.

"Can you teach me to make lights like that?" my young guide said as we entered a damp space beneath another building that was cluttered with cast-off bits of metal I couldn't even imagine the purpose of. I had been wondering how long it would be before he asked; he had been sneaking glances at the light the whole time.

"Do you have magic?" I forced my lips not to curl into the

smile they wanted to make. I didn't want it to seem as if I was making fun of him.

"No idea." He pushed open a decaying wooden door and we squeezed into a narrow passage with puddles of greenish water on the floor. My foot wraps soaked through, and I could feel the chill of the stone in my feet, all the way up to my ankles.

"Kiernan – my companion – once told me everyone has a little magic."

"So can you teach me?"

I thought about teaching Neeka and my guards, when we still barely knew each other, how we sat on the floor of the Eyrie library, and I talked the three of them through the process of connecting to the Realms and calling light into their cupped hands. How their eyes had shone when they opened them and saw they had succeeded. And I thought about sitting on the roof of my tower at the Abbey of the Moon, Kiernan's smoky voice in my ears as he did the same for me.

There was so much joy in magic that I knew I would never be able to deny a request to teach it to others.

"I can," I said. "But not while we're walking."

His shoulders slumped, though he tried to hide it, and I reached out to touch his hair. He looked up at me.

"If we have time when we reach the edge of the city, I would be happy to teach you."

"Does it take very long? We might only have a little time before your Prince finds us."

"If you can pay attention," I said, letting myself smile as he turned away to lead me through another basement, this time all wooden posts and walls. "It only takes a short time, once you know what to do."

"I can pay attention if it's important."

"Then I'll tell you what to expect while we walk." So as we

passed through basements and passages and made one more trip to cross a street above and moved quickly through an alley behind a housing block, I told him about connecting to the Three Realms, and how everyone had a different type of magic they were best at.

"That seems to take a lot of work just to get some light," he said.

"At first it is," I agreed. "But if you practice, it comes easier each time, until it hardly takes a thought."

"Easier than lighting a lamp?"

"Until you learn to call on fire to light the lamp for you, it's definitely easier than lighting a lamp."

"You can call fire?" He stopped and looked at me eagerly, and I only got him moving again by calling a flame into my palm. I was still not very good with flame – I could call it easily enough, but fine control was another matter – and tended to melt candles down trying to get them burning. I had seen Kiernan light a candle with the slightest gesture that barely disturbed the wick.

And that memory made me somber again. I had to find a way to help him regain his magic. Perhaps there was a way I could use healing magic to speed the growth of his antlers, instead of closing over the wounds.

"You're thinking, aren't you?" Jinta asked. "You gotta be careful about that. Too much thinking can make you dull, like Nimue. She thinks too much."

"I must be terribly dull, then," I replied. "I like thinking quite a lot."

"But it's making you sad." He stopped in front of a heavy door with a big iron handle.

"There are a lot of sad things in the world."

"Well, here's one to make you happier." He gestured at the door. "We've reached the last building before the wall. Up these stairs and out and we're at the edge of the City Beneath."

I looked at the door. "Will there be guards?"

"Could be. Could be they're waiting to see if you try to leave, though if Joss did his job, they'll be looking for you closer to the Eyrie."

I looked at Jinta, so small, grubby, and defiant. "What's the 'resistance'?" I said, raising an eyebrow.

He blushed. "Forgot I said that. It's just a game me and Joss and some other kids play. Nimue used to play, too, but she says she's too grown up now." He leaned on the wall next to the door. "We pretend we're rebels, fighting for justice against…" He paused.

"Against what?"

He chewed his lip. "Pa said we could be tried for treason, if any of the Guard heard us."

"Against the King?"

He nodded. "It's just a dumb game, I know. But it made us feel like maybe we really could help people, one day."

"You're far too young to think your games are dumb," I said. "Though your father was right. Be careful about who might overhear you."

He nodded again.

"And you have done good." I gestured back the way we'd come. "You and your Pa, your friends, all of you have created a way – two ways – for people to move more freely around the City. And you helped me. I hope I can help all of you someday." It was my turn to hesitate, but then I said, "When I return to the Eyrie." Because I realized I *did* have work to do in the Eyrie and in the city. The whole Monarchy. I had people who believed I could help them, so help them I must.

I knew I didn't want to do it without Kiernan; we had tried that, and it was agony to be apart. Surely there was some way we could both fulfill our obligations to our Monarchies and help our people *and* still be together.

The two of you together are worth fighting for, Magnus had said, certainty strong in his voice. If he could believe in us, never having met Kiernan, then I also had to believe it. What was I even doing, if I did not?

"Me an Joss, old Magnus, too, we'll tell everyone. The whole City will be behind you when you return." Jinta pulled himself up to his full height and raised his chin.

"I know you will," I said. "Will you come with me to wait outside the wall, or do we part ways here?"

"I'll come," he said. "I promised I'd see you safe outside the City and I will. Let me go out first and check for King's Guard. I know a place we can wait, where we can see the beach."

"The beach?"

"Sewers come out in the sea, so I figure someplace with a view of the beach is the place to wait."

"Oh, of course."

He reached for the door handle and turned back to shoot me a serious look. "Stay here, my Seer. I won't be a moment." Then he pulled open the door, slipped through, and closed it again.

While I waited, I let my wisplight trickle away and leaned against the wall. I reached for my connection to Kiernan, feeling it warm in my belly, and the faint tug that told me he was somewhere behind me, probably still making his way through the sewers. I felt no fear or pain or anxiety, only the strength of his presence.

I pressed my hand to my stomach and closed my eyes. He was so close, so *real*. It had been terrible to be away from him, not knowing when I'd see him again. I never wanted to feel that again, even if I had to live the rest of my life as an outlaw. I shivered at the thought and pushed away the fear that tried to engulf me. I would *not* let us be separated again.

The door cracked open again and I opened my eyes to see Jinta's shape against the brightness of the afternoon. How was it afternoon already?

"My Seer?" Jinta stepped back inside and pulled the door most of the way shut. He sounded confused.

"I'm here," I said, though surely he could see me.

He startled. "I didn't see you there."

It was dim in the building's entry, but not dark, and the light that spilled down the stairs from outside had fallen into my eyes, so I must have been illuminated.

"I didn't mean to startle you," I said, not sure how I possibly *could* have startled him.

"My Seer," he said, a note of awe in his voice. "You're covered in shadows."

I stared at him, then looked down and stared at my feet. I could see the dim light from the crack in the door, could feel it in my eyes, yet my body was hidden in shadow. As I watched, the darkness ebbed, slipping away back to the corners and depths of the hall.

"Oh," I said. "I've never done that before." I looked back up at Jinta. "Kiernan called shadows to hide us when we were fleeing the Alfar, but… I don't even know how *I* might have done it." I had been thinking of him, had been afraid of the thought of being apart. Had the shadows felt him through me? Had they sought to keep me safe when I was afraid, for his sake?

"I guess the shadows like you," Jinta said, his voice returning to its usual cheerfulness, as if summoning shadows was perfectly normal. "Maybe I can learn to cloak myself like that, too?"

"If I knew how I did it, I'd be happy to share."

"When you return, then. Maybe?"

"When I return, if I figure it out myself. Kiernan told me

he'd always thought of shadows as his friends, when he was a child."

"Then they're your friends, too." Jinta nodded towards the door. "There was only one Guard, and I watched him follow the wall back towards the Eyrie. If we're quick, we probably won't meet another."

I followed him again, out the door and up a dirty stone stair into an alley. What had once been a huge, well-built stone wall formed one side of the alley, and the building we'd come out of was the other. Now, the wall was a tumbled heap in more places that it was solid, with more gaps here than there had been where Kier and I had entered the city.

We slipped into the gap directly ahead of us and were about to pass through to cross an open stretch of meadow to a copse of trees when Jinta hissed, grabbed my hand, and pulled me back. He pressed against the wall, and I copied him.

For a moment, I didn't understand why he had stopped me, but then I heard footsteps and muttering.

<Go patrol the wall,> said a gruff voice. <Go walk around looking official in the fucking cold,> it continued, low and irritated. <Fuck them. There's nothing here. No one who kidnapped a Seer in the first place is going to be stupid enough to walk out of the city in full daylight.>

The footsteps and muttering grew closer until they were directly on the other side of the wall. I held my breath and Jinta pinched his lips together with his fingers to tell me to keep quiet. The footsteps paused and the Guard scuffed his feet.

<I should just go back,> he muttered. <Captain would never know if I went all the way 'round anyway.> He shuffled some more, then swore, and finally began to walk again, back the way he'd come.

Jinta relaxed and took my hand, and we slipped through

the gap. This time it was my turn to hiss and pull him back. The Guard had thought better of his decision and had stopped only a short distance away. His head whipped around at the sound of my breath, and I desperately hauled Jinta back behind the wall and down into the stairwell. I didn't dare open the door to go back inside.

<Who's there?> said the Guard. I heard his footsteps approach again and Jinta huddled close to me at the bottom of the stairs. If he didn't come too close, he wouldn't see us there.

<Fuck,> the Guard said. <If that's you Kinsa, you can fuck right off. I wasn't really going to go back without checking the road.>

Again, the footsteps moved away. Jinta and I stayed crouched at the bottom of the stair for long while before we dared move and when we did, it was to creep slowly and silently back to the gap in the wall. I waited while he peered around the edge then motioned at me to stay where I was and slipped all the way through. I heard the shift of a pebble on the hard-packed earth as he checked one direction, then the other.

When he returned, he beckoned for me to follow, and there was no one to see us cross the meadow. The grass was cold-dead and flattened and we hardly left a trail. The trees were bare of leaves, but thick enough to hide us from view once we reached them.

"We have to cross the road to see the beach," Jinta said in my ear once we were hidden in the copse. I nodded and looked where he pointed, though I couldn't see much through the branches. "More trees that way," he said. "And a ditch runs along beside the road. Just around the first bend, there's a place where a stream runs down to the sea from the hills, and the road crosses it on a bridge. We wait there, under the bridge. We'll see your Prince when he comes up from the beach."

I nodded.

"Then you'll follow the road, but not *on* the road; stay in the trees. From there you can walk right into Tronven."

"Easy as that?" I said, letting a smile touch my voice.

"A bit of a walk, I hear," he said. "And winter coming soon. But me an' Joss will make sure those guards think you never left the city."

"Thank you."

He waved his hand. "No need for that. Only teach me to make light like you said you would, and we're even."

"Are we, then?" I smiled some more.

He sighed. "I'da helped you anyway, but I sure would like to learn some magic."

"When we reach the bridge and can rest, I'll teach you."

"And maybe fire, too?"

"I must ask you to promise me something first."

"After I helped you?" He raised his chin, and I wanted to hug him for his fierceness, but I didn't think he'd appreciate the gesture.

"This is important," I said. "You must promise two things, if you wish me to teach you magic."

"You said 'something'; that's only one thing."

I hid my smile this time. "One thing for each lesson."

"Fine." He crossed his thin arms over his chest, and tucked his wings close to his back. I tried not to notice that even this child had bigger wings than I did.

"First, you must only use magic for good purposes. To help people. To protect yourself. To keep others safe."

"That's easy," he said. "You don't even need me to promise that, but I do."

"Second, you must promise to teach your friends, your Pa, anyone who wants to learn. Magic belongs to us all."

He laughed, then clapped his hand over his mouth and

looked around quickly, in case he had been too loud and attracted attention.

"I promise," he said. "Anyone who'll listen, I'll teach. And I'll make them promise those same two promises first."

"Good." I patted his shoulder. "Then let's go to the bridge and get started."

"Right this way, my Seer."

As I followed the small, defiant child, I was filled with warmth. I felt love and courage and – most of all – hope. Because if ordinary people – Vogel, human, and who knew how many others – could already live together in peace in the City, helping each other weather poverty and injustice, surely every good thing I could do would spread and find root and make the world better a little at a time.

If small children could be valiant and generous, then they would grow up to be valiant and generous adults, and my people – all people – could thrive and flourish and not simply survive.

I could hardly wait to tell Kiernan what I had learned.

21
Kiernan

I WAS SHIVERING so violently by the time I reached the shore that I had difficulty unstrapping my pack. Fortunately, the rocky beach was empty as it was evening and most of the docks were closer to the city.

I dressed as quickly as I could and stomped up and down the shore a few times to try to get my blood flowing again before I even tried to buckle on my weapons. What I needed was a good fire and a hot drink, but I didn't dare try for either until Fionn and I were well away from the City.

With that thought, I felt for my connection to him and found it steady, a comforting heat behind my belly button. He felt calm, maybe even hopeful, and the gentle tug of the thin silver ribbon told me he was somewhere not far ahead of me. Waiting, I hoped, and safe.

The serpents circled around my pile of things, keeping close guard over the thin bundle tucked into the top of my pack, and when I had reassembled myself, I let them nestle in the front of my coat. The chill of their snakelike bodies started me shivering again, until all three began to purr, and grew warm, warming me in turn.

And warming the tiny dryad child I had wrapped in a handkerchief and tucked in with them. The infant looked, while asleep, very much like a twig with long pale roots at one end and a few branches with tightly-closed buds at the other. They looked precisely like a seedling tree.

Thetis had told me their child would continue to look like a tree until they were somewhere around three years old, when they would uproot for short periods of time to explore the world around them. Each uprooting would last longer, and by the time they were nine, the young dryad would look like a smaller version of an adult, though with childlike features. By then they would be fully ambulatory and only needing to root for a short time every few days, and a longer period at the dark moon.

Infant dryads, I was informed, only woke very occasionally, and then one might see something of what they would become. This one had opened their eyes and looked at me as Thetis passed them between the bars.

"Hello, little one," I had said, and the tiny child had smiled, then closed their eyes and looked exactly like a twig again.

I had felt Thetis and Alnus's sorrow and hope as if they were emitting it like magic – and I had smiled as reassuringly as I could and promised, again, to see the baby safely planted.

Of course, I still didn't know where or how I would manage it, but I hoped Fionn would have an idea. He would probably want to adopt the child and, had it been possible, I would not have objected.

I glanced at the sky as I walked, though I didn't really need to in order to tell how much daylight was left. That much of my magic was intact. Here, on the west side of the Eyrie's cliff, daylight would last a little longer than on the east side, where the cliff's shadow would plunge the shore into darkness sooner. I hoped Fionn had been able to rest, because we would be traveling at night for a few days at least.

To my right, above the mark of the high tide, on an embankment built up long ago by ancient people, the road between Aven and Tronven was empty. It was past the evening mealtime and anyone who'd been on the road would have hurried to get somewhere they could rest and eat. I wished Fionn and I were going to be doing the same. It would be a cold evening meal for us and a long night of walking.

I heard him before I saw him, even with the sound of a burbling stream to cover his soft voice. It was only as I rounded the corner where the road embankment crossed a bridge that I realized I hadn't actually *heard* him at all – not with my ears. It was magic that told me where he was, and it must have told him I was coming, too, because he was standing, looking at me with a smile – the one that lit up his whole face – when I came into view.

I almost pulled him into my arms for a long tongue-filled kiss before I realized his wasn't the only magic I felt. Whoever was with him must have had a very good natural blocking ability, because their magic almost blended with Fionn's, hiding behind it.

"Beloved," Fionn said, and he took both my hands in his.

"Hi, pretty bird," I answered, looking past him to see one of the boys we had met on the street, cross-legged on the stream bank, concentrating on a pool of wisplight in his hands.

"And hello –" I looked at Fionn.

"Jinta," he said.

The boy looked up and grinned. "Told you I'd get him out of the City safe," he said. His wisplight dwindled when he turned his attention away.

"So you did. And I see you are a man of your word."

The boy's chin came up and his thin chest swelled with pride. "I'm learning magic," he said. "Seer Tokka told me I must teach it to everyone I know."

"Seer Tokka is very smart," I replied. "If he says you must, then you must."

I followed Fionn to a clear spot by the stream and let him take my pack off.

"We can't stay long," I said. "Just long enough to eat."

He nodded and began to rummage for the food we had brought from the Eyrie. I had more in my pack, but it would keep better, so we would eat it last.

"Will you eat with us, Jinta?" I asked.

"No, I best get back or Ma'll have me scrubbing the floors all tomorrow."

I tried not to smile. "I find it's best not to keep parents waiting. Mothers, especially." Then I did smile. "Mine, at least, is frightening when vexed."

Jinta grinned, then cocked his head and frowned. "Why's your jacket moving?" he said.

Fionn looked up from where he was kneeling to lay out food on a flat rock. "Why *is* your coat moving?"

I widened my eyes dramatically, as if suddenly in pain, and pretended to swoon, falling to my knees. I pulled my coat open with a flourish, tumbling three feathered serpents out into the air with a chitter of annoyance. All three of them aimed for Fionn and burrowed into the hood of his cloak.

"You saved them!" said Jinta.

"I said I would," I said, in the same tone he had used earlier, and buttoned up my coat.

"And you're obviously a man of your word," he replied, so seriously I nearly laughed. I liked this boy very much, and if there were many like him in the City Beneath, then there was good hope for the future of Fionn's people.

As I moved to do up the last couple of buttons, Fionn said, "What else are you hiding in there?"

I smiled softly then, and knelt in front of him, slipping the handkerchief out and handing it to him. Jinta crept closer to watch.

Fionn saw how carefully I handled the bundle and took it gently from me, unwrapping it slowly. He blinked at the twig he uncovered and looked up at me.

"You carry a wrapped-up stick in your shirt?" said Jinta.

"Look closely," I replied.

"I see magic," said Fionn. "My seer-sights sees this as… a person?" He looked at me again, white brows pulled together over his eyes.

"A dryad, beloved," I said, and he stared, searching my eyes, then looked back down at the seedling. "A newborn dryad infant."

Just then, the child opened their eyes, the same green of spring leaves that Syrinx's were, and suddenly it wasn't a stick Fionn held, or even a newly-sprouted tree. It was a tiny child, spindly and delicate. They smiled and Fionn's face lit up with the sort of expression he saved for the things that delighted him most. The smile I would spend my life trying to get him to turn on me.

The infant blinked slowly, then yawned and closed their eyes, and seemed all at once to be only a twig again.

"Goddess Above," said Jinta. "I guess I never knew what a dryad baby might look like. 'Course I never even saw a grown up one."

"What's their name?" said Fionn, tucking the handkerchief carefully back around them.

"Quercus," I said.

"It's a strong name."

I looked at Jinta, and said, "I thought you knew

everything about the sewers."

He looked at me, puzzled.

"There's a whole colony of dryads down there," I said. "Sent there generations ago, so long since they've been forgotten."

"I never knew," Jinta replied.

"They can be very still, and unseen in the shadows. And they have good reason not to be seen."

"How come they don't come out?" asked Fionn, still gazing down at the seedling he held cradled in his arms, a little smile tugging at his mouth.

"They can't." I settled on the ground and picked up one of the sandwiches Fionn had assembled. "Their last instruction was to maintain the sewers, and they can't leave until their master gives them new orders or assigns them a new master." I lifted the sandwich, but before I took a bite, I added, "Anyone who finds them can tell them what to do and they have to do it. But only if it doesn't interfere with their master's instructions."

"But surely their master is dead by now." Fionn picked up a sandwich and offered it to Jinta, who looked guilty, like he knew he should decline, but he took it and bit off a corner.

"And there's the problem," I said.

"How do you come to have this child?" Fionn settled the bundle on his lap, then picked up another sandwich for himself.

"This one has never rooted in the sewers, so it was hoped the magic that kept the others prisoner wouldn't apply."

Fionn swallowed a bite of food and laughed softly, but there was little humor in it. "And you, naturally, volunteered to test the theory."

"They asked, and I agreed." I ate a bite. "And now *I* have a dilemma. The infant can only survive a day or two without being planted. We can't take them with us, and I don't know of a safe place nearby." I brushed my fingers softly over the handkerchief that rested across Fionn's knees.

"The only place I can think of," I went on, "is on the other side of the Eyrie, a tree where people leave offerings. It will still be lonely, but when I was there it felt… good. Safe. And perhaps the fisherfolk I met there would help."

Jinta had been looking back and forth between us with bright eyes. When I paused to eat again, he said, "You mean the Dancing Dryads, don't you?"

"You know this place?" asked Fionn.

"Sure. Me and Ma go there to leave offerings on the holy days. They say it's the only salt-leaf tree left in our whole Monarchy, and the locals keep it secret. My Ma has family in the fishing village, or else we wouldn't know of it, either." He looked at me again and sat up very straight. "Sir, I could take the dryad there. I could plant them and watch over them."

I looked at him seriously. He couldn't be more than ten. "You know dryads are an enslaved people?"

He nodded solemnly. "It's not right." The defiance in his voice was strong and I saw out of the corner of my eye as Fionn lifted his sandwich to hide his smile.

"No, it's not right, but until someone finds and breaks the magic that chains them, there's nothing anyone can do about it."

"I bet I could find that magic." His pointed chin rose, and he glared at me, as if daring me to contradict him.

"Perhaps you could," I said. "And I also have people looking into it even now." Fionn looked at me sharply and let his smile show.

Jinta continued to meet my eyes evenly. "I know I'm only a kid," he said, "But I know what's right, and I know I could watch over that child. Ma would help, and Grandma. Lots of us think dryads should be free like the rest of us."

I put my hand on his shoulder and squeezed. "I was six when I decided I wanted to defend people weaker than I am. I know how you feel."

"And did you? Help people?"

I shook my head. "Do you know how tiny a six-year-old Sidhe is? I let my lips curve up a little. "But that day I started to study bladework, very seriously, so that when I *was* big enough, I would also be capable."

"You're saying no, I can't help," Jinta said, bitterness in his voice. "You're being nice, but you're saying no."

I shook my head again. "I'm saying you can't do it alone."

Fionn's head came up and the serpents hissed softly, exactly at the same moment I heard wingbeats and the sound of someone landing on the road above, some way down towards the City.

Jinta looked at me, then Fionn, and opened his mouth to speak, but stayed silent when Fionn made a gesture at his lips.

I got to my feet and crept slowly out from under the bridge and crawled up the side of the embankment. Peering between blades of dead grass, I saw a single figure walking along the road, looking from side to side down the edges of the slope. He had blue and green feathers in his wings, carried a long spear, and wore a gold bird mask. King's Guard.

I reached out to feel the magic around me, and the Guard showed up as a soft glow, not strong in magic, but with some. It was a *familiar* glow. I looked more carefully at him as he got closer and realized I had been mistaken. The mask was not gold; it only reflected the yellow of the setting sun. It was silver. He was Seer's Guard.

I didn't need to turn to know Fionn had followed me. He was a warmth and a crackling silver spark. "Trikta or Konta?" I asked.

"Trikta."

"Less blue in his wings?"

His laugh was almost inaudible. "Yes."

"Do you trust him?"

"With my whole being."

"Wait until he's closer, then call to him." I did turn to look at him then, to meet his beautiful silver eyes. "We may have a solution to our problem." I looked down the embankment to where I could see Jinta peering up at us through the brush that grew along the stream.

WHEN TRIKTA SAW FIONN he said, "My Seer!" loudly enough that Jinta hissed at him to be quiet. The Guard slid down the embankment and tore off his bird mask to throw his arms around Fionn. "Neeka is beside herself. She's alternating between cursing you for leaving her behind and weeping in worry."

He seemed suddenly to realize what he was doing, that he was embracing his Seer, and that such an advance might not be welcome. He let go and sank to his knees. He didn't even seem to notice me or Jinta.

Fionn put his hands on each side of Trikta's face. "Never kneel to me, my friend," he said, and kissed his Guard's forehead. Trikta's eyes closed, and he looked like he was having a holy experience.

I could hardly blame him; Fionn's kiss was capable of inducing euphoria in me, too.

I cleared my throat, and Trikta leapt to his feet and put himself between me and Fionn. I raised my eyebrows but didn't say anything.

Jinta stepped in front of me and glared up at the Seer's

Guard. "Don't you threaten Hraf na Tokka," he said.

"It's okay, Jinta. Trikta's a friend. Of Fionn's – of Seer Tokka's – anyway."

"Prince Kiernan," Trikta said. "If you've hurt him –"

"If I ever hurt him, Seer's Guard, you have my permission to kill me. In the meantime, I hope we can be allies in trying to keep *other people* from hurting him."

He seemed to lose his bravado at that and leaned on his spear instead of pointing it at me. "You're taking him away. Every Guard in the Eyrie is looking for him." His voice was accusatory, and I was glad he didn't mention the dead King. I didn't think I was quite ready for Jinta – and by extension the whole City Beneath the Cliff – to know I'd killed their King. Not yet.

"He asked me to," I said.

Trikta turned to look at Fionn, his eyes practically begging his Seer to deny it.

Fionn touched his arm. "I did, Trikta. It's not forever, but right now… I need to be away from the Eyrie. I can't… I can't bear to be there anymore."

"He hurt you." It wasn't a question, and I knew – as Fionn did, but Jinta would not – that the 'he' in question was not me, but the King.

"Yes," Fionn said softly.

Trikta nodded sharply and turned back to me. "If you hadn't done it, I would have." His lips pressed together, and he suddenly stuck out his arm. I clasped his hand in the Vogel fashion.

"I know you would have."

"I'll come with you," he said, looking back at Fionn.

My beloved bit his lip. "There's something else I need you to do," he said.

"My Seer, you can't ask me to stay at the Eyrie without

you. Me, Neeka, even Konta, we'll all come with you, protect you."

"No." Fionn lifted his chin and looked, for a moment, every bit the Royal Seer he was born to be. "I need you and Neeka and Konta to stay and be my representatives in the Eyrie while I'm gone. Go to Councilor Rocsh. He'll know what to do."

"But my Seer –"

"I said no."

Trikta stiffened, but in the way a soldier given a command does, not in affront at being brusquely denied. The Seer facing him was not the frightened, gentle young man Trikta and I had both fallen in love with. He was the commanding figure that I, at least, believed a whole Monarchy could rally behind. And I loved him even more for it.

"I need you," Fionn said. He turned to the Vogel boy who watched us with growing confusion. "And you, Jinta." The boy straightened in exactly the same way Trikta had. "I need you to be my Resistance." Jinta's chin went up.

"There is a dryad infant here." Fionn went to where are things were piled near the stream and lifted the handkerchief bundle in both hands. "I need you two to go to the Dancing Dryads."

Trikta looked confused and I realized that Jinta had been correct when he said the triple-trunked salt-leaf tree hidden behind the Eyrie's cliff was a secret kept safe by the fisherfolk.

"Plant this child in good soil there and take turns tending them. They'll need protection, and water. And company."

"*I'll* do it, my Seer," said Jinta, looking sidelong at the Guard.

"The only dryads in our Monarchy are in the lower gardens," said Trikta. "Brought to our King by the Sidhe Queen. Where did this child come from, and why not take them there?"

"There are dryads maintaining the sewers beneath the City," I said. "The child is theirs, and their presence there seems like something Councilor Rocsh should be informed of."

"Are you sure?" said Trikta.

Fionn held out the bundle. "This is a dryad seedling, Trikta. Kiernan was asked to keep them safe when he passed through the sewers. They want their baby to grow up with clean air. Will you do as I ask? Will you help me and assist Jinta here in taking care of this child?"

Trikta bowed his head and reached for the child, but Jinta got there first. "They like me," the boy said, taking the wrapped, twig-like infant carefully.

"You know I would do anything for you, my Seer," Trikta said. He looked at me from the corners of his eyes and a muscle in his jaw tightened.

"I know, my friend," said Fionn. He stepped towards his Guard and embraced him. Trikta was taller, and tucked Fionn against his chest tenderly. I had to admit they looked good together, two handsome, slender, feathered Vogel men. I almost felt bad that Fionn had chosen me.

Almost.

Trikta lifted Fionn's face with a finger under his jaw and, for a moment, I thought he was going to kiss my beloved right in front of me. But Fionn put a hand on Trikta's chest and stepped back.

"You'd best stop by Jinta's home on your way," he said. "Let his family know what's happening, and perhaps they, too, will help. You might even wait until morning and take Jinta's friends Joss and Nimue along as well."

Jinta nodded firmly. "I'll tell the ones I know I can trust and only them. We won't fail you, my Seer." He looked at me. "Or you, Sir. Prince Kiernan."

"Take Smoke and Flame," I said, and Fionn nodded.

The serpents chittered.

We guard YOU," said Smoke.

Fionn smiled. "I have Coal and Kiernan to guard me," he said. "And I know you'll return quickly and let us know that all went well."

We go then, said Flame.

We return swift, said Smoke.

We protect Guard, said Flame, and I laughed.

"The serpents think you need protecting, Trikta," I said, slapping his shoulder.

He scowled at me, then gestured to Jinta. "Let us go then, before our Seer starts to think maybe he should find someone else."

They were gone into the deepening gloom and Fionn and I just looked at each other for a long moment.

"They'll be fine," I said.

"It's us I'm worried about."

"I know." And then, finally, I could put my arms around him, and kiss him, and remind him of how important he was to me.

22
Fionn

WE DIDN'T DARE CLIMB up the embankment to watch Trikta and Jinta fly away. There was always the chance that other guards would be out, observing the road and the land around the City Beneath in case we tried to leave.

As I stood staring out into the grey evening, Kiernan put his arms around me from behind and nestled into my back.

"That boy is going to apply to train for your Seer's Guard," he said. "I'd bet my favorite throwing knife on it."

I laid my arms over his and squeezed his hands. "Either that, or he really *will* form a secret resistance to fight for those without power."

He chuckled softly. "You inspire loyalty, my heart."

I turned away from the dusk to face him and pulled him tight against my chest. Coal slipped out of my hood to drape himself over the top of Kiernan's head.

"Your heart?" I said, scratching Coal's chin and then tracing the shape of Kier's eyebrow.

"You are, beloved." He turned his head to kiss my palm.

"We'll stay here until full dark, and then we head for Tronven."

"Jinta said to follow the course of the road from in the trees."

"He's a smart kid." He studied my face, something unreadable in his eyes, so I felt for our bond, wondering what he was thinking. He must have felt it, because he smiled. "Trikta loves you so desperately," he said.

I opened my mouth to protest, half expecting him to put his fingers on my lips to stop me from speaking. He didn't, but I didn't say anything anyway. I couldn't exactly deny it; Trikta didn't hide how he felt when we were alone, and I had thought for a moment that he was going to kiss me in front of Kier, so I had stepped away.

I cared for Trikta, loved him as a friend, but I couldn't return his feelings, and he knew it.

"He would never betray you," Kiernan said. "And he would never hurt anyone you care about. He's a good man." He looked away, eyes focused on the evening sky, or maybe on nothing at all. "The people who love you want you happy above all else. It's the people who fall in love with me we have to be careful of."

I knew he was referring to Daphnis, but I couldn't help jerking back in his arms. He didn't try to hold me, and maybe it was *because* he didn't that I pulled him close again immediately.

"I didn't mean you," he said. "You don't even like hurting people who deserve it."

I flushed – not with shame, but with pleasure – and rested my forehead on his. Coal grumbled and slid off of Kier's head onto his shoulder.

"I like it when you hurt them *for* me," I whispered, and then I *did* feel shame, because it was an unworthy thought. But

I also felt a flush of lust.

He tilted his face to press his lips on mine. "I'll do whatever unpleasant things you can't," he said when he leaned away.

It was dark enough that I could only see his outline in the gloom under the bridge. "I don't like being apart from you," I said. "Not even for a day."

"I don't like it, either." But he let go of me and went to our things to weigh each of my bags in his hands. He tied one of them to his own pack as he had when we left the Eyrie. I wanted to tell him that I could carry my own bags, but I didn't want a repeat of last time, when he had simply said, "I know you can," and kept one of my bags anyway.

So I just cleared up the remains of our food, tucked my cloak around me, and slung the other two bags over my shoulders. The one with my medicines clinked and I opened it to rearrange the contents so the bottles were more protected by the other items and tucking the small amount of unspun wool I had brought more securely around them. My hand paused over the wooden box that took up much of the space. I wished I knew what I was supposed to do with it.

Our breath formed white plumes in the dark of the night, catching the faint moonlight as it drifted over our heads and dissipated like mist. It was cold, and it would only get colder. I followed Kiernan out from under the bridge, through the ditch, and into the trees. We had to go quite a way upstream to find a fallen log to cross the stream on, because we couldn't risk the bridge this close to the City. We walked without speaking and I concentrated on moving quietly, as he had taught me to do when we were fleeing the Abbey of the Moon what felt like lifetimes ago. It was hard to believe it was only a matter of moons, and not years.

My eyes were meant for daylight so I could barely see, only vague shapes and Kiernan's hands keeping me from walking into trees in the dark. I felt for the Realms to see if I could use my seer-sight and walk at the same time. I knew it was possible, because it was how Siona was able to move through the world so easily without physical vision and only a fox to warn her about obstacles. It was tiring, though, because I wasn't used to it, and before long I stumbled and almost fell, even with Kier's hand on my elbow to guide me.

"Okay, pretty bird?" he said softly, his voice almost blending with the sounds of the wilderness at night.

"Just tired."

"Do you need to rest?"

I wanted to hug him for suggesting it, even though I knew he wanted to get as far away from the Eyrie as we could before stopping.

"I'm fine. I was just trying to see in the dark with magic."

His laugh was a barely audible snort. "Did it work?"

"Almost." I looped my fingers through his belt, and he carried on walking, a little slower, so I could find my footing without seeing it. "I know it's possible. Seer Siona does it to see and she's blind." I didn't add that Kiernan, too, had used seer-sight in the vision I'd had of us as old men, even though he was not a seer.

"She's had a great deal of practice."

I heard a trickle of water and then Kiernan guided me across another stream – this time only a very small one.

"Kier –?" My foot slipped on damp moss, and he steadied me with an arm around my waist.

"Mmm?" His hand moved away, back to my arm, and I saw a faint glint of moonlight on the branches from a gap in the trees far above us.

"I called shadows today."

"Did you?" He sounded interested. "What made you decide to do that?"

"I didn't." He was quiet, waiting for me to continue, but I could feel his curiosity. "I was waiting for Jinta to check for guards before we left the City, and… I was thinking about you, and about wanting to feel safe."

He pulled me close to help me around the large spread of roots from a fallen tree and didn't move away again once we were clear of it.

"Jinta almost didn't see me when he came back, because I was hidden in shadows. When I spoke to him, they just slipped away."

"And you didn't call them?"

There was faint light ahead, and in a few more steps we were at the edge of a meadow, frost on the dead grass glinting sliver in the last of the moonlight.

"No," I said. "Not on purpose. I wondered if maybe they knew, if they came because I'm yours."

We paused at the edge of the trees, and he looked up at me.

"I know I talk about shadows as if they're my friends, as if they're alive," he said. "And as a boy, I really did think of them that way." He looked across the meadow. "But I don't know that they're really… sentient. They feel more like *forces*, I guess, than spirits. Or *a* force with many shapes."

"But even if they don't have awareness, they might still… recognize you. And me." As I said it, I realized that one of the things I loved most about Kiernan was that we could talk about things like this, things I could never discuss with anyone else I knew and have them just *understand* me. Yes, I missed his body, his touch, when we were apart, but more than that, I missed his *mind*.

"Maybe." He looked back at me. "You'd think, after so many generations of magic, our languages would have better words for speaking of it."

"Maybe they did, once. Or maybe there are ancient, lost

languages that did. Or maybe there's no way to really talk about magic because it's different for everyone." I tried to keep the excitement out of my voice, because it was hardly the time or place for a deep philosophical discussion about language and magic. But I tucked the thought away in my mind to examine more closely later, when we were safe and comfortable and had time for just thinking.

I could see the upward curve of his lips in the fading moonlight and the glint of his teeth as he smiled.

"Have I ever told you how smart you are?" he said, lacing his fingers with mine and turning away to lead me around the edge of the meadow so we wouldn't leave a path through the frost that would be easily seen from the air. Not that any of my daylight-dwelling people would be flying at night.

I snorted. "You're the one who designed me a pair of artificial wings. I didn't even think to try."

It was his turn to snort. "Wings that will never work because they're too heavy. As I recall, you were the one that suggested different materials to make them lighter."

"So you're saying we make a good team?"

He squeezed my fingers. "We do."

We walked again without speaking, and as dawn rose slowly behind us we left the trees for rolling hills, and fenced pastures with sheep and cows. Kiernan pointed out a barn built into the side of a hill. There was no house in sight, but the open door of the barn revealed golden grasses piled inside. Two shaggy brown cows stood in the doorway, pulling out mouthfuls and chewing placidly.

"Fancy a roll in the hay?" Kier said. I shoved his shoulder in mock indignation, and he laughed.

"Won't the farmer mind?" I asked.

"Maybe, but I'm betting that if anyone objects, they'll stop objecting when I offer them silver in return for shelter."

The cows regarded us from deep brown eyes and blinked their absurdly long lashes when we passed them to enter the barn. The whole building was full of bundled hay piled up on long wooden beams to keep it off the floor. Only near the door was it loose, presumably so the cows could help themselves and the farmer wouldn't need to visit every day.

Kiernan chose one of the back corners, out of sight of the door, and cut the bindings holding the nearest bundle of hay so it spilled thick onto the boards. He caught my uncertain look – I was feeling guilty at making a mess of the neatly-stored forage – and said, "I'll leave a few coppers near the door where the farmer will find them."

As we curled up together, surprisingly warm even with no fire, he pressed his lips to the spot behind my ear and said quietly, "I had Erith send to Tronven for reeds and spider silk, so we can build you wings that might actually work."

I wanted to roll over then, to kiss him, but I was so weary I could only murmur, "I love you," before falling quickly into sleep.

EACH DAY WAS MUCH the same, with a lot of walking, resting while leaning against each other in the dark, and walking some more. If we found a sheltered place to camp for the day, we might have a small fire for tea, but most of the time we drank water and ate cold food. After we ate, we curled up together and fell into exhausted slumber.

I knew that if I asked, Kiernan would go slower, let me rest more often, and even have more frequent fires, but I refused to ask. I knew we wouldn't be safe until we left Aven altogether, and maybe not even then.

Every evening when I woke as darkness gathered, I would

find Kiernan already up, practicing, blades whirling around him and making silver streaks in the gloom. The first night, I only watched, amazed as always by his grace and skill. The second night I took up his twin knives – *my* knives, now, he said – and began to practice, too. He finished the form he was on, then moved closer to join me, gently correcting my posture and then leading me faster and faster through the steps.

"You don't have to do this," he said, when we paused, and I tried to catch my breath. "You already have a long night of walking ahead."

"Yes, I do," I replied. "I told you I want to learn to defend myself, and I meant it. I want you to treat me like a real student."

He nodded. "Will you teach me to spin, then?"

I stared at him, trying to figure out if he was serious or teasing me. His face was blank – in fact, he wasn't even looking at me but was taking up a new starting position and waiting for me to copy him, which meant he was going to teach me a new form. He took my statement seriously, at least.

"You want to learn to spin?" I tried to put my limbs into the appropriate positions.

His lips curled up as he sheathed his blades so he could move one of my arms slightly. "Like this. There will be less strain on your wrist." Then he bent to shift one of my feet. "There." He stood back to look at me. "Balance over both of your feet, remember."

I moved as he directed, and he stepped into place next to me. "I won't really know if I want to learn to spin until I've tried," he said. "But it looks like a useful skill, and I *would* like to try." And then he was moving, and I was too busy trying to follow him to answer.

We settled into a pattern of practicing blade forms each evening before it was quite dark, then having a quick meal before departing. And walking. And walking. Then each morning as it grew light, we made camp, washed if there was water nearby, and I showed him how to prepare wool for spinning and began to teach him how to draft and spin, a little at a time. Soon enough, we ran out of even the wool in Coal's basket and the young serpent had to sleep on spun yarn instead.

It was only a start, but Kier had worked diligently, face serious as he tried to make his lumpy yarn more even. When his fiber got too thin and snapped, he looked up at me and grinned. "I refuse to be outsmarted by a sheep," he said.

"It's too bad we only have one spindle," I replied. "It would be nice to be able to work side by side like we do with our blades. Once we get more wool, of course."

His face lit up and he reached for the bag that held the last of the food we'd brought from the Eyrie. "You can spin this," he handed it to me, and I realized it was still quite full considering we had eaten most of the food. Hidden beneath the empty wrappers was a bit of cloth wrapped around more fiber. Cloud silk from my basket at the Eyrie. It was silver-white and was, of course, my own hair.

"Look underneath," he said, setting aside the spindle he was toying with and picking up one of the food packets to see if there was anything left in it.

I pushed the silk aside and at the bottom of the bag was a spindle of wood with moonsilver fittings. It was not one of mine, but the spindle we had found in the Seer's abandoned rooms.

"Happy Midwinter," Kiernan said.

"It's not Midwinter." I stared at the gleaming wood, smoothed by the hands of the long-ago ancient Seer, and somehow still solid despite the centuries it had lain on the floor of that abandoned room.

"It will be soon enough, and I haven't exactly had a chance to buy you a gift."

"I don't have anything for you," I said, then met his eyes, feeling the prick of tears in mine. "Kier, I was angry at myself for forgetting to take this, for leaving it on the floor like trash."

"You should have said." His touched my face, catching a tear on his finger as it slid free. "I'd have given it to you sooner."

"I didn't want to be annoying."

"I don't think you're capable of being annoying, beloved." He leaned over and kissed me, and I let myself revel in the feel of his lips on mine, of his tongue brushing my tongue. When I reached out to pull at his shirt, he leaned away.

"I haven't bathed properly for days, pretty bird," he said.

"I don't care."

"You will when you smell my armpits." He grinned and I swatted him and would have leaned in for another kiss, only two sinuous shapes streaked out of the sky and into the brush we were camped in.

We return, said Smoke.

We hurried, said Flame.

"Hello, little friends." I held out my arms and both serpents twined around my wrists and climbed to my shoulders.

"You call that hurrying?" said Kiernan, lifting Coal from his basket to greet his mothers. "I was starting to wonder if we should go back to get you."

Not funny, said Smoke, and I wondered if feathered tree serpents understood humor. Every day, they seemed to understand more, to have a better command of language.

"How did your mission go?" said Kiernan. "Is the dryad child safe in the earth?"

Is safe, said Smoke.

Is loved, said Flame.

Love, said Coal, as if he didn't want to be left out.

"Loved?" I stroked Flame's tiny head, then Smoke's.

Many Vogelfolk, said Smoke.

They help, said Flame.

They love, said Smoke. She looked into my eyes and then at Kiernan and purred. *They… slaves…* She paused, as if she was trying to think of the right words or the correct order to put them in.

Bad, said Flame.

"They believe slavery is bad?" said Kiernan.

Slaves bad, said Smoke, her voice conveying agreement.

They care, said Flame.

Humanfolk too, added Smoke.

And others, finished Flame.

That day as the light grew, we curled up together, me and Kiernan and the three serpents, and I felt more hopeful than I had since we left the Eyrie even if I didn't like that Kier kept evading my advances.

"I'm frustrated, too," he said suddenly the next night as we resumed walking. I wondered if we would be walking forever.

"What?" I tried to piece together how he had arrived at that thought and what, exactly, he was referring to.

"I can feel your frustration, pretty bird." He put his hand on my belly, just a brief touch that sent heat through my limbs. "I can feel your desire."

I couldn't see his face in the dark, but I could imagine the curve of his lips and he tried to keep back a smile.

"I don't like not being able to bathe." It came out whinier than I meant, and wasn't quite a response to his comment, or even what I had meant to say.

"I know you hate not being clean." He reached for my hand. We had been walking on the road for the last several nights, since we were far enough from anywhere that travelers were uncommon, even during the day. At night the road was entirely deserted. It meant we made better time, and I tripped much less frequently.

"So do you," I said, squeezing his fingers.

"I hate not touching your skin when we lie next to each other," he said.

"You still can."

He stopped and pulled me close. "I can barely stand to smell myself when I drop my trousers to piss, pretty bird."

"I don't care." I pressed closer and felt him grow hard against my thigh. "Vogel have a poor sense of smell, anyway."

"Liar," he said, his lips brushing mine as he spoke.

"It's true." I traced his lips with my tongue, glad we had at least been able to clean our teeth, even if we couldn't bathe.

"You'd have to have *no* sense of smell with the stench I'd loose if I undressed now. I ran out of clean undergarments days ago."

"Me, too," I said, and bit his earlobe.

"Fuck, Fionn," he said. "I want you. You know I do." He breathed in slowly and then stepped back, turning to lead me along the road again. "We'll be on the coast of Archipelago Bay soon, if the maps I looked at in Great River were correct. There are supposed to be hot springs along the shore, and if there aren't we'll risk it and find an inn somewhere. Most fishing villages have someplace for travelers to stop."

"I hate this."

He didn't stop, but he did look at me. "Which part?"

"Being filthy, and not being able to touch you the way I want to."

"I'm sorry."

"No." I shook my head and he turned back to look the way we were headed. "We can't stop at inns like normal travelers do, I know that. And I couldn't stay at the Eyrie." I walked a way in silence, taking what comfort I could in the warmth of his hand on mine. "There was no choice, and even if there had been, I would still have chosen to leave with you."

"Even knowing you'd go so many days with no proper bath and no sex?"

I snorted. "Even then."

The next day, we both slept badly. My skin itched and I couldn't stop scratching between the feathers on my groin. That evening, we didn't even speak as we practiced, and Kiernan stopped us early in favor of getting back to our journey. It was a long, miserable day, too cold, and with too many rest breaks because I kept tripping even on the smooth surface of the road.

Kiernan didn't say anything each time we had to pause so I could sit. He didn't get angry or even annoyed, but I could feel a tension growing between us that I didn't understand.

Finally, after we had stopped yet again so I could rest, I burst into tears. I tried to stop them; before I left the Abbey, I hardly cried at all, and then only when I was alone and hidden in my bed. He knelt in front of me and took my hands. He didn't say anything; he just brushed his thumbs over my fingers and rested his forehead against mine.

I felt thick and stupid, cranky as a selfish child, but I couldn't stop crying for several long moments. When I finally did, he brushed my tears away and kissed one cheek, then the other.

"I'm okay," I said.

"You're not." His voice was so gentle I almost started weeping again. "Pretty bird." I met his eyes and he smiled. "The smell of the sea is different tonight. I think we've almost reached the Bay." He kissed my forehead. "I even thought I smelled hot water a moment ago. There must be a hot spring not too far off."

"You can *smell* hot water?" It seemed like a stupid thing to say, but it's all that came out of my mouth.

"I can, and I'm fairly sure I did. Which means it's only a little farther, and then there will be hot springs, and maybe a nice spot to camp where we can bathe and wash our clothes and make a proper cup of tea."

I looked into his eyes, searching to see if he was telling me the truth or only trying to make me feel better. I saw no lies, and when we carried on and had walked only a little farther, leaving the road to climb up and down a hill, then up another, we stopped.

The sun was just rising behind us and there at the bottom of the hill was an expanse of sand and sea grass, and beyond that, an enormous bay, so huge the other side looked like a whole different land. It was full of islands in all shapes and sizes, and as I watched, the sun struck a colony of sea birds and they rose into the air like a pale cloud. Their harsh cries echoed across the water to reach us.

Then the bright light of the sunrise cast our shadows dark before us, and I felt disoriented, as if I had been here before, only the sun was in a different part of the sky. My shoulders ached from the weight of my bags and my feet hurt and I was scared. But Kiernan was beside me, holding my hand, and I knew I could believe everything would be okay.

I smiled at him, and he smiled back, and the wind tossed a lock of his hair over his forehead. I reached up to push it back and he flinched even before I touched him.

"I'm sorry, pretty bird," he said. "They still hurt. Like I'm missing part of my skull."

I bit my lip. "I forgot. Even though it's still strange to see you without antlers. How could I forget?"

His smile was small. "You *have* mostly seen me in the dark, lately." Then he turned away to continue down the hill and I followed eagerly to cross the sand to the shore. Off to the right, there were ridges of stone, like the layers of a fancy cake, that came right down to the shore, and to our left the sand and rocks curved far away to meet the open sea.

Where the layers of stone met, the sea had carved fantastic shapes and, as Kiernan had said, caves. Some way away, far enough the thought of walking there made me even more tired, a waterfall cascaded over the edge of one ledge to fall onto another where it formed a pool, then overflowed to fall again, eventually dropping into the sea. Where it met the cold ocean, steam rose.

"Look!" I pointed, and Kiernan paused to see. He had stripped off his pack to stretch and was unbuckling his swords.

"That looks like it comes from a hot spring," he said. "And if there's a spring, it will be a warm place to camp, too. I think I see a cave nearby." He bent to tie his boots to his pack and leaned his swords against it. "We'll rest here a little," he said. "I think that waterfall is farther away than it looks, and it will be nice to bathe our feet in the sea, as cold as it is."

"Okay," I said, too entranced by the sight of the hot water spilling over the edge of the stone to look away for long. I let him take the bags off my shoulders and wrap my cloak tightly around me, then I heard his soft footsteps retreat and the quiet splash as he waded into the waves.

Then I heard a louder splash and wondered if he had decided to swim, despite the danger of getting too cold.

"It's awfully chilly for –" I started to say as I turned to tease him. I stared at the empty beach. Our bags were there, his swords and even his knife leaning against the pile of gear.

Kiernan was gone.

THE
III: DROWNED FOREST

23
Fionn

KIERNAN?" I TOOK A STEP towards the incoming waves. Indents in the sand showed me where he had walked out into the water. "Beloved?" I hated how weak my voice sounded. How afraid.

I pressed my hand below my belly button and felt his presence, still strong. I felt alarm, but not fear. I felt… I couldn't breathe. *He* couldn't breathe.

The clasp holding my cloak shut at my neck stuck as I tugged at it. It finally gave and I dropped the heavy fabric to the sand and waded into the water, fear clutching at me. I was fairly sure I couldn't swim.

"Kier?" I knew he couldn't hear me, but speaking aloud helped me focus. I stared into the water but could see nothing; the rising sun only reflected the too-bright sky at me.

He couldn't breathe. I made myself pause and call on my magic, made myself look with my seer-sight and saw the fine silver ribbon of our bond trailing out into the water, and there, I saw the deep green glow of his forest magic. Near him was something else, something storm-grey and… angry.

I sucked in a deep breath and pushed it out again, wading forward into the bone-numbing water of the bay. I took three steps, and the bottom dropped away beneath me, plunging me under the surface, the frigid salt water closing over my head. I barely had the presence of mind to draw in another breath and hold it before I was submerged.

I nearly lost all that precious air when something flicked across my vision and the blurry sting of ocean water was replaced by crystal clarity. I almost reached up to touch my own eyeballs but managed to shove the surprise aside. That was something for later.

My hollow bones wanted to float me to the surface, but my sodden clothes dragged me down. That was good. I needed to go down; I couldn't look for Kiernan if I was above the waves and he was below. I thrashed my arms against the water and managed to propel myself forward awkwardly, no doubt wasting far too much energy, but I didn't know how else to move.

There was a dark shape ahead. Was it Kier? A sudden current brushed against my skin and the shape vanished, but then there were hands on my arms, pulling me away. Was I being pulled away from shore or closer to it? I no longer knew which way was which and only knew *down* because I was sinking.

I tried to twist around to see who held me, to see if it was Kiernan and I could relax, but I couldn't glimpse anything beyond a shape, dark against the glare of the sun from above. I looked down at the hands that held me, clawed fingers digging into my arms. They were large hands, dark-skinned with bright patches of scales scattered across their backs.

Not Kiernan.

I thrashed again, kicking out with my legs. Now *I* couldn't breathe. I felt fear, but not my own. *I* was angry, suddenly and overwhelmingly. It wasn't Kiernan's fear for himself, either, but his fear for *me*, and that made me angrier. I twisted, trying to find him in the stark bright-and-dark contrast of the water, but the big hands held me tight, like I imagined shackles must feel.

I kicked. I kicked for the surface, desperate to breathe; and kicked out behind me at whoever held me prisoner. I kicked and my talons met flesh.

A burst of bubbles from behind me tickled the back of my neck, my ears, and my scalp. Then another pair of hands gripped my arms, these ones firm but gentle, and I opened my eyes, not realizing I had closed them, and met deep forest green.

Kiernan.

His hands moved away, down to my waist, and I felt a tug at the straps around my thighs as he pulled my knives free. A swirl of water enveloped me as he swam past.

There was more swirling water, currents curling around me, and the hands let go. I kicked again, met flesh again, and used the body behind me to push against, to resist the weight of my clothes pulling me deeper. I aimed for the surface and kicked one more time.

I tasted iron in the water and saw a reddish bloom from the corner of my eye and then familiar strong arms wrapped around me, bronze hands and grey-green wool sleeves. He pulled me to the surface where I tried to breathe but could only cough.

"You're okay, pretty bird," he said, his voice sounding hoarse, like his throat was as scoured by salt as mine felt. He somehow kept both of us afloat despite our heavy garments, somehow got us both to the beach almost exactly where we had entered the water.

I felt a ripple along the surface from behind, but didn't have the energy to turn and look. My feet touched bottom, and I stumbled. Kiernan helped me onto the sand, and I still couldn't breathe properly until I coughed, and a gush of water erupted from my throat. Then I sucked in air greedily, hardly noticing as Kier guided me farther up to dry sand, past the heap of seaweed and detritus that had been left behind by the tide.

He turned me around and held my shoulders, examined me closely, then nodded and let go to pull my knives out of the front of his coat and slide them into their sheaths on my thighs. Smoke and Flame swirled around us in the air and Coal scolded from his perch on Kiernan's pack.

"Get those wet clothes off, beloved," he said, bending to pick up his sword and draw it with the whisper of moonsilver against leather. "Then wrap yourself up in your cloak."

One-handed, he unbuttoned his coat, turning his back to me and facing out across the bay. He stripped off his coat, three layers of shirts, two layers of trousers, and even his undergarment. He stood guard between me and the water, sword held ready, watching, naked and utterly magnificent.

I undressed quickly and pulled my cloak around me, grateful for the soft warmth of the wool. Then I went to him and pressed myself to his back, draping as much of the cloak over him as I could without interfering with his sword arm.

His skin was icy against mine, but pressed together and wrapped in the most luxurious wool the Isle could produce, we gradually began to warm. Slowly, our breathing eased, and I stopped feeling like salt was burning through the lining of my throat.

For a long while, nothing happened, and I was about to suggest we move along the beach. The hot spring beckoned, and there we could get properly warm before looking for a good cave to camp in. But then I saw a ripple out where we had first come up for air. Then another ripple appeared on the calm water of the bay, closer to shore. Another and another, and then a head broke the surface.

He had gleaming dark skin sprinkled with bright orange freckles or scales. His eyes were large and wide and some dark color I couldn't make out from this distance, and his thick brown hair was arranged in twisted locks held back from his face by what looked like golden-yellow coral – though whether it grew from his head or was an added adornment, I couldn't tell.

He was compelling, but something about him made me profoundly nervous – something beyond the fact that he had recently tried to drown me.

"You'll stay away, if you're smart," said Kiernan. All three serpents arranged themselves on his shoulders, reared up, and hissed softly.

"You come into my realm and threaten me, little man?" The stranger's voice was deep and musical, with a lilting accent unlike anything I had heard before. It was the sort of voice that could mesmerize a person, but again, something seemed off, a deep undercurrent of hatred and anger, and I shivered.

"I only waded in to bathe my feet," Kier said. "*You* pulled me in."

The stranger cocked his head, and a wicked smile crossed his face, accentuating his high cheekbones. "Maybe I did," he conceded. "But you made me bleed, when all I wanted was a closer look at the little bird Seer." He turned his eyes to me. "Nobody lives who makes me bleed." His gaze was bright, *too* bright, and there was something feverish in the way he looked at me. I had to force myself not to press closer to Kiernan.

"You could have introduced yourself, like a civilized

person."

The stranger's eyes narrowed. "Will you call me a beast, like the rest of your conquering kin?"

"You look like a man, and you speak like a man, but every beast I know has better manners than you do. So no, I don't think you're anything but a very rude person." I noticed that, as Kier spoke, his words grew a little more formal and his accent more refined, like the rough-mannered Kiernan Druison was transforming into the Prince of Morven Forest right in front of me.

But of course, he wasn't two different people, not really. He only had different ways of approaching the world, depending on circumstances. In his actions, he couldn't be anyone but himself.

"And you look like a little boy with a grown man's tackle," said the stranger.

Kiernan snorted. "I haven't been a little boy for some time."

The man lifted a thickly muscled arm from the water to point at me. Blood dripped from a deep cut across his biceps. "*He* looks like a tasty snack." Then he looked at his arm, as if just noticing the blood. "And now, thanks to you, I'm going to attract sharks, and I'm in no mood to fight off sharks today. They don't even taste good."

"I can heal you," I said, and almost clapped my hand over my own mouth. This man's magic felt strange, and he hated us without even knowing who we were, and yet I felt responsible for his injuries, even if he had been the one to attack us first.

The stranger turned his eyes back on me and I held very still so as not to shudder at the malice in his look. "From all the way over there?" he said. "You must be the Isle's most prodigious healer if you can do that."

Kiernan twisted his neck to look at me. "Pretty bird? Are

you sure?" His voice was soft, and I knew only I could hear him.

"I don't fancy seeing you get eaten by sharks," I said, pressing a hand to the small of Kiernan's back in reassurance. "Come out of the water until the blood clears, and I'll heal you." I put as much confidence in my words as I could, even though I felt exactly none.

"Why?" His voice was challenging, but he drifted closer.

Kiernan didn't lower his sword.

"I told you; I don't want to watch you get eaten."

The man lifted his other arm to reveal a long spear, tipped with pale bone and studded with coral to match that on his head. "I won't get eaten, though I'll make a bloody mess avoiding it."

Kiernan stayed firmly between me and the water, his sword never wavering.

"Do you plan to finish me off, little man?" said the stranger. He paused where the bottom dropped down to deeper water.

"Not if you leave your spear at the water's edge, and don't try anything stupid."

"You think you *could* finish me off?" With a sudden lunge, the man was in the shallows and then at the edge of the sand.

Kier didn't even flinch, even though he must have felt the pinch of my claws when I gripped his arm tighter in startlement.

"I don't *think* I could," Kier said. "I'm quite sure of it."

Out of the water, the man was even bigger than he had seemed. His arms, shoulders, chest, and belly were powerful with muscle. Below the waist, he had even darker skin, a deep brown-black body that didn't split into legs, but instead widened into something like a seal's shape, with two broad flippers and a wide tail. He seemed to be entirely aware of his own fearsome presence, and I found myself blushing and looking away.

"Like what you see, little bird seer?" he said, meeting my eyes when I looked back up. His were deep brown and bottomless, and the strange light in them made me shiver again. He laughed, a deep rumbling I felt in my bones, and laid his spear down just above the reach of the waves.

"I'm heart-bonded," I said, much more lightly than I felt. "I have no opinion on your body." Kiernan's soft snort of amusement was almost inaudible.

I moved cautiously closer to the Siegel man – for what else could he be than one of the sea folk? Now that he was out of the water, I recognized his shape from a book I had read in the Abbey, and I refused to think about how I knew exactly the way his reproductive organs were tucked away below his belly button, in a sheath not unlike my own.

"Careful, pretty bird," Kier said softly, walking with me until the point of his sword tucked under the man's chin. He looked tiny next to the other but faced him calmly. "You even twitch the wrong way, and I end you," he said, a growl in his voice. I felt a flush of pleasure across my skin but shoved the thought aside.

The sea folk man smiled with all his impressively large teeth showing. "You're welcome to try."

"Oh, stop this," I said, suddenly irritated. I was tired and wanted a soak in the hot spring. I wanted to curl up with my lover and sleep, and fuck, and sleep again, and I *didn't* want to deal with dominance posturing. "Hold out your arm."

The Siegel turned his smile on me, and it seemed to soften a little. He held his arm out and I took it between my hands. His skin was surprisingly warm and smooth, the scattered scales making an interesting change in texture. I breathed in, calling on the Realms, and breathed out, sending healing magic into the man's wound.

It was a clean cut from a sharp weapon and as it closed it knitted back together until only a thin line was left to show on his skin, and that would soon fade without even a scar. But as I healed him, I was reminded of how strange he had looked to my seer-sight, how different his magic was, and how even his voice and his glance felt off, as if he was so full of hate it seeped into his very spirit.

Suddenly, I wanted to be very far away.

As I let go and stepped back, he met my eyes again and nodded. I thought I saw respect, along with the anger.

"Will you not heal the damage you did yourself?" he said as I stepped back.

I blinked. "What?"

He gestured at his chest and belly, where two sets of parallel scratches decorated his skin. They were shallow but bleeding sluggishly.

"Oh." My kicks had been more effective than I had realized. I moved forward again, remembering just in time not to bite my lip, and pressed my hands to his chest. He was built like Kiernan, well-developed with muscle, but on a larger scale. I concentrated on healing and ignored the way his skin felt on my palms. The ragged nature of the scrapes made them harder to heal, even though they were much more superficial than the cut on his arm.

Finally, weariness dragging at me as surely as the water had, I stepped back again and let Kiernan guide me away, back up past the tide line. His sword never once wavered.

The Siegel man nodded again, first to me, then to Kiernan. Then, with a sudden kick of sand, he grabbed his spear and slipped back into the water, flicked his tail, and was gone.

With the Siegel man gone, or at least out of sight, I sagged, and Kiernan held me up with an arm around my waist.

"We can rest here if you need to, pretty bird," he said. "But if you can make it, we should head for that ridge where the caves are. I don't think the sea folk can climb up there. They're the wrong shape for scaling cliffs."

I nodded and pulled my cloak tighter around me. I had forgotten how much healing could drain me. I tried to help as Kiernan piled our sodden clothes on top of his pack and shrugged it onto his back, but all I managed to do was get in the way. He pushed me gently aside, then picked up the bags I had been carrying and took my hand. I knew he was tired, too – I could *feel* how tired he was – but I couldn't seem to make my limbs work well enough to do anything more than follow as he led me down the beach.

I had never walked on sand before and might have enjoyed it at another time, but now it made the walking harder. Every step was a fight for stable footing. We could have walked closer to the water, where the sand was firmer, but I didn't think either of us wanted to get that close to where the sea folk might be lurking.

When we reached the bottom of the first rocky shelf, Kiernan left me to climb up with our gear. "I'll be right back," he said, and I watched him climb, moving more quickly now that he didn't have to help me. He paused to look into caves as he walked along the ridge, then climbed higher up to the next shelf, and kept going. He stopped at last, in front of a wide, low opening into the rock. It wasn't quite as far along as the waterfall, but close enough it would be convenient. He dropped everything except one sword, then started back.

I stared at him, gleaming in the sun and completely at ease in his unclothed body. I wished I could have that much confidence in myself. I supposed, though, that the fact that I could enjoy him looking at me now, instead of trying to hide as I used to, was a good start. Eventually, maybe, I would be rid of the Abbess's belief that nudity – even when alone – was sinful.

He moved easily, even though I could see the slight tremors that might be shivering or might be weariness – or might be both. When he climbed back down to me, I wanted to put my arms around him and press our bodies together, but it was all I could do to take his hand again and follow him up the rocky slope. I would never have made it – especially up the steeper second ridge – without his help. Even *with* his help I had trouble, and I was so tired I was hardly conscious of the distance we walked.

Perhaps it was a mercy, because the next thing I knew we were standing in front of a cave entrance and the nearby splashing of a waterfall filled my ears.

"There's a pool at the base of the waterfall," Kiernan said, and I blinked stupidly at him. "It's hot. Get in and warm up while I collect some branches to make a bed in the cave." He walked me along the ridge to where the water hit the stone, collected, and then ran over the side. I looked at it.

Kier snorted, unclasped my cloak to let it fall to the ground, and lifted me in his arms to take me the last few steps. I must have looked ridiculous with my long legs dangling from his arms, but I didn't care. I clung to him, even when he stopped at the edge of the pool, so instead of setting me on my feet, he just stepped right into the water with me.

The heat – not as hot as my pool in the Eyrie or even the baths at the Abbey, but still much more than merely warm – felt delicious on my chilled skin. Kier dunked us both up to our necks and then moved across the pool until the waterfall tumbled down onto the tops of our heads, washing away the travel grime and sea salt.

My eyes blurred, then twitched and were suddenly clear again, even with the water running into them. I buried my face against Kier's shoulder, and he moved us out from under the fall and sat on a ledge under the water with me on his lap.

"Okay, beloved?" he said.

"My eyes." I lifted my head and looked at him. He looked confused a moment, then peered more closely, and grinned.

"That's new."

I blinked and the odd feeling was gone. "What's wrong with them?"

"Have you ever opened your eyes under water before?"

"Only –" I gestured at the bay, "When I got pulled under. It happened then, too."

"You have a second eyelid, pretty bird," he said, leaning his forehead against mine. "Like a… what's that thing natural philosophers use to look at the night sky? A lens. An extra lens to protect your eyes under water." He freed an arm so he could stroke the side of my face. "Though I suppose it's really to protect your eyes when you fly."

I bit my lip and looked away, then remembered I was trying to stop biting my stupid lip, and I frowned instead.

"I know, pretty bird," he said gently. "But you still have all the parts for flying, even if you can't."

"How come I only learned this now? Why did no one tell me?" The hot water was making me sleepy and slow, but Kiernan's naked body was giving mine other ideas.

"Probably because you've never needed them before and… well, I suppose everyone at the Eyrie would assume you already knew."

I sighed. "Are we safe here?"

"I think so. As safe as we can be. I think we should stay a few days, to get a proper rest."

Smoke landed on the ridge and slipped to the edge of the

pool. She sniffed it, sneezed, and launched into the air again, Flame and Coal following.

We guard, she said.

We watch, said Flame.

Protect, said Coal.

"How many words is that now?" I said, drowsing with my head on Kier's shoulder and watching the serpents play in the warm updraft from the pool.

"I've lost count," he replied. "But he seems to learn a new one nearly every day now."

"Will you kiss me, handsome Prince?" I said, lifting my head from his shoulder.

"Handsome Prince?" He smiled and kissed the end of my nose.

"You *are* my fairytale Prince," I said.

"And you're a sleepy bird." He kissed my forehead.

"Not all of me is sleepy." I lifted his hand from where it rested against my hip and pressed it against my sheath, then relaxed my belly muscles to let my erection out.

I smiled at the hiss of his breath when he felt me hard against his palm.

"You don't want to sleep first?" he murmured against my lips.

Instead of answering, I pushed my mouth harder against his, slipped my tongue in next to his, and pushed my hips against his hand.

He smiled and tightened his fingers around me, and for a while there was no more talk of sleeping.

24
Kiernan

I could feel Fionn's exhaustion in my belly, adding to my own until I could have laid down exposed on the cold stone and not cared. But I cared that *he* would suffer. I cared that he was cold and tired and sore, that he was worried about the Siegel returning, so I helped him climb up the ridges and finally resorted to carrying him to the hot spring.

He wouldn't let go of me, even in the water, so I rinsed away the salt and grime and held him in my lap, my heart so full it almost chased away the weariness.

Almost. When he insisted he wasn't sleepy and put my hand on his cock, I stroked him slowly, kissed him softly, and in moments – despite his arousal – he was asleep in my arms.

I stayed in the water until I was certain he was warm and then I lifted him, awkwardly slung his cloak over us both, and carried him to the cave I had chosen. It was dry inside, with a smooth stone floor and an entrance that dipped down at the bottom and flared up at the top, with the next ledge overhanging. If I built a fire in just the right spot, the smoke would be carried out of the cave, but much of the heat would stay in.

Once I had laid him on the floor and tucked his cloak around him, I dragged our gear under the overhang and ventured, as quickly as I could, to the beach below for some driftwood to burn. It lit easily with a spark from my flint and steel. In a moment, I would go back out to cut branches from the nearest clump of fir trees so we wouldn't have to sleep on the stone floor. I slipped under his cloak next to him, chilled from my trip to the beach. In a moment, I would go back out. I needed to wash at least one set of clothes for each of us, so they could dry while we slept. In a moment.

I woke when a cold tree serpent slithered under the cloak and around my neck. I opened my eyes to bright silver. Fionn was awake and watching me, though I don't think he had been awake long.

"Hey, pretty bird," I said, and rubbed my eyes. Everything – every muscle, joint, and tendon, and even my *skin* – ached, and I hated to think how much worse it would have hurt without the hot soak in the spring. Or how much worse it *did* hurt because I'd fallen asleep on a hard stone floor.

He smiled, and it made the aches fade a little. "Hi," he said. "I think I fell asleep before I was done with you."

"And I fell asleep before I had a chance to make a more comfortable bed for you to have your way with me on."

He twined a leg over mine. "We're awake now." His smile grew mischievous.

"Shall I make you a bed of fragrant fir boughs, my heart?"

His lips parted slightly and his smiled faded to a different expression altogether. "Will you make love to me on it?"

This time it was my smile that grew cheeky. "Aren't you hungry, though?" I could feel the emptiness of his belly and my own, twin rumbles that reminded me it had been a long time since we'd eaten.

"I'm *very* hungry." He slid his hands up my chest to wrap his arms around my neck and press his body against mine.

When he kissed me, he pushed me onto my back, onto the cold stone floor, and I flinched away from it, closer to him. He pressed me down harder, his mouth devouring mine, and the cold of the stone only added to the heat of his desire, and I felt like I might melt into nothing. There was nothing more important, just then, than getting as close to him as I could, touching as much of his skin as I could.

"Fionn," I said when he lifted his mouth. "Don't stop."

He studied my eyes, then leaned down to kiss me again, this time so softly it was like a feather brushing my lips. I slid my fingers into his hair and pulled him closer; it was my turn to be hungry, to slide my tongue into his mouth, to moan softly when he abruptly rolled over, pulling me on top of him, and slid his hands down my back to grip my ass.

His claws dug into my skin, and I lifted my head from his mouth to bury it in his neck, to nibble the long lines of muscle and tendon, to taste his earlobe.

"Beloved." He sighed and dug his claws in harder, pulling my ass cheeks apart so I could feel my asshole stretch.

"Tell me what you want, pretty bird," I said, almost a growl, into his perfect, elegantly pointed ear. "Tell me what you want me to do to you."

The sound that escaped him was almost a whimper. He let go of my ass to caress my back, to trail the tips of his fingers over the shape of each muscle, up and up until he reached my shoulders. Then he suddenly rolled again, pinning me under him.

"Tell me what *you* want," he said, kissing his way down my neck to trace my collarbone with his tongue.

I followed the curve of his arm with one hand and ridge of

his spine with the other, brushing over his ragged wings, folded tightly on his back as if he didn't want me to notice them. I stroked one of them again, firmly, not reacting to the feel of the cut edges of his feathers on my palm, trying to tell him with my touch that he was still entirely beautiful.

"I want to make you feel good," I said.

He bit one of my nipples, sharp but not hard, and I sucked in a breath. He kissed it, then sucked gently before lifting his head to meet my eyes. "No," he said. "You always make me feel good. This time, I want to make *you* feel good."

I stroked his hair and arched my spine as he moved across my chest to my other nipple, nibbling more gently this time.

"Goddess Below, you always make me feel good, too. Fionn, touching you, just sitting near you, feels good."

He raised his head again and his pale eyes were hot. "You know what I mean. You never ask for things. I want you to *ask*." He was breathing hard, and I wanted him to keep touching me, to never stop touching me.

"Tell me what you want *me* to do to *you*," he repeated.

"I want —" Too many things swirled through my head, and I couldn't pick out any one of them. I wanted his hands on me, on every part of my skin. I wanted to taste him, to suck him, and I wanted him to taste and suck me. I wanted to fuck him, and I wanted him to roll me over and pin me to the stone with his weight and *take* me, to remind me that I was his and only his.

"What do you want?" He traced my belly muscles with his long fingers, his blunted claws creating a delicious tingle on my skin. "Listen to your body and tell me what it's asking for." He followed the path of his fingers with his tongue, lower and lower until I threw my head back and moaned.

"Fionn. I want —" I reached for his hair, but he didn't touch me again, didn't move his perfect mouth lower to engulf my cock. "Please."

"Tell me," he demanded.

"Fionn."

"Tell me." He flicked his tongue over the very tip of my cock, pushed the skin of my hood back from my head with his fingers, letting them linger where I was most sensitive, and finally slid his lips over me, but only my very tip.

"Goddess, Fionn." The words were probably unintelligible.

He let me feel his teeth, just barely, and I groaned.

"Tell me," he repeated.

"I want – Fuck." I gasped for breath, opened my eyes to find him watching me, one hand teasing my cock.

"Fuck me," I said.

"Pull your knees up."

"No, I –"

He raised an eyebrow.

"I want –"

He sat up, still stroking me, so softly I almost couldn't feel it. His own cock was erect and slick with lubricant and I wanted him in my ass so badly I ached.

I lay limp, staring at him, trying to force myself to move, to talk, to do *something*, but all I could do was look at him.

"You're so fucking magnificent," I managed, finally. "Fionn, I'm yours. Everything I am is yours."

His lips curved up, "I'm yours, too, beloved. Always."

My hands curled, trying to find something to hold onto. One hand found his cloak and bunched it in my fist, and the other found only stone. My claws scraped against rock.

"Take me," I said. "Pretty bird." I panted, my breath harsh and loud. "Roll me over and take me. Fuck me until I can't remember my own name, until I remember only that I belong to you."

He stared at me for a heartbeat, and another, then he crawled over me until he was above me on his hands and knees, not touching me, but close enough I could feel the heat of his skin.

"Beloved," he said. "My Kier. You *are* mine." He bent and kissed me, long and slow, his tongue hot against mine. Then he raised his head and looked at me again, looked *into* me and saw everything I was, and smiled.

"Yes," I said.

"Roll over."

"Yes." It was as if his words freed me to move, finally, and I rolled onto my belly, felt the scrape of cold stone on my cock, and pressed the side of my face into a fold of Fionn's cloak where it lay on the ground.

"Take me," I said.

"Tell me you want me." His voice was as rough as mine, but his hand was soft on the skin of my back.

"I want you, my Seer," I said, and heard his breath hitch.

"I'm your Fionn," he said, and scooped a hand under my belly to lift me up onto my knees.

"You're my Fionn," I repeated, pushing my ass back against his hips. "And my Seer. My Tokka tanKarshanka, and my heart-bonded love."

His hand slipped away from my back, and I tried not to whimper. I heard a soft, slippery sound and then his fingers slipped between my ass cheeks, slick with his lubricant. If I could have decided which deity to pray to, I'd have given thanks then and always for a lover who produced his own lubricant. But then I couldn't even *think*, let alone pray, because his fingers were pushing into my asshole, deeper and deeper until I felt his knuckles against my cheeks. He massaged me, found that spot that feels so fucking good, and I thought for a moment that I might come right then.

"Please," I gasped.

He pressed his lips to my spine and slid his fingers out of me. A moment later I felt the press of his cock on my asshole, rubbing in circles, teasing me.

"Fuck me," I said. "Please, Fionn, I need to feel you inside me."

He pressed forward and I dug my fingers into his cloak, buried my face in the fabric to smell his lingering sweet scent.

"Goddess, yes," I groaned. "Fionn, take me."

He thrust gently and I reached back with one hand to find his ass, to pull him against me harder.

"*Take* me, Fionn," I said. "Please."

"Goddess Above," he whispered, and I felt his first pulse as he throbbed inside me.

"Please, my heart," I said into the cloak. "Fuck me hard."

He gasped at that and pulsed again. "You're mine, Kier," he said, voice ragged.

"Yes. I'm yours."

"I –" He pulsed again. "Goddess." His fingers tightened on my hips, and he thrust harder, faster. "You're fucking mine, fucking Prince of fucking Morven fucking Forest," he said, growling the words. He wrapped an arm across my chest and pulled me up, sat back on his heels, and settled me in his lap, never once stopping his thrusts.

"Yes," I said. "My Fionn, my Seer, I'm yours."

He cried out softly in my ear. "I'm so close. Goddess."

"Fuck me," I whispered in return, too lost in pleasure to yell. "Please don't stop."

He groped at my thigh, found my cock, and wrapped his fingers around it. His hand was still slippery from fingering my ass and his grip slid over me with each thrust into me.

I opened my mouth to say his name again, but all that came out was a groan as he slammed into me, deep and hard, and I felt him pulse again. Then I was gone, too, spunk spurting out onto the stone, pleasure making me stupid.

He clung to me, and somehow, we remained sitting upright for a few more heartbeats before I reached for his cloak and lowered us both onto it, wrapping us in it.

We lay, limbs twined together, staring out at the sky. Most of the day had passed while we slept and more as we fucked, and soon it would be growing dark with evening again.

"I need to cut some boughs for our bed," I said, finally. "And gather more driftwood for the fire."

"Yes," he said. "And we should eat." He laughed softly, his breath tickling my neck. "And bathe again."

I touched his face, no less full of wonder than I had been the first time we made love.

"You said I was magnificent," he said, butting his nose on mine.

"You are."

He licked his lips. "I was thinking that about you." He touched my lips with his fingertips. "Watching you hold your sword against that Siegel man, naked and beautiful."

I kissed his fingers.

We lay a bit longer, until the hard stone finally got too uncomfortable. We bathed again, but quickly, and I left him rinsing our clothes while I unstrapped a hatchet from my pack and climbed the rest of the way up the cliff with his cloak wrapped around me, clasped at the neck and belted at my waist. It probably looked ridiculous, especially as it was too long, but it kept me warm while I walked to the nearest copse of trees to cut fir branches and collect as many of the fall's dried ferns for our bed as I could manage.

When I got back, all our clothing was spread out on the ledge, and some of it was arranged near the fire to dry quicker, and Fionn had made tea and was examining the packets of food I had brought with me from Great River.

I slung his cloak around him and piled up the boughs and ferns, covering them with a blanket.

"How do I prepare this?" he asked, holding up a packet.

I sat next to him. "These ones," I said, pointing out wrapped parcels with a particular knot holding them shut, "You just add to water. They're like dried stew. You can eat them cold, but they're much better hot."

"Oh, that's clever!"

I held out the larger of our pots and he opened the packet carefully and smelled it. After he emptied it into the pot, he started to get up. "We need more water," he said.

I pulled him back down. "Let's use what's left in the waterskin. I want to refill it with fresh water anyway."

We prepared the stew together and ate it right out of the pot, and watched the sky grow dark. Then we settled on our now-comfortable bed, spread Fionn's cloak over us and lay down.

"That Siegel man," Fionn said, tracing the crease between my chest muscles.

"Mmm?" I closed my eyes, enjoying his soft touch.

"He felt… wrong. Angry. Full of hate."

I opened my eyes again. He was frowning, his silver brows crowded close together and his lips pulled down just a little at the corners.

"Hate for us? Why?" I tried to think if I had felt anything off, but I'd been too busy fighting and protecting Fionn to notice anything with my magic.

"I don't know. I used my seer-sight to find you in the water and… he was grey. I've never seen grey magic before. And I could feel how angry he was, so full of it that it tainted his very spirit. I think that the hatred that fills him has twisted his magic somehow."

I nestled my head into his shoulder. "I didn't like him," I said. "But that's because he tried to drown me, and then he tried to swim away with you." I pulled him tighter against me. "And he didn't even thank you for healing him."

"Maybe he didn't think I deserved thanks, since we wounded him in the first place."

"Maybe," I said. I shivered when the serpents swooped into the cave and wriggled between us. Then I raised my head to look at Flame and Coal. "Where's Smoke?"

She guards, said Flame. *We take turns.*

Turns, said Coal.

"Oh, that's good," said Fionn, pulling my head back down onto his shoulder.

"Mmm." This time, *I* fell asleep with my beloved holding me.

I WOKE TO STINGING COLD and cracked open my eyes to see that the fire had gone out. My breath made plumes of white, and I sat up, tucking Fionn's cloak around myself and making sure the blanket still covered him. He stirred and made a sleepy sound, but didn't wake.

Smoke poked her head out from next to his shoulder, and Coal clung to my hair, even as I sat up. His tail dangled down over one eye and I lifted him down and settled him next to Fionn.

Flame guards, said Smoke, and I reached out to scratch her chin before turning to contemplate the fire. I could have sworn I'd left my flint and steel out where I could find them easily, but a quick glance didn't reveal them.

I shifted off the bed of boughs, careful not to disturb Fionn, and crawled to the fire, peering between the chunks of stone I'd arranged around the inner edge of the coals to keep them contained.

"Have you seen my flint?" I said softly.

No see, said Smoke. Coal didn't stir and I thought about poking him awake to see if he could start the fire. He hadn't made flame again since the night he'd melted my candle to a stub, but I knew he *could*. What I didn't know was how feathered tree serpents processed magic, or if it might be dangerous for him to attempt too much, too young.

So I reached for my own magic, breathing slowly in and out to touch the Three Realms as I arranged driftwood and dry tree branches into a good shape for starting a fire. How long had we slept that there wasn't even a single coal left smoldering?

Of course, it hadn't helped that I'd fallen asleep, sex-weary, without making sure the fire was properly banked for the night.

When the wood was arranged in a way I was happy with, tinder and kindling ready to light, I held out my hands, cupped as if I were a child learning to summon wisplights. I closed my eyes and let magic fill me. I breathed it in, Land, Sea, and Sky, and then I reached out and called fire. My palm warmed, and when I opened my eyes, a tiny yellow flame danced there. I tried to transfer it to the tinder, and it just trickled away.

"Fuck," I said softly.

"Kier?" Fionn stirred in the bed, then sat up, pulling the thin blanket tighter around himself. He shivered.

"I'm here, pretty bird," I said. "The fire went out, and I can't find my flint and steel. I can't stop shivering long enough to start it with magic." Also, I simply couldn't call enough magic, or hold onto it long enough, but I didn't say that part out loud.

He crawled over to sit next to me. "Let me help. I can call

flame."

"I know," I said. "I know. I was just hoping my magic was strong enough I could do it myself."

He leaned his head on my shoulder. "I'd love that," he said. "But I'd also love if we didn't freeze to death while you try."

That stung, though I knew he didn't mean it to. I just hated that I couldn't even call the magic a child could use. When *I* was a child, I had called fire so easily it was frightening. I'd set fire to a lot of things that shouldn't even have been able to burn before I learned to control it, to lock it away in the core of my spirit.

Forest magic was my deepest heart, but my spirit was fire and shadow, and I had been able to call on all of them from the first moment I touched my magic.

Fionn took my hands in his, cupping his under mine, and I felt him call his own magic as clearly as I had felt mine. He poured it *through* me and for a moment I could use his magic as I had not been able to use my own. With his help, I summoned a big, bright flame and transferred it to the tinder, which caught easily and spread to the kindling with a snap and crack.

I swallowed, hard. "Thank you, pretty bird. That was sure a long way from setting my Queen's favourite couch on fire."

He smiled and squeezed my fingers. "We'll be okay. We make a good team."

"I have a thought about that," I said, following when he crawled back to bed and settling next to him again. I was awake now and thought about getting up to practice forms on the ledge outside the cave. But Fionn was warm and soft and smelled nice. I kissed his shoulder, then tucked the blanket and his cloak over him.

"What was your thought?" he asked.

"We're connected," I said, kissing his cheek. "Magically."

"Yes, by our heart-bond." He pushed away a curl that fell over my forehead and threatened to poke me in the eye.

"What if…?" I put my hand on his chest over his heart and felt it beating, strong and sure. "What if that bond is why you called shadows, and why I… Why you *saw* me in a future vision, blind but using seer-sight to see, like Siona does. Maybe you borrowed my magic, and I borrowed yours. Maybe that's why you can use my named blades without burning your hands."

He cocked his head slightly and his eyes went unfocussed, so I knew he was thinking, especially when his eyebrows drew together. "Like our magic is… blending? We're connected, so our magic is, too? That seems… reasonable," he said. He opened his mouth to say more, but a sudden gust made the fire flicker, and then a rush of soft sound filled the cave as it began to rain large, hard drops that hit the stone in great splashes. Then whatever else he might have said was drowned out completely as the rain turned to a downpour.

25
Fionn

Tʜᴇ sᴏᴜɴᴅ ᴏғ ᴛʜᴇ ʀᴀɪɴ muffled what I had been about to say, and almost as soon as the large drops turned to a torrent, one every wet, very annoyed feathered tree serpent fled into the cave and burrowed into my cloak.

Is wet, said Flame.

Kiernan smiled and sat up to poke the fire and check that we had enough wood to last a good while.

"Oh!" I said, sitting up behind him. "The clothes!"

We both stared out the mouth of the cave. The water was falling so thick I could barely see the ledge outside.

Kiernan sighed. "Well, we can't leave them out there." He got to his feet and let the blanket fall.

"No, I suppose not. Not unless we want to go around naked for the next few days."

He turned a grin on me. "I'm happy to be naked with you, pretty bird, as long as I don't have to leave the warmth of the fire."

I poked my tongue out at him and got up. Together, we

ducked out of the cave and were immediately drenched. The water was colder than the ocean had been, and I started to shiver almost immediately. I couldn't help but laugh, though, as I grabbed trousers and shirts and undergarments and bundled them in my arms without even looking to see what they were.

Through the blur of falling water, I saw Kier doing the same, laughing as he grabbed sodden clothing off the ledge, and shivering at the downpour on his bare skin. Fortunately, we hadn't brought that many clothes with us, since we had to carry it all, and it didn't take long to gather everything.

I almost walked into him as we both ducked back into the cave. He dropped his armful on the floor with a wet plop.

"We should wring them out," I said. "Or they'll take forever to dry." He took my bundle and dropped it next to his, then pulled me into his arms and closer to the fire.

"Warm up first," he said. "You're shivering."

"So are you." I pressed close to him, close to the heat of the fire. He let go long enough to grab a cloth that had been hung overnight on top of his pack and rubbed me dry with it, ruffling my hair until it must have been sticking up in all directions, but wiping carefully over my feathers.

I laughed and snatched the towel away to dry him in turn. Then I hung it up again and pulled one of the blankets off the bed to wrap us in, accidentally disturbing the serpents, who looked at me in annoyance.

Pressed close together and slowly turning in front of the fire, the icy chill gradually left our skin.

"No regrets?" Kiernan said, his voice barely audible over the rain.

I shook my head. "I would still have left."

He smiled and shifted position to slide his fingers into the damp feathers on my back. "Even if you knew you'd be dragged into the ocean by sea folk and end up cold and miserable in a cave?"

"Even then." I adjusted the blanket to block a draft that was tickling my backside with cold air. "And I'm not miserable." I kissed him, letting my lips linger. "Though I might be once we finish wringing out all those wet clothes."

His fingers were soft on my face as he stroked my cheek. "I wouldn't be anywhere else," he said.

"Even if I wasn't here?" I teased.

His face was smiling, but his voice serious. "If you weren't here, I wouldn't be either." His eyes moved over my face, intent, and I wondered what he was looking for. He traced my eyebrow with one finger like it was the most wondrous thing he'd ever seen, and my face flushed.

"When I was following Jinta through the city," I said, and his eyes met mine. "He took me to see another Seer. A human man."

"Did he welcome you, this Seer?"

I nodded. "He told me that Seers look out for each other, protect each other, that we even keep one another's secrets." I licked my bottom lip and Kier's eyes flicked to my mouth, then back to my eyes. "He said our first loyalty as Seers is to other Seers, because we are the ones who must help the powerless."

He nodded, some of the seriousness leaving his face. "Siona said something like that to me once, though she couldn't tell me anything more because I'm not a Seer myself."

"Maybe you should have been."

His finger left my eyebrow to brush across my upper lip, then my lower, and I tightened my arms around his waist.

"What else did the Seer tell you?"

"He wanted to help me. He could feel my… my hurt, and he wanted to help me heal. Only I couldn't tell him about all the things that happened to me. I wanted to, but the words wouldn't come out."

He moved his other hand from under the blanket to cup both around my face. When his thumbs brushed my cheeks, I realized I was crying. Then he blinked rapidly, and I realized *he* was crying, just a few large tears. "Pretty bird," he said softly, and his voice was sad.

"He said he could read me, if I would allow it, so I wouldn't have to speak. I let him." I turned my face, so my cheek pressed against his palm. "He could see how much I was hurting, and it felt… it felt good to let someone else *see*, even though I was ashamed." I sniffed and my voice dropped to a whisper so soft I wasn't even sure he would hear. "I was so ashamed."

He stroked my hair and held me close. "You have nothing to be ashamed of, beloved."

"I know. In my head I know that, but I still *feel* it."

He stroked my back, my ragged wings, and kissed my forehead.

"After he had read me, had seen everything that had happened to me, that my King did to me, what he said was…" I pressed my forehead harder against his. "He said that you and I are worth fighting for. They we, together, are worth everything we have gone through."

"He said that? Even though he's never met me?"

"He saw what you are to me, and I felt how strongly he believed his words. Kiernan, I must believe that we two – I won't say we're *meant* to be together, because I refuse to believe in fate."

"Our choices *do* matter, my heart," he said, his voice strong with conviction.

"I *do* believe you and I can be… can be more together than we are alone." I leaned away just enough to see his face again. He wasn't crying, but his eyes were still bright.

"You make me believe we can be, too," he said.

I nodded. "I don't think the Seer meant our magic; I think he just meant… how we can change the world, and help people. But I think our magic is stronger when we're together, too."

"You helped me make fire when I can barely use my magic at all, pretty bird." He smiled again. "I think you could be right." Then he sighed. "If I could use my magic, I would ask the water to leave those clothes, and we wouldn't have to wring them out one by one and spread them all over the cave to dry."

I laughed. "Would you use magic to do such mundane tasks?"

"Usually, no, but I very much want to lie down in bed with you right now, and I very much *don't* want to do laundry."

"Well, the sooner we do laundry, the sooner we can go to bed."

So we tackled the wet clothing and then huddled, again, in bed together, after digging through the blankets to make sure we weren't about to crush a tree serpent beneath us.

I watched Kiernan as he got up to add wood to the fire and pile up the coals to keep it going as long as possible. When he turned back, he saw me watching him. I met his eyes and – feeling daring, as if he hadn't already seen me naked and wanton many times – I slowly pushed the blanket down, running my hands over my body as I did.

"Fionn," he said, his voice low and rumbly. Backlit by the fire, he was little more than a shape to my day-dweller's eyes, but it was a familiar and beautiful shape.

"Kier," I replied, pushing the blanket lower and stroking

my hands over my belly.

He shifted closer, but not to lie down with me. Instead, he sat on the end of the bed, stretched his leg out next to mine, and picked up one of my feet. His hands were warm from the fire, and his fingers strong as he rubbed my sole.

"Are you warm enough, with no blankets?" he asked.

"I'm a bit flushed," I said, and ran my hands over my thighs, pushing the blanket the rest of the way off.

"Are you trying to torment me, beloved?" he said and raised my foot to his mouth to kiss the delicate skin right in the middle of my sole. Then he kissed my ankle.

"Do you want me to stop?" I stroked my hands back up to my belly and traced the seam of my sheath with one finger.

"Goddess, no." His hands moved to rub my calf. I shifted my other leg to stroke his thigh with my foot and he drew in a quick breath. He traced his fingers back down my leg to brush across the bones of my ankle, then draw over the bottom of my foot, making me stretch out my toes. He smiled and did it again.

I let my thighs fall apart and touched the feathers of my groin with one hand and the inside of my thigh with the other. His eyes followed my movements, and his breath hitched when I stroked my seam again and my fingers came away moist with lubricant.

"Pretty bird." He lifted my foot again and this time his tongue slipped between my toes, to that place that should not have felt so sexual, but did, intensely. It was my turn to gasp.

I bent my other knee and pulled my foot closer, dipped two fingers deep into my sheath and spread the lubricant between my toes and on my sole. He watched me, eyes bright with curiosity and tongue pulling absurd amounts of pleasure from my toes that zipped up my leg to my groin until I couldn't keep my erection in any longer.

I stretched out my leg again and pushed apart his thighs with my foot, sliding my toes into his crotch. He was already hard, and wrapping my toes around his length made him even harder.

"Fuck," he whispered. "Oh, fuck." I adjusted the grip of my toes so his erection was sliding between them and slipped my rear toe between his legs, between his buttocks, squeezing his testicles against my heel and settling my toe against his anus. "Oh, Goddess," he groaned, closing his eyes. "Fionn."

"Kier," I said, and he opened his eyes and followed my gaze when I looked down at myself. As soon as I knew he was looking, I touched myself, slid my palm over my erection and stroked, slowly down and up and down again.

I moved my foot in time with the rhythm of my hand, stroking him as I stroked myself.

He kissed the inside of my ankle and held my foot in both hands, sliding his thumbs between my toes, and then his tongue. When the sensation he caused tingled up my leg to my crotch it brought with it my first pulse, slow and warm, creeping up from my toes to my testicles and then my erection, finally erupting in a spurt of semen onto my belly.

I made a sound I think I intended to be, "Oh!" but it came out as more of a soft moan. Kiernan answered with a rumble from his throat that I felt between my toes as he licked here again. Warm tingling spread though my leg again and I quickened the movements of my hand and the foot that gripped Kiernan's hardness.

"I am very thankful," he murmured against the sole of my foot, "to all three of the Goddesses, that my beautiful lover has such long and flexible toes."

My second pulse came like the first, slow and warm, but I spurted more and harder, filling my belly button and decorating my stomach with pearly white fluid.

My third pulse came faster, burning up both legs from where his thumbs and his erection rubbed between my toes and erupting through my groin with more force and more semen, leaving me splattered to my ribs.

"You're fucking beautiful," he said, rocking his hips against my foot and grinding his behind onto my toe until my toepad pushed open his anus. I didn't dare slide my toe inside him, for fear of hurting him with my long talon, but the movement of my toepad against him, circling him and rubbing, made him moan and gasp, and thrust between my toes until I felt my fourth pulse build and build and I couldn't stop the arch of my back or the rubbing of my own hand, couldn't – didn't even try – to stop the cry that tore from my throat as I pulsed and splattered myself to the sternum.

He let go of my foot and braced an arm behind himself to thrust harder between my toes. "Fionn," he said, then he stiffened, and I felt his erection throb in my grip and watched the semen spurt from him to splatter my foot.

I lay, panting, and he sat, chest heaving. We stared at each other. I licked my lips, hesitant then, as if he might decide he didn't like what we had just done, despite the obvious pleasurable result.

But he swallowed and grinned, and gently uncurled my toes from his crotch, reached for a handkerchief that was drying nearby, and wiped my foot clean. Then he crawled up the bed to wipe off my belly and chest and pull the blankets over me.

"Kier?" I said as he turned away. He looked back at me and the smile he gave me was so full of love I almost gasped aloud.

"I'm going to add wood the fire," he said, "And see if I can make it so it won't burn out while we sleep."

"Okay." I watched as he worked and even though he was

only a few minutes, I fell asleep before he returned.

"Look, pretty bird." Kiernan's voice pulled me out of sleep, soft but full of delight.

I opened my eyes and blinked at how bright it was. How long had I slept?

"What is it? Is it day already?"

"Only sunrise."

It was still cold, but the fire was crackling and snapping, and I could feel its heat on my skin.

"Why is it so bright?"

"Come look." He twisted around and tossed me a shirt. It was dry and warm from hanging near the fire all night. I pulled it over my head, stuffed my arms into the sleeves, and settled it between my wings, then crawled over to where he sat just under the overhang of the ledge above. Our breath made white clouds to match the white that blanketed the beach outside. Sometime during the night, the rain had turned to snow.

"Oh!" I said.

The sky was vivid pale blue, and the sun must have been a burning disc behind the cliff to make the snow so bright it was hard to look at. The sea looked nearly black in comparison, except where ripples and waves caught the light in bright shifting lines and curves.

I didn't want to look away from the wonderland the snow had made, but I was also tired of being cold, so I turned back to the fire and pulled on the rest of my clothes.

By the time I was dressed, Kiernan had buckled on his weapons and was standing just outside the cave waiting.

He held my belt in his hands and wrapped it around my

waist, handling me like I was something precious. I did up the clasp on my cloak as he did the buckles around my legs. Then he held out a hand and we stepped out into the bright morning.

I looked over at him and saw his face relaxed and content and knew that this was a small glimpse of that elusive thing we had both being trying for since we met. Just this, the simple joy of getting up in the morning with the one you love, and helping each other dress, and going for a walk in the fresh air, hands clasped.

He noticed me looking and turned to smile at me.

"I love you," I blurted, and his smile broadened to a grin.

"My beloved," he said, and helped me climb down the ridges onto the beach. The cold had rendered the sand hard, and it made a firm footing. "Practice?" he asked.

I nodded and slipped off my cloak to hang it from the roots of a driftwood log then moved into place beside him.

"That's good," he said as we finished the first form. "Now see if you can go a little faster." We went through the form again and sped up, and I pushed aside the thought that I wouldn't be able to do it correctly if I tried to go faster.

When we finished, he stopped me with a hand on my arm. "Let's try something different," he said. "Instead of face-to-face to simulate combat, we'll go back-to-back, as if we were fighting a foe together." His hand slid to my elbow. "You won't be able to see me most of the time, so you'll have to try to *feel* where I am."

I shook out the arm he wasn't holding. "Like seer-sight?"

He cocked his head. "A bit like seer-sight, but you're not trying to look so deep, only widen your awareness." He let go of my arm to brush his fingers across my cheek. "Ready?"

"Ready."

He shifted his sword from holding both in one hand to one

in each again and stepped into place behind me. I tried to feel out where he was without fully committing to seer-sight.

"With enough practice," he said, "You'll be able to sense not only me, but those you're fighting as well."

"That's how you seemed to know where Sean and Padraig were, when the Queen made you put on a show for my delegation."

"I had no magic then, so I had to manage without. Now begin." I almost messed up the first steps when I *felt* him move, but managed to get them right, if a little shaky, and brought up my arms for the first lunge.

As I fell into the rhythm of movement and got used to *feeling* Kiernan move too, I wanted to laugh out loud in delight. We stepped and swung and thrust, we lunged and skipped back and slipped to the side, and the whole time, I felt him there, keeping pace, moving as I moved, as if we faced an invisible foe together, our motions compensating for each other's vulnerabilities.

And I understood in a way I never had before the joy and calm that Kier found in studying bladework. It was something like I found in spinning, but also nothing like it at all. When he reached the final move and went still, I was flushed and panting and completely at peace.

We remained in the final position for a long moment, the world still around us, catching our breath. Then as one we straightened and turned around. Kier's face echoed the peace I felt and I didn't want to spoil it with words, so I slipped my knives into their sheaths, letting a smile show as I managed it without looking, and moved closer until my chest brushed against his.

He looked up at me, his lips slightly parted, waiting to see what I would do. I leaned down and touched my lips to his. The tip of his tongue flicked out and traced my lower lip, so I kissed him more firmly and tilted my head to one side to fit my mouth on his more tightly.

He moved closer, just a half-step that pressed his chest hard on mine and opened his mouth to my tongue. I was happy, filled with a sort of contentment I had felt only once before, briefly, when we were sheltering at Moira and Col's house in the werewolf village, just figuring out what we meant to each other.

I pulled away a handswidth and rested my forehead on his. Neither of us said anything. There was no need for words. Everything was perfect right then, even if we both knew it was fleeting, that more hardship would come before we found lasting peace.

Then I felt the brush of magic and jerked my head up just as Kiernan leaned to look past me and out into the bay.

"Fionn," he said, softly, a warning in his voice. "We seem to have company."

I turned slowly and he moved to stand next to me, swords still bare and gleaming in the sun.

Out in the bay, between the shore and the nearest island, was a group of sea folk, only their heads showing above the waves. For a moment they just watched us and when they saw we had seen them, they began to move closer.

Though my night sight was poor, my daylight vision – including distance – was excellent, especially in light this strong and clear. I saw that one of the approaching Siegel was the one we had met the day before. He swam with two other men and two women, and ahead of them was a man who looked enough like him they were probably brothers, or relations of some kind. The coral around this man's face had gleaming golden tips, and swirls and curls of the same metal made a sort of crown on his head and around his cheeks.

What caught and held my attention, though, was the

woman swimming next to the golden-crowned man. She had a narrower face and much paler skin and long, twisted hair the color of steel, not quite as close to silver as mine. She looked at me curiously with shining silver eyes.

26
Kiernan

THE PALE ONE IS A SEER," Fionn said quietly. I could hear the excitement in his voice, tinged with caution, and felt it in my belly.

"She's silver, like you," I said, keeping my eyes on the approaching sea folk. I realized that greeting these people with drawn swords might been seen as a threat, so I sheathed them one after the other, knowing that they could see me do it without taking my eyes off them. And hoping they knew that meant I knew what I was doing with a blade.

Fionn shifted closer to me, but not so close as to be touching me.

"Okay?" I said.

"Yes. Just nervous."

I didn't smile, though I wanted to. I could feel his anxiety, but only through our bond. In every other way he appeared calm, collected, and serene. With one hand, I reached for his cloak, then deliberately took my eyes off the approaching sea folk to drape it over him and do up the clasp. I smoothed it over his shoulders and adjusted the way the hood lay. If the sea folk had spent any time among land-dwellers, they would know exactly the message I was sending them.

By turning away as they approached, they knew I didn't see them as a threat. By taking the trouble to put Fionn's cloak on him and making sure he was warm, they would know he was my priority. They would know I respected and cared for seers, and that *this* Seer was especially important to me.

It might have seemed like revealing a weakness to some onlookers; by letting them know what was most important to me, I was also showing them how to hurt me. But I was betting that they also revered their Seer. And it was a warning that if they tried to hurt him, they would suffer.

I turned back to face them, to show courtesy by not keeping my back turned on them. I stood side-by-side with Fionn to show that we were equals.

They paused in the water where the bottom dropped off, just a few paces offshore.

"A bright morning and calm seas to you," said the Siegel Seer, glancing from the man with gold around his face to us. She had the same lilting accented Islish as the man from yesterday had.

"Good morning," said Fionn.

I inclined my head.

The Seer rose a little out of the waves as she came closer, climbing up into the shallower water. She wore no clothing except a small carry pouch tied around her waist and, though she had small breasts, she was otherwise nearly as heavy with muscle as the men.

"I am the Seer of Archipelago Bay," she said. "And this is our King." She offered no names, and I remembered one of my lessons with the diplomacy tutor my Queen had hired for me. The sea folk considered names to be sacred and used only titles with anyone other than their close family and friends. It meant everyone among their people had some kind of title.

"I am…" I hesitated, not really wanting to reveal myself if I didn't need to, but unsure of how else to refer to myself that wouldn't be seen as deception. I decided to gamble on the truth. Fionn and I would be found out eventually, anyway, and I doubted the Siegel were going to spread gossip about us. My studies informed me that, although they welcomed outside news, the Siegel seldom bothered to associate with land-dwellers.

"I am the Prince of Morven Forest," I said. "And this is the Seer of the Eyrie." I touched Fionn's arm and let my hand slide down until I wrapped his cold fingers with mine.

The Seer's eyes widened slightly when she saw me take his hand, and her lips curled into the barest smile. "We have heard of both of you, even here in our waters. I would not have expected to find you together, however."

The King of Archipelago Bay climbed into the shallower water next to his Seer, not trying to hide his curiosity as he looked at me. The Seer tilted her head, as if listening, then said, "My King says he has heard that you were in Great River acting as Morven Forest's ambassador, Prince of the Woods. He asks me to read you to find out how you came to be here, and I have told him you would probably prefer to be asked instead."

"I am glad you didn't simply try to read us without asking," said Fionn, his voice cool and regal.

The Seer turned her eyes to him and inclined her head in respect. "That would have been rude," she said. "He asks only because it is how we communicate in the water. He forgets, sometimes, that land-dwellers prefer to speak aloud and have no need to touch minds in open air." She looked back at me. "Our King has had no speech since birth, but in the ocean, it hardly matters."

I nodded. "We're here because my Seer desired to leave the Eyrie."

She smiled. "And yet, he is not *your* Seer. That he decided to leave the Eyrie explains why *he* is here, or at least why he is not there. But what of yourself?"

"Does my business concern the sea folk?" I said it mildly, not wanting to offend, but also needing it to be clear that what we did was our business and no one else's.

"Perhaps not," the Seer said. "Only you encountered one of our warriors, and I hear it was not a friendly meeting."

I shifted my gaze to the five people behind the Seer and the King and focused on the one who had tried to drown me yesterday. He met my gaze with disinterest, no reaction at all on his face.

"It's hard to feel friendly towards someone when they drag you into the sea and try to prevent you from breathing again." I looked back at the Seer. "It's especially hard to feel friendly after they try to steal your companion."

The Seer's eyes flicked to our joined hands, then back to my face. "Companion?" A smile touched her lips.

"Among other things," I said.

"You are heart-bonded." She said it as if it was an obvious fact, and perhaps to a Seer it was. Perhaps to a Siegel it was. "When our Royal Warrior returned to tell me, I did not believe him."

"Why not?" said Fionn. "Heart bonds are rare, but they do exist."

"Of course," said the Seer, turning a brief smile on her King before looking back at Fionn. "All First Peoples have heart bonds, though it is, as you say, rare and precious. But this is the first I have ever heard of anyone heart-bonding with another people. Especially someone who is *not* from a First

People, but from a colonizing people."

"Perhaps the spirits are telling us that the only way to achieve real peace and prosperity for all peoples is to join together and work for it, whether our ancestors arose here, or whether they arrived on a ship generations ago."

The Seer's smile grew into something genuine and friendly. "That is something to think on, for certain. Will you walk with me? I would speak in private, Seer to Seer."

Fionn looked at me. I could feel his uncertainty, but to anyone observing he would simply look like he was asking me to wait where I was. I let go of his hand, bowed slightly, and stepped back.

"I'm afraid my people don't speak mind-to-mind," I said. "Except our seers. So I won't be able to have much of a conversation while you're gone." I directed my words as much to the King as to the Seer.

The Seer gestured at the others of their people, who waited in the deeper water. "One of them can interpret." She looked more closely at me. "Or…" She glanced at her King. "My King can attempt to teach you, if you are willing."

I met the King's eyes. They were blue and stood out in his handsome face like a patch of clear sky in a storm. If a smiling face could be said to resemble storm clouds, which it really didn't. There was good reason I was not a poet.

I had been trained very young to hide my most vulnerable self and to lock my thoughts away if I needed to. Siona was kind and gentle but could be a tough teacher when she needed to be, as she had with the wild creature I had been as a child.

"I would like that," I said.

As Fionn walked along the beach, placing his feet carefully on the icy strand, and the Seer paralleled him in the water, I stepped closer to the King and relaxed my guard, allowing my surface thoughts to be revealed.

Hello, I tried, and the King beamed.

You have a strong mind, he said. *I don't think I've ever spoken this way with a land-dweller on the first try.*

I've had excellent teachers. I didn't elaborate, but it was not only Siona I was thinking of. My Queen had made sure to test me frequently and the consequences of letting her know my thoughts were never pleasant. She could probably break into my mind even now, if she cared to exert the effort, but thankfully she hadn't tried in years. Her attempts to read my thoughts, it seemed, had given me better control over them in other ways.

I apologize for the actions of my brother, the King said. *He is…* He glanced over his shoulder and the Siegel man from yesterday glared at us both.

"*He* is standing right here," he said, as if he would not deign to touch minds with a mere fey.

He does not enjoy mindspeech, the King said, ignoring the anger in his brother's tone. *Especially with people he does not know.*

"Tell him," the Royal Warrior said. "I'm an embarrassment and a lunatic and you only keep me around because I'm a blood relative."

The King shook his head and ignored the other man. *Will you stay in the cave, or are you traveling?*

We haven't decided, I said, opting again for honesty. Likely I would never meet the King – or any sea folk – again once we left here, but if I could make an alliance, however tentative, I wasn't about to walk away from it. *I have kin, of a sort, among the Huldr.* I had originally planned to avoid Huldr lands, but the longer we travelled the more I realized we were going to have to seek refuge somewhere.

Ah, yes. The King sounded interested, as if courtly gossip was a favorite topic. I didn't suppose there was much courtly gossip to be had in his palace at sea. Not inter-Monarchy gossip, at least. *It is said that the Queen of Morven Forest had an alliance with a Huldr Lord, an engagement she had to break off before marrying the General of Dudoon.*

I considered not answering; my family arrangements were really no one's business. But then I didn't particularly care what people thought of my mother.

My sisters' father is Huldr, I said.

She builds quite a web, your Queen.

I looked at him sharply, but his face was open, and a gentle smile pulled his lips upwards. He looked at me, then at the bright morning sky. *Huldr, human.* He gestured down the beach at the two Seers, heads bent in conversation. *Her only son allies with the Vogel. Your human kin build relations between their Monarchies in Aven and Morven.*

I had to think about that last one, but then I remembered that my uncle, King Iain, had married the daughter of the King of Floodplains, the human Monarchy across the river in Aven.

"You'd think she was angling to take over the whole Isle," growled the Royal Warrior, and his King turned to scowl at him.

Now, brother, he said, mildly. He turned back to me. *He does have a point, though. You will have heard the prophecy, I imagine.*

That took me aback. The only prophecies I was aware of were in fairy tales and fiction. Prophecy was too much like fate for my taste. Even Fionn said his visions of the future changed as we made choices. If the future could change, what good was a prophecy?

I don't deal in guesswork I replied, though that wasn't entirely true. I had studied battle tactics with my father, and what was that but educated guessing?

He laughed, and it was deep and rich and merry. This man seemed far too *nice* to be a Monarch. Though I suppose his angry, glowering brother balanced out his goodness somewhat. For a moment, I even thought I could feel the man's hate and anger that Fionn had sensed, through the openness of my surface thoughts.

When your Queen agreed to marry the General of Dudoon, she also agreed to produce an heir to two Monarchies, and she has never made it a secret that she intends to marry you to whomever will add another Monarchy to her tally. He looked down the beach at the two Seers. *I cannot imagine she is pleased that you heart-bonded with a Seer and not a royal.*

I tried not to stare at him. What he said made no sense. Sure, I was a *Prince* in two Monarchies, but I wasn't heir to either of them. And while I knew my Queen intended to use me, and my future spouse, to her own advantage, I doubted any Monarch would hand over their own heir for that purpose. Not to a younger sibling.

She doesn't know yet, I finally said.

The King's smile grew as he watched my face. *Perhaps I am mistaken,* he said. He gazed down the beach at where his Seer had come out of the water and was bending over Fionn, their foreheads pressed together and their eyes closed, as if they were sharing an unspoken communion.

I am not a particular friend of the King of the Eyrie, he said.

Nor am I. I watched Fionn, a thought coming into my head unbidden. No one knew besides Fionn and Councilor Rocsh, but Fionn was his King's oldest child and as his son – legitimate or not – he should by Vogel law inherit the throne of the Eyrie upon King Sarkot's death. And Sarkot *was* dead. For a moment, I felt like I couldn't breathe because of what that might mean for the two of us.

Once, we of the ocean and those of the sky were on good terms, as we were with the Hirsch of the Plains. But the fey and human Monarchies separate us and keep us from ever joining against them.

I frowned. I had never considered the geography of the

Isle in that light, but it was true. At least one human or fey Monarchy physically separated the Monarchies of the First Peoples from each other.

Would you ally against us? I said, more curious than alarmed. Of course I wanted to protect my people, but not at the expense of other innocents.

The King snorted, the first actual sound I had heard him make. *Only if necessary for self-preservation. War benefits only the wealthy and the strong. I would much rather all our peoples on the Isle could find a way to co-exist. I believe, as your Seer does, that it is the best way to bring prosperity to us all.*

Behind him, the Royal Guard snorted, too, only his was a sound of disagreement and disgust, not amusement.

Fionn and the other Seer were moving again, heading back along the beach towards us. Something in their conversation had excited Fionn and I could feel a crackle like static in my belly.

Even without a heart-bond, you would love him, the King observed.

Yes.

But you didn't say if you knew the prophecy.

That again. I had already forgotten, but obviously it was of interest to the King. *Tell me, if you would.* I kept my eyes on Fionn, not caring if my joy showed on my face, not caring if I was grinning like a love-sick fool.

There is a sword, he said, and then I did look at him.

The Sword of Dragons, I replied.

You have *heard of it.*

I shrugged. *In legends and fairy stories. They say whoever wields it will unite the Isle, maybe even all of An, under one ruler and bring about a golden age for all.*

Indeed, the Prince Who Will Unite An. And does that not seem like an event to work towards? he asked

The Sword of Dragons is a myth. Something from the realm of ancient gods, not something for the here and now. And the last thing the world needs is one person telling everyone else how to live.

He laughed, and no sound came out, but his shoulders shook slightly, and his mouth opened in mirth. I thought I could come to like this King very much.

Yes, it is a myth, but some Seers believe there is truth in it. They – and I – believe the sword exists and if it is found and brought together with the other legendary weapons, the people will unite behind its bearer, because in their deepest hearts, all of our people want peace.

I frowned at his mention of other legendary weapons. Perhaps I hadn't read enough fairytale books as a child – I had had a favorite I read over and over until the Archivist had to re-bind it – but the Sword of Dragons was the only one I knew.

I looked away towards the sea. *Speaking of ancient blades.* I pulled out the knife sheathed at my waist and before I could hold it out, the big Royal Warrior had lunged out of the water and levelled his spear at me. He would have impaled me if I hadn't felt him coming and moved out of the way.

I heard Fionn shout from down the beach and held out a hand to reassure him. I was about to knock the spear aside and go for the Warrior's throat when the King said, *Enough!* with sufficient force to make my ears ring, though he had made no actual sound.

The Warrior scowled but allowed his King to push him back into deeper water.

I resisted the urge to stick my tongue out at him and turned back to the King, flipping the blade around to hold it out to him hilt first.

He looked at it curiously, reaching out to touch the antler handle, but he didn't take it. *I wondered if this blade was still among the humans somewhere,* he said.

You know it? My father gave it to me. He said it once had two others to match.

Indeed, I know of it. He dropped his hand and looked at me, then Fionn, then at his Seer. She frowned and tilted her head, and I was fairly sure she and the King were speaking in a way none of the rest of us could hear.

"Are you okay?" Fionn said softly, taking my free hand in his.

I grinned. "He's big, but he's slow." I grinned wider when I heard the Royal Warrior growl.

"I'll spit you and roast you and eat your tender flesh, little man," he said, and Fionn's hand tightened on mine. "I'll give your tackle to the sea birds." I felt a surge of something not quite fear through my bond with Fionn, something tinged with disgust.

The King turned back to me. *Your weapon was indeed one of three, but not three daggers,* he said. *Long ago, before the Founding, before your people came to the Isle, three weapons were made by a process now lost. It was said the weapons were made by dragons, or else they were made by fey and humans working together, to conquer dragons. When fey and human arrived on the Isle they brought the three weapons with them. When the alliance was made with those of us already here, when the Founding Laws were established, one weapon of the three was given to humans, one to fey, and one to the First Peoples.*

Fionn moved closer, pressing his shoulder to mine, not for reassurance but unconsciously, because he was enthralled with the tale.

The Spear of Dragons went to the First Peoples, who decided it would be safest in the sea. It is, even now, on display in my throne room. He gestured behind him at the Bay. *It is a weapon that guards, that upholds the peace between peoples.*

The Dagger of Dragons, he continued, *was given to the humans, who sent it to Great River because it was envisioned to someday become the biggest human city, a center of commerce and diplomacy. I had assumed it was still in the throne room there.*

I looked at the blade in my hand. *My father said it was given to my uncle, the King, by his grandfather. My uncle, I suppose, didn't know what he had, and gave it to his General, who stored it in the armory at Dudoon.*

The King nodded. *And so it came into your possession. It is a weapon of balance, meant to even the stakes and protect the people.* He looked away down the beach, as if caught by some errant thought. Then he turned back to us. *The Sword of Dragons was given to the fey, who could never agree on who was to keep it. They eventually decided to take turns, and presumably it was mislaid and disappeared from history. It is a weapon of rulership, symbolizing just governance.*

"So all three weapons together represent the unity of the Isle?" asked Fionn and the King looked at him for a long moment.

"Our King says they do, indeed," said the Seer. Apparently, mind-to-mind communication with land-dwellers was tiring and I could see weariness on the King's face as he nodded.

"I don't suppose you have an opinion on where the Sword of Dragons might be?" I said, suddenly feeling tired myself. A headache was creeping in behind my eyes.

"He says to ask the Huldr. They are a people of secrets and might know. Otherwise, ask your Queen, or the Alfar King."

The King gestured and his guards slipped back into deeper water.

I enjoyed meeting you, Prince of Morven Forest, he said.

"I enjoyed meeting you, as well."

Then he moved away into the water after his guards, leaving only the Seer facing us on the beach.

"He wishes to give you a gift," she said. "But he does not

want his Warrior to know." She glanced behind her, where the King and his guards were swimming quickly away. One by one, they disappeared beneath the surface.

"It's not necessary," I said. "Meeting him, and you, is gift enough."

She smiled. "And yet he wishes it, and he is my King." Her smile grew and she looked from Fionn to me and back. "And I am his Seer."

"Oh," said Fionn softly, as if understanding something from the exchange that I had missed.

"You will not see us again before you go but know that if you do as you say you wish to do, and bring good to all of our peoples, he will stand with you should you need it."

I felt a sudden gratitude and bowed deeply. "Please thank him for me. That is, indeed, a rich gift."

She chuckled. "That is not the gift." She opened the pouch at her waist and withdrew an object wrapped in waxed linen. "The one in the throne room has been a replica since before my grandsire's time. I carry the real one for safekeeping, because my King does not trust his brother." She looked at the packet in her hand for a moment and then held it out to me. "By all the Goddesses of your people, and by all the spirits of mine, be sure you are worthy of it."

Then she pressed the item into my hand and was gone in a swirl of water.

27
Fionn

KIERNAN AND I WALKED back to the cave, each lost in our own thoughts. The serpents were draped over the stones by the fire, toasting their bellies in the heat from the coals.

"Aren't you going to open it?" I said, when Kier set the waxed cloth packet on top of our gear and turned to stir up the fire and add more wood.

"I know what it is," he said. "And 'thank you' hardly seems enough gratitude in exchange for it."

I knelt to fill a pot with water for tea and dug out a loaf of bread. The Sidhe had a sort of cloth wrapping that could keep bread fresh for much longer than seemed natural, so the food Kiernan had brought with him was still as tasty as it had been the first day we'd eaten it.

"What is it?" I asked.

He took the pot of water and hung it over the flames. "Open it, if you like."

I wanted to wait him out, to pretend I wasn't interested, until he got tired of waiting and opened it himself, but I was

379

too curious. Once I had found a piece of sausage and a block of hard cheese to go with the bread, I picked up the packet.

I sat cross-legged with it in my lap for a moment, like I might have with a birthday gift, if I had ever received birthday gifts as a child, savoring the anticipation.

Finally, I folded back the sides of the waxed cloth to reveal another layer, this one of a burnt orange fabric that felt impossibly smooth to the touch. "Is this sea silk?" I had never seen any but had read of it. It came from a sea creature, they said, and was so rare and beautiful that it was even more expensive than cloud silk, if you could even find any to buy.

Kier paused in making the tea to look more closely at the bundle in my lap. "I don't know. I've never seen sea silk. I've never seen cloth like this, either."

I unfolded a corner, and the surface of the fabric seemed to shimmer. It was breathtaking, even on such a small piece. I was almost too caught up in studying the cloth to finish revealing what was inside, but eventually I folded back the other corners and there, looking almost primitive next to the textile on which it lay, was a spearhead.

"While you were speaking to the Seer," Kiernan said, looking down at the object in my lap, "the King asked me if I had heard of a prophecy."

"The Sword of Dragons," I said. "And the Prince Who Will Unite An."

Kier pulled his dagger from his belt and laid it on my knee. It matched the spearhead, both made of the same dark metal that gleamed like moonsilver but was the wrong color, and both decorated with similar designs. I peered closer and realized the twisting interlaced decoration was of a stylized dragon.

"A sword, a dagger, and a spear," he said, and told me of the rest of his conversation with the Siegel King, before I had returned to hear the end of the tale.

"I always thought the Sword of Dragons was just a legend," I said, carefully picking up the spearhead and turning it towards the light.

"Me, too."

"But if the dagger is real, and the spear is real, it follows that the sword must also be real."

He didn't answer and, when I looked up, he was gazing out the cave entrance towards the bay.

"The Siegel King thinks you will unite the Isle," I said, as the realization occurred to me.

"I'm not sure the Isle needs uniting, or wants it," he replied. "Not under a single Monarch, anyway." He poured tea into the cups and picked one up, but didn't drink. "And anyway, the Siegel King thinks I'm heir to Morven Forest and Great River."

"But you're not heir to either. Not unless your sisters or your cousin die."

"Exactly. So the Siegel King must be wrong."

"Still, the legend says that whoever finds the Sword of Dragons will rule the Isle, maybe even all of An. And if the weapons exist…" I didn't finish the sentence.

He looked at me, and his eyes were troubled. "I don't want to be King, not of nine Monarchies or only one."

"You may not have a choice."

"I thought you didn't believe in fate." One corner of his mouth twisted upwards.

I poked his shoulder, then wrapped the spearhead up again and handed it and his dagger to him. "I don't, but a lot of people do, and they might not let you choose."

He poked my shoulder in return. "I am very tired of not being able to choose."

I picked up my tea. "So, choose where we go next."

He looked back out the cave entrance. "To the Huldr, I suppose. Maybe they can help us."

"Are you going to look for the Sword of Dragons, then?" I teased.

"No." He met my eyes. "I'm going to ask their Seer to marry us."

HE REFUSED TO SAY any more on the subject of marriage, even when I teased him that maybe *I* didn't want to get married.

"What's wrong?" I finally asked, after watching him carefully re-pack our clothes and other gear so it was no longer strewn around the cave.

He shook his head. "I thought that by going to the Eyrie to steal you away, I was finally choosing something for myself."

"You were," I said. "You did." I waited until he met my eyes, then smiled. "You chose me."

His return smile was fleeting, but he said, "I will always choose you, pretty bird. Now tell me what you talked about with the Siegel Seer." He paused and touched my shoulder. "If you want to."

"Are we leaving now?" I said.

"I thought in the morning."

"Then let's have one more soak in the hot spring before we go, and I'll tell you the parts I understood."

In the hot pool below the waterfall, we sat side-by-side, our thighs and shoulders touching. For a long moment, Kiernan was tense, as if he was thinking – or over-thinking – his plans for the coming days. Then he relaxed all at once and leaned his head on my shoulder.

"The Siegel Seer told me most Seers have visions on

purpose, by putting themselves in the right state of mind and asking the spirits to show them the things they need to see."

"But you knew that." Under the water, he took one of my hands between his two and traced the length of each finger.

"Yes, but she showed me *how*. She didn't just tell me that was how it was supposed to be. She reached out with her mind and *showed* me." I tried to keep my voice calm, but I was too excited by what I had learned, and I realized that it didn't matter if I babbled it out like a giddy child; Kier would not think less of me for it.

"Did you try it? Right then?"

"I did. Kier, I… I fell into a vision, and I didn't have a seizure. I just… *saw*. And after, my back didn't hurt, and I didn't have a headache."

He leaned away far enough to look at my face and raised one hand from the water to touch my cheek. "That's wonderful," he said, and his voice told me he meant it, the feeling in my belly told me he meant it. "But why are you suddenly sad? What did you *see*?"

I shook my head. "Most of it… it's hard to describe. I'm not even sure what some of it was. But I *saw* seers. Vogel seers." He slipped his arm around my waist and pulled me close to him. I knew he could hear the sorrow of what I had *seen* in my voice, just as he had heard my excitement before.

"Do you know when this happened?"

"The past. I think… I saw eggs, like mine. And Alfar. The Abbess, and other women, other Abbesses from before her time, I think. And… the eggs. Some were left too long, and the unborn seers died. They suffocated." I had to pause, to let tears fall for a moment. Kiernan wiped them gently away with a wet hand.

"What else?" His voice was soft, gentle, and I knew I didn't have to say anything more if I didn't feel I could.

"Some eggs, the Abbesses broke open too soon, and the infants weren't mature enough."

"How many?"

"I don't know. I didn't… I couldn't count. But several. Kier, they all died."

He pulled my head onto his shoulder and held me while I cried again.

"The Alfar tried many times before they succeeded with you," he said, stroking my hair.

"Yes."

"Six or seven times, I'd wager," he said. "One for each generation since the last Vogel Seer."

"Yes," I whispered.

"The spell you *saw*," he said thoughtfully. "When they sacrificed the last Seer, what was it meant to do?"

I lifted my head from his shoulder and frowned at him. "To enslave the dryads."

"That's what the Founding Monarchs used it for," he said. "But you told me the Seer said something. It seemed to me they changed the purpose of the ritual, that originally it was meant to so something he approved of, something he was willing to sacrifice *himself* for."

"I don't know," I said, "but I think you're right."

"You saw something else that made you happy, though."

I blushed. "I saw our wedding. And… what happened after."

A sly smile spread across his features. He moved until he was facing me and climbed onto my lap. "And what happened after?" He leaned closer and kissed my neck.

I bit his earlobe, catching one of the rings in my teeth and tugging gently. "Guess," I said into his ear.

"This?" He took my face in both hands and kissed me, soft at first, and then more firmly.

"For a start," I answered when he leaned away to look at my face.

"This?" He slid forward on my lap until his erection poked me in the belly. Instead of answering, I grabbed his hair with both hands and pulled his mouth to mine again, so I could show him some of the things we'd done in my vision of our possible future wedding day.

WE LEFT THE CAVE EARLY the next morning, bundled up in our warmest layers. To my delight, Kiernan pulled out the hood, gloves, and leg warmers I had given him at Autumn Balance and put them on. I thought they went very nicely with his grey wool coat and dark trousers. Coal evidently thought the hood was perfect for nesting in and immediately curled up around Kier's neck, cuddled inside it.

"Will we follow the road?" I said as we climbed up the cliff instead of down and stood looking out over the bay, squinting into the reflection of the rising sun off the water.

No one comes, said Smoke.

Is safe, said Flame.

"This far from anywhere and this deep into winter, we aren't likely to meet many other travelers. Even the villages will be quiet, and we'll move faster on the road."

He meant *I* would move faster. I had no doubt he could move as fast or faster through the forest and over the pastured hills as on the road. But I wasn't made for long-distance walking, and I obviously couldn't fly, either.

What followed was hardly worth recounting. Long days of walking were punctuated with stops to rest and eat or to curl up somewhere out of the way to sleep. Each time we passed a village with an inn – which was seldom – I looked at it longingly, but I refused to ask to stop. I knew we were taking enough chances just by being seen on the road, and the longer we travelled, the more likely we would encounter someone who might think they could profit from telling someone else about who they had seen. Stopping at an inn full of wintering travelers would increase the chances that word would get back to the Eyrie.

But once, after days on the road, sleeping in barns and hay piles, Kiernan said, "Do you want to sleep in a bed tonight, pretty bird?"

"Can we risk it?" The town we were approaching looked busy, even from a distance.

"If you need a rest, we can." He twined his fingers around mine and his touch felt comforting, even through two layers of thick woven wool.

"No," I said. "There seem to be a lot of people about. Let's not even walk through the town."

"It's ninthday," he said. I must have looked confused because he added, "Market day. There will be enough people about that no one will even notice you."

"They don't notice strangers?"

He smiled. "Did you not study maps of Tronven in your Abbey?" His voice was gently teasing.

I frowned at the town ahead. Had there been a sign as we approached? I was too bone-tired to have noticed, and I felt stupid. I should be noticing everything, as Kiernan did. *Not* noticing something could be dangerous.

I pushed the thought aside and tried to picture our journey as if we were markers being moved across a map. The Eyrie was there, and the road ran west and a little north, and then there was Archipelago Bay. We had bypassed the towns and crossroads inns on that stretch of road. The high road then turned more northerly and real towns were scarce until the

Huldr cities deep in the Drowned Lands.

But between the bay and the forest was… "Markettown," I said. Of course. Markettown on market day.

Kiernan grinned and swung our joined hands. "Markettown," he agreed. "Where humans and Huldr and peoples from the two land-bound Tronven Monarchies mingle and gather."

"But it's winter."

"The market will be smaller, of course, but people still need bread and pastries and beer. And we could use more supplies, too."

"And if someone recognizes us?"

He shrugged. "It will happen eventually, but we're far enough from the Eyrie I'm not worried we'll be dragged back there. And I have no doubt someone will report to my Queen once we reach Huldr lands, anyway. Assuming she hasn't already figured out I've left Great River."

"Aren't you worried?"

He considered. "Yes. I told my people before I left what could happen, that some of the blame for my absence could fall on them. And I told them they were free to return to Morven Forest if they wished."

"They all chose to stay." I freed my hand from his to pull my hood more fully over my hair and to make sure my cloak hid as much of the rest of me as possible.

"They did. I'm not sure I deserve such loyal staff."

"You do," I insisted, taking his hand again. No one else was approaching the town from the same direction we were, but three other roads led towards it, and all had groups of travelers and wagons making their way to and from the center of town.

"Fionn," he said, his voice serious. "I have to stand up to her eventually, and she knows she has to let me make my own decisions sometimes if I am to be an effective ambassador."

"And stealing the Seer of the Eyrie away and fleeing to Tronven is such a decision?"

He laughed softly. "Yes, I think it is. Or at least I think I can convince her it is."

"How?"

He laughed again, more loudly this time, and he actually sounded happy. "You'll see," he said, and he led me into the market.

WE DIDN'T END UP spending the night, but we did leave Markettown for the Drowned Lands with all our packs and bags filled again, and with each purchase Kiernan had asked my opinion so we ended up buying foods we both liked, as long as they were things that would keep.

And we kept going. The land gradually changed again, from rounded hills on which wandered grazing sheep and cows, and between which was bare earth ready for planting spring crops, to a wilder land of rivers and ponds and wide beds of reeds and marsh grasses where the road was up on an embankment, like it had been leaving the Eyrie.

I lost track of the days, and I didn't care to ask. It didn't matter. Sure, we were often cold and sometimes too uncomfortable to sleep much, and I started to miss sex again, though Kier was careful to make sure I knew how he felt with comforting kisses and promises that we'd soon find someplace to bathe again, but we were together. For now, that was all I needed.

One morning, after a quick cup or tea and a handful of coal-roasted nuts for our morning meal, Kiernan said, "It's Midwinter, pretty bird. I had hoped we'd be somewhere by now, and that I'd have a gift for you." He touched my face. "Except I have this: I think we'll reach the Drowned Forest today and if I can find my near-father, we might even get a hot bath and a bed to sleep in."

I got to my feet and shouldered my bags, then opened my hood so Smoke and Flame could nestle inside. At the Abbey, they had vanished in the winter, I had supposed to hibernate somewhere. They had never wanted to go within the Abbey walls.

"What does near-father mean?" I asked. The Abbey had not been rich with books on family relations.

"It's what we say in Morven for a parent who is related by marriage only, or who is the birth parent of a sibling. So I have a near-mother who is my brother Duncan's birth mother, and a near-father who is my twin sisters' birth father."

"So your father, General Druison, would be your sisters' near-father, and your mother would be your brother's near-mother?"

"Yes, though none of them would be likely to claim it so."

"Is he a good man, your near-father?"

"I've never met him," he said. "But my Queen seemed to think so."

I gave him a look that said I didn't think much of the Queen of Morven Forest's opinion on anyone's goodness or lack thereof, and he smiled in amusement.

"He's a Huldr Lord, and he may not think much of me, but I *am* a Prince, so he'll be sure to offer me hospitality, at least."

"Do you know where he lives?"

He frowned and looked away. "He is Lord of the Drowned Forest, so I should be able to find him."

I tried, unsuccessfully, to stifle a sigh. "Do you know his *name*?" I asked.

"His title will be enough."

We kept walking and as the day drew on, the trees closed in and the ground between them grew ever wetter, until huge puddles and ponds took up more space than dry ground.

"Is the Drowned Forest dead?" I asked, suddenly imagining trees standing in endless water, starved of air and nutrients by the wet around the roots until they rotted in place. I shivered. I tried to remember what I had read about the place and could only think of passages about the secretiveness of its inhabitants. A memory tugged at my thoughts, of something I had *seen*, but I couldn't hold onto it.

"No," said Kiernan. "At least, not most of it. It's made of trees that love water and it's not wet all year. In the summer it dries out, I hear."

"That would make for a short growing season." I said it absently, something niggling at my mind, at my magic. "Kier…"

"I feel it, too," he said. His hand went to the dagger at his waist. "Just keep walking."

I did as he said, but he let go of my hand to have both ready to fight. I rested my fingers against the hilts of my knives.

Then, as clearly as if I saw them, I felt people around us in the trees where they were out of sight, and I realized I was feeling our surroundings as Kiernan did when his magic was at its full. The forest was vast and quiet and alive, and a handsworth… no, more than that, three threes of beings surrounded us.

Kiernan stopped and drew both swords in one smooth motion. "Like we practiced, pretty bird," he said.

I had to force myself to keep breathing slowly, to stay calm, to turn around so I was back-to-back with him, and to draw my knives and move into position. Some of his calm must have seeped into me along with his sense of the world around us, because when several masked figures stepped up onto the raised road on both sides of us, I didn't move. I just watched and waited.

"Calmly, pretty bird," Kier said.

And then the creatures advanced.

28
Kiernan

I FELT THE EXACT MOMENT Fionn's magic joined mine and he felt as clearly as I did the people – or creatures – gathering around us.

They felt something like the wolves of Morven Forest – like wild animals, but with nearly person-level intelligence and understanding – and something like spirits, with a more-than-mortal connection to the land. They made me intensely curious, and very afraid.

I pushed aside my fear so Fionn wouldn't feel it. The last thing we needed was for him to freeze in terror, though it was also very possible he would handle it better than I did. Still, fear was an emotion best set aside for now, for both of us.

I drew both swords, Winterborn solid and familiar in my right, non-dominant hand, and Brightheart – less familiar – in my left. Best to balance the blade I knew least with the hand I was best with, though my father claimed his tutoring had worked out any tendency to favor one side over the other.

"Like we practiced, pretty bird," I said softly, letting no

trace of uncertainty into my voice. The first time *I* had faced a real enemy, I had puked my guts out after.

Fionn fell into place at my back and drew his knives, the buzz of their magic and his reassuringly strong. I could sense him struggling to keep calm and sent him some of my own ease with my weapons through our bond.

"Calmly, pretty bird," I said, waiting for the beings that surrounded us to make their move. And they did, quickly and silently. They almost seemed to appear out of nowhere onto the road on both sides of us. Three faced Fionn, and four confronted me. Two more waited in the trees to the sides.

"There are three here," Fionn said, though he must know I already sensed them.

"Like we practiced," I said. "Keep your mind open to me, and let your body move. It remembers, even if you don't."

"Okay." He breathed, slowly, carefully, trusting me. I hoped I was worthy of it. I hoped the lessons I'd put him through held when faced with real danger. I hoped I had taught him enough.

I hardly had time to study our opponents, only had an impression of fur – whether grown or worn as a garment, I couldn't tell – long limbs, claws, and blank-faced masks. Then they were on us, and everything was movement.

I felt claws on my arm and struck back. They moved away. A slash, a counter, a lunge, and before long I couldn't tell my movements from Fionn's and it was as if we danced, us two and our opponents.

They fell back and Fionn became a separate presence again. The long, shallow scratch down the forearm had been his, not mine, but he said nothing. The quick, shallow breathing was his, too, and I stepped back enough to press my back against his.

"You did well," I said, and his breathing slowed and

deepened. "Is your arm okay?"

"I wasn't prepared for them to be so fast," he said. "But it's shallow. I'll be fine."

The creatures stayed out of reach, studying us. I didn't say so to Fionn, but I suspected they hadn't really been trying to hurt us. If they had, I was fairly sure as least one of us would be dead.

The creature closest to me crouched on its haunches, studying me with its head cocked. Now that they were still, I could see that they were mostly person-shaped, with legs that ended in furry shins and paws, and long arms with five-fingered hands ending in claws. Still, they seemed awkward both standing on two legs and crouching on four, yet moving they had been lightning fast in any posture.

"What do you want of us?" I said, and the creature in front of me cocked its head to the other side.

"Do you speak Islish?" Fionn asked.

The creature looked past me at him and put one hand up to its mask, then paused, glancing to the side, into the forest. It dropped its hand. Then, as suddenly as they had appeared, all but one of the creatures slipped back into the forest, subtle and silent as mist.

"Kier?" Fionn's voice was quiet.

"I don't know, pretty bird. Only one left here."

I felt him start to turn, then think better of it and stay where he was, guarding my back. "They're all gone on this side," he said.

The creature in front of me continued to watch, moving only occasionally to scratch its armpit or its head.

"Will you let us pass?" I said, taking a slow step forward.

The creature rose, shoulders hunched, and growled softly.

"You want us to wait here?"

The creature sat again and resumed watching me.

Coal poked his head out of my hood, and I wondered if he had been asleep the entire time. He saw the creature and hissed. The creature growled back, and Coal turned around and crawled down the back of my neck.

"Whatever they are, they frighten Coal, and I didn't think he was afraid of anything."

Smoke and Flame chose that moment to return from scouting ahead, chittering in excitement and swirling around us.

He comes, said Smoke.

Why stop? said Flame. Then she noticed the creature and flung herself to the road in front of me, reared up, wings spread, and hissed. Smoke circled Fionn protectively.

You go, said Flame to the creature. To my surprise, the creature responded by crouching low to the road, as if cowering from the tree serpent, a beast only barely more than the length of my arm. Otherwise, the creature didn't budge.

"It's okay, little friend," I said. "I don't think they mean to hurt us."

Hurt Bright, said Smoke. *Is blood.*

"I'm okay," said Fionn. "I think it was an accident."

"Who did you say was coming?" I said, suddenly remembering Smoke's first words on returning and wondering if they had anything to do with these creatures.

"*I* am, I suppose," said a deep voice, and a man stepped out of a swirl of mist behind the creature.

I DIDN'T MOVE, though my instinct was to step back, closer to Fionn, to protect him. Instead, I kept my swords raised and faced the man calmly.

"I think it's okay to turn around," I said, leaving off the

endearment I wanted to add to the end of my words.

The creature that had been watching us crept backwards until it crouched at the man's feet.

"I apologize for my scouts' ill-treatment of you, Seer," he said, nodding to Fionn. "I asked them only to delay you until I arrived, but they are not the most intelligent of creatures." His accent was cultured, and his Islish precise and elegant. He was taller than me, close to Fionn's height, but not so tall as an Alfar. A dark cloak of rich, soft wool embroidered all over in intricate designs in colors nearly as dark obscured almost everything about him except the horns or antlers that rose from his head, looking like two dark, twisted branches, like the limbs of an ancient tree stunted by time and weather.

"You must have strong magic and great trust between you to fight as you did, like one being in two bodies."

I ignored his statement, not sure what to make of it, and instead said, "May I know your name?" I let my royal Sidhe accent tinge my words in a manner of speaking I usually saved for those occasions when my Queen was observing me, and judging.

The man pushed back his hood with gloved hands to reveal a face even paler than Fionn's, almost bone-white and blue-tinged. His black hair was pulled back from his face and his ears were small and delicately pointed. His eyes were wide and dark and his cheekbones high.

I knew immediately who he was, but I didn't say anything. I just waited to see if he would tell me.

"Lioswright Tovarsson, Lord of the Drowned Forest and cousin to the Monarch of the Drowned Lands, over-Monarch of Tronven." He smiled, and it changed his face from cold to something almost friendly. I could see, I thought, what had drawn my mother to him, and wondered what had made her send him away.

"And you," he continued, amusement touching his voice, "are the errant Prince of Morven Forest and Great River." He bowed slightly from the waist. "And the lost, then found, then evidently lost again, Seer of the Eyrie."

"Kiernan Druison nicFia nor Dudoon nor Morven," I said. "And Seer Tokka tanKarshanka." I let some of the formality in my voice be replaced by cheek. "You're Caitlín and Sigrún's father."

"Which makes me your near-father, as your Sidhe relatives would say."

"How did you know we were here?" I sheathed one sword, then the other, though I was not so stupid as to lower my guard entirely. Beside me, Fionn sheathed his knives, and I reached for his arm to look at the scratch. It was, as he'd said, shallow, and had already stopped bleeding. I kept his hand in mine.

"My creatures have been tracking you since Markettown."

Fionn squeezed my fingers, and I knew he was thinking we should have stayed out of sight instead of shopping for supplies. I didn't think it would have made a difference.

Lord Tovarsson continued. "I got word of something happening at the Eyrie, something that, I was told, set the King's Guard all aflutter." He crossed his arms and looked down at the creature crouched at his feet. It gazed up at him, then suddenly moved away into the forest. "I'm afraid, good Prince, that news of your absence from your post at the new Sidhe embassy in Great River reached me the same day, and I had to wonder."

I didn't let my thoughts show on my face, but deep dismay pooled in my gut and Fionn shifted closer, so his shoulder pressed against mine.

"And why, Lord of the Drowned Forest, did you have to wonder, and about what?"

He laughed, and I didn't know if I should feel at ease or worried. "I have a Seer very skilled at marking patterns, and they told me the spirits whispered to them of Vogel Seers and forest Princes, and old things stirring in the wild places of the Isle."

I let my frown show on my face this time.

"Very cryptic, I know," he said. "My Seer speaks that way so often I'm not sure they're capable of simply stating anything." He gestured along the road. "You must be weary and cold. Will you accept my hospitality?"

"Will you send word to my Queen that I'm here?" I stepped forward and he fell in beside me on the side opposite Fionn.

"I have to assume she already knows you're absent from Great River, if I was informed of the fact." He said nothing more for a few steps. "But if you prefer I don't tell her, I will not."

"Why?" said Fionn, and Lord Tovarsson's eyebrows lifted.

"Why?" the Huldr repeated.

"Why keep it from her? Is she not your ally?" Fionn's voice was cool and imperious, and I wanted to hug him. Sometimes I forgot the kind, inexperienced young man I had first met had grown into someone capable of facing even my royal mother without flinching.

"We have children together," Tovarsson said. "But I do not owe her fealty. That I reserve for my own Monarch." He looked at me. "Your Queen once hoped to marry you to my Monarch's daughter. It would have been an excellent match." He looked pointedly at my hand, clasped tightly around Fionn's.

"I have other ideas," I said.

"Our children always do." He gestured ahead. "Boats await. The rest of our path lies by water." He sighed. "My

Monarch is inclined to let their child choose her own alliance, and she is not especially keen on marrying you."

"I'm sure she's lovely, but I'm not disappointed."

"Are your 'other plans' acceptable to your mother?"

"Do you care?" I let my words come out blunt, already tired of courtly manners and dancing around whatever it was he really wanted to know.

"I care about my people, my daughters, and my Isle. Believe it or not, that means everything you do concerns me."

"Which is why you've had me watched."

We stopped at a sort of crossroads, but instead of another highway, the road intersected with a canal that flowed under it and arrowed directly into the forest on both sides, a straight stone-sided waterway through the patchwork of standing water, trees, and soggy bogland around us. Two slender boats were tied up on one side, each with a dark-cloaked person in the stern.

"I have never had you watched, exactly," he said, voice mild and unoffended. "I have only asked my agents to let me know anything of interest they may have observed."

"Do my sisters report to you?" I knew they both kept up correspondence with a number of other royals and nobles, but it had never occurred to me that they might be their father's spies in our mother's court. They were too obviously my Queen's children.

"Not knowingly," he said. "They rarely write about you or anything particularly political at all, except to occasionally complain about your lack of princely graces and to lament how the Monarchy would suffer should you ever come into any significant power." He laughed suddenly and Fionn startled, then caught himself.

"Your sisters," Tovarsson went on, "are under the impression that you're their mother's favorite."

I couldn't keep in my snort of disbelief, and he looked at me curiously.

"You don't agree, obviously."

"Do you see my antlers?"

He looked at my head and frowned, so I reached up and pushed back my hood. Fionn had designed it to fit around the antlers I no longer had.

Tovarsson's face went still when he noticed the two raw wounds where my antlers should have been. He lifted one hand, but let it fall immediately. "Goddess Around," he breathed. "She didn't…"

"No," I said. "She didn't. *I* did, because it was the only way to escape the spellwork she put on them."

His eyes didn't leave my forehead. "Spellwork to do what?"

"To block my magic. No, to *steal* my magic, to siphon it off for her own use and to block me from even feeling it." I let go of Fionn's hand to pull my hood back up. "Do you still think I'm my Queen's favorite?"

He met my eyes finally. "I know Ríoghnach does nothing without reason," he said. "And I know her intention has always been to make you strong." He looked at Fionn, then back at me. "But this…" He shook his head. "Come, share my home. Rest. Eat. Bathe."

"You never said why you would aid us," said Fionn, letting me help him into the boat Tovarsson indicated.

"I did," the Lord of the Drowned Forest said, climbing easily into the other boat. "I said I care about this Isle, and my Seer is of the impression that the wellbeing of this Isle is somehow tied to the two of you."

I settled into the boat behind Fionn and then there was no more chance to talk as the silent cloaked Huldr poled us away from the road and along the canal, deep into the forest.

It was hushed with the held breath of winter, but like any forest it was not a true silence, only quiet in comparison to spring.

Wind high above made the upper branches of the huge old trees creak, and though the canal seemed to have little current of its own, small ripples and splashes showed the movement of birds and animals. The ice forming in the standing water between the trees cracked occasionally and a sort of audible hush fell as we approached and passed.

With nothing else to do, I let myself feel the magic around me and I heard Fionn's soft breathing and knew he was doing the same, looking around us with his seer-sight. I moved carefully closer and put my arms around him. He leaned back against me.

"It doesn't feel at all like Morven Forest," he said. "Or Aven."

"No," I replied softly, my lips brushing his ear. "It feels… strange. Familiar and foreign all at once."

"Aven Forest welcomed you," he said. "Even though it wasn't *your* forest, it still knew you and recognized you as kin, I suppose."

"Yes. This forest, though. I can't explain it, but… I don't know. It doesn't feel unwelcoming, only… secret. Like it hasn't decided if it accepts me or not."

"It frightens me, a little," he said. "But it also excites me. Like there's something here for me to discover." He shook his head. "That sounds silly."

"It doesn't. It sounds like you're having the same trouble I am, finding the right words to describe something that can't be told in words."

We sat quietly for a while and I smiled into Fionn's shoulder as he kept looking this way and that, as if to see everything we passed and take note.

"Those are willows," he said, pointing to a group of trees bending over the canal to dip their hanging branches into the water.

"Those are, too." I pointed at a group of upright saplings, their red stems bright against the grey winter forest and the soft white snow that stuck to their buds.

He looked that way. "Yes, but a different kind. Those make good baskets."

I kissed his cheek. "Perhaps you'll get a chance to make a basket you can carry on your back, instead of draping several bags from your shoulders."

"It would have to fit between my wings," he said, but he sounded thoughtful.

We glided quietly along the canal, only the soft splashes of the poles propelling us along and our lowered voices making any sound. The person who steered our boat didn't speak, and only moved to push the boat along. I resisted the urge to start asking them all the questions that popped into my mind.

Then ahead there was a bright light between two huge willows that leaned over the canal, and we slipped out into a large pond. In the center, on a smooth-sided circular island, stood a large, well-built house, rich-looking but not opulent. All around the edge of the pond grew reeds, like a living fortification, some with stalks the size of trees, forming a deep gold fence broken only by canals entering from several directions.

Our guide steered us towards the island and the house.

"Welcome to my home," said Lord Tovarsson as we glided up to the dock that projected out from the island. He had already disembarked and waited for us, surrounded by silent, cloaked Huldr.

I climbed out of the boat first and turned to help Fionn. As he climbed up beside me, I glanced up over his head and deeper into the forest. Towering over even the largest tree stood a huge fir, off in the distance but so big it appeared to be just past the edge of the reed palisade.

"What's that?" I asked, though it could only have been one thing.

"The Heart of Tronven," said Tovarsson. "Perhaps you would like to visit it, once you've rested."

"Yes," I said softly, not caring if he could hear me. "Yes, I would very much like to visit the Heart of Tronven."

Next to me, Fionn squeezed my hand so hard my bones ground together.

29
Fionn

ONCE WE ARRIVED at his home, Lord Tovarsson didn't seem inclined to talk. He had us shown to a large room furnished in pale wood with jewel-toned upholstery. There was a table with four chairs, a large couch in front of a huge fireplace, and a door on the far side that lead to a second room where I glimpsed a bed and a wardrobe.

"Make yourselves at home," he said. "I'll have food brought, and once you've rested, we'll speak again." And then he left.

Kiernan shrugged off his pack and walked around the room, looking at everything, as if to determine whether or not we were safe. He opened the door to the bedroom, looked inside, then continued back around to stand next to me again.

"I everything okay?" I said, placing my bag of medicines carefully on a small table next to the couch, and dropping the one with my clothes to the floor next to it.

"I don't know," he said. "But I suppose we're as safe here as we would be anywhere. The door has a lock, at least."

I glanced towards the door in question, where a sturdy bolt could be run across to keep out unwanted visitors, and almost jumped when there was a sudden knock, and the door cracked open.

Kier put a hand on his knife but didn't draw it. "Yes?" he said, and I was surprised at exactly how much haughtiness he could fit into a single word.

The door swung open to reveal a slender woman in a pale grey dress. Her dark hair was pulled back from her white face in a tight bun. She bowed and said, "I'm to show you to the bathing room, Prince of Morven Forest."

Kiernan nodded and took my hand. "Lead the way," he said.

"Together?" The woman sounded like she was offended but trying to hide it. Perhaps the Huldr didn't bathe together? They had given us a room with only one bed, so why should us sharing a bath be strange?

"We won't be separated," I said, using the tone of voice I used when I was trying to be regal. I realized I didn't sound so very different from Kiernan's princely voice. It must have had the intended effect, because something changed on her face, and she nodded and gestured for us to follow.

"I'll build up the fire while you bathe," she said. "And take your clothing for washing. My Lord has had fresh clothes laid out for you both."

We followed her down a long hall to the end, and she indicated a door that stood half open, then bowed and hurried away.

I smelled flower essences and soap and when we pushed open the door, we found a tile-lined room with a huge copper tub steaming with hot water and a second, smaller, tub surrounded by buckets for rinsing.

A shelf along one wall held an assortment of soaps and

lotions in bottles and cakes and powders. Each had a paper label with elegant writing on it, all in the same hand, and I realized I couldn't read a single word.

Behind me, Kiernan locked the door.

"Can you read Huldr?" I said, running a hand across a label written in green ink. He put an arm around my waist and leaned his chin on my shoulder.

"Very little." He pointed at the green label. "That says… amethyst rose? Maybe."

"Do you see any lavender?"

He kissed my cheek, then looked along the shelf. "That one, I think." He pointed to a tall, thin bottle of milky liquid. I lifted it and worked the stopper out.

"Definitely lavender," he said, before I even raised it to my nose, and I was reminded how much keener a sense of smell he had, because I had to bring it nearer to my face before I caught the scent.

I wanted to linger in the bath, to rub the stiffness from Kiernan's muscles and pleasure him slowly, but he was restless and hardly seemed able to sit still long enough to get clean.

"What's wrong?" I said, when I finally got him to let me scrub his hair.

He sighed. "I don't know. Something feels… not wrong, just… I don't know."

I let my magic slip out through our bond and immediately felt what he felt. "It feels as if something is going to happen." I worked my fingers against his scalp, and he relaxed a little bit.

"Yes. That's exactly it. I feel like it's the night before an important meeting and I don't know what the topic will be so I can't prepare. Or the moment before a sword fight against an opponent I've heard is very good, only I've never even met them, let alone sparred with them." He let me ease his head under the water to sluice the soap out of his hair. It was getting long enough for the curls to fall over his eyes when they straightened out with the weight of the hot water.

When he sat up, he said, "I'm sorry, pretty bird. You need to rest and I'm making you tense."

"I want to make love," I said, abruptly. "Not sleep. If not here in the bath, then in that very large, comfortable-looking bed in our room. I want to feel you inside me, Kier. I want to feel you take pleasure in me through our heart bond and I want you to know exactly how much fire you stoke in me."

He twisted around to look at me. I was breathing too fast, and I wanted to cry for no good reason. He smiled gently. "You know I want you, too, pretty bird." He touched my face, brushed fingers over my cheek and down my neck. "Let me pleasure you and tuck you into bed and watch over you while you sleep."

"No." He blinked at the suddenness of my answer. "Kier, I don't want you to give me pleasure and take none for yourself." He opened his mouth to protest, and I put my fingers on his lips to stop him. Then I stood and climbed out of the tub.

"Fionn?" He said it softly and I knew I had struck a blow without meaning to. He thought I was rejecting him.

I stepped into the smaller tub and emptied a bucket over myself to rinse off the soap. Then I met his eyes. "I want us to take pleasure in each other," I said, "and if you're too anxious for that, then I'll wait." I wrapped myself in a towel and held out a bucket of water until he got up and let me rinse him.

Back in our room, clad in the loose warm clothing provided by our host, we found that someone had left the table full of covered dishes of food, and had taken all our clothing for cleaning, leaving the rest of our things piled neatly on a side table. I didn't like that someone had gone through our bags, and from the look on his face, neither did Kier, but nothing seemed to be missing except clothes.

Kiernan bolted the door and paced back and forth across the room, stopping at the table with each pass to pick up something to nibble on.

After watching him for some time, I said, "You're making me dizzy."

"I'm sorry," he said. "I can't settle. I feel like something's pulling at me."

I got up from the table and walked to him, took both of his hands in mine, and pulled him over to the big couch by the fire, where I sat in front of him, looking up at his face. I could see the tension there, in the frown that bunched his eyebrows and the sharp downturn of his mouth.

"Let me in," I said.

He stilled and stared at me. "What?"

"You're blocking every slightest thought and emotion, beloved, and I can't even feel you here." I let go of one hand and pressed my palm to his belly, where our heart-bond connected.

His shoulders bunched, then slumped. "I —" He shook his head.

I reached out with my magic, let it brush softly against his, and felt him close me out, then slowly, gradually, he let me in and I sensed, all at once, that the feeling of unease he'd only let me glimpse earlier had grown. It was almost overwhelming, a sharp pull to go off into the forest.

I closed my eyes and brought to mind the Siegel Seer's lesson on how to ask the spirits for a vision. "Let me see," I said, hardly audible even to myself, a request and not a demand. I didn't direct it at Kiernan, but at whatever else might be listening.

And something responded. I almost pulled away, so clear was the sense of an ancient being hearing me, and answering me, and so sudden and full was the… not vision, exactly, but a flow of magic.

But I *was* a Seer; this was what I had been born for. I let out a breath and let the magic draw me in, into Kiernan and through him into the forest. I remembered what I had felt in the boat: that there was something for me to find here.

It was the same thing that made Kiernan so restless that he couldn't relax, and it rushed into me as if it felt me looking. For a moment, I stopped breathing.

When I opened my eyes, Kiernan's hands were tight on mine and his eyes were bright.

"I saw it, too," he said, his voice full of awe. "Fionn, you took me with you into your vision."

I stood up. "The Heart of Tronven knows we're here, and it wants us to go to it."

He nodded, then he said, "I'm afraid." He leaned closer and I tilted my head so our forehead pressed together. "I don't know why, but I'm afraid."

WE LEFT THE ROOM TOGETHER, hand-in-hand, our own outer garments layered over the borrowed clothing; my cloak and his coat, along with hoods and gloves, were all the Huldr had left of our own. We had our weapons buckled on, and the serpents perched on our shoulders.

At the last moment before leaving the room, something made me grab my bag of medicines and sling it across my shoulders. I shouldn't assume we might not come back, but if we didn't, there were things in that bag I wanted to keep with me.

We retraced the route we had taken to get to our room and found ourselves back in the large entryway of the house. Two guards, cloaked and hooded despite being indoors, barred our way.

"Are we prisoners here?" Kier asked.

"No, Prince of Morven, said one guard. "But it isn't safe to wander the Drowned Forest at night."

"Then give us a guide," I said. "We need to go out."

"I can't allow it."

"Call your Lord, then. We're not fleeing." I let my exasperation creep into my words.

The guard said nothing else, but only stood with their arms crossed, blocking the door with their companion.

Kiernan growled under his breath. "There must be another door." He turned and stalked towards a hallway on the other side of the entryway, and I followed.

"Prince Kiernan, I presume," said a voice not belonging to the guard. It was musical sounding and light. "Seer Tokka. Surely you aren't leaving so soon. I had hoped we might converse once you had slept. Are you rested already?" A figure, cloaked in black and grey as everyone here seemed to be, stepped out of the shadow of a doorway.

Kiernan moved between them and me. "Who are you?" His courtly manner was entirely gone, replaced with the brash manners of the young agent of the Queen of Morven Forest he had pretended to be when we first met.

The person facing us didn't seem offended. They didn't even seem to notice Kiernan's rudeness.

"I am the Seer of the Drowned Forest." They stepped farther out of the shadows and revealed themself to be an average-looking Huldr — if the guards and servants we had seen so far were any indication. The only difference was that they had a face on which a smile seemed to be the most natural expression, and a head shaved to a dark stubble on a very round skull. Their wide silver eyes gleamed.

"Do you have a name?" I asked, then snapped my mouth shut, realizing the question might be taken as rude. But the Seer only laughed, and the sound immediately put me at ease. Even Kier's restlessness seemed momentarily suspended.

"Seer Stígandr," they said, and bowed slightly.

"I am Seer Tokka of the Eyrie, as you apparently already know," I said, a little dismayed at how naturally I introduced myself with my Vogel name instead of the one I'd had my whole life, the name Kier whispered to me when we made love.

They cocked their head at me. "Silver, yes? It suits you."

"You speak Trillka?" I couldn't keep the surprise out of my voice.

"Does anyone really speak Trillka anymore?" they said, another smile brightening their face.

I couldn't help but return the smile. "No, even we Vogel use it only for names, now."

"And you," the Seer said, turning to Kiernan. "Shadow. Did your mother the Queen know the darkness protects you when she gave you that name?"

Kier only shrugged, but the Seer didn't take offense.

"Something has stirred you from your rest," the Seer said. "Something will not let you sleep but pulls at your thoughts until you can't be still but seek to escape into the darkness between the trees." They looked at me, but I knew it was really Kiernan they were speaking to.

"The Drowned Forest can do that, to those who can feel its currents," they said. "I have spent many a night and day wandering aimlessly, pulled here and there, feeling as if there is something important I should be doing." They turned their sharp gaze away from me to Kier, who had been fidgeting with the hilt of his knife. Kier went still.

"But this is no soft notion plucking the strings of your mind until you wake restlessly from your slumber. No, Prince of Morven Forest, child of magic, something does not merely pull at you, it demands your presence."

I shivered as they moved closer to Kiernan until they were looking directly into one another's eyes. "What is it, I wonder, and why?"

Kier stared back, utterly still where he had been unable to stop moving before, as if entranced by the Seer's words, the rhythm of their speech, and I wondered if they had worked a subtle sort of magic on Kier. I wondered if it was good or bad.

But they were a Seer, and if I could trust anyone, I reminded myself, it was another Seer.

"The Heart of Tronven calls us," I said, and both Kiernan and the Seer turned their eyes on me. I felt a blush heat my cheeks, but I ignored it.

"Indeed?" said the Seer. "That is not a call to be ignored at all, and I think even my Lord would agree. He will lend you a boat in the morning, when the creatures of darkness have gone to to their rest, I'm quite sure."

"This can't wait," said Kiernan.

"All things can wait, young Prince."

Kiernan held out his hand. "This can't wait," he repeated. "See for yourself, if you like."

The Seer looked at his hand, then at me, then back at Kier's hand. Finally, they took the proffered fingers delicately in their own and closed their eyes.

The Seer swayed. "Oh," they said. "I have never felt the like. Even when I was called to my magic the Heart was not so demanding." They suddenly dropped Kiernan's hand and stepped back, eyes wide and no trace of the smile that had seemed so perfectly suited to their face. "You must go. She calls and you must answer." He tilted his head to one side, then the other, and frowned. "Why she wants a Prince so stuffed with magic already, I can't say. But yes, you must go. I will find you a boat and a guide. Only be wary of the creatures in the dark. The Drowned Forest is very old and not all its inhabitants are friendly. Even some of the trees are best avoided."

"No guide," Kiernan said.

The Seer's eyebrows rose. "No, I suppose not. You two must follow this call alone. Prince of Three Realms and Seer of Spirits." They swayed again and I thought they might fall, so I stepped forward to catch them, but they suddenly straightened and their whole face changed, smiling and merry again.

"Come, let us find you a boat." They led us back to the entryway, waved off the guards when they would have stopped us, and continued out and down to the dock we had arrived at. Several boats were tied up there.

Another guard stood watch at the end of the dock, flanked by two of the strange masked creatures that had attacked us on the road. The guard looked at us, then at the Seer, and said nothing.

"That one, I think," said the Seer, pointing to a boat half the size of the others, fitted with a pair of slender oars.

Kiernan nodded and knelt to untie the little craft and climb carefully aboard. He held it steady for me to join him.

"Thank you," I said.

"If you get lost," said the Seer, their teeth flashing in the light that spilled down the hill from the house, "I'm sure your serpents can guide you back."

Smoke poked her head out of my hood. *Is odd*, she said, and I thought she might have been commenting on the Seer, but they didn't give any indication that they had heard.

"I will inform my Lord of your errand. I'm sure he will be most interested to hear about it when you return." Then they turned and walked back to the house.

"Ready, pretty bird?" Kier's voice was carefully neutral, though I could feel his impatience in my belly, layered on top of my own, now that he wasn't blocking me out. Though I didn't feel quite the same intensity of pull as he did, once I had felt it through him it became an insistent tug on my mind.

"Always," I said, and took the hand he held out to help me settle in the boat. As soon as I had tucked my cloak around me, he pushed off from the dock and began to row. He seemed to know exactly which canal to head for and where to turn and when the canal we followed ended at a broad pool of ice-rimmed water, lit by a partial moon high above, he didn't even hesitate to find his way into the next passage.

I wished, as I had often done when traveling at night with Kiernan, that my night vision was even half as good as his. The trees around us were only vague black shapes to me, lit here and there by silver outlines from the moon. The water gleamed softly, and the ice sent back sharp reflections like gemstones caught in candlelight.

The forest made me feel very small and I was glad Kiernan was with me, because even restless he was a solid presence keeping me grounded.

I looked upwards and between the tree branches the stars were bright points of light, hardly dimmed at all by the glow of the moon. It was a glorious night, if a sharply cold one, and I felt full with wonder.

And then, a tall broad shape blocked out even the stars and a feeling of deep awe clutched at my belly.

"Is that it?" I asked, my voice hushed.

"The Heart of Tronven," Kiernan answered softly.

"Is it bigger than the Heart of Morven? It seems bigger but I can't see it well in the dark."

"It's taller." The boat stopped suddenly as we ran aground, and Kier slipped the oars from their locks and laid them in the bottom of the boat. "It's thinner, and there's no ramp into its branches, but I think I see a platform high up. Can you climb?"

"In daylight, I climb very well," I said, stepping carefully over the side of the boat onto the mossy ground of the forest. Ice crackled beneath my feet, and I dug my talons in. "I suppose I'll manage if I call wisplights to help me see."

"Fionn." I turned as Kiernan straightened up from tying the boat's rope to a small tree growing on the shore. He put his hands on my shoulders, and checked to see that my cloak was properly wrapped and fastened, as if he was worried I might get cold.

"What is it?"

"I'm afraid."

I put my palms on his chest and felt the solid muscle there. That was the word for Kiernan. *Solid*. He was my foundation, and for the second time that night he had admitted fear. Usually, I was the frightened one, and he was the one easing my fears. But this time I was not even a little afraid. I was eager to see what awaited us high in the branches of this huge fir tree, excited to find out what the insistent call meant.

"I'm here, beloved," I said. "You can be afraid because we're together."

He swallowed and moved closer, and I opened my cloak to wrap him in it with me, to pull him close against me.

"I want this so much, Fionn," he said. "To be together."

"You have it."

"Everything I've wanted this much has been taken from me."

Once, I had asked Seer Siona how to avoid hurting him, and she had said – as if it were both the easiest and the hardest thing in the world – "Don't let yourself be taken from him."

"No matter what happens," I said. "I'm yours. If we're

separated, I'll find you. If I'm taken from you, I will give myself back. Always."

He lifted his head from my chest to look at me. All I could see was his shape and the reflection of the moon in his eyes.

"Always," he repeated.

We stood so a long moment, then he stepped away, re-wrapped my cloak around me, and said, "Shall we climb this tree, pretty bird?"

"Yes," I said. "Show me where to put my hands, and we'll climb this tree together."

30
Kiernan

My hands were shaking when I turned away to look at the trunk of the massive tree, so I closed them into fists. Fionn's certainty was calming, though it had never been his strength or resolve I doubted, but my own.

I tried to keep my breathing slow and even, to ignore the urgency of that tug of magic that had only gotten stronger after we left Tovarsson's house.

The Heart of Tronven had no spiraling ramp like the Heart of Morven did and, being a fir, there were no branches low enough to reach. But I was certain people came here to celebrate, to worship – and not only around its roots. I walked around the huge trunk slowly, trailing a hand along the bark, feeling the rough texture, the huge flat plates and deep fissures, under my fingertips.

Fionn followed behind me, not speaking, his feet soft on the deep carpet of fallen needles. He summoned a group of wisplights and sent them ahead of me to help me see, but I didn't need light for this task. In fact, partway around the tree

I closed my eyes to better feel the texture of the bark and the currents of magic that swirled around the tree.

"Here," I said, feeling a smooth edge on one of the bark plates. I ran my hands over the trunk and found more at various heights, hand- and foot-holds, where many before me had found purchase to climb the straight trunk.

I took off my boots and socks and left them at the base of the tree.

"Go ahead," said Fionn. "I'll follow."

I closed my eyes and leaned my forehead against the tree, letting its magic wash over me. It was strong, and it was aware of me. I felt tiny and afraid, but I wouldn't have resisted its call even if I had been able to. And, afraid as I was of what it could mean to be summoned by this ancient forest presence, I didn't *want* to resist.

The Heart of Tronven wanted me for some purpose, and my whole life I had been desperate to be wanted. So I drew in a breath, let it out, and began to climb. I didn't open my eyes, but placed my hands by feel and by instinct. It was as easy as walking up the ramp into the branches of the huge old oak at home in Morven Forest and before I had realized it, I had left Fionn behind.

I reached the first horizontal branch high above the forest floor and forced myself to stop, to wait until Fionn caught up. However urgent the summons felt, I wanted to face it with him next to me, as I wanted to face the rest of my life. I made myself *breathe* and let my magic flow out to *see* the forest around me. Like Morven and Aven, Tronven Forest teemed with life, only it wasn't a life of leaf and soil, but of water.

Fionn was a bright silver presence climbing up the trunk to meet me, the thin ribbon of our heart-bond suffused with the green of my own magic. For a moment, the insistent tug of the tree's call faded beneath an overwhelming love as he glanced up and I opened my eyes to meet his gaze.

"Kier?" he said, and I held out a hand to pull him up onto the wide branch with me.

"I love you," I said, and his beautiful smile spread over his face, highlighted by his soft blue wisplights.

We climb, said Smoke, leaning out of Fionn's hood to peer up into the branches.

"You could fly," I said.

Up, up, said Flame, poking her head out of the other side of Fionn's hood.

"Yes, we climb." I turned back to the tree.

Nyah, said Coal, sleepy, and he draped himself over the top of my head. *Magic*, he said. *Secret*.

I wanted to rush to the top, to the platform that I knew was still above us, but I also wanted to linger, to draw out the climb all night. Something powerful awaited us, and for just a little longer, I wanted nothing to change.

At last, I pulled myself up onto one of the huge branches that supported the platform and walked along it to the edge of a flat space built of giant split reeds like a larger version of a child's playhouse. It had no walls or roof, only the branches and needles of the great tree, and it curved around the trunk in a sweep of pale flooring. I pulled myself over the edge and stood.

Fionn climbed up after me and stood close enough that his hand brushed mine. His breathing was quick but not loud and I could feel that he wanted to say something but didn't want to intrude in whatever I was experiencing.

"What do you feel?" I asked.

"Spirits," he said, his voice barely audible, like he was nervous of disturbing the quiet. "So many spirits and… something bigger. Older." He slipped his hand into mine. "I feel like I should pray," he whispered.

I turned to look at him and his face was full of wonder, his eyes unfocussed, or maybe focused on something I couldn't see. I touched his cheek, and my fingers trembled.

"You can pray if you like," I said, and he turned his gaze on me.

"You don't think it's silly?"

"Why would I think that?" I let my hand fall back to my side. "You're a Seer, pretty bird. Spirits are your business, and I think you would know if prayers are needed." I squeezed his hand. "And if you want me to pray with you, I will."

He bit his lip and immediately let go, as if realizing what he was doing. "Do you still feel restless?"

I looked around us, at the tree, the branches, and the forest below. "I feel… observed, as if whatever called me here is waiting to see what I'll do. As if I'm being… not judged, exactly, but evaluated."

"I feel it, too," he said. Then he seemed to come to a decision and moved away from me, farther onto the platform, circling the tree, and unbuckling his knives as he went.

I followed more slowly, but I decided to do as he did. As a Seer, spirits really *were* his business, and if he thought we should be unarmed here, then I would remove my weapons.

As I neared the trunk, swords and belt in hand, Fionn laid his knives down carefully on top of the bag he had brought from our room.

"Here," he said, in the exact tone I had said that same word, far below, when I knew exactly where to begin climbing. He took a step away from the trunk and knelt on the floor, tree to one side, open air to the other.

I put my swords and all my knives down with his, finally pulling the cloth-wrapped Spearhead of Dragons out of the inner pocket of my coat and adding that, too. When Fionn held out a hand to me, I went to him and knelt in front of him and took his hands in mine.

"What if I say the wrong words?" he said softly. "I never learned the right way to pray, to commune with the spirits as I *saw* the last Vogel Seer do in my vision. At the Abbey I only learned how to address the Alfar Moon Goddess, not the appropriate way to address spirits."

I brushed my thumbs over the backs of his hands. "I think the spirits will know your intentions." As the words came out the sense of urgency began to build in me again, only now it wasn't a summoning; it was something else, something I couldn't put a name to. Magic swirled around me, through me, into me, and I had no way to let it out again, to use it or to direct it back to the Realms.

Holding Fionn's hands seemed both to make the magic build faster and to give me a bit of release, as if the magic concentrating in me was able to seep away a little through him, just enough to keep it from being too much.

"Close your eyes," he said, so I did. Then he said something in Vogel, uncertain, like he was feeling his way with words. He said something else, longer but hesitant, in a language I had never heard before. But no, that wasn't true; I *had* heard it, when he stopped to say farewell to the Eyrie in the same place where he had *seen* the last Vogel Seer praying.

Then he began to sing and something tightened in my belly. It was the same song he had sung on top of the Eyrie, only I thought some of the words were different, and it made me want to weep, though I had no idea what it meant.

His voice was sweet, high, and pure, but somehow still soft, and even though I didn't understand the words, I *felt* them. I felt his plea to the spirits nearby for understanding, his welcome to them, and his hope that they would welcome us. And when he stopped, I realized his song had once more drained away the pressure of the magic building up in me. My face was wet with tears.

"Beloved," he said, his voice almost still a song. I opened my eyes to see that he had wept, too.

"I feel welcome," he said. "And… I think I need to have a vision. I think if I don't try to have one, I'll have one anyway."

"What do you need me to do?"

He opened his mouth to answer, but instead of words he let out a soft sigh and crumpled to the floor, back seizing.

I reached for him, to cushion his fall, but at that same moment the magic I had felt building rushed back all at once to fill me, to take over me, and it was all I could do not to sprawl on the floor myself.

Magic like roots reaching up from the land took hold in me, pushed into my body in green and brown and black tendrils. I felt every tree in the forest, every animal that sheltered there, and every bit of soil that breathed as much as any creature did.

Magic like tinkling streams and soft rain seeped and fell and absorbed into me, and I felt how the icy waters around us were filled with fish and insects and plant life. I felt the lives of a myriad of tiny organisms so small I couldn't properly imagine them, yet I knew them as intimately as I knew myself.

Magic like a breeze as soft as feathers and a wind as cutting as a blade scraped against me, pierced into me, blew into me. I felt every bird that caught an updraft, every winged insect and speck of pollen, every slightest stirring of air.

Somehow, I managed to stand up, so full of the magic of Three Realms I was sure I would burst into flame, and took two steps closer to the tree. I laid a hand on the trunk and even more magic poured into me, so much that I knew it would burn me hollow if I didn't find a way to release it back into the world.

And something still watched me, observed me, waited to

see what I would do.

The wounds where my antlers had been burned, pain stabbed into my head and spread like a wildfire until my whole head might have been aflame. I might have screamed, but the only sound I heard was the rush of power in my ears.

My knees hit the platform with a shock that travelled up my spine and distracted me just enough from the magic burning me alive that I found Fionn, sprawled on the floor and twitching, and I crawled to him, and took his hands in both of mine so I could kiss his fingers one more time.

And then I did what I had always done when I couldn't cope. I let the shadows hide me and escaped into darkness.

OF COURSE, SOME THINGS cannot be escaped so easily. I opened my eyes to a dream where Fionn and I walked hand-in-hand across a wildflower meadow to where a tall, elegant Vogel with amber yellow feathers and a dark-haired Sidhe boy with small antlers waited.

As we got closer, I realized the Vogel had paler feathers on one side of their body, divided neatly down the middle, and I knew I should know who they were. They smiled when they saw us, a soft look of love on their features.

And the Sidhe boy… for a moment I thought I was looking at my younger self. But then I realized his eyes were not the dark green I had inherited from my mother, but were instead deep grey, and he was taller than I had been at that age.

He was about to speak when suddenly all sound was gone from the world and a spike of pain pierced my forehead and I fell to my knees and screamed again. And this time when I opened my eyes, the gaze that met mine was not the grey of my possible future son, but the pure bright silver of my beloved.

"My Seer," I said, finding a smile somewhere despite the magic that made my head ring and swirled inside me, threatening to ignite my spirit in a blinding burst of fire.

"My King," said Fionn. Then a look of confusion crossed his face. "My Prince," he corrected himself. "My beloved." We lay on our sides, face-to-face on the floor of the platform high above the Drowned Forest.

"My head hurts," I said, and he reached up to put a cool palm on my brow, his touch a caress like water to the burning heat.

"You're so full of magic," he said, wonder in his voice.

"I'm going to burn hollow," I replied. "I can't *use* it. I can't channel it away, and it's going to burn me to a cinder inside."

"Oh, beloved," he said. "Maybe I can draw some of it off." He pushed himself up and then helped me sit. I wanted to curl into a ball and disappear, but for him I would try to exist.

He reached up to touch my forehead, then stopped suddenly, hand still outstretched. "Oh, I'm so stupid."

I wanted to tell him no, he wasn't stupid, he had never been and could never be stupid, but I couldn't make my mouth shape words. I reached for the sounds, but they slithered away.

He moved away from me, and I couldn't reach out after him. He crawled to where our weapons lay and I toppled over slowly, unable to even put out an arm to stop myself.

"Ow," I said, or tried to say, unsure if sound came out or if I just *thought* the word. I lost track of what Fionn was doing until I felt his arm around my shoulders, helping me sit up again.

"I know what she meant now. The Lady of the Forest. She promised to help me again and I was so overwhelmed by everything that's happened that I didn't even feel her here among all the spirits."

I knew the meaning of each of his words, but I was having trouble figuring out how they made sense together, so I stopped trying and just concentrated on staying upright and not screaming again from the pressure of all the magic building up in me.

He knelt in front of me and placed a wooden box between us. I *knew* that box; I had seen it somewhere. Was it Siona's? My thoughts drifted again, and I started to fall over, but somehow managed to right myself.

Fionn lifted the lid of the box and the weave of the cloth inside caught my attention. I could see every smallest detail of it in a way I never had seen anything before. And then I caught the scent of what was wrapped *in* the cloth.

"Have you stuffed me in a box, pretty bird? Put me away for later?" I knew I wasn't making sense; the magic was too distracting.

"Do you trust me?" he asked, which seemed like such an absurd question that I laughed.

His hands on my face forced me to pay attention and a little of the magic drained away into him and I could think again.

"I trust you," I managed to say.

"Then… don't move." He lifted something from the box. Antlers. *My* antlers, one pair of child-sized spikes and one pair of branched youth prongs. He held them so each of the spikes sat at an angle to the forked tines, making shapes approximating the antlers I had made Daphnis tear from me, that had burned in the blaze of my Queen's revenge for thwarting her.

"I killed Daphnis over those," I said, trying to keep myself focused.

Fionn shook his head. "Daphnis chose death. And this will give you your magic back, not take it away." He held up my antlers, one set in each slender, pale hand, and he closed his eyes.

I felt his healing magic gather as he connected with the Three Realms, and the magic filling me eased off.

"Beloved, you can't heal me. If you heal me, my antlers will never grow back."

"I *can* heal you," he said. "But you must let me. You must trust me, trust that I know what I'm doing, that I've figured out why Siona gave me this box, and what I am meant to do with it. I *know*, Kier, and you must trust me."

I stared at the antlers in his hands. They were mine. They had been mine, and all these years I hadn't known that Siona had saved them, had kept them safe.

"I trust you," I whispered, and I reached out and put my hands over his, not to hold them away from the raw wounds where my antlers had been, but to pull them closer, to *show* him that I trusted him.

"Close your eyes," he said, and I realized I had forgotten they were open. I closed them. "Breathe deep," he said, so I breathed. "Do you feel the Three Realms?"

"I can't avoid them, Fionn. "Their magic fills me and I'm going to burn to nothing."

"No," he said gently. "You're not. That magic is yours and I know how to return its use to you."

"I trust you," I said again, and I knew that whatever happened next, I *did* trust him. Even if his plan didn't work, it didn't matter, because I would do anything he asked.

"Feel the Realms and see the bright flame at the center where they meet that is you," he said, telling me what I had told him when we first met, and I showed him he was not without magic as he had believed.

I made myself turn my awareness inward, to really feel the magic gathering in me and to place myself at the center of it, burning bright green in my spirit.

"I'm ready," I said.

For a moment, I felt the cool silver of his healing magic swirl between my green flame and the magic of the Realms, then it slipped up my spine to my head and bathed my antlers – where my antlers had been – and it felt so good, so right, that I might have said something aloud.

Then I felt the bases of my childhood antlers press against the raw wounds where my adult antlers had been and all the magic – mine, Fionn's, the Three Realms – all rushed to those two points and flared up, and I suppose I must have screamed again because Fionn flinched. But he held firm, pressed the antlers to my forehead, and flooded me with healing.

I knew he had said to keep my eyes closed, but something made me open them. His face was relaxed as he bathed me in his magic and I could have gazed on him forever, despite the pain in my forehead and the magic burning through me. But something made me look away, over his shoulder, where I met eyes as deep green as my own.

I jerked, and Fionn said, "I'm almost done, beloved. Hold still for me just a little longer," but he didn't open his eyes.

I breathed carefully and made myself study the face peering at me over Fionn's shoulder. It was not, as I had first thought, my Queen. The woman watching me resembled my Queen, or perhaps it was that my mother resembled *her:* green eyes, flowing hair the color of dried blood, large elegant antlers.

No, not my Queen, my mother, my bane; instead, the Lady of the Forest watched me, watched Fionn heal me. Behind her, I could see the vague shapes of other spirits hovering, and there, just on the edge of my perception, that ancient force that had summoned me here, content now to observe.

I felt my old antlers fuse to my skull, as vital and alive as they had always been, and the built up pressure of all the magic that had filled me eased off as I could finally let it flow back into the Land, Sea, and Sky.

Then the Lady of the Forest smiled and said, "Awaken, child of my forest. Your people have need of you." Then she vanished, and all the other spirits with her. The ancient spirit of the Heart of Morven lingered a moment longer, then she, too, was gone, and I fell forward into my lover's arms.

31
Fionn

ONCE I REALIZED what I was meant to do with Kiernan's childhood antlers and how the Lady of the Forest intended to help, I felt stupid for not seeing it sooner. It was so *obvious*.

And it was so easy. Perhaps I should have done the healing in spirit form, in order to better manage the flow of magic, but I was in a hurry and the rest of the vision faded as I opened the box and pressed the antlers to Kier's head and let all the healing magic I could call up flow through me and into him.

Smoke and Flame stayed perched on my shoulders, pressing their heads against my cheeks and purring, as if to help me, while Coal slid from his favorite perch on the top of Kiernan's head to wrap himself around his neck.

Kier was so full of magic already, and so unable to do anything with it save endure it that we must together have lit up the forest like a beacon to anyone with any ability at all to sense it.

I knew it was working when he screamed and, terrible as

it felt to bring him pain, I kept on, kept pressing the antlers against the wounds on his head, and kept sending healing into him. The moment the Lady of the Forest added the magic of the trees to mine, Kiernan flinched, but I was too close to stop, too nearly finished giving him back what had been stolen.

It seemed a kindness when he lost consciousness and fell forward into my arms. I turned him carefully, so his head rested in my lap, and I brushed his hair back. Coal crept from around his neck to settle across his forehead, purring fiercely, as if to add his healing – if serpents had any healing magic – to what I had already done.

Kiernan's antlers were firmly re-attached, subtly different in shape from what they had been, but the baby spikes had fused to the larger pair, giving him the same three points he had before.

The bumpy-smooth texture was the same as I remembered as I ran my fingers lightly over them. I reached out carefully with my mind to feel his magic and it was strong, pulsing like green flame in the core of his spirit. It still filled him to bursting, but no longer seemed about to burn him hollow.

Around us, the spirits drifted away, and I could no longer sense the Lady of the Forest, nor the ancient power that had observed and summoned us. They were all quiet, as if they had seen what they came for, and now had other things to attend to.

Kiernan opened his eyes, blinked up at me, and smiled.

"How do you feel?" I asked.

"Whole. Thank you."

I bent over and pushed Coal aside so I could kiss Kier's forehead. The serpent grumbled softly, but moved away.

"You called me your King." His lips curved in a smile. "When you woke from your vision."

"Did I?" I tried to remember what I had *seen*, and my back

twinged, as if just now remembering the abuse it had suffered. "I *saw* myself healing you," I said. "And I *saw* us walking through a field of flowers. Lisna was there."

"The Vogel child you told me about?"

I nodded. "And your son."

"If I have son in the future, pretty bird, he'll be *ours*."

It made me glad, that he assumed that whatever future child he might have would call me "father" also, and that he kept insisting on reminding me. "Our son, then."

"I saw that, too. I think I shared your vision."

"Then perhaps I called you 'King' because I saw you in a possible future, as King of Morven Forest."

"I will never be King."

I shrugged. "I don't remember that part of my vision, but I'm happy to call you my King if you want me to."

He smiled wider and raised a hand to lay his palm on my face. Then he frowned and moved his hand closer to his eyes to examine the back of it.

"What is it?" I asked, shifting Smoke and Flame off my shoulders where they were leaning over so far they were about to slide off anyway.

He didn't answer but rolled off my lap, dislodging Coal, who followed his mothers to our weapons where they all curled up as if to guard them. Kier tugged impatiently at the buttons on his coat and pulled it off, fumbled with the sleeve of his borrowed shirt, then pulled it off, too.

Goosebumps rose on his skin, but his ignored them to lift his left arm. "Look."

The green leaves tattooed – or magically grown, perhaps – had spread, covering the back of his hand where he had seen them when he touched my face. They also curled, now, up past his elbow.

He stared at the green design, then met my eyes, so I

smiled and reached for his hand. "Your magic has grown," I said. I brought his hand to my lips and kissed it. "You're going to get cold."

He cupped his hand around my face and said, "I seem to have magic to spare," and the air warmed around us until I unclasped my cloak and let it slip off my shoulders.

"It still wants something from me," he said. "The magic, the… ancient presence that watched us. And…" He stared into my eyes. "Pretty bird." Something in the way he said it, deep and growly, made me flush.

I reached out and put my hand on his chest, felt his smooth skin and his hard muscle and something in me answered the look in his eyes. I felt pressure behind my belly muscles, in my sheath, as my body woke to his.

"Fionn," he said, voice soft. "Goddess Below, I want you."

"I'm here," I said. "I'm yours." I stroked my hand over his chest, felt his nipple harden under my palm, and heard his breath catch.

"I'm afraid," he said, as he had said so many times lately.

"To make love to me?" I let a teasing note into my voice, but he still looked at me seriously.

"The magic is still so raw, and it fills me, makes me want… Makes me *want*. Pretty bird, I'm afraid that if I touch you, I'll wake something dark in me, and I won't be able to stop."

"If you touch me, I don't *want* you to stop."

He leaned toward me, then tensed to pull away, as if he was fighting his own self. "What I feel inside me… I'm afraid I might hurt you. What if I hurt you?" He moved his hand away from my face and it shook.

I reached for it, guided his touch to the hem of my shirt and under, pressing his palm to my side. "You won't hurt me, beloved, and I want you, so much."

For a moment he was still and then, suddenly, he was

yanking my shirt over my head and pressing me onto my back, my cloak the only thing between my skin and the floor.

His mouth on mine was hard, insistent, demanding, and so unlike the usual care he took with me that I was startled. But I didn't push him away. I felt the fire building in my belly flare up to meet the fire burning in his, and I grabbed his hair with both hands and answered the demands of his kiss with demands of my own.

He pulled away, looked down at me, and breathed hard. "My beautiful Fionn," he said. "Push me away, now, because I can't do it myself."

"I won't." I reached for the tie on his trousers and tugged it free.

"Fionn, please." His arms, braced on each side of me, strained to hold him up, to keep him from crushing my body with his.

"Do you want to stop?" I rested my hands on his waist, slid them lower to push down his trousers, and when the garment was as low as I could reach, I moved to my own, wiggling out of them until we were both nearly bare.

Still, he held himself away from me, looking into my face with burning eyes. "What if I can't stop? The magic is driving me, like a fire burning deep inside, and I don't think I can stop."

"I don't want you to stop." I bent one leg to grasp his trousers with my toes and pull them the rest of the way off.

"What if I lose control? What if I hurt you?"

"You won't hurt me."

"Fionn." He let his head drop so I felt his hair brush my chest. "What if I lose control?" he asked again.

"It's okay to lose control with me," I said. "Sometimes, maybe you *need* to lose control, and it's safe to lose control with me. *You're* safe with me, and I'm safe with you."

I slid both hands down my thighs and grasped my knees, pulling them up almost to my chest. My spine curved and I tucked one knee under Kier's arm and wrapped my other leg over his back.

"Fionn." His voice was ragged, his breathing harsh.

"Lose yourself in me, beloved," I said. My erection was pressing insistently on the inside of my sheath, and I let it slide slowly out, and he moaned softly at the wet sound it made. I moved a hand from his waist down my belly and dipped my fingers into my sheath, withdrawing them covered with my lubricant. Then I curled my fingers around his hardness, spreading my slick onto him until he slid easily through my fist.

He groaned and shifted between my legs. "Fionn."

I reached up with my other hand and combed my fingers through his hair and curled them around one of his antlers.

"Goddess," he breathed. "I can't. I might –"

"No." He blinked at my strong tone. "You won't hurt me, Kier. I *want* you. I want you inside me, deep and hard. I want you to come undone fucking me. I want to pulse with you fucking me." Pronouncing those words I had been raised to believe were sinful left me flushed, but I was glad I said them. I tugged on his antler and tightened my hand around his erection, moving it lower until its tip pushed against my anus. "Do you understand?" My voice was almost angry, and he focused his eyes on mine.

"I –" He seemed unable to say anything more.

"Remember in the cave when you wanted me to *take* you?"

He nodded and whispered, "Yes."

"And did I?"

"Yes."

"Did I hurt you?"

"No."

"No. So fucking *take* me." I didn't swear often, especially not so many times in so short a moment, and it made Kier pay attention.

"I love you, Fionn," he said, still holding himself back.

"And I love you." I pressed my heel against his buttocks and felt him resist me, so I eased off, then suddenly tightened my leg again, catching him off guard and pulling him towards me, into me.

He cried out and buried his face against my chest and the feel of his tip pushing me open and then stopping, hesitating, made me pulse, spurting a little onto my belly.

"I felt you, Fionn," he said, voice soft.

"Make me pulse again," I demanded.

He relented, but pushed forward slowly, too slowly, until I wanted to yell at him for making me wait. But finally, he was buried as deep inside me as he could go, and I pulsed again.

He looked at my belly, decorated with pearly white, and it was as if seeing the pleasure I took from him inside me freed him from his fear of hurting me. He slid out and plunged in and I wrapped my legs tightly across his back and gripped both his antlers in my hands.

He kept his face pressed against my chest as he thrust his hips, hard and fast now that he wasn't trying to resist the magic driving him. His belly slid over my erection, and I pulsed again, harder, and he jerked a little, and I realized I had hit him in the face.

When he raised his head to look at me, splotches of my fluids dappled his chin. He met my eyes, then ducked his head and licked my skin, meeting my eyes again as he swallowed my semen and licked his lips.

"Don't stop," I said, feeling the slow build of my fourth pulse. "I will never forgive you if you stop now."

He grinned like a wild creature and slammed into me again

and again, my pleasure building each time his hard length rubbed me inside, each time his hard belly muscles rubbed over my erection. He was fierce and lost in it, in a way he had never dared to be before, and I felt fierce in return, wild with desire.

When my fourth pulse came, it spread from the tips of my fingers and toes all through my body, concentrating in my testicles and pushing through me to spew semen up my belly to my chest, slipping over his skin and mine as we rubbed together.

I thought to relax, to enjoy the aftermath of my orgasm and watch him finish, but my body had other ideas.

"Goddess, Fionn," he said. "I need to come, please, I can't stand it. You feel so fucking good."

My fingers and toes tingled, and my erection did not subside.

"Please make me come," he said.

"Don't stop, Kier. I'm not done, either." I grabbed at his shoulders, his back, his buttocks, trying to pull him farther into me, trying to satisfy the insistent need building again. I dug my heel against his behind, letting my rear toe slip between so my knuckle pressed against his anus.

He moaned and thrust. "Please."

"Don't stop."

He didn't stop, and I felt magic building in both of us, between us, swirling around us, as pleasure built and built, and we both begged to be released. And then his green spirit flame blazed half orange and swirled together with my silver, and we both cried out at the same time. I felt my own pulse and his orgasm together and I knew he felt mine, and somehow our heart-bond became stronger, though I would not have thought it possible.

I flooded my belly and chest with so much semen it pooled

in the hollow of my throat and ran down the sides of my neck. I felt Kier strain against me and go still, and something wet dripped out of me to tickle my backside.

He met my gaze, and his pupils were so big his eyes looked black. But then a sudden rush of wisplights swirled around us and he laughed. His arms trembled to hold himself up and finally he gave in and sagged on top of me, sliding in the mess I'd made of my skin.

It seemed an impossible effort to move my arms to embrace him, and I was certain it took several days to accomplish, I felt so disinclined to move. We lay together for an eternity before he stirred, and I felt a trickle of cold air as the warmth he had gathered around us began to fade.

I shivered and pried open my eyes. And almost shrieked.

All around us, the strange masked creatures that served the Lord of the Drowned Forest crouched, waiting.

"Kier," I said, and he lifted his head, peeling his face off my chest.

"Oh," he said. "I hope you haven't come to kill us, because I don't have to energy to reach for my swords."

Smoke and Flame slid across the floor to put themselves between us and the creatures, but they didn't rear up or hiss as they had before. One of the creatures crept forward a little and cocked its head.

Kiernan slowly sat up, making sure I was behind him, though it made little difference as the creatures were on all sides. He wiped his chin with one hand and reached out with the other. Coal followed the other serpents and growled softly as the creature crept forward a little more.

"It's okay," Kier said. "I don't think they mean us any harm."

The creature edge forward again and made a soft noise in its throat.

"I… I can almost understand," Kier said. "But it's like there's something blocking me. My magic lets me speak to all the creatures of the forest, but something prevents me from understanding this one."

The creature raised a clawed hand to touch its mask. Then it cocked its head.

"What if —" I stopped myself from saying what seemed absurd.

Kiernan didn't look at me, but he said, "What if what, pretty bird?"

I hesitated, but remembered how, every time I felt I had a stupid thought, he encouraged me to voice it anyway, and usually it turned out to be not so stupid.

"What if it's the masks?" I said.

The creature turned its head towards me and tapped its claws against the rounded wooden mask that covered it.

"Can you take your mask off?" Kier asked.

The creature raised both hands and gripped the sides of the mask, but it didn't come free. It made a motion with its shoulders, something like a shrug, and put both palms on the floor.

"Can I try?" I said, and the creature looked at me again.

Smoke and Flame edged closer to me, very obviously putting themselves between me and the creature. It cocked its head, then looked at Kiernan.

"I think it wants you to do it," I said.

Kier scooped Coal off the floor and handed him to me, grabbed his shirt to wipe off his chest, then closed the distance between himself and the creature. I shivered, realizing the warmth he had brought had completely faded, so I pulled my cloak around me. The creature glanced at me again, as if waiting for something.

I moved closer to Kiernan, slipping behind him and

putting my hands on his shoulders. He was tense, big muscles straining, but he looked calm. I felt our magic swirl together, as if preparing for something, and he leaned back, just slightly, into my touch. He reached for the creature's mask and started to lift it away.

"I would not do that, were I you, Prince of Morven Forest," said a familiar voice and we both looked over to see Lord Tovarsson standing on the edge of the platform as if he had just stepped out of a swirl of darkness. All the creatures scurried away save the one crouched in front of Kiernan, disappearing over the edge of the platform and down into the forest.

I wrapped my cloak over Kiernan as best I could, though I knew it didn't bother him to be naked.

"What don't you want me to see?" Kier said. I could feel the tension in him and the magic he held near, keeping it ready in case he needed to defend us, since our weapons were behind us, against the trunk of the tree. But despite how he felt to me, his voice was calm and reasonable.

The creature kept its face turned towards Kiernan, gazing at him as if he might shield it from its Lord.

"We Huldr are called the Hidden People for good reason," Tovarsson said. "Lift that mask, and you will learn things we have no wish for you to know, and that you will regret finding out."

Kiernan shifted slightly under my hands but didn't move his grip from the creature's mask. His head moved, but I couldn't tell what he was looking at from where I sat behind him.

Tovarsson strode forward. "This creature is being punished for its crimes. They all are."

"You have a curious way of treating your criminals," Kier said. "What happens if I remove the mask?"

"You free it."

"And why is that something I would regret seeing?"

For a moment, every line of Tovarsson's body expressed hostility, anger, and… something more elusive.

"Is this something you would hide from the Queen of Morven Forest as well?" I said, and Tovarsson flinched.

"That was a cruel blow, Seer," he said. "But well struck. These creatures are the shame of our people, but the Queen of Morven Forest already knows. I would have her son think better of me. Of us."

"Is this why she sent you away?" Kier asked.

"She did not send me. I left. But yes. When she learned the truth, it changed how she felt. She *pitied* me, because it was my task to cast the spell that created the masks, and I could not bear her pity." He looked away, out over the forest. "And then she fell in love with a human man, and married him, and I knew I had no hope of ever winning her back."

"What did the creatures do, that you punish them with masks they can't remove and with magic that prevents them from being understood?" I said it carefully, trying to find the right words, the right *questions*.

Tovarsson seemed almost to deflate. "Come back to my house, and I will explain it all to you, only please do not remove the creature's mask."

Kiernan still didn't move, and I understood why. On the surface, it seemed reasonable to step back, to go with the Huldr Lord and let him explain. But the creature had asked for help from us, and I knew that if I had difficulty refusing such a request, Kiernan would also. He had been the champion of those who could not help themselves since we had first met, me in my spirit body, when we were only tiny boys, and he had set aside his own fear and grief to comfort me.

"If you plan to tell me, what difference does it make if I remove the creature's mask or not?"

"It matters to me," said Tovarsson.

"Why?" Kiernan jerked his head up and his fingers tightened on the wooden surface.

The creature itself waited, still and silent, and I reached out a tendril of magic towards it. I found a barrier, like the mask blocked even my *sight*. The creature shifted slightly, and I saw the gleam of its eyes watching me from inside the mask.

"Take it off," I said, suddenly certain that it was the right thing to do.

"Yes," said a new voice, light and feminine, that made me shiver and caused Kiernan to go rigid under my hands. "Take off the mask and let us see what the noble Lord Lioswright Tovarsson has been hiding from everyone but his Monarch these many years."

The Queen of Morven Forest stepped around the trunk of the tree to look from the Huldr Lord to her son and then back again.

Kiernan hissed under his breath, and I felt his dismay, confusion, and anxiety through our bond.

"Beloved," I said softly, keeping my voice low for only him to hear. "I know you don't trust your Queen, but I believe it needs to be done. Remove the mask, and then let everyone explain."

His shoulders relaxed a fraction under my hands, and he lifted the mask gently away from the creature's face.

A twist of magic swirled away, and there, instead of an animal-like being of fur and claws, there sat a woman, muscular, with shaggy hair, tanned skin, and freckles across her shoulders.

"Hello, brother," she said, grinning, and then in an eyeblink, she was a wolf, huge, wide-eyed, and regal.

32
Kiernan

THE WOMAN BEFORE ME was almost immediately a wolf again, but I would have known her in either shape. What I didn't know was why she was in Tronven in the first place, or what she could possibly have done to merit punishment.

I opened my arms and the huge wolf pressed herself against me and rested her head on my shoulder.

"Where are our siblings?" I said, but I didn't really need her to tell me. She was the leader of the three, and they would be wherever she was, which meant they, too, were trapped in masks.

She turned her head to look back over her shoulder to where Tovarsson stood on the edge of the platform, looking extremely guilty.

I stood, absently taking and donning the trousers Fionn handed me. I didn't know who to get angry at first. Tovarsson took a step forward, so I focused on him, "Why?" was all I said.

"I told you, for their crimes."

"What crimes could a wolf of Morven Forest have committed against Tronven that would merit such barbaric punishment?"

"I wonder that myself," said my Queen, moving to stand next to me.

"And you knew," I snapped, whirling to face her. "You must have known the wolves were here, and you certainly know who else is hidden behind those masks." Fionn handed me a shirt and I pulled it over my head with angry movements, almost tearing one of the seams.

"Calmly, my son," my Queen said, holding out a hand. I wanted to say more, but the fact that she looked amused and not angry at my outburst made me force my breathing to slow. I needed to remember she was the most dangerous person present, and though I hated to follow her command, she was right: I needed calm.

My wolf sister pressed against my side, so tall her shoulder reached well above my hip.

"If you found a spy from another Monarchy lurking in your forests, would you not punish them?" Tovarsson said.

"My wolf siblings are not spies," I growled.

"My son," said the Queen and I realized all at once what must have happened and how the three wolves who had nursed beside me as infants had come to be here.

"You sent them," I said, feeling calm start to slip away again. Fionn's hand on my back steadied me enough that I didn't yell, didn't pick up my sword and threaten her with it. For now, she still seemed to find my reactions entertaining; the moment I offended her, my safety ended.

"I asked them to follow a trail of betrayal that went back a great many years, most recently manifesting with the death of my beloved nephew by your hand." She didn't sound like a grieving aunt to me, and I knew she used "beloved" more as an obligatory title than a true description. "The trail led here, to Tronven." I glared at her, and the corner of her mouth quirked up. "Your wolf sisters and brother offered to help investigate, because it was a betrayal of *you*."

"But you," and Fionn moved even closer to me, directing his words to Tovarsson. "You said these creatures are the shame of the Huldr." He turned to the Queen. "And you seemed surprised at who was revealed when the mask was removed."

The Queen regarded Fionn with mild astonishment, as is he was a piece of furniture that had suddenly come to life.

"Please," said Tovarsson. "Return home with me, and we can discuss this in comfort."

The Queen inclined her head and made to follow the Huldr Lord down off the platform. When he had preceded her into the darkness, she paused and turned back to me and I made myself set aside my fear and anger and really look at her.

She was dressed much more simply than usual, in trousers and a long tunic suitable for travel, which told me she had likely just arrived here, and Tovarsson's surprise at seeing her was genuine. A fur-lined cloak covered her shoulders, her hair was pulled back in a simple braid, and her feet were bare. If it weren't for the fact that her face looked thin and more drawn than I had ever seen, she might have looked no older than I was. But she looked tired, ill, even.

"Are you well, my Queen?" I said, not sure what impulse made me ask, or why I even cared.

Another brief smile touched her mouth. "I am still recovering from the backlash of your magic," she said. The smile became stronger. "I had hoped my spellwork would force you to turn to your sisters for aid. I miscalculated your determination to do everything yourself."

I wanted to stare at her in disbelief, but I made myself

speak. "You may also have miscalculated my sisters' inclination to help me." I rubbed my left ear, deliberately drawing her attention to the deep nick in its edge, caused by my elder siblings' desire to make me look more like the half-human I was by trimming the points off my ears.

She reached out and touched softly where my fingers had just been, and I managed not to flinch. "They are no longer children," she said. "And if you let them, they could become your staunchest allies."

I snorted and she frowned.

"Do you know why I gave you to Siona to raise?" she said, and I had to work hard not to gape at her.

"Because you hated to be reminded that you married a human man and had a child with him." I turned away to pick up my weapons and found Fionn already holding out my belt, ready to buckle on.

The Queen didn't reply until I turned back, and then she took my face in both hands, and I stood very still. "No, my son. I loved that you reminded me of your father. We couldn't live together – we are too much alike – but I *do* miss him." She took a curl of my hair between her fingers, then dropped her hands and stepped away. "I gave you to Siona because I am not given to softness. I knew I could make you strong, but I needed Siona to teach you compassion."

I felt tears building up behind my eyes, tears I had not even thought to shed since I was a child, desperate for a mother's love. I blinked them away and looked at Fionn instead, to ground me and make me feel strong again.

The Queen moved to the edge of the platform, then turned back one more time.

"Tell me why I find you here," she said.

"Did you not expect to?" I took Fionn's hand in mine.

Her mouth quirked again, almost making another smile.

Her eyes flicked to my antlers, then back to my face. "I came here to find out why your wolf siblings had not yet returned to Morven Forest." She glanced at Fionn curiously, then back at me. "I was aware you were not at Great River, where you were supposed to be, but I assumed you would return there and report to me once your… errand was complete."

I hesitated to speak. Last time I had lingered away from where she wanted me, she had taken my magic.

"I'm afraid it's my fault Prince Kiernan is not at his embassy," Fionn said.

The Queen raised an eyebrow. "Indeed?'

"I needed help," he said, his voice calm and cool. "Prince Kiernan was good enough to assist me."

"Help that your own people could not provide?" she said. "And has this… help anything to do with the rumors of something significant happening at the Eyrie?"

"Just so," Fionn said, but he declined to specify which of her questions he was answering. He held out a hand. "I have heard you are strong in magic, Queen of Morven Forest. If you wish, you may look for yourself."

I wanted to wrap my arms around him, to protect him from even having to think about what had made him flee the Eyrie. But perhaps my Queen was less cruel than I had believed her to be, because she shook her head.

"That won't be necessary, Seer Tokka. Your word as a Seer is sufficient. You required my son's help and he, being the generous man he is, went to your aid." She glanced between us again. "Which does not explain why I find you rutting together in a sacred tree."

The tips of Fionn's ears and the tops of his cheekbones turned pink, and I was glad my own complexion didn't show blushes easily.

"We are…" I started to say, but then didn't know how to

explain our relationship in a way the Queen would accept.

"Your son and I are heart-bonded," Fionn said.

"You offer me a fairytale as an explanation?" Her voice went up a note at the end, as if she was offended. "I care not who my son couples with, but I *do* care who he makes promises to."

Fionn looked down at her — he was taller than I was, and I was taller than she, so he nearly towered over her. It made it easy for him to look haughty, and he made his voice match.

"Heart-bonding is not a fairytale to my people," he said. "And if you care to look, ours should be visible to your magic."

Her eyebrows rose, but her eyes lost focus and her gaze drifted down from the level of our faces to that of our bellies. She blinked and focused on me again.

"How curious," she said. "This does not change the fact that you cannot marry him."

"It may not," I said. "But other facts will."

"Even if I were to allow it," she said, "Vogel law forbids him from marrying outside his people."

She raised her hand when I would have spoken again. "Your hand is mine to give away, my son," she said. "You will make the alliance *I* choose when you wed."

"You once suggested I marry the Vogel King's daughter," I reminded her.

"And you pointed out then that not only was she still a child, but that their own law forbids Vogel from marrying non-Vogel." She scowled as if annoyed at having to repeat herself.

"The existence of our heart-bond will make it necessary for my people to repeal that law," said Fionn, sounding like a diplomat discussing simple politics and not a young man pleading to be allowed to marry his love. "Along with the law forbidding same-sex unions. Neither law is of any great antiquity, anyway, and most of the ordinary citizens believe both are unjust."

"Even so," said the Queen. "My son is a Prince, and my heir. I have deep respect for Seers, but you are not a fit match for a royal Sidhe."

I knew her words would hurt Fionn, who had once believed himself to be an unwanted orphan and an ineffectual Seer, but he didn't show it.

"He's not just any Seer," I said. "And I am only your third heir."

She looked at me with a thoughtful expression, but didn't reply.

Fionn said, as she was about to turn away to descend the tree, "It is true that the two children King Sarkot had with this Queen are still too young to make marriage alliances." He glanced at me and smiled slightly. "But they are not my King's only children. By Vogel law, a child need not be born in marriage to inherit, as long as a Seer verifies their parentage."

The Queen studied Fionn, calculating, and I wanted to tell him that he didn't have to say anything, that we could find another way. But he was only going to tell her the very fact I had planned to use myself, to convince her to give me what I wanted.

"There are only the three of us here," the Queen said, glancing at my wolf sister, who remained pressed against my side, then away, as if deciding she didn't count. "Speak plainly if you will, Seer Tokka."

"I am King Sarkot's oldest child," Fionn said. I squeezed his fingers.

The Queen let out a breath, long and slow. "I see. Perhaps this does change things." She turned abruptly away. "Let us return to Tovarsson's house where we can discuss this, and other things, in comfort."

"My Queen?" I said, surprising myself by speaking up

when it might have been better to be silent.

She waited for me to continue.

"I will not deny that I want this alliance for love." I jerked my chin up. "But I believe that it is also a politically advantageous one."

Her face softened for a moment, and she moved closer again to touch my cheek. "You are so like me," she said, then she moved quickly away, off the platform and disappeared down the trunk of the tree.

All at once I felt weak and I leaned against Fionn.

"That was terrifying," he said, and I laughed.

"Yes, it was."

"Will she punish you?" He wrapped an arm around me, and I turned my face to breathe in his scent. I could smell his skin and our sex, and I tried not to think that the Queen had probably smelled it, too, that she had probably also heard us. Fuck, the whole forest had probably heard us.

"She seemed…" I shook my head. "She seems different since I had Daphnis take my antlers."

"Do you think —" He hesitated, then turned away to gather up the rest of our things. I looked at my wolf sister, who had moved to sit waiting at the edge of the platform. Fionn turned back. "I don't dare hope," he said. "That she'll let you marry me."

"She isn't our only obstacle, pretty bird," I said. "There's still your Vogel laws to change, and I don't think every one of your Councilors will be eager to do away with them, no matter what the common folk think."

I took my coat when he handed it to me and shrugged into it, ignoring how awkwardly it fit over my weapons, because it felt like too much work to unstrap them all to put them back on over the garment. "Siona told you one of my wet nurses was a wolf?"

"You're changing the subject," he said, but he looked at the huge wolf crouched on the edge of the platform and smiled. "Siona didn't say your siblings were werewolves."

I let a smile onto my face, and it felt good. "Morven wolves can take two-legged shape when they need to, but they are still very much wolves."

"Oh."

"Werewolves are people who can put on wolf shape, which is sort of the opposite."

"I see."

"This is… well, her Islish name would be Grace. My other siblings are Hunter and Ranger." I looked at my wolf sister. "The others were punished by Tovarsson, too?"

She nodded.

"Bring them to Tovarsson's house and I'll free them."

She nodded again, and then too fast to follow, she took human shape and disappeared over the side of the platform.

"Shall we go find out who the rest of the masked creatures are and why Tovarsson didn't want us to know?"

It was my turn to nod, "And see if we can convince my Queen that an alliance between our peoples is a good idea?"

"Yes."

I HAD HOPED TO GO FIRST to our rooms, to wash and change into my own clothes, but it seemed Tovarsson was not inclined to wait, and we were escorted into a large sitting room as soon as we arrived back at the island inside the reed palisade.

The Queen looked irritated, as if she had hoped to wait as well, and in the improved lighting of the room – lit by firelight and lamps and floating orbs of wisplight – she looked even more ill. It made me uneasy. Except for immediately after having Daphnis remove my antlers, I had never seen her show weakness of any kind. If she was still afflicted by the magical backlash and neither Siona nor our most skilled healers could help her, then… Well, I didn't know what it meant, and I didn't want to think about it too carefully.

I paused to let Fionn precede me into the room, and he entered as if the house and everything in it belonged to him, never mind the borrowed clothes that trapped his wings beneath them or the twigs in his hair. He looked far more like a Prince than I did. He always had, and I thought even my Queen could see it.

Her eyes followed him across the room as he went to the fireplace and held out his hands to its warmth.

"May I make some tea, Lord Tovarsson?" he asked, and the Lord of the Drowned Forest hurried forward, looking mortified to be called out as a poor host, though I was sure Fionn hadn't meant it that way. It was simply that he was cold and wanted a hot beverage.

"I will have someone bring a fresh pot," Tovarsson said, turning and snapping his fingers at a groggy-looking servant who hurried from the room.

I stood next to Fionn near the fireplace and waited. Tovarsson made to sit on the couch next to the Queen, but she shot him a look that made him hastily move to a chair on the other side of a low table from her.

No one else seemed eager to bring up any of the subjects we had proposed to discuss, so I finally just said, "My Queen, what did you learn of my cousin Sean's betrayal and his attempt to murder Seer Tokka when the Vogel delegation visited us in the fall?"

She looked at me with eyebrows raised, probably as surprised by my boldness as I was. But she had already done the worst thing to me she possibly could have when she took my magic, and I had survived and even grew stronger. I couldn't say I was no longer afraid of her – I was rash, but not stupid – but I was tired of trying to function with only partial knowledge.

"I questioned my sister's husband, as you suggested." I noticed that she didn't refer to him as my uncle, or even as my cousin's father. "I learned that he had close ties to the man who paid to have you assassinated when you were a boy."

"But why not try to kill me again? Why target Seer Tokka instead?"

She stretched her legs and rested her bare feet on the highly polished table between her couch and Tovarsson's chair. I refused to show surprise at her un-queenly behavior – she had reason for everything she did, and I suspected in this case that she was trying to provoke her former lover. From the look on Tovarsson's face, it was working.

"It seems that someone besides you determined that an alliance – even a trade alliance – between the Vogel Monarchy and Morven Forest would benefit us both and thought that killing the Seer to stir up animosity was the easiest way to prevent it." She stretched her toes. "These same people once wanted to ensure you never had much power but have perhaps realized you are now too strong to touch." She looked thoughtful. "Your cousin, too, would never have dared kill you, anyway, no matter how much he wanted to. But he had already killed a lover of yours once and suffered no real punishment for it. No doubt, he thought he could repeat the process, though I don't think even he guessed your friendship was anything more than two young men working for the same end." She paused, then said. "Even I did not guess the two of you were… entangled."

I felt my whole body go still at the mention of my cousin killing my lover. I had mourned Dec already, but it hurt to be reminded that I had failed him. Fionn put a hand on my back as he always did when he sensed my distress, and I felt steadier.

The Queen, seeing my look, raised a hand. "I know. I prevented you from taking your revenge, but I could hardly allow you to kill my sister's only child over the death of a commoner, and a werewolf at that."

I clenched my jaw and shoved hurt aside. "I thought perhaps Sean was trying to prevent the Alfar from attempting another blood sacrifice by killing Seer Tokka first."

She looked thoughtful at that. "Perhaps. Perhaps these conspirators thought they could take care of two problems with one death."

"So you sent my wolf siblings to Tronven?"

"There were indications that the other fey Monarchies were involved. If you are correct about the Alfar plot, it is even more a tangle than I had thought." She looked sidelong at Tovarsson, who looked uncomfortable, but didn't comment.

"We have our conflicts in Tronven," he finally said, when she turned her full stare on him. "But to my knowledge we have never harbored anyone seeking to act against you, Queen of Morven Forest."

"Perhaps not, but you do have the habit of keeping anyone who opposes you prisoner." She paused for a heartbeat. "Along with anyone who knows information you don't want anyone else to learn."

"By forcing them to wear those masks," said Fionn. "You turn them all into mindless half-animal servants." Something in the way he said it, the soft horror in his voice, plucked at my memory, but I couldn't quite draw out the thought.

Tovarsson looked embarrassed.

"And thus, my agents were prevented from carrying out their mission here," said the Queen.

"If only you had *told* me they were coming," Tovarsson started.

"You would have assured me that you would take care of it," the Queen retorted. "I would have learned nothing useful, and you would have made excuses for *doing* nothing useful." She paused while a servant brought in a pot of tea and a tray of cups and then quickly retreated from the room.

"I suspect the very traitors I was looking for are among your prisoners," she said. "Along with those who knew the true shame of the Huldr."

"Are they truly traitors if they are not your subjects?" he said.

"Wait." I held up my hand and everyone looked at me. I pushed away from the fireplace and took two cups of tea from the tray, handing one to Fionn.

"Thank you, beloved," he said, ignoring the looks from both Tovarsson – surprised – and the Queen – calculating.

"You know who they were," I said, losing the thought that had made me speak up and substituting another until I could catch hold of the fleeting notion.

"There were Alfar scouts in the Drowned Forest last autumn. More came a moon ago. I suspect they hoped to sneak into Morven Forest via the hills."

"And you didn't think to inform me?" The Queen looked affronted. "I could have uncovered this conspiracy long ago."

"You're hiding something," I said to Tovarsson. "You implied that my Queen already knew this shame you speak of, but there's something you don't want even her to know." Something, I was beginning to suspect, that reached back much farther than my childhood escape from an assassin.

"Not all the Monarchs agree that the Isle should be united under a single ruler," Tovarsson said. "And very few of them think that yours should be the lineage to provide such an overlord."

"Not all the Monarchs agreed the dryads should be enslaved at the Founding, either," said the Queen. I felt Fionn go still, but when he spoke his voice was calm.

"What is this shame of the Huldr that you've mentioned?" Fionn asked, and we all looked at him. I almost grinned, because he had captured at least half of the thought that had been plucking at my mind. The juxtaposition of it with mention of the dryads filled in the rest.

"Seer Tokka had a vision," I said. "That the last Vogel Seer was sacrificed to enslave the dryads."

"That is something only the royal heirs of the fey Monarchs are told," said the Queen. "You would have learned of it eventually."

"Some few others know," said Tovarsson.

"Yes," said the Queen. "The heirs of those who were responsible for the spell." She looked at the Hulrd lord pointedly and I realized that she was referring to *him.*

"The spell was originally supposed to grant them true seership," I said, remembering what Fionn had told me of his vision and finally fitting it together with the other pieces. "Is that the shame of the Huldr? That your people made that spell, changed it to one of enslavement instead, and now you silence anyone who might make it widely known with those masks?"

Everyone went silent, staring at me. Fionn looked horrified, Tovarsson looked mortified, and my Queen... She looked delighted.

"My marriage was the first step in a plan to unite the Monarchies," the Queen said, and I was about to say something about her changing the subject, but Fionn's hand on my arm stopped me. He saw how it all fit, even if I didn't quite yet. "That plan was agreed on by the Council of Six."

She set down the cup she had been holding with a thump. "If they didn't intend my lineage to produce the one Monarch, why begin with me and Druison?"

Tovarsson shifted in his chair. "Perhaps the Alfar changed their minds again. They always did like to dissent after the council had already decided. It was they, if you recall your history, who suggested changing the spell to enslave the dryads instead of awakening their seers and offering them a Monarchy." He turned his gaze on me as he said it.

Fionn made a soft strangled noise in his throat, but when I looked at him, he shook his head slightly.

I sorted through all the questions that leapt to mind to find one I could most easily put into words. "What is the Council of Six?" I finally asked.

"Have you told him nothing?" said the Huldr Lord. "No wonder he seems such an innocent."

"It wasn't the time," said the Queen.

"Does he even know who *he* is?"

"Of course he knows. He is the son of the Queen of Morven Forest and the General of Dudoon, nephew to the King of Great River."

"I've known that since I understood words," I said. "What wasn't it the time to tell me? What more is there?" I set my cup on the mantel of the fireplace, carefully, afraid I would smash it if I let my frustration show.

The Queen sighed. "I suppose you'll have to know soon enough, especially if I'm to offer your hand to the Vogel."

Fionn squeezed my fingers hard, and I squeezed back.

"What?" I managed to get out.

"I have decided," said the Queen. "An alliance with the Vogel will, as you said, benefit our two Monarchies in matters of trade. It will also unite the First Peoples with the later settlers and bring us closer to a single Monarch for this Isle."

Tovarsson sat up suddenly and drew breath, to protest perhaps. My Queen silenced him with a look before he could get a single word out. A hard smile curled her lips. "And it would annoy the Alfar King no end. Especially if I offered a Mother-of-the-Heir alliance to the Huldr instead of to *his* daughter." She looked at Fionn. "If you can convince the Vogel King and Council to change your laws, Seer-Prince Tokka, I agree that my son shall marry you and join our two Monarchies."

I took a long breath. I wanted to smile, to hug Fionn, the thank my mother, my Queen, for allowing this. But I couldn't, not yet, because she had still avoided more than one of my questions, perhaps hoping to distract me with the news of her decision. It had nearly worked.

"What is the Council of Six?"

"The Council of Nine is the Nine Monarchs of the Isle," said Tovarsson, after a glance at the Queen for permission to answer.

"Of course, and the Council of Three is the three Triarchs, the three fey over-monarchs." I shifted my weight impatiently. Fionn let go of my hand to cover his mouth, and I watched his eyes widen.

"It's the fey and the humans, isn't it?" he said. "The three fey Monarchs and the three human Monarchs make decisions about the Isle without consulting the First Peoples."

The Queen smiled. "Indeed."

"That's –" Fionn shook his head.

"Perhaps," she replied, before he could finish. "But it is how the Isle has been ruled since the Founding."

"And what else was it you hadn't told me?" I said, taking Fionn's hand again.

She stood and walked to me, took my hand out of Fionn's and held it in both of her own.

"You are my heir," she said.

I frowned, confused. "Of course. Your third heir."

She smiled. "You know well that your sisters would never rule separately. I had once thought to marry them both to your cousin, to keep them together. They think of themselves as one spirit in two bodies."

I shook my head, no more enlightened.

"Together," she said, "they are my second heir."

I still didn't understand, but Fionn drew in a sharp breath and pressed his hand between my shoulder blades.

"You, Kiernan, are my third heir publicly, but secretly and truly you are my first. My marriage to your father was only the beginning of the alliance with Great River. To complete the peace treaty, we were to produce a child, a half-human half-Sidhe heir for two Monarchies. It is why I was at first supposed to marry your uncle." She squeezed my hands, and I desperately tried to make her words fit together in my mind in a way that made sense.

"You are," she said, "the Crown Prince of Morven Forest and, much to your uncle Iain's disgust, by the terms of our alliance, you are also the Crown Prince of Great River, with your cousin Eamon as second after you."

I couldn't seem to manage to do anything but stare at her, a whole flood of emotions filling me until I didn't know *what* to feel. I had spent so many years believing myself unwanted, when all along I had been her heir? How many others knew? How many had laughed at my ignorance? It almost made sense that Sean had been disgusted by my behavior, my former determination to fuck my way through two courts and most of the surrounding countryside.

How could she have kept this from me? And why had my father never said anything? The comments of my cousin Eamon, and of the Siegel King, and various others suddenly made sense. My thoughts stilled, and all that was left was rage.

I jerked my hand from the Queen's and turned away, threw open the door, and walked out. I knew if I stayed a moment longer, I would do or say something I'd be sure to regret later.

I wanted to go outside, to seek solace in the forest, but I didn't know *this* forest, so instead I sought our guest rooms. At least I could be alone there. When I turned to shut the door behind me, barely controlling the urge to slam it, Fionn took it gently, closed it, and slid the bolt across.

He said nothing; he just waited to see what I needed.

That kindness, that unconditional love that made him wait for me to tell him what I needed, was what finally broke me. He caught me as I fell to my knees and held me as I sobbed into his shoulder.

33
Fionn

MY ELATION AT THE QUEEN'S decision to offer an alliance of marriage to the Vogel Monarchy, with Kiernan and I to wed, was short-lived. As soon as the Queen told him he was the heir not only to Morven Forest, but also Great River, so many things fell into place. Odd comments and strange looks, hints and innuendos suddenly had new meaning.

It made sense, too, why the Queen had raised Kier the way she had – though of course I didn't *agree*. She needed him strong and to her mind not offering any hint of kindness would best achieve that goal. I was only glad she had enough motherly feeling for him that she'd given him as an infant to her Seer, so that Siona had provided the love he craved.

I knew, too, that when he went still, he was trying to control the flood of conflicting emotions. Even if I hadn't been able to feel them through our bond, I'd have known. He was hurt and wanted to lash out but, being who he was, he chose instead to walk away.

I thanked Tovarsson quickly and aimed a hasty curtsey in

the Queen's direction, then hurried after him. I knew he would want to be alone, but that he would also *not* want to be alone. I could not offer him any solutions, but I could still be there.

So I held him while he cried and said nothing except to softly whisper that I was there and that he was loved. And then I put him to bed and crawled in next to him, wrapping him in my arms until he fell into a restless sleep.

I stayed awake long after, until the sky began to grow light, feeling the unstoppable urge to watch over him. Finally, the stress and anxiety of all the past day's revelations overcame me, too, and I drifted off.

I woke much later, my eyes gritty but my back warm from Kiernan nestled against me, his face tucked into the feathers between my wings. His hand stroked my arm so softly I barely felt it, and when I stirred, he did, too, and kissed the back of my neck.

For a moment we just breathed together, and then he said, "I don't want it, Fionn. I don't want to be King. Not of Morven Forest, not of Great River, and especially not of the whole fucking Isle."

"And I don't want to be King – or even Prince – of the Eyrie."

He laughed, a strained and unhappy sound. "I'm even afraid to be happy that the Queen supports our marriage."

"Me, too," I said, starting to roll over. His arms tightened around me, so I lay still.

"I couldn't stand it if you were taken from me, too." His voice was muffled by my feathers.

"I won't be," I said, with much more confidence than I felt.

"Will you promise me, pretty bird?" he said, still speaking into the space between my shoulder blades.

"I promise," I said. "But you must also promise me."

"I promise." His arms relaxed and he traced his fingers

over my hip and down my thigh. I wished I had undressed us completely before getting into bed, but all I'd managed was to pull our borrowed shirts off.

"I want your hands on my skin," I said, and he kissed the back of my neck again, then helped me wriggle out of my trousers. Again, I made to roll over, and again he stopped me.

"I like how we fit together," he said, once he'd removed his trousers, too. And he was right, his belly fit in the curve above my buttocks, and his arms fit snug around my waist.

"We fit together in other ways, too," I said, and reached back to find his thigh.

"Yes, we do." His palm pressed flat on my belly, pulling me back against him. "I like all the ways we fit, but right now I especially like how my cock fits along your ass crack." And he gently folded my tail to one side and shifted position until his hard length pressed exactly there, then slid his hand down over my sheath to pull us snug together.

"That *is* very nice," I said, pushing my hips backwards and gasping when his fingers found the seam of my sheath and slipped inside then out again. He stroked down my thigh, slowly, as if savoring the feel of my skin under his hand the way I was savoring that same touch.

We lay that way a long time, as the sun rose higher and passed noon, slowly touching, pressed together, talking only about sweet and gentle things.

My erection stiffened in my sheath and slowly – agonizingly slowly – pushed out. He didn't even touch me there, only caressed everywhere else he could reach until I pulsed just from his soft touch on my hip and again when he stroked my belly. The third came when he paused to transfer some of my lubricant from my sheath to my buttocks and slid his erection between them.

Finally, sliding between my buttock muscles slowly, then

faster, he wrapped his fingers around my erection, still touching me only lightly, and I cried out when I felt him go still and his semen spilled under my tail and dripped. I spurted onto the sheets, and he slipped his arms tight around me again.

"Feel good, beloved?" he murmured into my neck.

"Mmm," I said. "I do feel good. And loved."

"You *are* loved." His breath stirred the hair on the back of my neck. "So very much."

"You're loved, too," I said.

He pressed his lips to my shoulder. "That knowledge keeps me going," he said. "It gives me hope."

Neither of us showed any inclination to get out of bed, though the day wore on. There were things we needed to face, soon, but for that moment we stole the day for our own and spent it in bed, lazy, together.

Smoke and Flame and Coal had left through the window, very early. They came back once, saw we were still in bed, and left again. Apparently, the pond that surrounded the house was rich in dragonflies even in the depths of winter, and the serpents found them to be both delicious and good sport.

Finally, Kiernan sighed and said, "Will you return to Great River with me, Fionn? While the Queen makes arrangements for our alliance?"

"I suppose you must go back."

"Yes."

"I should return to the Eyrie, sooner or later." I would need to, in order to convince the Council to change our laws, and to have them confirm, via a Seer, that I truly was King Sarkot's son. And then there was the matter of his death and my part in it.

"But not yet," he said.

"No, not yet."

Again, we lay in silence until I broke it when I said, "We'll also have to explain my King's death."

He took a moment before answering. "I'll have to tell my Queen about it. And my role in it."

I started to turn, to roll over so I could kiss him, when I felt pressure behind my eyes and the back of my neck tightened. I managed to say his name before my back seized and my whole body convulsed, and my mind was carried away.

For a moment I thought that somehow my vision had stopped before it truly started.

I lay in bed, Kiernan curled at my back, his hand stroking my thigh and his erection slipping between my legs. But the bed was bigger and softer, and the room was decorated in soft greens and greys with accents in blue and purple, and the wood of the furniture was dark.

The sun slipped through a crack in the curtains and Kier grumbled when it hit his eyes. Soon, the embassy staff would be making breakfast, and the building would fill with the scent of fresh bread, but for now we had time alone. Beginning the day with slow lovemaking was a luxury I intended to indulge in as often as possible.

I closed my eyes when his hand moved from my hip to tease my seam, and I laughed when a gust of air caught me and tossed me higher into the sky.

The beach below the Eyrie stretched out below me and a group of fisherfolk had stopped their work to shade their eyes and watch me. One of them grinned and waved and I grinned back. I shifted my weight and tilted my wings and the reed-and-silk prosthetics I wore responded smoothly and I circled and soared back to where Kiernan waited, knee-deep in the surf.

Smoke and Flame dipped and swirled around me, chittering in excitement, and a moment later Coal joined them, the red feathers in his wings catching the sun and gleaming as if they really did radiate heat.

I swooped lower, changed the angle of my tail to slow myself down, and landed solidly on my feet a few paces in front of Kier, who grinned and opened his arms.

I flung myself at him, splashing into the surf and laughing. "They're perfect!" I said. "The last adjustments Erith and Syrinx made worked!"

"I saw," he replied. "Beloved, I'm so happy for you."

"You gave me flight," I said.

"You gave me life," he retorted.

Then I said, feeling cheeky, "I'd like to give you something else." I wiggled my eyebrows up and down and he laughed, throwing back his head and opening up in a way neither of us had in some time.

When he stopped, he was still grinning, and he said, "Race you home," and let go of me to run full tilt down the beach towards the cliff where the Eyrie was built.

"You'll never beat me," I called after him, but by the time I got turned around, he was halfway down the strand. But he still had to climb the cliff. And I still had to get airborne again, when I had never managed it from the ground. Yet.

I positioned my wings and tail and then began to run after him. I slipped my arms into the straps that would let me use them to add strength to my flapping, because my stunted wings didn't have the force necessary to get me off the ground. I swept my wings down and felt my footfalls lighten. Again, and my feet just lifted off the ground. Once more and I leapt as I flapped and pushed up into the air and off the beach. I beat my wings furiously and, assisted by my arms, I slowly lifted from the beach and turned to soar out over the sea to circle and gain distance from the ground.

Below me, Kiernan had reached the path away from the beach into the trees and I lost sight of him, but I could still hear him laughing between gasps for breath.

Kiernan's laugh was not merry in my ears, but at least it wasn't grim. We stood on top of a hill, looking down at a group of tents in the valley.

"They're here for you, pretty bird," he said, putting an arm around me and pulling me close against his side.

"Perhaps," I said, then pulled him around to face the other way. "But *they* are here for you."

Seafolk seemed to fill the bay, basking in the sun on the beach and on several of the islands, waiting for him to go speak to them.

"I didn't really expect them to come," he said, leaning his head on my shoulder.

"We may not believe in fate," I said, "but *they* believe in prophecy."

"So do they," he replied, and turned me as I had turned him, to point at what at first looked like a flock of birds. But my distance vision was good, and I could see that it was a group of bird folk, my own people, coming to see if one of our oldest legends had come true.

And then I stood on top of a tower, watching a Seer like me – Vogel and silver-feathered, only taller and with full-sized wings – kneel in ropes before three fey Monarchs.

"This is not what we decided on," he said.

A tall Alfar woman with elaborate moonsilver decorations on shiny black horns curled close to her pale hair said, "We changed our minds."

"All of our Seers determined that dryads have potential for Seers too, and the Council of Nine determined to try to awaken that potential and to offer the dryads a Monarchy of their own. I only agreed to sacrifice myself to make that possible. I did *not* agree to this change in plans."

A Huldr man with long black hair, cold brown eyes, and horns like twisted bog oak said, "And the Council of Six decided the dryads are too volatile to make good citizens of the new order we are founding."

"I did not agree to offer my lifeblood and to leave my unborn child fatherless to enslave a whole people."

"Ten is such an ugly number," said the Sidhe Monarch, a man much smaller than his Alfar and Huldr peers, with deep red hair and leaf-green eyes. He looked enough like Kiernan that I knew he must be an ancestor. "So the Council of Three decided that a tenth Monarchy simply wouldn't do. Where would we put them, anyway?"

"They resisted our rule," said the Alfar Monarch. "And they must be punished."

"Many people argue they had every right to resist conquest," the Seer replied.

"Your people gave in easily enough," said the Huldr.

"You offered an influential councilor a Monarchy to rule, of course he agreed," the Seer scoffed. "And I agreed because I didn't want to see any more of my people killed. The Siegel gave in because they live on islands and in underground caves at sea and lose nothing by letting humans and fey have the land. The Hirsch agreed because they don't concern themselves with worldly things when they can avoid it." He lifted his bound hands. "I do *not* agree to this."

The Alfar glanced at the other fey Monarchs, then smiled a tight, cold smile that reminded me of the Abbess's. "You aren't required to agree. Our Huldr friends have seen to it that this ritual will succeed as we wish it to."

Darkness swirled around me, and I thought I would wake, but no. I was deep in a cave lit by pools of water that glowed like wisplights, only reddish instead of blue. The air was so dry it hurt my nose, and I wanted to sneeze, but some feeling in my gut told me I needed to be quiet. Something touched my elbow, and I almost jumped out of my skin, but of course it was only Kiernan.

He put his hands on each side of my face and tilted my head, so our foreheads touched. *You feel it, too?* he said in my mind.

There's something here, I replied. It was difficult to speak mind-to-mind, but we were getting better at it, as our magic blended and bled one into the other.

He nodded and gestured, and we continued to creep silently along the passage. There were symbols painted on the walls here and there, that reminded me a little of the ancient Vogel writing in the caves below the Eyrie. Only these were more complicated, as if the language they represented was a complex one, with multiple layers of meaning. I wished I had taken more time to study the Vogel symbols – perhaps they would have given me insight into these.

I let my seer-sight creep over me as we walked – I was getting better at that, too – and could feel Kier's magic reaching out as well. There was no one else here that I could sense, but there was still *something*, ancient and powerful, and it terrified me.

Kier stopped me again and this time I pressed my forehead to his immediately, closing my eyes to concentrate on putting words to the substance of my thoughts for him to hear. *There are no spirits*, I said, feeling a hint of a headache creeping over my temples.

None? His fingers pressed on the sides of my head, massaging, his small measure of healing magic easing the pain. He knew where my head ached, because his would be hurting there, too.

I shook my head. There were nearly always spirits around, sometimes close, sometimes not, but always detectable. Here, I could feel none.

Smoke and Flame pressed close to my neck, their narrow bodies wrapped tight, and I could see Coal doing the same with Kier, only his whole body was tucked into Kier's collar, leaving only his tiny feathered head visible.

This has to be the place, I said. *I remember it.*

He nodded and pressed his fingertips to my lips. I knew that he meant for me to stop talking, even though I was not making any actual sound. He wanted me to conserve my magical energy and keep from giving myself too bad of a headache.

I kissed his fingers, and he smiled and pressed them to his own lips. It was as good as saying "I love you" aloud.

We continued until the passage suddenly opened out into a huge cavern. It reminded me of the one beneath the hills of Aven, only it felt even more ancient.

A line of carved stone lanterns shaped like dragons with their heads turned to the sky led across the floor, forming an intricate path that ancient people must once have followed in a sort of ritual procession. Or so I imagined, anyway. I couldn't think of any other reason why they would not simply lead directly to the middle of the cavern, where a platform rose from the cave floor, its top in deep shadow. Light grew around the edges of a hole in the roof high overhead but didn't yet penetrate the cavern.

It must be day again, then. It was hard for me to keep track underground.

Kiernan took my hand and was about to cross the floor directly to the platform. I pulled him back and shook my head, pointing to the stone lanterns.

He held up his hand and summoned a tiny flame, then

pointed. I bit my lip, unsure, but believing that we should try to approach as the ancients had, if we could. I nodded and he gestured at the nearest lantern.

It leapt into flame and then suddenly everything was bright, blinding, and I was blinking in the glare of pale blue wisplight.

My head was in Kiernan's lap, and someone was rubbing the ache from my legs with a deliciously cool touch.

"Kiernan, I saw —" He put his fingers on my lips, and I wanted to tell him exactly what I thought of that until he smiled and pressed those same fingers to his own lips.

"The Huldr Seer is here, beloved," he said.

I tried to sit up, realizing that must be who was flooding my sore muscles with healing magic.

"Roll over, Seer Tokka, and I'll rub your back."

I would have preferred Kiernan do it, but he didn't have much healing ability and when I moved, the pain was so bad I yelped.

"You were gone a long time," said Kiernan, taking my weight and helping me turn over.

"And seizing the whole time, I hear," said the other Seer. "You must be in great pain."

Their touch was soothing, their magic easing the ache of my back muscles.

"That is helping," I admitted.

"Good." They worked quickly, but gently, and I was glad their touch was impersonal. "I have heard that Vogel Seers suffered seizures when they had spontaneous visions," they said. "It's said it makes their visions stronger."

"How could you have heard that?" Kiernan said, as if he knew what I wanted to ask. "There hasn't been a Vogel Seer since the Founding."

"There are stories passed among Seers," the Huldr said.

"And among the Hirsch of the Plains, who are said to hold stories in their original form far longer than the rest of us." They helped me sit up and smiled at the look on my face. "I trained with a Hirsch Seer," they said. "It is unusual for the plains folk to do such a thing as train one not of their own people, but they saw potential in me, I suppose." They stood up. "Now you should rest and see if perhaps meditation can make sense of your vision. If you have any other need of me, only ask."

When they left, I heard Kiernan bolt the door. He came back with a tray that smelled of pain relief tea and warm bread with honey, and he was draped in feathered tree serpents, which made me laugh despite the headache when they all slithered off to curl up next to me on the bed.

"Tea?" Kier said, setting the tray down on a table.

"Yes, please." I gathered my thoughts while he poured the tea and when he handed it to me, I nearly spilled it because I suddenly knew where we had been in that last vision, and what we had been doing.

He steadied my hands and helped me sip, and then I pushed the cup aside.

"I know where the Sword of Dragons is," I said.

About the Author

NICO SILVER LIVES like a hermit on the edge of the woods, but haunts used bookstores like a wraith. They fully expected to be found someday as a mummified old corpse crushed under a toppled to-be-read pile, but the rise of e-books has made that somewhat less likely, though the books will always outnumber even the dustbunnies. Nico will read just about anything, including the instructions on the back of medicine bottles, but has a particular fondness for good stories with a hint of magic. They write dark, sexy urban and romantic fantasy, and sometimes dream in black and white.